A Rite Of HEARTS UNDONE

CHILDREN OF THE GLARING DAWN
BOOK 2

LAUREN C. SERGEANT

A RITE OF HEARTS UNDONE

CHILDREN OF THE GLARING DAWN
BOOK 2

LAUREN C. SERGEANT

INtense Publications
www.intensepublications.com

INtense Publications
A Rite of Hearts Undone
Copyright 2020 Lauren C. Sergeant
Paperback ISBN-13: 978-1-947796-60-7

This edition published by arrangement with INtense Publications LLC. The opinions expressed by the author are not necessarily those of INtense Publications LLC.

www.INtensePublications.com

For Kimberly, whose suggestions breathed life into these characters and their world.

Chapter 1

A DAINTY RED FAWN MADE timid steps into the wide clearing where Jasper had sunk down onto a rotting log. The fawn didn't see him, and he didn't move. He sensed something so innocent and uncorrupt about the animal, it held him motionless by its grace. He didn't want to scare it away.

She'd had the same look about her, Miss Marchand, that of bewitching purity and goodness. She'd wanted to help him. She *cared* for him. A painful lump formed in his throat, and he coughed. The fawn's head twisted toward him in an instant, and seeing him, it bolted and disappeared among the trees, leaving him blinking.

Why was it he drove away everything worthy and beautiful in his life? What was it about him that repelled whatever he loved? He wanted nothing more than a life uncomplicated by the Shadow, something simple and straightforward in which resolve and effort could accomplish his pursuits. That was not what he'd gotten. No, he'd received an existence of secrets and snags in the most inconvenient places where a mistake could cost him his life, or worse, Oerid. This wasn't how it was supposed to be for Oer's Chosen Son, Oerid's sovereign.

Jasper exhaled an exasperated breath through his teeth. Anyway, it didn't matter that he'd destroyed Miss Marchand's affections, if they'd existed in the first place. It didn't matter because it could never be. He was betrothed.

The log beneath him gave way, and he swore, then stood and brushed himself off, muttering more curses under his breath. Besides being engaged to Jessica Cibelle, he realized the Lady of Shadows seemed intent on tormenting him around Miss Marchand. She wanted the girl dead. Maybe Cor was right. Maybe Oer's Blessing *was* supposed to battle the Shadow, which would make Miss Marchand a threat to the Lady. But why did Jasper have to be the one the Lady was pressing to dispatch her? Why did it fall to him, of all people, to endure that agony? He knew the answer—because of his blasted connection to Hell's Mistress, because she knew her power over him. What was wrong with Oer to allow this? What in the name of the Light was Oer's problem that he let his *Chosen Son* suffer the harrowing compellings of Light's nemesis? Why wasn't Oer fighting? Was Jasper in this alone?

Jasper realized he was standing in the middle of the clearing and that dawn's brightness had replaced the starlight filtering through the trees. He shook his head. Futile wonderings, that was all these were. They were unimportant. No, what mattered was that he needed to find Lady Cibelle and make that confounded journey to the Shadowed Realm to retrieve what had been rightfully his all along. Then he would return to rule Oerid in peace. Maybe after it was all finished, he'd find his life the way he wanted it. He doubted it, though. Things never turned out right for Jasper Thesson Aurdor.

Chapter 2

IHVA SAT ON THE GROUND at the edge of camp while her companions gathered their things. Having awoken before dawn, she was alert to her surroundings while the others were still rubbing their eyes. Warm pink and yellow clouds surrounded the rising sun through the sparse treeline, though the air was still cold and left her shivering.

She hardly noticed though; her mind consumed by thoughts of her argument with the Prince half an hour ago. Her heart ached. She'd ruined everything between them. First yesterday morning's incident with her foolish little "I'll miss you, too," now this morning's estrangement. It was all over because she'd been trying too hard to care.

His expression toward the end had struck her. He'd appeared transfixed on her somehow. He hadn't turned his gaze from her until he'd reached the edge of the clearing, and then he'd fled. What was so wrong about her questions that he'd had to run from her? Was he that afraid she'd learn about whatever he was hiding?

Ihva looked around and spotted everyone but the Prince and Yidda. Malach was saying something to Kronk, which Ihva couldn't hear, but Kronk laughed, and Cor smiled next to her. Ihva wished she was part of the conversation, but she couldn't bring herself to join their gaiety. She was too troubled in her current state, and she didn't want them asking questions.

"You needn't fret, child."

It was Yidda who spoke. It dawned on Ihva that the Jini woman might have overheard her entire conversation with the Prince, and she flushed at the thought.

"What do you mean?" she asked the woman.

"Your distress is clear, and if you sit here on your own much longer, the others will start to ask about it."

Yidda's voice was kind and gentle, and Ihva realized the woman was trying to help her. Anyway, it was no use hiding anything from Yidda when she might have watched the whole thing. Ihva decided to be forthright.

"I don't know what I did wrong," she said, misery in her whispered words.

"Nothing, dear. You've done nothing wrong."

"But it's all ruined now. All of it." Ihva buried her face in her hands. She was *not* going to cry again.

"Nothing is ruined, Ihva."

Ihva turned toward Yidda's voice, but of course she saw nothing. It was disconcerting not to see the person she was talking to, but she didn't have long to think about it as the woman continued.

"As I told him, there is far more to this than what you see. You are Oer's Blessing, Ihva. Of that I am certain. As for what that means, that remains to be seen."

Ihva shook her head. She wasn't talking about being Oer's Blessing. She was talking about her relationship with the Prince, but since Yidda wasn't addressing it, she wondered whether she should avoid the topic as well.

Instead she said, "I can't seem to do good anywhere, though. I've seen a king assassinated and left two nations without their next leaders and a third one facing impending doom. What if I'm nothing but a force of chaos and destruction like everyone believes?"

"Is that what you believe, Ihva?"

Ihva was silent for a moment. Something inside her was contending hard against her, telling her she was the destined ruin of Gant, but there was another part of her, a deeper part of her, that believed something else. That second part reminded her about how she'd found Malach and saved his life, how the magic within her had helped Heal her, and how Cor had said her Power was strong. It reminded her that she'd sounded the Horn and saved them all from the Shades.

"No, I don't think so," she said in a quiet voice. Yidda was silent for another moment, so Ihva added, "I think maybe I *can* do some good, if I try."

"I believe you can, Ihva," Yidda replied.

Ihva nodded. Then there was a pause.

"I also wonder whether your destinies aren't intertwined more closely than you think," Yidda added.

Ihva flinched. Was Yidda talking about her and the Prince? What could Yidda know? Ihva flushed as she realized how unsettled the woman's words made her feel.

"What do you mean?" she asked, but there was no response. It seemed the woman was gone, leaving Ihva to mull over her words. She hated how one little statement could thrill her hopes, bringing them to life to flutter inside her once again. Their destinies intertwined? How? And how close was "more closely than she thought"?

At that moment, the Prince stepped out from the treeline in the center of Ihva's line of sight. He was scowling, but when he caught sight of her, his eyes widened, and he froze for a second. She tried to frown to cover her flustering, but he looked away and made his way over to Cor. He said something to the dwarf, at which Cor nodded and straightened, then spoke.

"We have a journey ahead of us today. Let us make haste."

Ihva and the others nodded and shouldered their packs. Yidda instructed them on which direction to walk—northwest—and they made their way out of the enshrouding M'rawan forest into the barren hills toward the sands of Jinad.

"Alm'adinat is a port city," Yidda was saying. "Jini alone may enter and leave the gates, and then only to transport goods to and from the ships. We must sneak into the city by the dock from the south and enter through the gates. We will camp a few miles away on the beach and begin our entry an hour or so after nightfall."

They had been trekking through the sands of Jinad for an hour. It was hotter than in M'rawa but not nearly as sticky—a dry heat.

"Where will we head once we are inside the city?" Cor asked.

"To my home," Yidda replied in a soft voice. "I need to find someone there. If he will receive me, he should have information about any humans entering the city or at the port. He will know if Lady Cibelle is in or has been to Alm'adinat."

"Can we trust him not to give us away?" the Prince asked Yidda, his words quiet.

"He serves the higher cause. Explain your purpose, and as much as he begrudges me his help, he will assist us in any way he can," Yidda answered.

Cor's gaze was on the Prince, and Malach tilted his head. Ihva knew they were just as curious as she would have been to know what the Prince and Yidda were talking about, but neither of the dwarves spoke a word of inquiry. Instead the conversation died, and they continued in silence.

By early afternoon, the temperature had become sweltering, and the glaring sunlight reflecting off the ground made it so she had to shade her eyes. She'd never considered headwear an important piece of attire as hats were more her mother's style, but at this moment, she wished she'd brought one. Soon, the heat of the sand began to filter through the soles of her boots, thick as they were. Cor suggested digging each step down into the ground where the sunlight didn't reach. Ihva took his advice and found the bottoms of her feet met a more comfortable temperature.

They journeyed on through the heat of the day and blinding brightness of the sun. The view was the same in every direction— hazy desert dunes without a plant or creature in sight. At one point, Kronk grew tired and sat down. She refused to move, complaining she needed water. Ihva lent the woman her own waterskin, wincing as she watched Kronk drain a good portion of it. She hoped they would find a spring or something of the sort soon.

Thankfully, around late afternoon, they found one. Ihva saw something shimmering in the distance. Peering ahead, she thought she could make out something other than sand.

"Are we close, Yidda?" she asked.

"Not yet, dear, but we do approach an oasis. It would be advisable to take some water there," Yidda replied.

Malach exclaimed his thanks to Esh, and Ihva breathed a relieved sigh, then continued forward with renewed energy. The others picked up their pace as well. Within ten minutes, they arrived at a small pool of water with tall stalks with wide leaves surrounding it. Ihva kept herself from rushing toward it but only barely. She'd never before noticed the smell of water like she did now, not of fresh water at least, but at this moment it washed over her like enveloping waves on the shore. It was refreshing, rejuvenating, invigorating even. She drank her fill, then stepped aside for the others to do the same.

"Well, now that's what we call thirst-quenching!" Malach proclaimed, grinning at Ihva as he gave Cor a hearty pat on the back.

Ihva laughed and nodded her agreement. The moment seemed to release some of the tension she'd been feeling since that morning. She smiled at Cor. Maybe it was the discovery of water and shade amid the burning Jinadian sands, but everyone appeared more at ease as they sat beneath the leafy vegetation. A moment's reprieve was just what they needed, and Ihva was thankful they'd found it.

Turning back to the water, though, she met the Prince's gaze for a second. It was an awkward second, an anguished second during which her heart beat out of rhythm and she forgot to breathe. She nearly shut her eyes against the sight of him to make it go away, but he seemed transfixed as well and it delighted her with a misery that twisted in the pit of her stomach. Something she interpreted as anger sparked in his dark eyes, and his mouth twisted into a frown. Afraid, she averted her gaze and fought to inhale a normal breath. Thankfully, Yidda interrupted her train of thought.

"We mustn't waste too much time. There will be time to rest at the shore," the Jini woman said.

Malach heaved a sigh.

"That is wise. We must be on our way," Cor replied. "Let us fill our waterskins and depart."

Everyone agreed with varying degrees of reluctance, and Ihva managed to nod and speak her assent as well. Her thoughts were still racing, and she couldn't banish the image of the Prince's expression from her mind. Did he hate her that much that even looking at her was abrasive? She squeezed her eyes shut at the thought.

"You alright over there, lass?" came Malach's voice from a few feet away.

She snapped her eyes open and gave a curt nod. "Yeah, I'm fine," she said, aware her tone wasn't convincing.

Malach peered at her for a moment.

"Really, I'm fine," she repeated in a firmer voice. "Just worried about Alm'adinat."

Malach gave a knowing nod. "Makes sense. Not looking forward to heading into a city full of those nasty, conniving, murderous devils myself—forgive me, Yidda." He gave an apologetic look to no one in particular. "Anyway, it's understandable you're ruffled. Just don't let it get to you, lass. No use letting the enemy defeat you before you've even met."

Ihva was staring at the dwarf, and when he finished, she shook her head to clear her thoughts and mustered a smile. "You're right," she said quickly. "We'll just have to see how things go." She gave a firm nod and another forced smile, then focused her attention on filling her water skin.

A few minutes later, they were all trudging through the sands once again. Ihva fell toward the back with Kronk, trying to keep as much distance between herself and the Prince as possible. Maybe then she could forget for a moment about him and the morning's incident and the fact that she was stuck traveling with him for the foreseeable future.

Chapter 3

"INDEED DEAR, WE ARE BARELY an hour from the sea. We will rest there for the remainder of the day before making our way to the city," Yidda was telling Ihva. "It is much cooler by the sea."

The "cooler" part sounded good, but at the mention of making their way to Alm'adinat, fear trickled into Ihva's mind again. Entering the Jinadian port was no small task, she knew. Leaving the city safely would be an even greater challenge. She thought back to the story that Marcia Polenya had written concerning her detainment in Alm'adinat. It was by outsmarting and outmaneuvering the Jini and with the help of a rebel Jin that Marcia had escaped. Ihva wasn't sure she possessed the same skills as Marcia and doubted she and her companions could escape the Jini if captured, even with Yidda's help. It would be best if they could move undetected instead.

Soon, the sand beneath her feet grew cooler. She shivered as a slight breeze hit her and smelled the salty scent of the ocean on it. She could make out the blue of the sea on the horizon whenever she reached the top of a sand dune. It was a much-needed relief after the toil of the day's journey.

About ten minutes later, they reached the top of another dune and found the beach Yidda had described. Ihva stopped for a second, marveling, then forced herself to take slow steps forward. She could taste the saline in the air and soaked it in. The ocean was one of her favorite places—so outspread and unending. Her friends in Calilla used to talk about how the ocean made them feel small, and Ihva felt similarly. She remembered standing side-by-side with them, watching the gulls skate along the surface of the water and seeing how tiny the birds were compared to the expanse. She knew she was as minute as they were by comparison, and that had always comforted her. She'd never wanted power to weigh her down and constrain her, and yet here she was, Oer's Blessing, forced into significance by a will not her own. Oer had placed an even heavier responsibility on her than what she was imagining, she knew, but she refused to grasp at an understanding of it. As it was, she knew she had a duty to Oerid, to all of Gant, and if she failed, who could tell what consequences that might have?

She was determined to succeed, though, and that meant she first had to survive Alm'adinat. She ought to be thinking about the present task and save such fearful wondering for later. She blinked away her reverie and walked to where the others had gathered. Yidda was speaking when Ihva reached them.

"This is where we will camp until evening. The city is two hours north of here by foot, so we can begin our journey as darkness falls," the Jini woman said.

The others nodded while Ihva's stomach churned. She'd faced danger before, but up to this point, she hadn't walked into a place with so many enemies at once. Even the Shades seemed less a threat when Ihva thought about it. She'd been confident Rawa or even Oer would guide her steps in that instance. The Jini, on the other hand, were a complete and horrible mystery. Tales were told of their heartless terrors—they were a chaotic race that tortured and held for ransom and killed on a whim—but no one knew the extent of the Jini's twisted ways. It had been hundreds of years since anyone had entered a Jini city, and only a few had returned. A shiver ran up Ihva's spine at the thought.

For the next hour, she and the others relaxed at the seaside. At least, they relaxed as well as they could in light of the journey ahead. After fifteen minutes or so, Ihva took off her boots and walked along the beach barefoot, feeling the waves lap at her feet. She needed to be alone.

Her first thoughts concerned Alm'adinat. What would they find when they arrived there? More important, though, was whether they'd find a way back out. The question brought on oppressive anxiety, so she turned her mind to the ocean instead. The water was peaceful, and the waves were quietly overtaking each other. The sound soothed her nerves as memories of Calilla suffused her mind. Boats full of fish sailing into port, the beauty of the sunset's colors peeking up from the water, and the way the moon seemed so large over the ocean as the stars twinkled all around—these remembrances mesmerized Ihva for a moment. She closed her eyes, breathing in the ocean air and giving herself a moment's rest. The memories were calming, and she let them wash over her like the waves at her feet.

After some minutes, she reopened her eyes and looked back at the others. Malach and Cor were sitting on the beach away from the water, conversing. Kronk was out in the waves, letting them carry her, and the Prince was standing at the shoreline similar to Ihva, looking out over the ocean. Shame crept over Ihva as a replay of the morning's events reentered her mind, and the words exchanged sounded afresh inside her. She turned and started down the beach once more, away from the others. She wasn't sorry that she cared about him. That had been a lie. She'd never be sorry for that. What she was sorry for was that she'd let him know. She felt like an utter fool. The past couple mornings had been the most humiliating moments of her life. Even trying to kiss Gregorio back to life couldn't top this.

She still felt the Prince's response in her gut. She had no part in his life, he'd said. According to Yidda, though, she did, or at least, that was what Ihva thought the woman had meant, but that didn't make any sense. How could their destinies be so connected when he'd have Lady Cibelle as his wife? Ihva wasn't sure anymore she could interact with him so closely and maintain her peace—not with Lady Cibelle around. Then again, would *not* having Lady Cibelle around make it any easier? This unapproachable thing the Prince was doing lately was convincing her that she wasn't satisfied with mere friendship. The more he pushed her away, the closer she wanted to be, but then when he'd shown a sympathetic side, that had made it worse, too. If she was honest, there was nothing that could slow her fall now. She was losing her heart to this man, and she could do nothing about it, nothing except flee from him the same way he kept fleeing from her. Yet everything in her clung to hope, that tiny hope, which had grown heavier than lead. She kicked the sand beneath her foot, spraying it into the water.

Crunching sand sounded behind her. She turned to look and found Kronk. At least it was only Kronk. This woman was the last one to cause trouble and heartache.

"Ihva okay?" asked Kronk.

"Just upset, Kronk," Ihva replied.

"Kronk no try to make Ihva upset!" the orc-blood woman cried.

Ihva turned to Kronk and patted her shoulder. "Not with you, Kronk. Never with you."

"Who make Ihva angry?"

Ihva flinched and glanced behind her at the others. The Prince was still standing at a distance, looking at the water. Her eyes settled on him before she could think to stop herself.

"Ihva hate frowny prince? Want Kronk to beat him?"

"No!" cried Ihva. "No, I mean, he just…" She shook her head. "It's nothing."

"What frowny prince do?" Kronk asked.

Ihva was at a loss for a moment. The Prince had done nothing wrong. He'd fled her advances, and well he should have. She hadn't meant them as advances, but it seemed she couldn't separate herself from her feelings, so it was for the best that he didn't engage her interest in him.

"I don't know," she said quietly.

Kronk watched her looking back at the Prince, and there must have been something in Ihva's demeanor that gave away her longing.

"Ihva like frowny prince."

"What?" Ihva exclaimed.

"Yes, Ihva do."

"He's the *Prince*, Kronk, and engaged to marry a nice young noblewoman if we can find her. Besides, he never would have given me a second glance if it wasn't for the fact that we're traveling together."

"Then good we all together."

Ihva looked at Kronk in exasperation. The woman was more clever than Ihva realized sometimes. Besides that, Kronk cared. She wasn't trying to embarrass Ihva or shame her. Ihva felt her guard lower as she replied in a quiet voice.

"I don't know, Kronk. It's just, sometimes he seems kind. Other days, he seems like he couldn't care less that I even exist, or worse, he's infuriated by my presence. I don't know what to do."

Kronk put her arm around Ihva and said, "It okay. Ihva pretty and nice and strong. How frowny prince not love her?"

"He would never." Ihva remembered his biting tone that morning. She couldn't explain the conversation to Kronk, not without crying. "Besides, he's engaged, Kronk. He belongs to Lady Cibelle."

Kronk took a moment to understand, then her expression turned downcast. Ihva looked up at the woman and tried to comfort her.

"It's okay, Kronk," she said. "When we get home, I'll find the perfect one. I'll have tales to tell, and boys will line up to hear them. They'll line up to marry the hero girl who came back from Jinad of all places. We just have to focus on getting through Alm'adinat safely."

Kronk looked up, and her posture lifted. "Ihva right. We get home, and good things come."

"That's right," Ihva said, feeling like a liar.

The two turned back toward the rest of their companions. Ihva had strolled thoughtfully down the beach, but now her trudging steps back up it were despondent. She couldn't bring herself to tell Kronk that she'd probably never go home to Agda. As Oer's Blessing, she'd be shunned and even killed by the Oeridians. Whatever the elves believed about her, she was aware that men would see doom when they learned who she was. She braced herself for a life of exile, knowing that even so, she could never be prepared for the existence that awaited her.

Chapter 4

AS THE SUN'S SETTING RAYS turned the sky brilliant reds and pinks and purples, Jasper and the others ate a dinner of elvish bread. Even if there had been wood for a fire, no one wanted to alert the Jini to their presence.

Jasper knew he looked gloomy. He *felt* gloomy. Trying not to meet anyone's gaze, he just stared out into the distance over the ocean, taking in the colors that tinged it. The sunset had held nearly every color except green. It figured. Sunset never held any greens.

"Unfortunate, since I'd taken a liking to the lass," Malach was saying.

"Were there any you had not taken a liking to, Malach?" Cor asked, a smile in his voice.

"There were plenty," Malach replied with mock offense. "But why would I bring them up?"

The others laughed, including Miss Marchand. Oer, she needed to stop that. Her soft mirthfulness was only making it harder for him to ignore her, as he realized he was going to have to do. Anyway, how could they be in such good moods with a journey into Alm'adinat looming over them? It agitated Jasper to hear their lightheartedness.

He stood and stalked off toward the water. Looking out into the sea quelled some of his disquiet. The water lapped at the sand in front of him, and he positioned himself where the biggest waves would reach in front of his boots but not touch them. The rhythm was soothing. It was a cycle—the water came in, hesitated for a moment, then washed back out, just for another wave to do the same thing again. Something about it intrigued him. The ebb and flow reminded him of swordplay—first on the offensive, then switch to defense, then back to offense. Thrust, parry, jab, deflect. It was a never-ending duel between sand and water, between land and sea, like the duel between Light and Shadow. The battle never ended, only rebalanced itself in favor of one side or the other from time to time. The Light had been prevailing for a while now, and it was high time for the Shadow to overtake it. Jasper just couldn't be the reason for it.

The sun was out of view by now, and stars had begun to appear in the sky. The sky was becoming so black that the darkness nearly overwhelmed the little pinholes of brightness. The moon was almost full, but its light appeared somehow dim, and the air seemed laden with the gloom of dusk. He sighed.

The chatter behind him had quieted, and he realized he'd been gone from the group for a few minutes. It was probably best he got back to them. They were doing this for him, after all. For him and Jessica, for him and his betrothed. He felt strange associating himself with the woman like that. Their relationship seemed so detached compared to, well, compared to other relationships he had. He didn't want to think about her, about Miss Marchand that was, for fear of inciting the Lady again. Did Miss Marchand care for him like *that*? It was ludicrous to even consider—even if she did, it was worthless knowledge that could only torture him. The gods really did despise him, didn't they?

He smoothed his face and turned back toward the group. They were gathered in a semicircle, each staring out at the sea. He walked back to them.

"Is it time?" he asked in a soft voice when he got closer.

Yidda spoke from the darkness. "It is indeed time, friends. We must make our way to the city."

Cor and Malach looked to one another, and Malach sighed. Kronk looked startled, then her eyes widened. Miss Marchand's gaze remained on the water, and she gave an absentminded nod. What was she thinking about? A moment later, she came to and glanced around, catching Jasper's eye for a second. It was an agonizing second. In that time, Jasper detected surprise, then pain, then something like anger, then she cast her eyes north toward Alm'adinat. Yidda spoke again.

"We can enter from the southwest dock. There will be two guard towers, one on either side of the gates, each manned by a single guard. The gates remain open, so it will be no problem getting through them. We will just need someone to disable the guards. Prince, would you be willing?"

Jasper nodded, remembering the cloak the elves had given him. Laithor had told Jasper if he stuck to the shadows, he would be nearly invisible to anyone not looking for him. There would be no chance of the Jini seeing him before it was too late.

"Once we enter the city, it shouldn't be too difficult to remain hidden. I will lead the Prince, and the rest of you must follow and keep quiet. We are headed to the district right outside the palace. Alm'adinat in built in concentric rings, so we must pass through three to make it to my home. There we will find Ohebed. He will tell us what we might do next."

Cor gave a knowing nod and replied, "We follow your lead, Yidda."

The others nodded as well, including Jasper. He'd be at the front then. Good, fewer distractions, less to divert him from his purpose. He had to find Lady Cibelle. Nothing else mattered. He made his way to the front of the group and set his face toward Alm'adinat.

Jasper and the others traveled north up the beach for some time. After what seemed like half the night, Jasper spotted a distant change in the landscape. It was all shadows at first, but then something large protruded from the ground. As they drew closer in the moonlight, he discovered they were enormous city walls. Somewhere in the middle of the city rose a large, dome-topped building with a tall, thin spire. Beside it stood smaller domes topping shorter towers, at least as far as Jasper could make out.

Jasper turned his gaze toward the seaside and made out a number of ships in the port. As he and the others drew closer, he recognized the dwarven style of the vessels. Dwarven ships had always fascinated him with their abrupt, geometric frames. Everything visible about them above the water had sharp lines and edges. The bow was a triangle fitted onto the rectangular body of the ship, and the forepeak at the front was a smaller triangle with its base in the bow. Dwarven vessels looked almost as though they shouldn't be able to sail, yet sail they did, and well at that. Jasper figured the parts of the ship beneath the waterline must have been smoother.

Soon, he and the others neared the port. About a hundred paces from the closest ship, Yidda told Jasper to halt. He held up a hand for the others, and they all stopped and gathered together as Yidda gave them instructions.

"We must move as quietly as possible," she said. "The guards aren't too attentive, seeing as few other than the Jini have ever entered the walls of Alm'adinat. Nonetheless, if they suspect something out of the ordinary, they'll be fearsome opponents."

"Will they be invisible like you? How will we even see them to know where to avoid them?" Malach asked.

"I didn't explain to you, I apologize."

Malach's brow furrowed. "What were you supposed to explain to us?"

"Most Jini are visible. We perform a ceremony that consumes evadium to give us temporary, physical bodies made of the sands of the surrounding desert. The Sultan controls the evadium trade and therefore controls which Jini are allowed bodies at which times. He ensures the guards are equipped with bodies to combat any forces that would oppose him. You will be able to see the guards. That I can promise. Most of the Jini who might be without bodies will be the impoverished on the outskirts of the city. They shouldn't bother us. They live in terror of the Sultan and his forces. They will not alert the guards."

"You Jini certainly are something," Malach replied.

Meanwhile, Jasper was scanning the port. He looked back at the others, and his eyes went to Kronk. "You must be sure to keep quiet, Kronk," he told the woman.

Miss Marchand stepped between him and Kronk, avoiding his gaze and looking at the orc-blood woman. "We'll need to sneak, Kronk. Like we did to the temple at home."

She tiptoed to demonstrate, and Kronk gave an enthusiastic nod, then Yidda spoke again.

"We'll navigate through the port to reach the entrance to the city. Then, we must make our way by stealth through the outside of the city where the poor reside and find our way through the market district. We'll then make as straight a path as possible through the largest part of the city, where the commoners dwell. After that, we'll be in the district of the nobility. There, I'll lead you to my house where we'll be safe."

"Hopefully," Jasper muttered under his breath.

"Prince, if you will lead," Yidda prompted him as though she hadn't heard him. He nodded, and she went on. "I will remain near you and give directions."

Jasper nodded and turned to face the docks. "Let's go, then," he said and started forward.

Chapter 5

JASPER LED THE OTHERS THROUGH the docks where Yidda guided him. As they made their way across the wooden platforms, he looked around, realizing this might end up being their escape route. Better to know where they might be headed.

A large number of crates and chests littered the docks, waiting to be loaded onto the ships. Jasper also spotted a few platforms below the level they were on. Ladders reached the lower platforms, and he figured these must have aided in repairing ships.

"Stop here," Yidda told him as they were about to round a corner.

He held up a hand for the others and peeked around the pile of boxes in their way. A gap in the city walls held a tower on either side. They'd found the city gates.

He turned back and whispered to the others, "We're here."

Cor nodded and glanced between Malach and Miss Marchand, then said, "It falls to you to get us through, then, son."

Jasper nodded. It *was* up to him. He couldn't fail, for their sake, for Jessica's sake, for Oerid's sake. He put up the hood of his elvish cloak and looked around the corner again. The light from the moon and stars cast heavy shadows that reached all the way to the boxes. Perfect.

He stepped out into the walkway and stole away toward the southern stone tower. Getting across the fifty paces to it turned out to be easy enough, and once he reached its base, he found an opening about his height. He slipped through it. Inside, he found a spiral of stairs leading upward with a solid pillar coming up the center. The only way was up so he wasted no time. He ascended the stairs in quick, stealthy steps, trying to ensure his movements weren't audible. There were small windows every so often, for which Jasper was grateful as it would have been pitchblack in the stairwell otherwise. Finally, he saw a wider empty space ahead of him and slowed his pace. He quickly drew his dagger, but in his rush, he nearly dropped it, and its tip scraped the wall with a small grating sound. He froze for a second. Nothing happened. He strained his ears, listening for any small noise that might reach them, but there was nothing. He crept forward.

He made the final turn up the stairs and found himself face to face with a creature whose appearance both startled and disturbed him. Its eyes were inky black, looking at the same time like dark liquid and lifeless glass. Its face was roughly human in shape with a narrow nose and a mouth bearing needle-sharp teeth, but its skin looked nothing like flesh but rather rough and granular. Baring its teeth, it thrust a spear in his direction. He dodged in time; then thrust the dagger he'd drawn into its chest. It slumped to the ground, then disintegrated, deflating the rough, sack-like material it had been wearing as clothing. So much for getting a good look at the thing. Jasper noted the spear on the ground and a sword leaning against the outer wall of the small guardroom. A crossbow was also lying at the window overlooking the docks. These Jini were well-armed for not seeing many trespassers.

Jasper slipped back down the stairs and darted across the entrance to the city to the other guard tower. This time he kept his dagger out, trying to ensure he wasn't making any noise at all. When he reached the top, he used the central pillar to hide himself and peered around it.

There was the other Jini guard. Its limbs were on the bulky side, though Jasper remembered the dextrous movements of the last one and told himself not to underestimate the thing. He observed it for a moment. It was facing away from him, standing still while it watched and listened. Its stance spoke belligerence. Its ears came to points at the top like elvish ears, but other than this feature, the creature was in no way reminiscent of the residents of Rinhaven. For a moment, a strange emotion overcame Jasper, nostalgia and longing to return to the place where everything had made more sense. It had all seemed so clear in Rinhaven.

This was no time to be reminiscing, though. He needed to take the creature out before it saw him. He darted forward and put a hand over the creature's mouth, tilting its head back. Its skin was rough, made of sand like Yidda had informed him. Jasper slit its throat with his dagger as it tried to break free, and it crumbled in his arms.

Jasper looked around. There appeared to be no other guards, just as Yidda had said. Time to get the others and head inside. He descended the stairs and exited the tower, then waved for the others to follow him. No one moved, just kept peering into the space surrounding Jasper. He remembered the cloak—they couldn't see him. He moved along the shadows back to the others.

"It's done," he said once he'd reached them.

He lowered his hood, then turned and led the others up the walkway to the entrance to the city. The gates made him feel small as they towered overhead. He hated the feeling, the sense of his own powerlessness. Instead of dwelling on it, he slipped forward into the city.

Everywhere around him stood small dwellings made of what looked like sand. The houses looked just large enough to each contain one tiny room. The multitude of them overwhelmed his vision, but he forced himself to look ahead.

"Straight through you will find the gate to the market district," Yidda said in a quiet voice.

He nodded and led his companions through the Jini slums. After creeping along for five minutes or so, he found that a short, clay wall, and beyond the wall, many shops. Yidda told him to keep heading northeast, so he did, giving vague attention to the details of his surroundings. The buildings bore signs displaying everything from cut gemstones to ingots to barrels. The scene made him wonder what the district looked like during the day, but he didn't care enough to consider it as he slipped between buildings along through the streets. They were here for one task, and it wasn't exploration.

Soon, though not soon enough for his anxiety, they arrived at another clay wall and a short wooden gate. The ring of commoners' dwellings came after the market district, Jasper remembered. Nothing in particular stood out about the commoners' district except that the homes looked roomier and more stable, their walls consisting of sand bricks. It took a short while to navigate through the commoners' district, but eventually Jasper stopped at another, taller gate.

"We'll now enter the noble's district," Yidda whispered. "Turn left after the second house, and mine will be the third one on the right."

Jasper nodded, and with soft steps, he made his way to the gate and eased it open. It made no sound. The others followed him through the gate, and he shut it behind them. Then he crept forward, keeping low to the ground.

These houses were made of stone and glass, and they dwarfed the homes he'd seen so far. They had two or three stories each and opened to the street by wooden doors with elaborate carvings. Their roofs resembled the roof he'd seen from outside the city, domed with small spires extending from the tops. They looked like small palaces, and their height blocked his view of anything beyond the noble district.

He led his companions around the corner, counted three houses, and stopped at a three-story dwelling. Its door was carved with an image of an elaborate shield. Jasper didn't stop to wonder at its meaning as Yidda spoke.

"This is my home." There was a tremble of emotion in her voice.

Jasper looked in the direction of the whisper.

"You may open it," Yidda said.

He nodded and eased the door open. It swung on its hinges without a sound. He drew a deep breath and stepped inside.

Chapter 6

IHVA WATCHED AS THE PRINCE entered the house first, and the rest of them followed. Someone shut the door behind them with the slightest creak, and everyone froze. Nothing happened, though. The Prince remained still another second and Ihva could hear that Yidda was whispering something to him, then he called out in low tones.

"Hello?"

There was no answer. He called out in a still tentative but louder voice. Again there was no answer.

Ihva heard Yidda speak again and could make out her words this time. "The lower level is for entertaining among my people. He'll likely be upstairs in the living quarters."

The Prince moved at a cautious pace through the downstairs rooms toward where Yidda indicated there would be stairs. They traveled through the mansion by the dim light of Kronk's elvish ribbon, reasoning Cor's light would be too bright and might call attention to them through the windows. There seemed to be no one there, and Ihva wasn't alone in feeling suspicious of the situation. The others were tiptoeing as well. They walked through the foyer and found everything neat and orderly. Tasteful pastel paintings with flowing, non-organic designs lined the walls, and a table rested on the right side of the room with an ornate vase atop it. They continued to walk down the hallway. Looking into each of the two other rooms along the way, they found everything in a state of tidiness with tables and chairs placed to create an open space and rugs with similar designs as the paintings. After a few moments, they reached the staircase. Everyone stopped and waited.

The Prince glanced back, then led the way up the stairs. Ihva and Kronk walked beside each other behind him, and Malach and Cor took up the rear, hands on their weapons. Ihva heard Yidda murmuring from the front of the group, though she couldn't discern the Jini woman's words. Reaching the top of the stairs, they found a door blocking the way. The Prince hesitated, but there came no sound from Yidda. He knocked—no answer. He rapped his knuckles harder, and the door creaked open. Bracing for someone to cry out, all Ihva heard was silence. The Prince opened the door further and motioned the others to follow him into the room.

Ihva allowed Kronk to go ahead of her, then quickly followed. The ceiling was the first thing that drew Ihva's attention. It was tall— the room must have taken up two of the three stories—and it had starry jewels glowing in it amid more of the flowing designs Ihva had seen downstairs. It reminded her of the sky with the colors of dawn swirling amid the twinkling gems. After staring for a moment, Ihva made her way farther into the room.

"We need more light," the Prince said from her right.

At his suggestion, Cor created a small, bright orb and centered it in the room. Ihva continued to look around. The Jini must have appreciated open floor plans. At the far end of the room there looked to be some sort of altar, and nearer to Ihva and the others rested a large couch-like bed colored in the same pastel color scheme. A couple chairs and ornate woven rugs were arranged in an orderly fashion against the walls of the room with a large, round, central rug depicting the shield Ihva had seen on the front doors. There was no sign of anyone present except herself and her companions. She shifted her stance, uneasy. Where could Ohebed be?

She walked over to inspect the altar as it intrigued her the most after the ceiling. The altar was a solid piece of stone carved with the image of the sun on its front face and topped with a slanted surface. The stone was polished, and Ihva could see a vague reflection of herself in the angled top piece. She drew closer. A folded piece of parchment lay on the slanted surface. Curious, she crept forward and picked it up to inspect it, flattening the paper to read to herself.

Are you heading to the Prison of Souls?
Tell my love I will meet her there.
Tell her I will pay our tolls,
And we will head to the Palace of Air.

Are you going to the spirits' hell?
Tell my love that I seek her yet.
I'll break her from the jail cell
And bear her on to where she'll forget

The suffering of morning, before our hope's light
Springs into being through the substance of white.
She'll no more remember withdrawal's pain
When we live where Light and graceful hope reign.

The Voice will be but a far recollection
When she recalls again her deep affection.
We'll no longer need Evadium's objection
To foment our rebellion, the Voice's rejection.

Are you going to the Prison of Souls?
Tell my love I will meet her there.
Tell her I will pay our tolls
And we'll be free and live in Love's Air.

There was no signature or any indication of the note's author, but Ihva immediately knew who had written it—Ohebed.

She called out, "Yidda, I think I found something."

"What is it, Ihva?" The Jini woman's voice came from across the room, but she sounded like she was approaching. Ihva held up the parchment.

"Oh," was all Yidda said at first.

No one else said anything, and Yidda began to read aloud, her voice wavering but gaining strength until the final few lines, at which she dropped to a mere murmur.

"...And we'll be free and live in Love's Air," she finished. Her voice cracked with the last two words.

A heavy silence fell on them all, and it was the Prince who spoke first.

"I thought you said he hated you," he said, his words quiet.

"He did," Yidda replied. Her voice shook.

"You didn't tell him you left," the Prince came back with a sharp tone.

"No. He would only have tried to stop me, but he was better off without me. I knew I had erred, and there was nothing that could reverse it. He needed to start afresh without me as a restraint."

Cor interjected at this point. "This was Ohebed?"

"Yes. He was my Companion." Yidda's voice had gained strength and was steady now. "I loved him, and a part of me withered when he discovered my betrayal and turned to anger and self-protection. Whatever infatuation he might have felt for me died that fateful night when Eliyah passed on. He kept careful watch over me after that. He threatened me that the guards would find me if anything like that ever happened again. He spoke with fear in his voice, and I knew why. He was afraid of me."

Silence filled the room. Malach looked at Cor, his expression still confused, while Cor's face showed something more like careful consideration. Ihva turned her eyes to the ground, and Kronk kicked something on the floor.

The Prince spoke however, his voice soft, though it still had an edge. "Did you really know why?"

"Yes, Prince," Yidda replied with a tremor to her words again.

"He wasn't afraid of you. He was afraid *for* you." The Prince gestured at the note.

"But he never left my side. He watched me constantly, instructing me every hour how to overcome the Voice."

"He loved you," the Prince replied in a flat voice.

A short pause ensued, and no one spoke, waiting for Yidda to answer.

"Certainly someone as pure as him could not love someone as tainted as me," she said finally. "Certainly not after—"

The Prince cut her off. "It's not impossible for the innocent to fall for those touched by evil. Some say they can even redeem them." His strained voice contained something as near to emotion as Ihva had ever heard in him, but she didn't have time to wonder about it as Yidda replied.

"But if he did, if he does, then…" she said, trailing off.

"Then what you've come for is more possible than you believed," the Prince replied.

No one said anything for a moment, and since Ihva couldn't see Yidda, she glanced at the Prince. His expression caught her gaze, though she tried to mask the fact that she'd seen him. She held her breath, confused. He had his lips pressed together and his brow deeply furrowed, but it was his eyes that drew her attention. They were hard and showed none of the emotion his voice had been suggesting. She caught herself watching him but couldn't seem to turn away. A split second later, though, recognition sparked in his eyes that she'd seen him. He jerked back, then cast his gaze past her toward where Yidda's voice had seemed to originate.

"We must find him," he asserted.

Yidda didn't respond.

"Where might he be if he is not here?" Cor asked in a calm voice.

"On duty, maybe, but his shifts always began at sunrise…" Yidda trailed off.

"He wouldn't have been one of the ones in the towers, would he? He's not one of the ones we offed to get in here?" Malach blurted out.

"No, he couldn't have been!" Yidda exclaimed.

"But then where is he?" Malach asked.

"I don't know!" the Jini woman replied, sounding flustered. "It doesn't make sense."

"There's someone outside," the Prince said suddenly.

Everyone froze, and apprehensive silence seized them. Ihva wanted to go look out the window, but she was terrified to move and give them away. Instead, she remained as motionless as possible, her breath becoming shallow and irregular with fear. Nothing happened for a long moment, and finally she began to relax her stance and breathe more normally.

"We have to get out of here," the Prince whispered into the stillness.

Chapter 7

"TO THE STAIRS," YIDDA INSTRUCTED the others.

Ihva turned toward the one door in the room and was about to rush toward it when it burst open with a crash. She stopped short, paralyzed, unsure which direction to go. Her eyes fixed on the door, she watched as a pair of sand creatures lumbered through it. They were human in shape, having two legs and two arms, and were carrying themselves with a domineering aggression. The sight of their rough, light-colored skin beneath the unshapely, tan-colored clothing they were wearing evoked memories of the abrasive sands she and the others had traversed to get here. These had to be Jini. The first two made way for five or six more to step inside as Ihva watched, petrified. They were bulkier than she'd expected and carried torches, whips, and spears.

"Not so fast, Yidda," one of the first two guards said with a foreboding calm in his deep, grating voice.

Yidda let out something that sounded like a curse.

"You'll be coming with us, though first you must use this. Follow me." The guard held out a handful of glaring, white evadium and proceeded toward the altar at the end of the room. The ritual used evadium, Ihva remembered. They wanted Yidda to take material form, but that would only make her more vulnerable. Ihva froze.

There was silence.

"Come, Yidda!" the guard commanded her again. "Or don't you think you've done enough damage already, *Hero*?"

"Where's Ohebed, Askari?" Yidda demanded.

"You don't know?" the other Jin said.

The other guards had begun to circle around Ihva and the others, enclosing them. Ihva shifted nervously, watching the Jin named Askari.

"He wrote you a letter, didn't he?" the leader said.

There were a few cruel chuckles from other Jini around the room.

"A final note, a last message—" Askari went on.

"He's not dead, Askari," Yidda cut him off. "Don't toy with me. There was no reason to condemn him." Her tone was icy.

"Disobedience to the Sultan in any form incurs penalty, Yidda. Surely you know that. Refusing to divulge knowledge of a fugitive's whereabouts was quite enough."

"He had no knowledge of my whereabouts!" Yidda replied, an angry strain in her voice.

The leader faltered and jerked to a stop in his approach to the altar.

"I left without telling him," Yidda said. "I told no one. If he said he didn't know, he was telling the truth!" Her words were forceful, but then her voice grew softer as she added, "He always tells the truth."

Askari remained frozen facing the altar, ten paces away from Ihva.

"Askari, tell me. Where is he?" Yidda was pleading now.

"Just tell her, Captain!" a guard on the other side of the room demanded impatiently.

Askari didn't say anything, but Ihva watched his unnatural mouth grimace.

"He's not dead. Please tell me he's not dead!" Yidda cried out.

At that, Askari shifted his gaze to where Yidda's voice had last been, and he replied, "You desire the truth. I will not lie."

Yidda's voice choked out a simple, "No."

Askari didn't respond.

"Please no!" Yidda cried. "He can't have. Not another. Not Ohebed!" She began sobbing now. "Light help me, I am forsaken. There is no mercy large enough! Ohebed, no! Please no!"

Askari stared, unmoving, and Ihva watched as horror crept over her. Yidda was giving up. Ohebed was dead, and Yidda was giving up. They couldn't make it out of Alm'adinat without her!

"Use this," Askari said after a moment in a voice devoid of emotion. "Please," he added in a softer voice as he started again toward the altar, holding the evadium.

Yidda's sobbing subsided enough for her to reply, "You would dare act remorseful, Askari? What did Sasar promise you? My Companionship? A place in the Court? Don't dare act like you care more than for your own gain. Ohebed is dead, but you'll never pry me from his memory!"

"Just do it, Yidda!" Askari shouted.

Everything went silent, then Yidda spoke in a quiet voice from a pace or two away from Ihva. "Take me then."

Ihva froze. "Yidda, no!" she cried out.

Yidda didn't say anything, and Ihva couldn't tell where the woman was so she just stepped back in front of the altar. Putting her hand on Darkslayer's hilt, she readied herself.

"Keep your peace, Ihva," Yidda said fiercely. Her voice came from a few feet away.

Ihva stopped, still perplexed. Why was Yidda yielding?

"Move aside!" the woman demanded.

Ihva glanced toward the others for help, but her gaze didn't move past the Prince. He was staring at the space before the altar where Yidda's voice was originating, but when Ihva looked over, his eyes met hers. Seeing his face twist into a strange combination of a grimace and a frown, she hardly noticed as Askari approached. The Jini guard shoved her to the side, pushing her to the ground, and she lost track of the Prince as she panicked. She scrambled to get up, to stop Askari, but as she began to stand, she found another Jini guard between her and the altar. He was brandishing his spear at her, and she couldn't find a way around him. The next thing she knew, she heard Askari's harsh voice.

"Now. It is time." His words were sharp and curt.

The guard in front of Ihva shoved the point of his spear at her, forcing her backward. There was a glint of malice in his glassy black eyes. His sandy expression had an outlandish yet familiar look to it, as though someone had pasted the desert onto a human face. Or an elf's, really, with his pointed ears, but the guard's features were heavy and brutish, unlike the winsomeness Ihva had encountered in Rinhaven. She glanced again at his eyes. They shone with something, but it was not life. No, they looked unalive, otherworldly, and at this exact moment, they gleamed with savage intent.

"Go on. *Speak!*" Askari commanded.

Ihva held her breath, praying Yidda would refuse, but then Yidda's voice began to sound. Her words came softly at first, and they had a rhythm to them. Ihva didn't understand the woman's speech, though it had a haunting sense of familiarity. For a moment, Ihva wondered whether it was her hearing that was the problem. She glanced around at the others, at Cor. His face showed no recognition of the words either.

Before Ihva could sort through her confusion, Yidda let her words trail off, and a white light appeared over the altar. The brightness grew more intense with the passing seconds. Then, it pulsed outward, creating a sphere larger than Ihva hovering a few yards above the ground. Ihva had to close her eyes and look away for a moment until the light dissipated.

As she reopened her eyes, she heard a thump and looked back at the altar. In front of her stood a new figure. It was in the shape of a Jin, but its skin was pale with yellow undertones such that Ihva could have sworn the creature had flesh rather than sand for a body. Its figure was feminine, and as it lifted itself from the ground, Ihva knew—it was Yidda.

No one moved for a moment. They all had to be wondering the same thing—what had happened to Yidda? She was tall and thinner than the other Jini but appeared strong. Her body glowed with warm light as the flames of the guard's torches reflected off of her skin. Ihva watched the woman take stock of her new body, limb by limb. Her arms were long and lithe as she spread them in the air, and her abdomen was fit and powerful. Her strength seemed to center there. She spun around; her eyes wide. She was elegant and well-built, a Jin but without the barbaric look.

"Come here!" Askari called out in a loud voice.

Yidda looked at him without saying anything, her expression blank.

"Yield and surrender yourself!" Askari shouted again, though Yidda was five paces from him.

The Jini woman's face became hard. "He has not abandoned me."

"Who, Ohebed?" Askari asked, his voice wavering.

"No. He has neither cast aside nor deserted his champions. Neither has he renounced me," Yidda replied. "My Exchange is made."

Ihva's bewilderment was increasing with each word the others spoke. It seemed Askari felt confused as well, though his puzzlement was leading to discomposure.

"Give yourself up, you and your companions, Yidda. The Sultan's purposes will not be subverted," the Jini leader threatened.

Ihva saw the thought of escape cross Yidda's mind, as the woman's face was not used to masking her feelings. It was a look of daring and defiance, her eyes narrowed, and chin set firm. The guard next to Ihva brandished his spear, and Yidda made a menacing move forward. The guard threw his weapon toward her to force her back into place. It hurtled out of his hands toward her and grazed her upper thigh.

All at once, everyone in the room moved toward Yidda, either to help or constrain her. Then, as though each one thought better of it, they all froze in place.

In a voice cracking with anger, Yidda cried out, "Oer aid me, I am not going with you! No Sultan will, in hypocrisy, deliver me to the same fate as those whom he murdered in the Rebellion." She picked up the spear.

"You force my hand, Yidda," Askari said quietly. Then, loud enough for them all to hear, he commanded, "Seize them!"

Chaos broke out in the room. Each of the guards on the perimeter of the room launched their spears at Ihva's companions, who'd gathered in the center. The Prince dodged to avoid a spear aimed at him and knocked it to the ground with his blade as it passed. Kronk batted another out of the air as she flailed her club. Cor used his hammer to divert the incoming projectiles, and two more spears fell harmlessly feet away. Malach dodged out of the way of another.

The next moment, a rough rope whipped around Ihva's feet, tripping her. She fell to the ground, then looked around for Yidda. She and Askari were circling each other, brows furrowed and a look of concentration on their faces.

"I'm alright. Go help the others!" Yidda called to Ihva. Her voice, at least, was still the same.

Ihva heeded the woman's instructions, threw off the rope, and ran toward the others, drawing Darkslayer on her way. She stopped at the edge of the fray and took a moment to search for where she might be most helpful.

Kronk seemed to have her guard well handled, pinned to the ground with her foot and beating him with her club. Ihva didn't have time to wonder how the woman had become battle-worthy after all her cowering the past many weeks. Back to back, Cor and Malach fought three more guards. Cor heaved his hammer across, and the first guard spun to avoid the blow. Quickly, Cor came around on the backswing and pummeled the guard into the one next to it. Malach threw his dagger at the third guard and narrowly missed him. The dagger was back in Malach's hand a split second later, and he appeared undaunted.

Two guards also beset the Prince. Despite his expert rapier-wielding and maneuvering, their attacks seemed to be overwhelming him. Ihva took a deep breath and brandished Darkslayer. She stepped forward and swung with swift confidence, striking one of the guards on the Prince. The guard's arm was sliced in two, and the lower part fell to the ground. Ihva looked up in time to see a spear hurtling toward her chest. She sliced through the air again and deflected the blow. Using the momentum she'd built up, she moved her blade toward the guard's chest and buried Darkslayer up to the hilt. The guard disintegrated on the ground, lifeless.

At the same time, Ihva glanced in the Prince's direction and saw him knock aside a guard's thrust of a spear. The Prince looked at Ihva for a split second, and something registered on his face that Ihva couldn't identify. His eyes contained a fire she hadn't encountered in him before. Her heart beat faster, and she regretted looking at him.

Glancing around, she realized that Kronk's foe had died, Cor's and Malach's had been disabled, and the Prince had his blade ready to impale the guard on him. Ihva felt relieved reassurance flood her body. Suddenly, whips of energy burst forth from some unknown source and wrapped themselves around her. She fell as her feet were bound together. She looked around and found that the same thing had befallen the others.

"Do you *want* to see me kill her?" asked a voice from Ihva's left.

Ihva turned her head and saw Askari from the other side of the room holding Yidda tight against his body with his spear to her neck. Ihva stopped breathing.

"You wouldn't." The Prince's voice was steel.

"Then you'll follow where I lead you," the guard replied.

He and the Prince stared each other down for a moment, but Askari pressed the point of his spear into Yidda until she flinched, and the Prince relented. He glared at the guard but nodded his assent. They would follow.

Ihva felt the bindings around her feet loosen and fall off. She went after the Prince as Askari led them out into the night.

Chapter 8

JASPER DID HIS BEST TO appear submissive as the guards filed him and the others out the front door. In reality, his thoughts were racing as he tried to come up with ways of escape. Where were the guards taking them? Askari still had his spearhead to Yidda's neck. Surely he would never hurt her. There seemed to have been something between them, at least on Askari's side, and Jasper wondered if those sentiments would stay the guard's hand. Even if not, there had to be some way to get Yidda free without hurting her or anyone else in the process.

Askari and the other guards escorted them up the road until they reached a much taller stone wall. A Jin swung open the door and led Jasper and the others through, and the sight of a huge palatial structure interrupted Jasper's plotting. It must have been the dome-topped building he'd seen coming into the city. Made of polished white stone and roofed with some shining metal Jasper couldn't distinguish for lack of light, the building rose four or five stories tall. Everything about it was rounded—its edges, the heights of its dome, the top of its doorways. It was grand and majestic in a way as foreign to Jasper as the palace in Irgdol, but he couldn't think to awe over it now. The guards were guiding them toward the huge space that was the front doorway, out of which poured a flood of firelight, so much that Jasper wondered at first if the place wasn't aflame. After a moment, he gained a better angle and decided it had to be just an overabundance of torches inside the place. The thought didn't comfort him.

He turned his attention inward again, trying to discern their situation. It seemed they were being taken to the Sultan. Jasper realized he'd have to rely on diplomacy to worm their way out of whatever the Jini had in store for them. That wasn't going to go well, if Jasper knew anything about the creatures. They knew they had the upper hand. There was no way anyone would come after Jasper and the others, even if he was the Prince of Oerid because no one would risk starting a war with the Jini on Jinadian soil. Perhaps the Sultan would hold him for ransom. What would happen to the others then? Jasper could protect them, promising a higher price to free them as well. Whatever happened, there was no way they were going to escape from the guards now, not inside the palace walls. Jasper would have to rely on his own prudence and clever speech to get them out of this.

They reached the front of the palace and proceeded through the doors into what was obviously a throne room. It had a wide hallway lined with painted columns and all the decor pointing one's eyes toward the far end of the space. As Jasper had imagined, there were torches lining the walls, though he hadn't expected the trenches of fire along the walkway. It was a moat of flames hemming them in, directing them in the only direction they could go. Jasper couldn't see beyond the Jin in front of him, so he glanced around. The brightly colored embellishments on the columns and ceilings grew more intricate the more he looked at them. It was as if the patterns were drawing themselves as he watched. He nearly ran into the guard in front of him when they stopped.

The guard moved aside, and Jasper found himself before a towering, bejeweled throne. He looked up and the gaudiness of the creature before him repelled him. If the outside of the palace was the majestic splendor of an Eshadian mountain range and the inner decor was the intricacies of M'rawa's flora and fauna, the Sultan was a circus of creaturely ornamentalism Jasper interpreted as uniquely Jini in nature. Above Jasper and the others, the Sultan had to be ten feet tall when he stood. Right now, he was lying, sprawled and unconcerned, on the gilded throne. His sandy body was set with many jewels like the outside of the palace. However, without a real pattern, they failed to give a sense of intentionality. It seemed more as though the gems were worthless pebbles carelessly strewn about, and Jasper realized that might have been exactly what the Sultan was intending. The creature also wore a crown of evadium and gemstones. It looked thick and heavy, and there was hardly a spot the gemstones didn't cover. They were rubies and diamonds for the most part with sapphires, emeralds, and amethysts on the sharpened points that rose from the top. Altogether, it gave Jasper an impression of greed and cruelty. It didn't surprise him, though.

The Sultan's eyes were closed and remained so even when the guards stopped in front of him. Askari's voice interrupted Jasper's scrutiny of the scene.

"We have located her," the Jini guard said, his eyes down and words emotionless. "Yidda."

The Sultan opened his eyes, and his gaze fell on Yidda. His eyes were the same inky, glassy, lifeless black as the other Jini's, but their size filled Jasper with a sort of dread as though the creature was watching him, too.

"I see you have, indeed," the Sultan answered, stroking his chin with long, spindly fingers. "It seems the ceremony malfunctioned for you somehow, Yidda? You certainly couldn't have intended that." He waved his hand in a nonchalant gesture at her general figure. "But forgive me. Let us introduce ourselves. I see you have company, Yidda, whom I would be delighted to meet."

"You have no business with them. Let them go," Yidda replied, her voice hard, though Jasper could hear it trembling

"Are you unaware, Yidda? Sultan Sasar *always* has business with his guests, and the guests of my subjects I count as *my own* guests." The Sultan's voice was oily. "So who have we here?"

The Sultan was going to find out anyway and being forthright might aid in their negotiations. Jasper decided to interject before Yidda could respond.

"My name is Jasper."

Out of the corner of his eye, he saw Yidda recoil. It wasn't like he'd told the Sultan his station. Being honest didn't mean he had to confess everything—it would have only complicated matters.

"Ah, what a polite young man. See, he has no problem telling me who he is." The Sultan aimed his sarcasm at poor Yidda who was now shaking her head at Jasper. The Sultan turned back to Jasper. "You lead this company, I assume?"

Jasper gave a firm nod, not taking his eyes off the Jin.

The Sultan smiled. "Then tell me—what brings you so presumptuously into my city? Surely a man of your station is aware of the consequences of appearing before a sovereign uninvited."

Jasper stopped breathing. A man of his station? So the Sultan knew who he was, then? "I am aware," he replied coolly, then stopped, searching for words. The Sultan knew who he was. "We are seeking someone," he said finally. "We must know if you have seen her. Surely a man of your station would be aware of such comings and goings." He watched the Sultan, pleased with his wording. If Jessica had come here, the Sultan would be aware of it, and Jasper's phrasing implied that any uncertainty would evidence a shortcoming on the Jin's part.

The Sultan shifted so he was sitting facing Jasper and the others, resting his elbows on his knees and his chin in his hands. He peered down at Jasper. "I suppose you are referring to a certain young woman who came through our blessed gates a short while back," he said. "A certain Jessica Cibelle of Hestia? To be your wife, if I remember correctly."

Jasper stilled the shiver that rose within him. The Sultan was much too aware of the situation. Could he know why Jasper was seeking Jessica? Before the Sultan could say anything about it, Jasper spoke.

"And what do you know of her?" he asked, his words tinged with sharpness.

"What do I *not* know of her?" The Sultan's leering smile invoked immediate revulsion in Jasper. "I *know* her well, Jasper Aurdor, better even than you would have."

The Sultan turned his eyes to Miss Marchand, his expression vile and suggestive. Jasper nearly jumped in front of her to protect her but caught himself in time. The Sultan was playing with him. Surely the Jini sovereign hadn't done anything to Jessica as vulgar as he was implying. The way he was looking at Miss Marchand wasn't reassuring. This couldn't be happening.

"Where is she? Have you allowed her to be harmed?" Jasper was maintaining his composure. Barely.

"Oh, only a little. She doesn't mind it now," Sasar said.

"Where is she?" Jasper demanded.

"Do not fret, young prince. She is better off now."

The Sultan was definitely playing with him now, and horror at the creature's implication blasted all Jasper's thoughts of diplomacy aside. He forgot himself and put his hand to his rapier, about to draw it when a cord whipped around and caught his wrist.

"Oh, killing me will not do anything. You see, there's no real way to reverse what's been done. She prefers it this way, anyway." Sultan Sasar began to laugh.

"What have you done?" The words burst from Jasper's mouth. There were so many questions cluttering his mind, he felt dizzy. The Sultan couldn't have done what he was implying. If he had… But he hadn't. He couldn't have. "Where is she?" Jasper nearly shouted.

The Sultan had to calm his maniacal chortling to manage the next words. "I'll answer your questions. No need to act so cross." He paused; his eyes now turned to Jasper with a pointed, savage glint in them. "She is dead. I killed her." Then the Sultan was laughing again.

Jasper felt the blood drain from his face. He hardly noticed as he wobbled, then stabilized himself. Jessica was dead. No, it couldn't be. Sultan Sasar was playing a sadistic joke on him.

"But you couldn't have," Jasper whispered.

The Sultan calmed himself enough to answer. "Oh, you would have appreciated her dying words, Jasper Thesson Aurdor, Prince of Oerid. They were something to cherish, her trust that you would come for her."

Jasper shook his head, trying to drown out the Sultan's voice, but it didn't work. Sultan Sasar had killed her. It never would have happened if it hadn't been for him. Jasper had killed Lady Cibelle, and with her, the hope of Oerid. Panicked, he sought answers to questions he wasn't conscious of asking. He had to gather himself for the others' sakes. Cor and Yidda must have known how terrorizing the news was, but the others didn't, and he couldn't bring them down into the black with him. They had to get out of here.

Shaking, Jasper was about to speak when he found himself surrounded by guards. He jerked as he felt his hands roped together. Grainy fingers enclosed his arm.

"Now off with you. I will have you severed in the morning," the Sultan said as he waved his hand, again untroubled.

The proclamation only vaguely fazed Jasper. What did severed mean anyway? If he was honest, it couldn't get any worse than it already was. The pit of his stomach the weight of a boulder, and something painful lodged in his throat so he had a hard time breathing. Jessica was dead, and he was the reason for it. What had he done? The guards shuffled him and the others out of the room. Dazed, Jasper noticed little as they were escorted away, and not ten minutes later, he found himself with the others in a dark, sandy dungeon.

Chapter 9

STILL STAGGERED, JASPER WATCHED AS Yidda stared through the bars of their prison cell.

"It's not your fault, Yidda," he told her. "The blame is mine. You wouldn't have been caught if we hadn't accompanied you."

It *was* his fault. He'd killed Jessica, and now he was going to kill the rest of them. Or get them "severed," that was, which Yidda had explained was the tearing of the soul from the body. No one asked what happened to the souls then. Maybe none of them thought they could handle knowing.

"I'll never again see Ohebed. He's most certainly in the Palace of Air, a place an evil soul may never enter," Yidda replied, her tone severe.

Her mouth twisted, contorting her face. If Jasper hadn't been so distraught, it would have evoked wonder that he could see the woman's face at all. As it was, he realized her physical form only meant she would die along with the rest of them, all because of him.

"What is the Jini understanding of the afterlife anyway?" Cor asked in a calm voice.

Yidda looked at the dwarf, frowning, but something must have diffused her exasperation as she answered him.

"We believe in two realms of the afterlife—the Prison of Souls and the Palace of Air. The Prison of Souls is for the spirits whose evil has overcome them. They have obeyed the Voice, or else they have become agents of the Sultan. In either case, they have served Evil herself. The Palace of Air is reserved for the few who can maintain their dignity and nobility and live in peace and goodness. We don't know where we come from, we only know what is now, and now is hellish. The Prison of Souls is a continuation of what we experience in this life."

"Evil is a woman, then?" Malach asked.

Yes, she was a woman, Jasper thought to himself. It crossed his mind again that he might hear the same voice as the Jini.

"Evil is an entity, yes, and a female one, if that is what you are asking. She is real and present with us. Hers is the Voice that afflicts us with terror and coercion. She drives us apart and forces fear into the crevices of our beings. We find ourselves compelled to listen to her, and she put in a safeguard—should we take material form to escape her Voice, she installed a Sultan who serves her and who controls our access to the material body. And should we die, the evil within us constrains our spirit to the Prison of Souls, where she reigns. She owns us."

Indeed, it had to be the same woman who spoke to the Jini as spoke to Jasper. The Lady of Shadows. People didn't normally associate the Jini with the Lady, not directly. The Lady had created the Jini, perhaps, but they were two separate evils, related but independent in most people's minds.

"How can a Jin attain good and peace, then?" Cor asked.

"I don't know," came Yidda's answer. She stared into the distance.

"Dwarves have it simple," Malach said after a moment. "We all go to Esh's Forge when we die. We are reborn into the occupation that befits the honor we achieved for ourselves in this life. All dwarves are equal before Esh. The sovereign and the servant, we are on equal footing. The level of integrity with which we lived our lives dictates which profession we have in Esh's Forge. There is no heaven or hell, no dichotomy but a continuum of glory." Malach's tone changed, his words quieter and more subdued. "And yet I wonder if there's a place for me among the workers of Esh."

Cor looked at Malach with softness in his eyes. "I have often wondered the same about the Courts of Oer."

Cor's forlorn tone irritated Jasper. They were talking nonsense. It wasn't that Jasper doubted whether the gods existed. He merely believed they took no interest in the lives of their creatures, certainly not in the way the others were describing.

No one spoke for a few moments. Instead, they all looked ruminative, probably wondering about Cor's implied question. Jasper couldn't stand the false hope they were buying into. It would fail them, and then where would they be? It would be cruel to disillusion them, but it would be perhaps more cruel to let them cling to such falsehood. He broke the silence, speaking with slow, quiet words.

"There are no Courts of Oer. And there's probably no Palace of Air or Forge of Esh or Prison of Souls."

He looked at the others. They were all staring at him with rapt attention. He went on.

"They're all just myths to make us feel better, to give us an answer to the question of death. We all want there to be a happy ending, and if we cannot find that, we'll be satisfied with any ending that prolongs the process of life. We're not comfortable with the notion that this is all there is, but this is it. This is all there is."

"How do you know?" It was Miss Marchand who challenged him. "You don't have the courage to believe in something more than this?"

Jasper turned his gaze to her. She was so naive. He'd known that, admired her innocence even, but right now it irked him. He wasn't angry at her, just upset in general as he answered her.

"Yes, I have courage. I have the courage to stand by this life and say it is all I am given. I have the courage to admit I've failed, that what I've received I've wasted. Despair takes the daring to accept that things are dreadful, utterly and horribly dreadful."

At that, everyone was quiet. Jasper looked to Cor and saw something shining in his eyes, something like sorrow, something like pain. Jasper told himself he didn't care, but he did. Cor was disappointed with him, he knew, but he couldn't accept what Cor believed. It didn't make sense. The gods didn't care about him except to toy with him. He knew, somewhere deep down, Cor was wrong about Oer. Kronk's voice interrupted Jasper's brooding.

"Kronk no like quiet. Grumpy ones no fun. Need song." She didn't look around before she began what sounded like a lullaby.

Night come, night fall
Sleepy, sleepy, one and all,
Moon out, moon bright,
Baby sleep by moonlight.

One day soon, all be right,
Orc will see by heartsight.

Spirit come, Spirit fall
Enter, enter one and all,
Sun out, sun bright,
Orc will wake by sunlight.

One day soon, all be right,
Orc will see by heartsight.

Kronk quieted and glanced around at each of the others. "No one sleepy?"

Everyone shook their heads. How was one supposed to think of sleep on the eve of his execution?

"Ihva have pretty voice. Ihva sing with Kronk!" Kronk demanded.

Miss Marchand sighed and looked at Kronk's pleading face. The woman's beseechment must have persuaded her as she nodded her assent. They began the chorus again.

"One day soon…"

Miss Marchand helped Kronk tune herself by singing in a louder, more confident voice, if that were possible. Her singing was so clear and bright, it didn't fit with the darkness that surrounded them. The flickering shadows from the torch flames on the wall held a stark contrast to the radiance of her melody, and Jasper felt a twinge of regret over his words. He was sure he'd hurt her with them.

"Quiet in there!" a guard yelled, moving into the room and clanging his spear against the bars of the prison cell.

Miss Marchand gave the guard a defiant look, and she and Kronk kept singing.

"Night come, night fall…"

The guard rattled the door to the cage and shouted, "Some of us need rest before the morning. Not everyone gets to die tomorrow. Life goes on, you know?"

Miss Marchand watched him as she continued, "Spirit come, Spirit fall, enter, enter one and all."

Something caught Jasper's attention out of the corner of his eye. Some sort of light appeared where their weapons lay in a pile on the ground. Turning toward it, Jasper found it was a blade, Darkslayer to be exact, which was glowing. He watched in startlement as the sword rose from the pile and unsheathed itself.

"What? Who's doing that?" the guard burst out.

Jasper turned to Miss Marchand. It was her blade, after all, but her eyes were wide and mouth agape as though she had no idea what was going on either.

"Stop!" the guard began to cry out, but then his mouth clamped shut as Darkslayer moved toward him.

"Orc will see by heartsight," Miss Marchand finished softly, almost in a whisper.

The guard's eyes grew even bigger, if that was possible, and the blade traveled to him. No one said anything, and no one moved. Jasper held his breath as Darkslayer eased forward and its point touched the Jini guard square in the chest. The guard swallowed, and everything became deathly still.

Then an even brighter light—a deep, translucent green glow—appeared at the tip of the sword. The light was the color of dark summer grass, of the M'rawan leaves they'd so recently left behind, of emeralds and of Miss Marchand's eyes, which Jasper was certain were as transfixed on what was transpiring as his were. He watched as the brightness grew in size. It looked almost as if the sword was drawing the light from within the Jin, and indeed it might have been. The guard, his mouth agape, stared down at his chest as though immobilized, unable to even reach a hand up to stop what was happening. A few seconds later, Darkslayer drew back, taking the green ball of light with it. As soon as the light detached from the Jin's body, though, the guard disintegrated and crumbled to the floor.

Jasper kept his eyes on the sandy remains for a moment, waiting for someone to speak. His attention shifted, though, when he saw Darkslayer come hurtling through the bars of their cell, the brightness with it. An almost imperceptible whisper accompanied it, so soft Jasper could only make out a couple words—*come home*. Mostly he gained a general sense of timbre, reminding him of a voice he'd heard recently, though whose he couldn't recall. The only ones he'd heard of late had been those of his companions and before that, of the elves. He didn't have time to puzzle over it any longer, though, as Yidda broke the silence.

"He left the keys," she said quietly.

Jasper glanced over. Indeed, the guard's keys were lying on the ground at the edge of the pile of his remains.

"We can't reach them," Malach replied. "Not unless we can manage to hook them with Ihva's blade."

"It's too far," Miss Marchand said.

Jasper kept his eyes on the keys. Maybe seven paces away, they *weren't* too far, not for him. He could reach them, he knew, but then he might incite the Lady's whispers. He cringed at the thought.

"Can you do that trick you pulled back in Irgdol again?" Malach asked. "Use your blade and work some of your magic?"

Jasper looked over and saw Malach's eyes were on Miss Marchand.

"I don't know," she replied, her words unsteady.

Jasper turned his attention back to the keys. He could reach them and draw them over. Half-conscious of reaching for the pendant around his neck, he listened to the anxious conversation beside him.

"I can't do it," Miss Marchand said with tension in her voice.

"You've got to! Try it again, and this time we'll pray to Esh, too," Malach came back.

"Jini prisons are shielded to magic," Yidda cut in.

"Well what in the name of the Light just happened, then? That was magic, or I'm a toadstool!" Malach exclaimed.

Cor hushed the other dwarf, but Jasper stopped listening. He had to get the keys. Maybe he could try to forget Miss Marchand was there and protect her that way. He nearly snorted. As likely he could forget the warp of his reality, the hollow within him. There was no way to avoid what was going to happen. He had to take the leap, knowing he had no wings. He steeled himself and grasped his amulet.

Taking care to position himself as far from Miss Marchand as he could, he looked at the keys, which were ten paces away now since he'd backed up. Wanting nothing more than to shut his eyes, he called on the Power hanging from his neck. Magic began to seep into his consciousness—a dark, filthy magic smearing itself across his mind. He forced his eyes to remain open, fighting the instinct to hide, and wordlessly called the keys closer to him. To his surprise, nothing more happened than the keys lifted themselves from the ground and moved toward him. He outstretched the hand not holding his Power and caught them. There was no voice, no violent impulses, just the feeling of cold metal against his palm and a sudden silence from the others.

He turned toward them. They each had a different expression. Malach had his mouth open as though he'd been mid-sentence and struck silent. Cor had a grim frown and Yidda a sympathetic softness in her gaze. Kronk had flattened herself against the wall away from Jasper. It was Miss Marchand he was afraid of, though, so he avoided looking at her.

"Ha, and you thought magic doesn't work here!" Malach said finally.

Jasper froze. He'd given himself away. Oer's magic didn't work here, but the Lady's apparently did. He was about to redirect the conversation toward escaping their cell when it started.

Slay her.

The Lady's voice jolted him, and he flinched.

Cut her down.

He became intensely aware of the sword in Miss Marchand's hand and of a dozen ways to disarm her and take her blade for himself.

Take it and destroy her.

Now he did shut his eyes, squeezing his eyelids tight together.

Eliminate her. Only one shall stand.

For the sake of everything good in Gant, don't let him do it! Desperation so overcame him that he almost cried aloud his distress. Then something touched his arm, and he jerked back, terrified it was Miss Marchand, that she was trying to help, that he would strike her, hurt her, kill her. A voice beside him shook that fear from him.

"Jasper," was all it said, but he knew it was Cor's voice. It had always been Cor's voice that had broken him from these fits. Their years of training flooded back to him, and he released the breath he'd been holding, then inhaled slowly, deeply, and opened his eyes.

All attention was on him still. He didn't dare look at anyone too closely for fear of seeing what their faces held. Instead he spoke.

"We need to get out of here," he said.

The others nodded, still silent.

"Do you know the way, Yidda?" he asked, forced to look her in the eye.

Her eyes were sorrowful, but her tone was pragmatic as she replied, "Yes. This is where they kept me before. I can get us out."

Jasper nodded, then made his way to the cell door. Fitting the keys into the lock, he found the right one and twisted it. With a click, the lock came open, and the door to the cell swung wide.

"After you," he said, motioning for Yidda to take the lead.

The others quickly followed the Jini woman, all except Miss Marchand. He caught her gaze on him and found she was watching him with a hesitant stance.

"Miss Marchand," he said.

She flinched and gave him a wide-eyed look.

"We have to go," he told her.

She nodded, and he looked away as she stepped out of the cell. As she passed, he moved aside with his eyes on the ground, guilt washing over him. He couldn't banish the echoes of the Lady's voice. She'd felt so near, her compellings so strong. What if he'd let down his guard? What would have happened? Now was not the time to think about that, though. He turned his gaze to the others, who were picking up their weapons from the corner of the room and strode over to join them.

Chapter 10

IHVA AND THE OTHERS MADE it out of the palace dungeons and nearly out of the palace itself before she heard the sound of shouts and footsteps pursuing them.

"Hurry!" Yidda called out as she led them out the palace doors.

Ihva turned her head and saw a group of palace guards following them brandishing all types of weapons, from spears to swords to crossbows. A bolt whizzed past her ear, and she decided to focus on fleeing.

They rushed past the nobles' houses. Ihva had no chance to gaze in wonder at their strange splendor on this pass-through. Reaching the district of the middle class, Ihva heard the sounds of their pursuers gaining on them. She redoubled her pace. They reached the market district. The city went by much faster as they fled, though the way seemed twice as long. Yidda led them on a straight path toward the docks. A few more crossbow bolts whizzed past, and one sank into the building next to Ihva. She didn't dare look behind her.

They reached the lower-class section of the city. Ihva grew more worried as they approached the ships in port. She couldn't swim and had never been on a seafaring vessel before—her father had never allowed her on his ships. If this was their means of escaping the Jini guards, she had serious doubts about their success.

By the time she and the others reached the docks, her heart was pounding, and she wasn't sure which scared her more—the pursuing Jini or the escape route before her. In front of her, Yidda skidded to a stop near the edge of the wooden platform over the water. The woman turned to face the pursuing guards, and the others stopped to turn toward the approaching Jini, too. Ihva drew Darkslayer, and the others readied their weapons as well. Looking at Yidda, Malach lent her one of his daggers, and they all faced the oncoming attack.

As the Jini guards rushed toward them, Ihva noticed movement out of the corner of her eye. She looked up at the guard towers to see two watchmen taking up crossbows and training them on her and the others. She braced herself.

One of the Jini on the ground, which had another crossbow, stopped forty paces away and aimed. He shot a bolt, and it came flying right past the arm in which Ihva held Darkslayer. The Prince, Malach, and Cor stepped in front of Ihva while Kronk positioned herself to Ihva's right and Yidda appeared on Ihva's left. The remaining Jini guards rushed forward with their spears and short swords.

Ihva tried to even her breathing as they approached but managed only one deep breath before they arrived. The Prince parried the first guard's sword with his rapier. The two blades met with a clang of metal. Another Jin shoved his spear toward the Prince's chest. He had just enough time to dodge, and it grazed his side.

Malach took the upper hand with a third Jin. He flung his dagger before the guard could manage to move his sword. The knife buried itself in the Jin's chest, and the creature disintegrated. The dagger hurtled back through the air into Malach's outstretched hand, and he turned to face a new opponent.

Ihva took a short moment debating who to help. She saw Cor's hammer hurtle sideways into a guard's belly and knock it into another Jin. Both toppled over. The Prince had two assailants, and he didn't seem to be faring well. While he was fending off the one, the other managed to slice his arm with its sword. Ihva slid between the Prince and Malach. The Prince didn't seem to notice as he parried the Jini's strikes. He was on the defensive and had no space to attack. As Ihva raised her blade, the Jini with the spear grazed the Prince's right shoulder. He grunted, and she struck out at the Jin. Her aim was true and pierced the guard in its belly. The creature put a hand to his stomach, and something granular poured out. He turned his attention toward her. Raising his spear arm, he stepped back and hurled it at her. Fear clenched within her as his eyes flashed. She jerked out of the way. The spear flew and clattered to the ground, harmless. Ihva's eyes turned up in time to see the injured Jin stumbling away. No matter, she told herself. He would find his end soon with the wound she'd dealt him.

The clang of metal and the thuds of Kronk's club and Cor's hammer filled the air. Ihva looked for Kronk and saw she was striking out with her club, blind, with her eyes closed. Somehow, her swings were connecting, and no other Jini were daring to close with her. Satisfied the woman was handling things well on her own, Ihva turned to see the Prince's progress with the other guard. He was more on the offensive than he'd been with the two guards. He knocked the Jin's sword away and struck the guard's upper arm. The rapier didn't sink in as deeply as it would have in flesh. Ihva knocked the guard's head with the flat edge of Darkslayer—not a normal use of her weapon, but she found it effective. The guard stood stunned for a moment, and she took advantage of those few seconds to sink the point of her blade into his throat. He crumpled to the ground and disintegrated.

Ihva looked quickly at the Prince. A weary look was in his eyes, and his eyebrows raised as he watched the Jin collapse. That was two Jini guards Ihva had put out of commission this fight.

The Prince jerked back, and she saw a crossbow bolt protruding from his left shoulder. She gasped. He eyed the bolt and grimaced. Ihva heard a couple more bolts whiz past. She looked up and saw three crossbow-wielding guards on the ground shooting in their direction. Hesitant to rush forward alone, she looked around. She knew she couldn't take on three guards by herself. She saw Kronk open her eyes and lift them from a disintegrating Jin to the archers. The woman screwed up her face in a resolved expression and started toward them. She was certainly becoming more daring. Beside Ihva, Yidda appeared with a spear. Ihva looked at her. The Jin's face was hard, and she and Ihva started forward after Kronk.

Kronk was sprinting and drew far ahead of the others. She barreled into a Jini crossbow-wielder, knocking him over, then proceeded to beat him with her club. He curled up, trying to protect himself but to no avail. After a moment, Kronk moved away and he lay still, then crumbled. Ihva saw an archer in one of the towers aim his crossbow at Kronk. Ihva cried out to warn Kronk, but it was too late. A bolt grazed Kronk's arm, leaving a bloody gash.

Meanwhile, the Prince made it to the bottom of the northern guard tower, and Malach started up the stairs in the southern tower. Ihva looked behind her for Cor. A guard wielding a spear was severely injured but putting up a tremendous fight. With Cor occupied, Ihva ran after the Prince while Yidda went after Malach. Passing Kronk, she saw the woman lumbering forward determinedly. Up close, she recognized Kronk's wound wasn't fatal. There would be time later for tending to it.

Ihva reached the base of the tower behind the Prince and bounded up the staircase. Reaching eye level with the floor beneath the Prince and the Jin, she halted. They were circling each other slowly. Each one's face spoke the death of the other, and there was blood flowing from the Prince's shoulder. She gauged the best way to join the fight.

Before she could move, the Prince lunged forward, then caught sight of her. Her presence must have startled him, as his blade missed the Jin. He slipped and fell to the ground, and the Jin dashed over and pinned him down by his bloodied shoulder. The guard loomed over him, and for the first time, Ihva saw unadulterated fear in the Prince's face. His dark eyes widened, and he struggled to break free without success. The guard raised his sword above his head in both hands and prepared to stab the Prince in the chest.

Ihva felt a scream rise in her throat. As the Jin's sword started down, she shrieked and lunged forward. The Jin turned his black, lifeless eyes toward her, the movements shifting his aim. She didn't stop. His sword pierced the Prince, and she was certain it killed him. She stopped thinking. Turning her full attention to the Jin, she swung Darkslayer wildly, forgetting all her training in her terror. The point of her blade drew a long cut in the + stumbled back. Shock and anger over the Prince threatened to distract her, but she struck again at the Jin. Her blade pierced his chest. Sand began pouring out of the wound, and he fell and disintegrated. She breathed a quick sigh of relief.

Then, without stopping, she turned back to the Prince. She didn't even steel herself against what she might find, but when she turned, she found his eyes on her. He was still alive. His breathing was heavy, and she found a puncture wound below his ribs. It wasn't bleeding as much as she'd expected, but she didn't want to take a chance. She went and knelt beside him.

"Can you walk?" she asked, her voice trembling. Looking back into the city, she wondered when the next onslaught of guards would arrive. "We have to go," she said.

The Prince looked up at her, pain glittering in his eyes. He coughed and squeezed his eyes shut, wincing. "Don't worry about me," he said, then sucked in a breath. Blood bubbled like foam from the puncture in his side.

"You're wounded. We need to get you somewhere safe!" she exclaimed.

"I said don't worry about me!"

"I just want to help. That's all. I'm not asking you to give me anything in return."

The Prince watched her as she put a gentle hand to his wound.

"You'll owe me nothing," she added in a quiet voice.

As he stared at her, his hardened expression slackened. Something in how he was holding himself tempered, and she felt her breath catch. His eyes on her became soft. He was watching her, too.

"I just want to help," she murmured.

His look stiffened as he frowned and jerked away from her. "I don't need your help. Your help is the last thing I want." He grimaced as he pushed himself to his feet. "Why can't you leave me alone?" he muttered under his breath, barely loud enough for her to make out.

She rose to her feet alongside him. He started toward the staircase, his breath rattling. He coughed and stumbled. Rushing forward, she caught his arm to keep him from falling.

"I don't know," she whispered.

She placed his arm around her shoulders and waited for him to walk, avoiding his gaze. His body was cool against her, and he winced. She expected him to lash out in frustration or anger. She expected him to take back his arm and leave her like he had that morning when she'd asked her prying questions, but he didn't. Instead, he leaned his weight on her and took a step forward.

She walked with him down the winding staircase. His weight was heavy on her shoulders, but she bore up under it with determination. Three quarters of the way down the stairs, they met Malach and Cor. Seeing Ihva struggling, Malach took the Prince's other arm and helped guide him down the rest of the flight.

When they reached the bottom, Yidda and Kronk met them. Kronk was bleeding from a few places, but nothing looked too serious. Yidda appeared unscathed. Kronk hurried over to Ihva when she and the others reached the ground while Yidda looked around. In the distance, shouts sounded. With no further hesitation, Yidda pointed to a nearby ship.

"We'll have to board that to escape. There's nothing in front of it to be loaded. I suspect it'll sail in the morning for Eshad."

Ihva looked at the ship. It was one of the larger vessels in the port. Yidda meant for them to board it? Ihva hated to admit it made sense. She suspected the Jini would be reluctant to come aboard a ship without the express permission of the captain. Seeing as it was the middle of the night, it was unlikely that they'd receive such permission. If Ihva and her companions escaped quickly enough, the guards wouldn't even know which ship to search.

"We would be stowaways?" Cor asked.

He seemed reluctant, and Ihva suspected he was wondering if Oer would permit such a thing. Ihva felt hesitant as well, though for different reasons. She loved the seaside, to be sure, but she'd never been out to sea. The thought of water surrounding her without a sure way back to land terrified her. Still, she'd known this expedition would require courage. She mustered as much as she could.

"If we don't escape by ship, our only option is to flee by desert. The Jini will follow us there. We'll be recaptured within hours," Yidda replied.

Cor gave a hesitant nod. With no other objections, everyone moved toward the ship Yidda had pointed out. Malach took the Prince's left arm, and Yidda took Ihva's position supporting his right arm as they hurried ahead. He was beginning to look gray, but his eyes shone with desperate energy. They made it to the gangplank and aboard the ship without hearing any shouts behind them. Then they ducked out of view.

Once on deck, everyone came to a stop. They all looked around. Ihva saw a couple of trapdoors in the floor of the deck. One was closed and off to the side. The other was in the center of the deck and open, but it was pitch black inside. Toward the front of the ship, Ihva found a number of cabins. The captain and first mate likely inhabited them. Ihva knew the rest of the crew would be below decks sleeping. She looked back at the two trapdoors. One must be for the crew and the other for the cargo, but she couldn't tell which was which.

Malach spoke first, saying, "The safest place will be with the cargo. They'll be least likely to find us there."

"Where would the cargo be?" Ihva asked.

"Probably in there," said Malach, pointing toward the closed trapdoor. "The crew's quarters will have been left open to let out the heat from the day."

Ihva nodded, thinking Malach's reasoning sounded logical. Still resting between the dwarf and Yidda, the Prince groaned and had a distant look as though he might fall unconscious at any moment. Cor rushed toward the closed door, opened it, and ducked inside. A moment later, light shone out of the hatch, and Cor's voice sounded softly.

"It is safe."

Ihva looked over at the Prince. His expression was stiff, and he didn't seem to be conscious of what was going on around him. His eyes had a distant look. Ihva wanted to let Malach and Yidda take him first, but Malach pointed out the Prince couldn't climb down the stairs himself and would need someone at the bottom to ease him down. Ihva nodded and made her way with Kronk down into the space below deck.

When she reached the floor, she looked up and found the night sky looked dark. Clouds must have rushed in to cover the starlight. She watched as Cor and Malach guided the Prince into the space below. Kronk was a few stairs up and wrapped one of her arms around the Prince's waist. She used the other hand to steady herself and climb down the last few stairs. When they reached the floor, Ihva positioned herself beneath the Prince's right arm once again. He felt like dead weight this time. She noticed his chin had slumped to his chest as she and Kronk moved him out of the way of Cor and Malach. His breathing was shallow and shaky. At least he was still breathing, but who knew for how long? Instead of the panic she expected, she felt numb, hollowed of emotion, even of fear. It was as though everything was waiting with bated breath for what would happen next, and Ihva felt the pressure of it all bearing down on her. When Cor and Malach reached the floor, they resumed their duties of carrying the Prince. Cor had a look of dreadful concern as they walked forward, a deep frown on his face and pain in his eyes.

He motioned the others toward the back of the space. They navigated between piles of boxes to follow him. It surprised Ihva to find that the room was rather disorganized. In a corner, they found a small pile of straw, and Cor and Malach set the Prince down on it gently. Cor knelt to determine the extent of the Prince's wounds. When he spoke, his tone was grim.

"I can do all I am able, but I am not sure that it will be enough," he said. "It appears his injuries are extensive and beyond my skill. He is fortunate to be alive at all, and he will not be for much longer without intervention."

Malach cursed, and Yidda muttered something under her breath. Kronk drew closer to Ihva and put her arm around her. Ihva felt as though her legs might give out. She leaned her weight on Kronk.

Still kneeling, Cor placed his hands on the bolt in the Prince's shoulder. He pulled it out. Immediately, he put one hand there, the other on the wound in his side, and spoke a quiet prayer. Light flashed from his hands. The Prince shivered, but his eyes remained shut.

"A lung has collapsed, and he has internal bleeding. I cannot mend such things. Ihva, it must be you, child," Cor told her as he moved aside, still pressing his hands to the wounds.

She felt something inside her jolt at Cor's suggestion. She, save the Prince? He'd said her help was the last thing he wanted. Would he ever forgive her if she indebted him? It didn't matter. There was nothing to do but Heal him.

She knelt opposite Cor and looked at the Prince's face. However off-putting the man could be, she knew she couldn't free herself from the web her feelings were spinning. His face was so pale as though all the blood had drained from it. He couldn't die, he couldn't. He meant something to her, much more than she'd allowed herself to admit. She squeezed her eyes shut. Aware that her Healing couldn't change his feelings toward her, she turned her focus to prayer. She silently pleaded for Oer to spare the Prince's life. She was disconsolate, desperate. The Prince couldn't die. She couldn't lose him. *Even if he never cares for me*, she prayed, *spare his life and bring him back. Let him live.*

She felt it before she saw it. Warmth filled her hands and spread from there. She opened her eyes. A second later, she saw a light appear extending from her hands to the Prince's wounds. Before her eyes, his flesh sewed itself back together. She was Healing him! The light expanded to fill his entire body, pulsed, then faded. His eyes fluttered open.

Ihva could hardly contain herself. He looked a mess still, blood staining his clothing, but he was alive! She'd done it! He would live. Forgetting herself, she leaned forward and hugged his neck. Joy all but overwhelmed her.

"Um." He cleared his throat softly.

She realized what she was doing and drew back, then fell from her knees backward and scrambled to stand. Her face must have been bright red. She tried to look anywhere but at the Prince or the others.

Her companions seemed to have hardly noticed, however. Malach extended his hand to help the Prince to his feet. Yidda clapped her hands, and Cor wouldn't stop beaming. Only Kronk's attention was fixed on Ihva. She looked at Ihva and shifted from one foot to the other, seeming unsure of herself.

The Prince stood with Malach's help and looked around. The color had re-entered his cheeks, and he could stand on his own.

"Where are we?" he asked. His voice was still weak.

"We are on a dwarven ship still at the port of Alm'adinat," said Cor, a smile spread across his face. He patted the Prince's arm.

"Are they gone, then?" the Prince asked.

"The Jini? We defeated the first round, but it sounded like there were more after us. That's why we hid here in the cargo hold," Malach said.

The Prince nodded his understanding. He turned his gaze to Ihva. "That was you who Healed me?" he asked her.

Ihva nodded.

"Thank you," he said in a quiet voice. His tone was surprisingly genuine.

Ihva nodded again. What was she supposed to say? She feared her voice would betray her, so she remained silent.

"Kronk will need some Healing too. Then we should get some rest," Cor said.

Ihva was grateful for his interruption. She looked at Kronk and instructed her to stand still, then placed her hands on the woman's shoulders and spoke a short prayer. The energy went out of her again, and she felt weariness overwhelm her this time.

"It must be nearly third watch by now. The ship will be out to sea in a few hours, and we will need to decide our plans from there," Yidda reminded the others.

Ihva and the others looked around for good places to sleep. They ended up spreading out in the back of the cargo hold. Ihva laid down with one stack of crates between her and Kronk, and as soon as her head hit the straw pillow she had created, she was fast asleep.

That night, she dreamed of kings, magical creatures, and adventure. In one of her dreams, a large, sparkling white dragon appeared and spoke to her. The dragon, a female, told Ihva she had to continue on her journey and warned her not to grow complacent. Ihva's mouth formed draconic syllables she'd never studied, and she replied that she'd remain faithful to her calling.

Chapter 11

JASPER WOKE TO THE SOUND of wood grating on wood.

"It's time to rise, Prince," came Yidda's voice from behind some crates.

He stretched and arose. He felt tired still, and his abdomen and shoulder ached with the pain of an old injury, but he was alright.

"We're having a meeting, everyone," Malach announced in a loud whisper.

Memories of the night before, of a few hours ago, filtered into Jasper's mind. Miss Marchand had Healed him. She'd saved him. She'd told him before that he'd owe her nothing, but he was indebted to her whether she wanted it or not. He'd almost gotten her killed, and in return she'd saved his life. Humiliation overtook him for a moment until Malach spoke again.

"Up and at 'em, lass. We've got things to discuss."

Miss Marchand was waking as well, then. What could she think of him except that he was an utter fool? Everything about the situation they were in was his fault, and he had no answers. Jessica was dead. They were stowaways. Jasper was lost, and so were they all.

He got up and stepped over the crate he'd been sleeping behind. He saw Cor, Malach, and Yidda already assembled in a space they must have cleared a few moments ago. Kronk was stretching, and Miss Marchand was moving toward a box to the side, looking meek.

"Is everyone ready?" Yidda asked.

Jasper was the farthest thing from ready, but he had no other options. These five—Cor, Malach, Yidda, Kronk, and Miss Marchand—were his only hope now. If they could ensure his survival back to Oerid, maybe he could lock himself away and rule in seclusion. He couldn't do what he'd done to Jessica again. He couldn't let another woman fall in love with him, not when it would cost her everything. Yet he knew he couldn't rule from solitude, and someday he'd need to choose a wife. He needed an heir almost as badly as he needed the woman who'd save him.

"We're as ready as we will be," said Malach.

Yidda glanced around at the others. "With Lady Cibelle gone, we'll need a new plan," she said.

A new plan? If Yidda wasn't careful, she'd alert the others to the fact that Jessica's rescue had been part of a larger operation.

"With Lady Cibelle gone, there *is* no new plan," Jasper replied before anyone could ask what Yidda was talking about.

"There must be. Your life depends on it, Prince, and your people," Yidda replied in a quiet voice, looking him in the eye.

Jasper flinched at the woman's forthrightness. "This is a conversation for in private, Yidda," he told her stonily.

Malach butted in. "We know you cared for her, but was there more attached to Lady Cibelle than sympathy, then?"

Jasper glared at Yidda as he replied, "If there was, it wouldn't be for you to know."

"So there was…" Malach said, trailing off.

Jasper turned his gaze and stared at the dwarf in silence for a moment.

"He has confided in you, son," Cor said from Jasper's left.

Jasper glanced over at Cor, who gave him a steady look. Cor was right, of course. Malach *had* confided his secret to them, but Malach had little to lose by revealing what he had to those whom he had. Jasper had everything to lose. If Malach knew, if he really knew who he was dealing with, he'd hesitate to offer his assistance and would likely regret his own confidence in Jasper. He might even use his status and sway to dethrone Jasper, throwing Oerid into confusion.

Jasper's eyes wavered in Miss Marchand's direction. If she knew the real reason he'd been chasing Jessica all over the continent, she'd never forgive him. He was already in her debt. Could he tell her now? Could he ever tell her?

"We're all you have left, Prince," Yidda told him in a soft voice.

Jasper bristled at the Jini woman's sympathy. Why did she insist on treating him like he was deserving, like he somehow merited her solicitude? Far from earning kindness and praise, he was dangerous, and he wanted to say Oerid would be better off without him except she wouldn't be. He was Oer's Chosen Son. By nature of his birth, he was to rule his people, and forfeiting the crown would throw the nation into the turmoil of an unclear succession. He had to fulfill his duty to the people of Oerid. That wasn't being noble, though. That was being responsible.

Jasper looked at Yidda again and then at Cor, then back at Yidda. Everyone was silent, waiting. He couldn't do this, but Yidda was right, these five were all he had, and it would be better to know who'd support him when it came down to it.

He spoke, his words halting. "There is much to lose and much at stake. If I tell you, I need you to pledge your support or your silence. I can't risk others knowing."

He looked at Malach and Miss Marchand, then at Kronk.

"You can't speak a word of this to anyone," he said, talking to the orc-blood woman.

Kronk nodded. Jasper looked back at Malach. The dwarf was peering hard at him as though trying to discern what Jasper was about to reveal from his demeanor. Jasper stared back at him, and after a moment, Malach nodded too.

Then Jasper looked at Miss Marchand. She was the one he was most afraid of, not because he thought she'd reveal his story to anyone else—she looked too scared for that—but because of what she might think of him upon hearing it. It was a selfish fear, and he knew it, so he pushed it aside and addressed her.

"You won't tell anyone what I tell you now?" he asked.

She shook her head, her eyes wide. Little did she know he felt the same way. He looked at Cor, who nodded. Then he drew in a breath, and the story began to spill out.

"It started the night I was born," he began. "The Lady of Shadows visited my father, or a Shrouded sent by her did. Something had happened that night, and the line of Aurdor almost ended. My mother and I had died while I was born. My father bargained with the Lady of Shadows, and she revived me. The price she required was my heart."

He paused. Everyone knew how Raising worked. Whoever possessed the heart of the Raised One had control over that individual. He saw Malach's eyes grow wide and didn't dare look at Miss Marchand as he continued.

"I would serve her, she thought. My father knew this, so he prayed." Oer had heard King Theophilus that night. The one-time Oer had ever intervened, and it had been to pain Jasper and complicate his life. No one else seemed to see it that way, though. "It seems Oer smiled on him somehow, and my father found a box to protect my heart." Jasper stopped again. He couldn't go on. They now knew who he was, but he hadn't gotten to the truly despicable part. He glanced at Cor with a pleading look, and Cor must have felt some mercy as he spoke for Jasper.

"Only one who loves the Prince, one whose heart he holds, can open the box. Oer intended it as a safeguard, and for twenty years, it has functioned accordingly." The dwarf gave Jasper a reassuring look and motioned for him to continue.

He picked up where Cor had left off. "When Lady Cibelle was captured, I knew the Lady of Shadows had taken her. I needed to head off Hell's Mistress and rescue Jessica, else the Lady of Shadows would use her to access my heart. If she did so, she would control me. She would control the kingdom of Oerid. I would be subject to her will, and thus so would the entire nation. It wouldn't be long before all of Gant fell to her."

Jasper shivered. He'd done it. He'd told them the detestable truth, the reason they ought to loathe him. They knew now he'd been after Jessica to save himself. He shook his head, trying to rid his mind of his self-contemptuous thoughts. That wasn't the whole of it, he realized. Now it was up to him to explain his new predicament, the new desperate truth. He drew in a breath and continued.

"Now there is no way for the Lady of Shadows to open the box and take my heart, no means by which she can control Oerid. There is also no means I can be freed of her influence, either. I live half a life, subject to fear and will rule with a weak will. I'll never be free with Jessica dead, and Oerid will suffer because of me."

Everyone was silent. Jasper's eyes were on the ground, but after a moment, he glanced up. Cor and Yidda were watching him with calm expressions, and Malach appeared alarmed, his mouth agape. Kronk squinted her eyes, and Jasper feared too much to look at Miss Marchand.

"You were Raised?" Malach asked after a long moment.

"Yes," was all Jasper replied.

"You are under the torment of Hell's Mistress then," Malach said.

"Yes," Jasper affirmed; the word feebler this time. He turned his eyes away from Malach to Cor as though Cor could somehow save him from the truth.

"That won't do. Oerid can't be governed by a king so entangled with the Lady," Malach said.

Jasper glanced over at the resolve in the dwarf's tone. Malach wore a heavy frown uncharacteristic of him.

"No, it won't. I'm aware," Jasper came back, sounding defensive. He didn't mean to, but that was how it had come out. Malach thought him weak. Maybe he was, but he'd done all he knew to do to escape his weakness. "I've done everything in my power to save myself and my people. There's nothing left to do." He looked Malach in the eye and continued, staunch. "The Lady has won." He repeated the prophecy he'd chanted like a dirge inside himself his whole life.

76

"To one whose heart he holds
Shall be this living token,
Shall the curse be broken."

He didn't pause after but rushed on. "The one whose heart I held is dead, Malach. What would you suggest I do? I will *not* put another woman through what happened to Lady Cibelle. I've had enough of the 'one whose heart he holds.' The one whose heart was mine is dead, and there will be no other. I will not stand for another woman to fall in love with me only to forfeit her life as the cost."

He stopped and inhaled. He'd forgotten to breathe. He kept his eyes on Malach, who had a serious look on his face. The dwarf wasn't quite dismayed but was certainly at a loss for words. It was Kronk who broke the silence.

"One who love frowny prince not dead." Her thoughtfulness had concluded, and she stood with a triumphant grin on her face.

"What do you mean, Kronk? Sultan Sasar told us that he killed Lady Cibelle," Cor said in a gentle voice.

"Cibelle lady not true love. Ihva is. Ihva's heart belong to frowny prince," Kronk replied.

All eyes shifted to Miss Marchand, including Jasper's. What Kronk had said didn't register with him at first except to single out Miss Marchand. He watched her eyes go wide and her face redden, then Kronk's words washed over him. Miss Marchand's heart belonged to him. Miss Ihva Marchand's heart belonged to him. That inkling he'd had back in the clearing in M'rawa swelled to a near certainty, but before he could process what that meant, Yidda spoke.

"Ihva," she said in a quiet voice. "Is it true, dear?"

Miss Marchand's gaze darted at Jasper for a fraction of a second, panic in her deep emerald eyes, then she quickly looked back at Yidda.

"No, of course not! I could never love such an unfeeling excuse for a man!"

With that, Miss Marchand fled, disappearing over some crates into a far corner.

"You need to go to her," Yidda told Jasper.

"But," he began.

"No 'buts.' She's upset with you. You need to reconcile," Yidda said.

There was a silence. What if it was true? Did Miss Marchand like him? Love him?

"If it's true, that changes things, right?" Malach ventured.

"Perhaps. For now, we need him to go talk to her," Yidda repeated.

They all looked at Jasper again. He froze. Why did it fall to him to talk to her? No one knew he loved her, though, or his desperation to have her and the measure of guilt he'd been carrying because of it. It wouldn't have been that hard if he hadn't held these feelings for her.

"Okay," he told them.

They all nodded. He glanced over them again and turned to go after Miss Marchand.

"I mean, she does seem fond of him," Malach said behind him.

"They have had much time together with their lessons," Cor replied.

"Besides, how could the lass not fall for the Prince? It's in every fairytale *I've* ever heard," Malach added.

Jasper had to tune them out. He strode toward the crates where Miss Marchand was hiding, carrying himself with feigned confidence. He paused a few feet away. She was on the other side of these boxes thinking Oer knew what. She hated him; he was sure. She'd said as much a few moments ago, and really, how couldn't she after all that had happened?

"Miss Marchand." His voice sounded weak, and he knew it. He bolstered himself with resolve and spoke again. "Miss Marchand, I know you're there."

She didn't answer. Taking a breath, he climbed onto the crate between them. She was below him. He shifted to the right, then lowered himself onto the ground beside her. He was having a hard time breathing deeply but forced a long inhale and exhale. Then he settled in, sitting cross-legged next to her, not looking at her face. He didn't want to see what he might find there. He cleared his throat.

"Miss Marchand, I."

"Don't," she stopped him and scooted away.

Jasper sighed and looked at his feet. He shifted, uncomfortable, then tried again. "Miss Marchand." He paused. She didn't respond, but at least she hadn't cut him off. "I don't think you understand," he said.

There was another pause. How was he supposed to explain? He'd been seeking Jessica for his own sake, for Oerid's sake, but even if Miss Marchand loved him, even *if* that was true, he refused to use her like that. He'd protect her, not send her into danger.

"*What* don't I understand?" She scooted farther away, almost against the crate that walled her in to the left.

He gave another soft sigh, then stood and walked over to sit down opposite her. "It's just, well, I've been afraid."

She turned her head up at him, her eyes wide, and he was tempted to look away.

"It's hard, you know, trying to protect those you care about when you're the one you have to protect them from." He stopped. He couldn't tell her what he felt for her. It wouldn't make sense. The situation was much too complicated for him to tell her that. He had to at least explain about Jessica, though.

"I tried to let Lady Cibelle off easily. My letters rambled and were rarely flattering to her. The gifts I sent had no meaning, and I hardly spoke when Father invited her family for dinner. Still, she took to me somehow. She fell desperately in love. I suppose the prospect of becoming Queen did nothing to deter her."

Miss Marchand's look was perplexed. He lost his breath again.

"What are you talking about?" she asked.

"I didn't stop Jessica. I didn't stop her, and now she's dead."

He inhaled. He couldn't do the same thing to Miss Marchand, even if she somehow returned his feelings, especially if she returned them. He'd protect her.

"Sorry, Your Highness. I don't mean to be rude. It's just other people have troubles and sorrows, too. It's not just you. If you expect any of my compassion, I think you should take a look at yourself and put a flame to the coolness of your manner."

He drew back. Was that what she thought of him? Cool-mannered, unfriendly, unfeeling? He clicked his tongue in frustration. Her words hurt.

"Do you love me, Miss Marchand?" he asked suddenly.

He wasn't sure why he'd been so blunt. All he knew was she'd lashed out at him and he'd reacted.

She flinched at his question. "What if I do?" The sharpness in her tone dared him to even try to get the truth out of her.

"I've been doing everything in my power to protect you," he shot back. "I haven't told you a word of anything so you could stay out of it. You asked me, but I couldn't bring you into this mess. I didn't want to keep a secret from you, but I had to."

What was he saying? He'd wanted to tell her? Of course he'd wanted to tell her. He wanted to share it all with her—the good, the bad, the curse, his love. He wanted to hold nothing back. That could never be, though.

"I just need to know," he added quietly.

Another pause.

"Fine, I like you," she said. "Is that what you wanted to hear? I might even love you. Not that you'd care. What is it to you? If you think you'll drag me into saving you, though, you're wrong. I won't be used." She crossed her arms in front of her chest, and her eyes flashed.

Jasper didn't comprehend what she'd said at first. It dawned on him slowly. She liked him. She might even love him. What terrible delight those words sparked in him. He trembled. She wouldn't be used, she'd said. That was the last thing he wanted for her. He wouldn't. He couldn't.

"I should start over," he said.

She broke his gaze and looked down.

"I'm sorry, Miss Marchand. The last thing I wanted to do was bring you into this." In his earnestness, he reached out and took her hand in his own. He had to make her understand that she didn't need to be frightened of him using her. He was a danger, but he wouldn't use her. "I tried; I really did. I tried to keep it all from you, but somehow, you're in the middle of it anyway. Still, I won't use you. You mean too much."

Miss Marchand's eyes rose to meet his, and there was pain in them. "Why?" she asked, sounding frustrated. "Why do you do this to me?"

"I'm sorry!" he replied, not knowing what he was apologizing for.

"You know letting me down easy is cruel. You pretend to care, you say you're sorry, but at the end of the day, I'm just a silly, prying girl to you."

"No, Ihva." Oh Oer, he'd used her name again. He took a breath to calm himself. "Miss Marchand," he started again in a serious tone. He squeezed her hand and looked her straight in the eye. "You mean a lot to me. As hard as I tried to discourage Jessica, I tried just as hard to protect you. I will not use you. I couldn't, not again, not you. You mean too much to Oerid, to Gant, to me. I—" *I love you*, he'd been about to say, but he stopped short and turned his eyes down.

"You what?" she asked.

"I care for you, Miss Marchand. I, um, I care a lot about you." His voice was soft. He didn't trust himself to be any louder.

She didn't say anything, so he glanced up. She was studying him.

"I don't want to hurt you," he added to fill the silence.

She stared at him, and he looked back at her. She appeared so unpresuming yet somehow bold. He couldn't help wondering at it all. She cared for him in a way that resembled his own feelings even if they didn't mirror them. The longer she watched him, the deeper her eyes became, and the more earnest their consideration of each other grew. After a long moment, he wondered whether she didn't love him after all. He came close to telling her what he felt for her, to just blurting it all out and hoping for the best. Thankfully, she spoke before he could.

"The first thing you can do is stop calling me Miss Marchand. My name is Ihva."

Her words caught him off-guard. Did she expect him to reciprocate? It wouldn't be appropriate for her to call him by name. It would be far from appropriate, but how gratifying, how heartrending, how pleasurable it would be to hear his name on her lips.

"Yes. And you will call me Jasper."

They weren't ruler and subject out here, he argued to himself. They were companions, and it was time for everyone to drop their courtly demeanor.

"I will do that," she stated in agreement.

They stared at each other again. He saw something cross her mind, a fearful expression run across her face.

"Don't tell them, please," she implored him all of a sudden. "Don't tell them, Jasper."

It *was* pleasurable to hear. He had to let go of her hand lest she felt him shaking.

"I won't, Ihva." He found it just as delightful to call her by her name. He wanted to go on, to make all the promises he'd been feeling for the past month, but instead he stood hastily. "I won't," he assured her again, then climbed over the crate and left her to consider things on her own until she was ready to emerge.

He made his way back toward the others.

"Did you reconcile?" Yidda asked.

"Yes," was all he replied.

Silence followed as the others looked at him, inquiring.

"Her feelings are hers to tell," he added.

He couldn't face them for too long before he had to turn and pretend to be looking through his pack for something.

Miss Marchand—Ihva—cared for him. Perhaps Oer had decided to intervene once again, and this time in Jasper's favor. Now Jasper just had to figure out how to protect her from himself.

Chapter 12

IHVA SANK DOWN, RELIEVED, DELIGHTED, fearful. It was enough for the Prince to know her heart. She'd rather not deal with questions from the others yet. He'd respected her confidence, she'd heard, and that reassured her he'd been speaking honestly.

Jasper. She was supposed to call him Jasper. It hadn't felt proper when she'd done it, though. Anyway, that was definitely not what she'd been expecting when she'd told him to call her by name. A lot of what he'd said had not been what she'd expected. He cared for her. That was what he'd said. She meant a lot to him. He'd had to keep his secret from her. Did that mean he'd wanted to tell her? What did it all signify? Was it like with Malach—the Prince saw her as a sister, dear to his heart, but nothing more? That had to be it.

The problem was their conversation had done nothing to assuage her longings. In fact, it had made them worse. She *would* help him, she knew. That she wouldn't had been a lie. Even if she hadn't liked him, she would have done it. She cared about him besides her feelings for him. Yet if she hadn't felt anything for him, she wouldn't have been able to help—the irony.

The others were waiting. She had to get back. She drew in a breath, tucked her thoughts away behind an attempt at composure, and climbed over the crates behind her. She wasn't sure what she'd say if they asked her anything, but she couldn't spend any longer dwelling on these questions, the answers to which would hurt her.

Malach gave her a sideways look as she approached but said nothing. Cor and Yidda were already discussing their next steps.

"We do not have sufficient provisions to last the trip. We must find food and water before too long," Cor was saying.

"There must be some around here somewhere," Malach said, turning back to Cor and Yidda. "The sailors have got to eat and drink, too, after all."

"Perhaps there are some rations among the crates," Cor replied.

Malach nodded. "Sometimes food is kept in the cargo hold. Other times, there is a separate compartment for food and water supplies."

"On a ship this massive, it is likely the dwarves have a second room for all their food and water," Yidda said.

Malach's face fell, and he sounded downcast as he replied, "Looking through these crates is worth a try. We've got nothing to lose."

The others agreed, and they spread out to start opening the wooden boxes. The tops of the crates were nailed in place, so they ended up having to work in pairs, prying open the lids with their blades. Kronk took her place with Ihva, and Cor joined Malach. Ihva quickly found the boxes too heavy to move so she stuck to checking the top crate in each stack. After a few minutes, she heard disappointed sighs coming from the others.

"Jewels, jewels, and more jewels!" Malach complained.

As for Ihva, she found her crates full of glassware—statues, bowls, figurines, and vases, among other things.

"Jini make jewels. Jewels and glass," Yidda said.

"This cargo must be worth a quarter of a city," Ihva exclaimed. "What do you dwarves do with all this stuff, anyway?" The ship's goods were probably worth a quarter of a year's trading for her father.

"Why do you think dwarven decor is so bejeweled?" the Prince asked from somewhere to her left. Strangely, he sounded amused.

"Good point," she replied in a quiet voice.

He'd taken such a familiar tone all of a sudden. Was this what it was going to be like now? She blushed and hid behind the crate she'd been checking. She almost missed when he wouldn't speak to her at all. Almost. At least then she hadn't had to deal with the fluttering in her stomach.

From behind Ihva, Kronk huffed in exasperation. "Kronk hungry!" She took a large glass vase out of a crate and hurled it in anger. The vase hurtled toward the staircase leading to the trapdoor, and Ihva braced.

It crashed into the rail and shattered into thousands of tiny pieces. The noise was even louder than Ihva had expected, and the shards of glass tinkled as they dropped to the ground. Everyone in the cargo hold froze except Kronk. She looked to Ihva and blurted out an apology.

"Sorry! Kronk not mean to break pretty vase!"

Ihva shushed her, then remained silent and motionless along with the others. She strained her ears, listening for any sign of commotion above deck. For a second, she held onto the hope the sailors hadn't heard the shattering. Then, a shout filtered through the wooden barrier between them and the deck, and the noise of feet pounding rushed toward the trap door into the cargo hold. Ihva shivered as the footsteps halted above them.

"Hide!" Malach said in an urgent whisper.

The light Cor had produced winked out. Ihva scurried through a maze of crates, moving to the right to hide behind a tall stack. She heard the hurried scrapes of boots on the floor behind her. Kronk followed Ihva. Ihva scooted over to make room for her and held a finger to her lips in the dim light of Kronk's ribbon.

As Kronk nestled into her hiding spot, the door to the cargo hold crashed open. Light poured into the room, and Ihva squinted her eyes as they adjusted. She shifted to her left, pressing against Kronk to remain out of view.

Ihva thought she could make out three sets of footsteps pounding down the staircase. Kronk hugged Ihva, and they held themselves still as wooden crates scraped against the floor. The dwarves were shifting the cargo in their search. Ihva's heart beat hard as they neared her hiding spot. She stopped breathing.

A dwarf cried out nearby. "Here's one!"

Ihva heard the dwarf dragging something heavy over a crate. She wondered who they'd found.

"Keep searching, there might be more!" another voice called out.

As the other dwarves continued moving around crates, the first dwarf asked in a loud voice, "What's your name? What are you doing here?"

"The name's Gregory, sir," Malach's voice said.

Fake names. That was a good idea. Ihva decided to reassume the name Esther like she had at the Eshadian farm if these dwarves found her.

"Why are you here?" demanded the dwarf.

"Escaping the Jini, of course." Malach spoke the truth, though not the whole truth, of course.

"Right." The word drew out, and the interrogating dwarf didn't sound convinced.

As the first dwarf conversed with Malach, a second dwarf called out in triumph. "Found another."

A third dwarf gasped as the sound of a crate being moved came from Ihva's left. "What in the name of Esh?" he yelled. "Look!"

Ihva heard him dragging something heavy across the floor for a second. Whoever was resisting must have realized there was no escape, however, and the dragging ceased.

One of the other dwarven sailors cursed. The first dwarf's voice trembled.

"It's a Jin!"

They must have found Yidda.

"But look at it!" said the dwarf who'd cursed, his voice quivering.

There was silence for the next few seconds. Then movement sounded from where the dwarves were positioned. The next moment, Ihva heard Yidda cry out. Ihva was torn between running to the woman's aid and remaining hidden. She stayed behind the stack of crates, took Kronk's hand, and squeezed it.

"Stay your hand!" Cor said firmly, his voice sounding from the center of the hold with the dwarves. He must have been the second one discovered.

"Why not? It's a Jin!" said one of the sailors.

"She's not just a Jin!" Malach answered. "She's, well, she's different."

"How?" The sailor's voice wavered.

Yidda cried out again, this time in genuine pain.

"Stop!" came the Prince's voice.

Ihva heard him crawling over a stack some paces away.

The room went silent. Dying to know what was happening, Ihva turned and peeked around the crates behind her. The Prince was standing with his rapier drawn. He trained his blade on a dwarf who was holding Yidda. The dwarf had her tight against himself and was pressing a dagger to her chest.

"That wouldn't be a wise move, lad," the dwarf who was holding Malach said. "We are but three of a large crew. You wouldn't escape with your life."

Jasper kept his rapier where it was and turned his gaze toward the dwarf who had spoken.

"You will not harm her." His tone was icy. "She's as good a creature as you could ever hope to be."

His response surprised Ihva, and Yidda looked down.

The first dwarf raised his own dagger to Malach's throat. "Are you willing to give their lives to prove it?"

The Prince was silent.

"Come with us, and you might have your lives spared. Try and fight, and you'll be easily slaughtered, if not by us then by our comrades," the dwarf said.

Ihva sensed the tension in the room building. She could hardly bear it, terrified for Yidda as well as for the Prince and the others.

After a few more moments of tense silence, the Prince called out. "Ihva. Kronk. Join us, please." He didn't lower his weapon or shift his gaze.

Ihva nudged Kronk to stand up. They climbed over the crates and took cautious steps toward the group. Ihva stopped a few paces from the guard threatening Yidda, next to the Prince. She held a hand up to stop Kronk as well and then grasped the hilt of Darkslayer.

"No, Ihva," the Prince said, glancing at her and then back to the dwarf at Yidda's throat. "If you swear not to harm any of us, not even her, we will come easily." With a threat in his voice, he went on, "It would be a shame for you to lose your own lives if it could be avoided."

The dwarf holding Malach eyed Jasper with a cold look. He dropped his dagger from Malach's throat and motioned for the sailor holding Yidda to do the same, then told the Prince, "Your lives will be spared." His eyes narrowed. "For now," he added.

With that, the dwarf pointed Ihva and the others up the narrow stairs. Looking up to the doorway, she noticed more faces peering in. Her anxieties heightened as she realized how outnumbered she and the others were. The others started up the staircase, and she followed them with the last dwarven sailor behind her.

The late-morning sun blinded her as she stepped onto the deck. She squinted and shaded her eyes. Before her, easily two dozen dwarven sailors stood, dressed in cut-off pants and off-white shirts and vests. Their arms showed generous muscles through the sleeves. The crowd of them parted to reveal a better-dressed dwarf. He sported deep brown cut-offs and a colorful, patterned shirt boasting blues and purples and reds. Over his shirt he had a yellow vest. A red bandana topped his head, pulling his dark black hair behind him, and a clasp ridden with gems adorned his braided beard. Ihva was thinking to herself how gaudy he looked when he spoke up.

"What have we here?" he said in a deep voice, his tone disapproving.

"Stowaways, captain," replied the leading dwarf who had been holding Yidda, looking pleased with himself.

"Stowaways from Alm'adinat? That's odd," the captain said, stroking his beard as he mused. A split second of hesitation flashed in his deep brown eyes as he looked in Malach and Cor's direction. Perhaps he hadn't expected dwarves to be among the stowaways.

"This one says they were escaping the Jini," the sailor who had Malach said, then snorted his disbelief of Malach's story.

"Escaping the Jini? They must have quite a story to tell then." The captain chuckled. "Tie them and bring them to my cabin. Stow their weapons in the hold. I'll see what I can get out of them."

"Would you like us to accompany you, Captain?" the first dwarf asked, fear showing in his furrowed brow. "They are well-armed and able-bodied. They could be dangerous, even tied."

"No!" the captain exclaimed; his response quick.

What was he intending that he wanted to speak to them alone? Ihva's ears started ringing.

"Thank you, Michael, but I'll be able to manage," the captain went on. "Besides, they might share more when they're not immediately threatened."

Quickly, some of the dwarves in the crowd supplied an ample amount of rope to tie all six prisoners. They paused a second at Yidda, seeming afraid to touch her. The captain motioned the sailors to hurry along after a moment, and the dwarves finished tying the Jini woman, then gathered the weapons and handed them to two dwarves to carry. Six more dwarves, one for each prisoner, escorted Ihva and the others to one of the cabins. The captain opened the door, and the dwarves led them inside. There they left them. Now Ihva and her companions were alone with the captain, the door shut behind them. The captain bolted the door and walked behind a small desk to face them, his mouth twitching as though he was fighting a smile. Ihva held her breath with no idea what to expect next.

Chapter 13

JASPER STARED AT THE DWARVEN captain as his eyes scanned the group.

"Welcome aboard the Wandering Whale," the dwarf said after a pause, then walked over toward Malach.

Jasper watched the captain in apprehension, then in confusion, and glanced at his companions. Everyone else looked as perplexed as him except for Malach, who instead had broken out in a wide smile, his eyes on the sailor. Malach looked downright jovial, in fact. Jasper found the situation strange.

The next thing he knew, the captain was untying the ropes restraining Malach. "What are you doing all the way out here in Jinad, Malach?" asked the captain in a familiar tone.

"In the middle of the Dihron Sea, you mean? I might ask the same of you with the nation in the state it's in, I presume, over the death of King Cherev-ad?" Malach replied.

"Trade is a never-ending business, and it takes no vacations for civil wars and chaos. In fact, it might be the only thing that keeps me sane in a time like this. But do introduce me to your friends, Malach!"

Malach peered at the other dwarf. "Right, well, everyone, this is Captain Emett Liktov. We grew up and served together for a while in the palace in Irgdol. His father was a member of the Council of Neved, but Emett always had a dream and knack for sailing, and he left us for the sea back seven years ago or so, wasn't it?"

Emett nodded.

"He's a dear friend," Malach continued. "Emett, this is Cor Gidfolk, who I presume you remember is the Dwarf of the East."

Malach paused to allow Cor and Emett to make their greeting. They nodded at one another with friendly smiles, though Cor hesitated.

"Sheal Liktov's son, I presume?" Cor asked, seeming about as taken aback as Jasper, which was an odd state to see the dwarf in.

"Indeed, his third," Emett replied with a hospitable smile.

"We also have Yidda as one of our companions," Malach went on, waving his hand at the Jini woman.

"A woman with an interesting story, I'm sure. She's quite different from the Jini I've met. How did she come by such an appearance?" Emett asked.

"We can tell that tale later. I'm not sure any of us really gets it, anyway," Malach said, glancing at Cor, who shook his head. "First, you must also meet Ihva of the Marchand merchant family of Agda. And her, um, guard, Kronk."

Miss Marchand waved at Emett, but she had to nudge Kronk into an enthusiastic greeting of her own.

"And finally, Prince Jasper Thesson Aurdor," finished Malach.

"I have the honor of welcoming two members of royalty, I see," Emett mused.

The dwarf knew about Malach, then. Strange, the folk Malach had decided to confide in. This sailor, the elvish Council, and their own little eclectic band.

"Mere princes, dear Emett. We have not been named nor crowned kings as of yet. I must fight for my throne, as you are well aware, and Prince Jasper here will ascend when his dear father, King Theophilus, passes on. Pray that is not for a good long while."

"Are you not aware then?" came Emett's reply. "King Theophilus is ill. Prince Jasper's kingdom seeks him." Emett looked at Jasper, his eyes kind and sorrowful.

Father was ill? How ill? Of course, Father had been growing weaker when Jasper had left, but he hadn't been sick. The way Emett was putting it, it sounded like Father was on his deathbed.

"Tell me everything," Jasper said, his tone more abrupt than he'd intended.

"Where have you been? It seems the whole world has turned upside down in the past couple months. First King Cherev-ad was murdered by infiltrators described much like your lot. The entire kingdom of Eshad is on the lookout for you. It's why I had you carried in here without a second to spare so the crew wouldn't recognize you and get any ideas about dragging you back to Irgdol for the reward. Thankfully, they seemed too distracted by this Yidda to think much on the rest of you lot."

Jasper was trying not to look impatient, but then Emett came back around to Father's health.

"Then the king of Oerid, King Theophilus, was struck ill a month or so ago. His condition has been deteriorating steadily. Some say it's because of the disappearance of his son. Others blame dark magic, and some suggest intrigue and poison. Really, the last does not make sense. The King hasn't named an heir in Prince Jasper's stead, so there is no one to immediately benefit by killing him. Still, the situation seems dire. In the confusion, the orcs have been invading from the south, attacking towns and villages and moving northward. There are rumors of Raised Ones. That's the darkest rumor I've heard. Raised Ones are said to have been spotted east of Irgdol all the way to Oerid's border. Needless to say, those who believe such rumors are in a panic, and many blame the unrest on the King Theophilus's weak reign. Civil war is near in Oerid, right alongside Eshad."

"What of the Eshadian throne, Emett?" Malach interrupted.

"The Council has not chosen a new king, but Arusha has named himself Commissioner and has taken the king's duties. He's

93

threatening to invade Oerid to keep it from being overrun. I suspect he is the source of many of the rumors concerning Raised Ones."

Malach interrupted Emett again, speaking in a hushed tone. "The Raised Ones are real, Emett. Arusha has been building an army. I believe he receives the bodies from Shadow Bandits and other Shadow-sworn. When he revives them, he takes their hearts and keeps them together somewhere, a place he calls the Vault of Souls. I wouldn't be surprised if he's deploying them to destabilize an already weak situation in Oerid."

Emett stroked his beard and furrowed his brow. "Indeed, anyone who really knows him knows he means to oppress and manipulate the Oeridian political system to his advantage. He certainly means to rule Oerid, and he'll do so as he rules Eshad, with a graceless, heavy fist. I don't know how he believes Esh or Oer would be pleased with such behavior."

"He's not of them anymore, Emett," Malach said with a sharp tone.

"He's always devoted himself to Oer and to Esh. What could have changed?"

"He went to the Summit. He was converted there somehow. He mentioned a sacrifice, and Exchange, but something must have gone wrong. He serves the Queen of the Mountain now."

Emett inhaled sharply.

"What of the people?" Malach asked.

Emett fixed Malach with a careful look. "Villages outside Irgdol and entire cities have been cut off and are soon to be starving under Arusha's rule. To fight the impoverishment there, I've taken to trading and distributing the revenue to the small villages for them to smuggle into the cities. This is my second trip."

Malach's expression darkened, and Emett went on explaining.

"I've traveled to Jinad with our evadium to trade for valuables there. I had to obtain evadium on the black market, as Arusha has restricted trade to his chosen few. After Jinad, I exchanged jewels and Jinadian glassware for food and other essentials at the few ports left outside Arusha's control. I have a few trusted contacts who'll distribute these goods fairly, and I'm relying on them to complete my work. As I told you, trade is the only thing keeping me sane in times like these."

"Oh, Eshad," Malach said, looking miserable.

"Malach." Emett until the other dwarf was looking at him. "You always said growing up you were not sure someone like you could ever serve your people in the manner they needed, but they need you now. Not just anyone, but you."

Malach turned his eyes down, but Emett waited for him to look back up to continue.

"Your people need the man your father raised to take his place. They need a ruler whose compassion spreads beyond his own borders. You are those things. You can repair the relationship between the Crown and the people, and you can restore relations with Oerid. You can bring peace to Gant, Malach."

At that, Yidda spoke up. "You've learned much of Eshadian history and culture, but you also have a tie to your mother's land. You seek a good that transcends borders. That is something only you can accomplish. You must return to your nation and claim your rightful place on the throne. Though bastard heir you may be to some, no dwarf has greater claim to the crown of Eshad than you. No creature of Oer has a greater claim to peace between Eshad and Oerid than you."

Stillness filled the room. Malach glanced between Emett and Yidda. The look in his eyes was woeful, and Jasper felt sudden sympathy. Never had he related to Malach more than in this moment.

"I can't do it alone," Malach said finally. "The elves pledged their aid, but they can't stand against such things. I fear I must ask your assistance as well."

He glanced at the others, and Emett was the first to answer. "Of course I'll help you, Malach."

"I'll aid you, Malach. I'll do anything in my power to assist your claim to the throne," Yidda added.

"You have my support, too, as you well know," Cor said.

Jasper had lost his voice in wonder and fear over the situation, but he recovered and spoke next. "I'll stand by you. Oerid will stand by you."

"Kronk fight with Firebeard!" Kronk exclaimed, nearly cutting Jasper off.

There was a short pause, then Miss Marchand spoke, her voice small. "You have me, for what that's worth."

Malach looked at her. "That's worth more than you know, lass."

Everyone was silent for another moment. Jasper felt a sort of compassion and respect for Malach as he watched the dwarf take in the others' words. Malach was always so unassuming, one could forget that he was a prince most of the time, but in this moment, it was clear that obligation to Eshad weighed on him, and he bore it well. The earnest look on his face revealed a certain dignity he didn't often show, and Jasper decided he'd underestimated the dwarf. He just might make a fitting king for Eshad.

"Thank you all," Malach said in a quiet voice. "I fear I will be forced to call on you before too long. It won't be an easy road. I'll do what I can to not let it conflict with any of your tasks." He glanced at Jasper, who was staring at the dwarf. "In any case, thank you."

Everyone murmured their assent, and they all rested in a solemn moment of silence watching Malach until he shook his head and smiled. "Now stop staring at me like I'm something noble, or I'll have to go proving you all wrong," he said.

And there was the real Malach again. Jasper glanced at Cor; the corners of whose mouth were turned up in amusement, and found himself smiling in return. Emett was chuckling but collected himself after a moment and spoke.

"The question remains, how will you leave this ship without being captured and turned in for a reward?" He looked around at Jasper and the others. "For that, I have an idea."

Emett went on to explain something about forcing them off the ship in a lifeboat somewhere near the northwestern edge of the continent. He discussed provisions and other details with the others, but Jasper stopped listening after a few moments.

His thoughts drifted back to his father. Father was ill, according to Emett, ill enough that news of it traveled to Eshadian ports and ill enough that Oerid was seeking her prince. It pained Jasper that they'd been gone so long. That had never been his plan. Nothing had gone according to his plan, though. Jessica was dead—he'd never forgive himself for that—Oerid was being attacked from inside and out, all of Gant was in upheaval, he was on a ship in the middle of the Dihron Sea with Eshad's prince and Oer's Blessing, he'd fallen in love with the latter, and there were Raised armies waiting for their return, for Oer's sake. Definitely not according to plan. He realized he was missing the conversation, perhaps something important.

"I'll need to split you up," Emett was saying. "Women in my cabin, men down in the hold."

"How'll you explain that to the crew?" Malach asked.

"One way in, one way out for each location, no way to escape without someone seeing you. Easier to keep track of you that way." Emett paused. "The women I can afford their freedom, but I'm afraid I must tie the men. The crew will be asking if you are let to roam free."

Malach nodded and replied, "Do what you have to."

"Make yourselves comfortable, then. I'll be back for you in a minute," Emett said smiling at them as he opened the door. Then he shouted with feigned anger, "And don't you think of moving even a toe until I get back!" He slammed the door behind him.

"Who would have thought? Emett Liktov, of all people. Luck's with us, eh?" Malach said, looking at the others.

The others laughed, and even Jasper let out a small chuckle, his anxieties easing for a moment. Even as they washed back over him, though, he had to admit he felt a sliver of hope for the first time in years. He glanced at Miss Marchand, at Ihva. Smiles became her well—he'd always known that—but today she was especially disarming. Just when he'd thought all was lost and it turned out things were worse than he'd imagined, he wondered if there might be a chance for them after all.

Chapter 14

IHVA LEANED ON THE EDGE of the bed across from Yidda, who was sitting on the floor cross-legged with her back to the wall. Kronk was in the corner watching the door. It was their second day in the cabin, and Ihva was growing fidgety already. Emett was still working on an escape plan so she and her companions could get back to the Eshad without the crew discovering their identities. Most things he'd come up with centered on using a lifeboat and setting them adrift somewhere near the continent. Ihva didn't say anything, but the concept of sitting in an even smaller, more vulnerable vessel on the sea for hours, maybe days, terrified her.

Something else—someone—terrified her almost as much, and she was thankful he wasn't here to make things worse. The Prince was down with Cor and Malach in the hold, as bored as she was in all likelihood. What was he doing? He probably hadn't had given a passing thought to her, yet here she was pining for him, bemoaning her affections for a man who couldn't wait to be rid of her. Sure, he'd been kinder than she'd expected, but she knew he hadn't meant anything by it. As soon as they arrived back at the continent, they'd part ways and she'd be lucky if he even recognized her a year from now. She squeezed her eyes shut. It wasn't fair!

With her eyes closed, a memory flashed in her mind, grabbing her attention. He'd miss her, he'd said. A lump formed in her throat, and her heart constricted. Why did he have to toy with her like this? He had to have been lying, but then, why would he lie to her about that? He'd miss her, yet he'd fled every opportunity for her to help him. Had it been because of Lady Cibelle? That was what Ihva had thought, but with Lady Cibelle gone, why hadn't things changed? Maybe she was expecting things to happen too quickly. They'd just learned about Lady Cibelle's death, and the Prince needed time to accept it.

Yet at the same time, another idea struck Ihva. What if he'd been telling the truth? What if he really was trying to protect her by keeping her out of it? He'd said he wouldn't use her. Maybe he'd been pushing her away because he'd suspected she was falling for him and wanted to deter her for her sake. Maybe he was even nobler than she'd imagined, forfeiting his good in hopes of saving her. He had a dilemma before him that no one should have to endure—to offer one in favor of many or to save one at the expense of the rest. Having fallen for him, she'd become that one, and he *was* trying to save her, she was sure of it. He did care about her in some strange way. Gratitude swelled her heart, and for a second she felt lighter than the air around her. He cared!

That was when she noticed how such a small concession on his part could kindle her desires to the point of agonizing frustration. She wanted so much more than he would give her she couldn't stand it. This wasn't about him being the Prince. No, all she saw right now was a man, an honorable, brave, self-sacrificing man whose dark looks and fearful stances only underscored his courage. A confession arose and submerged her consciousness in a wave of adoration—she loved him. She was certain of it this time, and it dragged her down into an ocean of miserable delight. It was a bittersweet realization, and it wouldn't leave her mind now that she'd allowed it inside. She loved him with an undeniable, enthralling, aching love. How was she supposed to endure this? When she thought she couldn't stand the feeling any longer, Yidda's voice broke into her consciousness.

"Are you alright, dear?"

Ihva opened her eyes and looked across the room at the Jini woman. It was still disconcerting to be able to see her with her almost human-looking skin, soft face, and pointed ears. It was even stranger to be able to discern her expression and not have to rely on her tone of voice to interpret her attitude and meaning. Ihva stared at her for a moment before remembering the woman had asked her a question, then hurried to answer.

"I'm fine. Everything's fine," she told Yidda.

"Ihva not look fine," Kronk interjected. "Ihva look very sad, very angry."

Ihva turned to the orc-blood woman. "I *am* fine. Really. It's nothing." Her words were a touch sharp. There was a long pause, and she grew uncomfortable, wondering if she'd been rude. "Sorry," she mumbled finally.

"There's no need to apologize," Yidda replied. "It's been a difficult journey for us all."

Ihva watched the Jini woman for a moment, then said in a soft voice, "Yes, it has." It struck her that she was being self-centered given what Yidda had been through in the past few days. Pulling herself together, she asked, "How are you doing, Yidda?"

The woman's gaze on her faltered, and after a moment she looked away. "I don't know."

Ihva waited for her to go on, but she didn't and Ihva realized she might not want to. "It's okay if you don't want to talk about it," she told the woman.

At that, Yidda looked back at her. "It's not that."

"Then what is it?" Ihva asked.

Yidda took a second to answer. "Everything changed. It was a room I knew well, but it became something different, a sanctuary of transformation and renewal. I don't know that I understand it. All I know is the wisdom given there changes things."

Ihva tilted her head in perplexity. She knew Yidda was speaking about the upper room of her house, but it seemed the woman experienced something quite different there than she had. "What wisdom?" she asked.

A corner of Yidda's mouth turned up in a half-smile, though her eyes were sad. "First, his letter, then the Exchange. There is much to be learned from these things and—"

Ihva stopped her, asking, "Wait, what Exchange? Do Jini make Exchanges, too?"

Yidda's smile became rueful. "Every time we take material form."

Confused, Ihva thought out loud. "But you have to go to the Temple to make the Exchange. How can you make one all the way in Alm'adinat, so far from Agda?"

"There is much you don't understand concerning such rites. Did the young prince's story not teach you? An Exchange can be made anywhere and can be struck with beings other than Oer." Yidda's voice was calm, but her words made Ihva shiver.

"So your Exchange isn't with Oer?" Ihva's words were strained, and her eyes darted to Kronk, who was glancing between the other two with an uncertain stance.

"No," Yidda replied in a soft voice. "No, it is with the one who Speaks, with the Voice. We give away a small piece of ourselves with every Exchange, and the pieces never satisfy her. Always she calls for more."

Ihva stiffened, and fear washed over her. Who was this she was talking to? All of a sudden, her gaze on Yidda was wary. The Jini woman looked back at her.

"What happens when you've given away all the parts of yourself?" she asked.

Yidda closed her eyes and spoke with a wistful tone. "We find ourselves in the Prison of Souls."

"I thought you said there was a Palace of Air. Who goes there? You said some Jini go there!" Ihva said.

"Some do. The good ones do. But there are very, very few who maintain their innocence. Very few. I've met only one who could."

Ihva paused, recognizing the pain in Yidda's voice. "It wasn't your fault, Yidda."

The Jini woman turned her eyes to the ground. "Yet if it hadn't been for me, they'd never have taken him."

Ihva opened her mouth to speak but shut it again. She wasn't sure how to argue with the woman, as convinced as she was of her own culpability.

"Not a mite of blame against him, and they murdered him. If I hadn't left, he'd still live," Yidda went on.

At that, Ihva interrupted. "Why *did* you leave?"

Yidda turned her eyes back to Ihva. "There was a dream or a voice or a vision, or maybe all three."

Ihva nodded. "It wasn't *the* Voice, though?"

Yidda shook her head. "No. It was a gentler voice, one that lifted rather than crushed."

"What did it say?"

The Jini woman thought for a moment. "It wasn't words so much as a picture. It showed me a city at the crossing of roads on a hill with fields all around—Agda, I later found out. It gave me the impression that I would go there and witness signs, that I would know them when I saw them, and that I would be among those who would redeem Gant."

"So you left and went to Agda?"

"Yes."

Ihva stopped for a second, remembering a conversation from M'rawa. "And you talked to Cor, right?"

"That was later, but yes."

"What did you talk about?" Wonder about Yidda began to dawn on Ihva.

The Jini woman smiled. "I don't know that you need to hear it yet."

Feeling chastened, Ihva looked away. "About this other voice— I mean I know who's *the* Voice is, but whose is the second one?"

"You don't know?"

"I mean I guess I have an idea," Ihva replied in a defensive tone as she looked back at Yidda.

"You are likely correct," came the Jini woman's response.

"Is it Oer?" Ihva asked.

Yidda nodded.

"What's he like?" Ihva said, her voice hushed.

Again, Yidda smiled. "Bright and dazzling with glaring light. Pure and refreshing, untainted. And good. He is very, very good."

Ihva detected a sort of marveling in Yidda's voice, a sense of awe and adoration. It caught Ihva off guard. As much as she'd wanted to believe Oer was good, she'd never had any real reason to. She realized that since they'd begun this journey, she'd been clinging more tightly to the notion of Oer's kindness and sympathy. She'd had to or she'd believe herself, his Blessing, to be a scourge on mankind and all of Gant. Now she had proof about him in a person, in Yidda, meager as it might be, and she wanted as much information to prove it as she could gather. She straightened her back and looked Yidda in the eye.

"What do you mean by good?" she asked.

Yidda's own posture stiffened and she seemed to withdraw. "There are many things I don't understand myself. He gives glimpses, brief insights into how things work, but there is something deeper. I don't know that I could explain it if I tried."

Ihva felt her face fall but tried to hide it from the Jini woman. If Yidda didn't want to talk about it, Ihva wasn't going to push her to. There was a lot Yidda had to still be dealing with, and Ihva wasn't going to interrupt that process with her own prying questions. She'd seen how that had gone with the Prince, and she wasn't about to repeat the same mistake.

At that thought, something twisted in the pit of her stomach. He'd been angry with her. Now she knew what he'd been hiding, and it made sense why. He'd been protecting her as much as protecting himself and knowing that threw her into a tailspin of longing. She tried to turn her mind to something else but couldn't. He cared about her, he'd said, and she was beginning to see it. It was torture. She almost wished he'd hate her again. At least then she could try to turn herself to forgetting him out of spite and resentment. Her feelings would be less complicated if he despised her as she could simply return his hostility. His acting unapproachable before had been a safeguard against her mistaking his intentions, but now that he'd shown kindness and concern, she couldn't help but hope. That terrible, tiny hope—it had sprung up again.

Ihva turned to Yidda and found the woman lost in thought. Then Ihva glanced at Kronk, realizing too late her look was miserable. She hoped Kronk wouldn't notice. Of course Kronk did, though, and furrowed her brow as she opened her mouth to say something. Ihva headed her off.

"What do you think dinner's going to be, Kronk?" she asked.

The orc-blood woman blinked her fawn-brown eyes and drew back.

"Probably the same old crackers and salted pork, huh?" Ihva prompted. "Not very appetizing compared to anything back home. Remember that beef and leek stew? It was delicious. I don't know what Nellie put in it, but I could go for some of that right now." She paused as Kronk's eyes were wide. "What about you?" she asked finally. "What do you miss the most?"

Kronk blinked again, then launched into a description of her favorite meal, "herb roast chicken," and went on in great detail about a number of other meals she wanted when they returned home. Ihva didn't show it, but every word the orc-blood woman spoke felt like it pounded her deeper into the floor. They weren't going home, but she wasn't going to tell Kronk that. Instead, she nodded along and made enthusiastic comments, pretending everything was going to be fine. If only everything was going to be fine.

Chapter 15

JASPER'S BACK WAS STIFF AS he leaned against the pole to which he, Cor, and Malach were tied. Emett had chosen the men to keep below decks in order to allow the women the privacy of the cabin. Jasper shifted his weight, but it didn't help. Wishing he knew what time of day it was, he tried to use the time Malach was quiet to think.

First, he wondered about his father. The man was ill, ill enough that news of it was spreading across the continent. Jasper shut his eyes and mulled over various memories—Father had always been kind and gracious if forceful at times. Maybe because of his own fault in having his son Raised, he never shamed Jasper for his mistakes. It seemed his own offense had produced mercy in him, or perhaps it was that Jasper was his only child and a living memory of his wife that inspired his leniency. He never failed to instruct Jasper when things went wrong, but he did so with a strange sort of gentleness, a special forbearing he didn't afford many others. Discord rarely arose in their relationship.

The only thing that really caused any contention between them was Theresa Aurdor, Jasper's mother. Father had often tried to speak of her when Jasper was younger, relating stories about her grace and beauty and tenderness. At first, Jasper had listened out of simple obedience, but the day he'd learned about the night of his birth, things had changed. He'd quickly realized that Father had had a choice and that he'd chosen to Raise him rather than Theresa. Maybe the king had been afraid of how his queen would react once she realized she'd been Raised, or maybe Father had been thinking of Oerid and determined to revive his heir instead of his wife. Both Jasper's parents had been older when his mother had him, and it had been unlikely she'd conceive again. Whatever the reason, the fact remained that Jasper's resurrection had precluded the Raising of his mother. He'd been rescued with her life as forfeit. True, the life to which he'd been recovered was nothing he'd want for his mother, but guilt still ate at him that he'd survived, and she hadn't. Father's remembrances of her gave prominence to this guilt, and Jasper had reacted strongly as a child against hearing anything about her. He hadn't known why he was doing it, just that he needed to escape the pain. Now he regretted acting that way, but there was nothing he could do. Father had long since stopped speaking of Mother, and Jasper wasn't sure if there was any way to repair the damage done.

Dwelling on it wouldn't help anything though, he told himself. Not that telling himself that helped him feel any less despondent. He tried to turn his mind to other things, and the first subject that sprang to mind was Miss Marchand. Ihva, he corrected himself—he could call her that now. Something inside him skittered at the thought of her, and memories of their conversation a couple days ago shifted his mood to something more buoyant, something almost high-spirited. Though her confession had been guarded, he'd sensed something genuine in her words. She had regard for him, was keen on him—she might even say she was taken with him. The notion thrilled him. She felt something more than friendship for him. Yet it could never be, and that truth threatened to undo him. All of a sudden desperation to tell her he loved her overcame him, and it was fortunate she wasn't in the room or he might have done it. As it was, he felt his breaths shorten as he thought of her—her soft face with its unfiltered expressions, her slender figure with a hint of shape showing through her loose clothing, the enticing fluidity of her movements, and her alluring emerald eyes. An overwhelming desire to hold her struck him, and he didn't know what to do with it. He couldn't, he reminded himself. The words came with fracturing force, and he struggled against their power. He couldn't, but he wanted to. How he wanted to! Why couldn't he tell her? Why couldn't she be his? There was no real reason, just something made up in his head, right? He wanted to kiss her, not her lips but her mouth. Why not? Oh Oer, why not?

Malach's voice startled him out of his agonizing rumination. "How long you think until the next meal?" the dwarf asked.

Jasper had to shake his head to refocus his attention. Even then, lingering feelings of frustration and distress made it hard to understand what Malach was saying.

"What meal are we even on? Lunch? Dinner? Surely not breakfast. I'm pretty sure we're past that one," the dwarf went on.

"We eat dinner next. There remains an hour or so until then," Cor replied in a calm voice.

They couldn't see each other, all tied with their backs against the same pole, and Jasper was glad of it. He knew his face was flushed, his breathing uneven, and his expression undoubtedly pained.

"An hour or so?" Malach exclaimed. "How do you know anyway?"

Cor answered with the same tone as before. "This is my fourth cycle through the morning prayers since the midday meal."

"You've been *praying*?" Malach replied, his voice strained. "Well, I guess there's nothing better to do. Pray away, then."

Jasper realized he'd tensed his muscles at some point, so he made a conscious effort to relax them. He didn't get a chance to before Malach addressed him, though.

"What about you, lad? What have you been up to, thinking about, doing? You know. What have you been using these blessed endless hours for?" the dwarf asked.

Jasper froze. He wasn't about to tell Malach anything about where his thoughts had taken him. He fumbled for words.

"Nothing much. Planning things," he said quickly.

"Things like what to do about the fetching lass upstairs?" Malach asked.

Jasper's breath caught, and there was a pause. It took him a second to remember Malach had no idea about his feelings for Ihva. The dwarf had to be talking about her sentiments toward him, but he wasn't about to reveal those either. She'd asked him to keep it secret, and he would.

"Just about where to go from here," he said.

"Oh," Malach returned, the word drawing out. "You're talking about that other lass, that Jessica of yours. My condolences, lad, my condolences."

Jasper wasn't sure how to respond. "Thank you," he said in a weak voice.

"I'm sure you miss her. Dreadful what Sasar did, downright ghastly," Malach continued. "Don't know what I'd do in your position myself. Don't envy you, that's for sure." He paused. "But if you need to talk about it, well, I'm not going anywhere anytime soon. And Cor here has some of that good Oeridian wisdom for you as well, I'm sure. Don't you, Cor?"

There was no response from the other dwarf.

"I'm fine," Jasper replied quickly.

"Not good to bury it, that's what Father always said," Malach came back, then rambled on about how bottling things up led to outbursts of anger and that hiding from one's feelings made them take over. Soon he was on a rant about some acquaintance of his and his "blowups," but Jasper was thinking about the irony of Malach's statements. The dwarf had seen his father murdered and never spoken a word about it, at least not in Jasper's hearing. Jasper's mind wandered from there.

Jessica was dead. He hadn't accepted that yet, and his thoughts scattered in the face of the concept. Catching hold of one fleeing rumination, he reeled it back in. Jessica was dead, but she wouldn't have been if it hadn't been for him. He cursed inwardly. What had he done? He'd known he never should have let her so close, that he never should have allowed her feelings for him to develop. He'd held her heart. It didn't matter that he hadn't wanted to, that he'd been indifferent toward her except for wanting to protect her from what he stood for. He'd failed. She was dead.

A resolution surfaced within him as he brooded—he couldn't do the same thing to Ihva. She was probably already a target of the Shadow, and he didn't want to make it any worse for her. Anyway, if he left her alone, maybe her feelings would dissipate. He couldn't have her. Why had he thought he could? The longing to kiss her returned with power, but he fought the notion, the imagining. He knew he couldn't think about her too long or his resolve might fade and he might convince himself it was possible. He and Ihva would never be. Oh, how gratifying it was to use her name, though. After all this time, she'd afforded him that intimacy, and he was going to cast it aside? He'd break her heart that way. How could he purpose to do such a thing? She wanted him, and he wanted her. Why wasn't it as simple as that?

"Don't you think?" Malach finished.

Jasper tried to snap himself back to the present. "Sure, that makes sense," he replied.

"You're saying she's right?" Malach asked, his tone incredulous.

"I mean no. No, you're right," Jasper came back quickly.

"Doesn't matter what I think. It's poor old Bunim we're talking about. I didn't take a side, though of course I think Bunim was on the mark when he said—"

"Peace, Malach. I think we all need a bit of quiet before the next meal," Cor interrupted.

"You mean like the hours of quiet we've had since lunch? Because I think we've had quite enough of that for one day. For one week, maybe—" Malach returned.

"Peace," was all Cor replied, his tone firm.

Jasper waited a second for Malach to say something else, but the dwarf remained silent. Thankful for Cor's intervention, Jasper was then able to distract himself wondering how in the world Malach ever planned to be king. The dwarf was so prone to tireless rambling, blathering on about things that had nothing to do with anything. It was rare he spoke of anything consequential, and even then, he had such a heedless manner about him. Jasper couldn't figure it out. After a while, a few of the sailors came down the stairs with dinner and untied Jasper, Cor, and Malach long enough for them to gulp down their meal. The sailors tied them again, binding their hands and feet for the evening, and Jasper knew they wouldn't come again until morning. It was probably better that way. As the trapdoor shut behind the sailors, Jasper did his best to find a comfortable position and drifted off to sleep.

Chapter 16

IHVA LOOKED BACK AT THE ship with longing. Minutes earlier, the dwarves had lowered her and her companions from the Wandering Whale in a lifeboat into the sea. They were left as castaways with a few days' supplies to accompany them. She felt nervous as the boat rocked back and forth with the waves and thought again about how she couldn't swim as she watched the ship sail away and out of view.

Everyone was silent. Kronk was looking at the water, her eyes wide as she streamed her hand along in it. The Prince looked into the distance after the ship. Yidda was playing with the dagger Malach had lent her, running her fingers along the sharp edges of the blade, and Malach was wringing his hands. Ihva was glad Emett had found a way to send their weapons with them. Cor looked pensive.

The moment Emett had re-entered his cabin with news of his success replayed itself in her mind. He'd convinced the crew that the stowaways deserved the disquiet of drifting in a lifeboat at sea rather than a trial once they returned to Eshad. Perhaps the uneasy political situation helped convince the dwarves to take matters into their own hands. Whatever the case, now they were suffering that disquiet. Ihva looked at the waters ahead. There seemed to be no end to them—

every direction looked the same. In secret, Emett had given them a compass and pointed them on the correct course. However, Ihva was no longer sure they'd be able to steer the tiny boat with the waves tossing them as they were. Cor's voice shattered the silence.

"We might not make it back as quickly as we would like. We must beseech Oer on behalf of our nations for peace until our return," he said.

It was Malach who replied. "Or pray for them to survive, for the menfolk to protect their women and lads and lasses in the stead of their princes." He glanced at Ihva. "And for courage for their women, too, of course."

"Maybe," the Prince said. "Or maybe we just need to do our best to get back."

"Kronk pray. Kronk pray very hard," Kronk interjected. "How Kronk pray?" Everyone looked at her, but the Prince went on.

"I doubt the gods would stoop to interfere with the lives of six individuals. That's what we are at the end of the day. We can't waste our time praying," he said.

Malach replied, his tone defensive, "I am certain Esh cares for his kingdom more than we know. It's his kingdom, after all. He'll do good for his children."

"Yes, but what if his good isn't your good?" The Prince's tone was cordial, but his words struck at Ihva's heart.

The rest quieted at his question, and Ihva turned his words over in her mind. What *would* good look like for a god? Did the welfare of humankind and of the other races matter to the deities in the end, or did the gods operate on a higher level, a more profound plane, than those of the lives of their creatures? Ihva wasn't sure of the answer, but she couldn't bring herself to believe that the Prince was right.

Yidda spoke, interrupting Ihva's thoughts. "One thing we do know is that we need a plan for once we get back to the mainland. Where will we go and with what purpose?"

"We must return to Agda," the Prince said. "Oerid needs her prince."

"Indeed she does, but to return unsuccessful with the likelihood you will soon rise to the throne could be inciting disaster," Cor replied. "She needs you, son, but she needs you whole."

The Prince gave Cor a steady look and replied. "There's one way for that to happen."

Cor nodded.

"I'm not sending anyone after the Lady. I'm not," the Prince said, his words forceful.

Ihva was grateful he didn't look at her. Even so, her heart fluttered—he cared.

"You have no other choice," Cor answered him.

"We can bring it back. We can take the box and bring it to the safety of Agda," the Prince came back.

Cor regarded the Prince with a patient look, then Yidda interrupted them. "We must head south, then. I can give you a general heading."

They'd head to the Shadowed Realm then. A brisk breeze rushed past, and Ihva shivered. She'd follow again, it seemed. She had no direction herself, anyway.

"What about Ihva?" Malach asked as though he'd heard her thoughts. He was looking at her. "She's Oer's Blessing, you keep saying. Does she keep tagging along, or is there something we ought to be helping her with, too?"

Cor turned his eyes to Malach, then to Ihva. "There shall be a final stand, I believe, but I pray it is not yet. Once Oerid has her peace and Eshad has her king, we might aid Ihva more aptly with guards and armies. There shall be a final stand with the Lady of Shadows but let us pray it is not for a while yet."

Ihva stopped breathing. She would face the Lady of Shadows? Cor had failed to mention that. He'd only spoken of the signs of Oer's Blessing and her Powers. He'd described some sort of final victory, but did it have to be against the Goddess of Hell herself? The Lady of Shadows was cruel, sinister, and dominating—some said she'd arisen and murdered Oer's wife, of whom they knew tidbits from elves and dwarves who'd wandered into Oerid in millennia past.

The Lady of Shadows was certainly not an individual one should underestimate, and Ihva knew she could do little against such an opponent. She put a hand to Darkslayer for comfort.

"My fear is that the situation will get worse before it gets better, and we cannot lose her," Yidda said, then looked at Ihva. "You are far too valuable to throw yourself into a battle that's not your own."

Ihva gave a slow nod, unsure what to say. She was going to face the Lady of Shadows. The thought paralyzed her.

"Then we must protect her until her time has come," Cor replied.

The others murmured their agreement, then Malach said, "Aid me as you will, Ihva, but I will guard you twice as fiercely. We won't be losing you, lass."

Cor and Kronk nodded, and Yidda said, "Indeed, I will protect you."

"As will I," the Prince said softly.

Ihva looked around at the others. This was reminiscent of their pledges to Malach, but he was to be King. She wasn't. Their promises overwhelmed her, and she looked down.

"Thank you," she managed.

"Do not fear, Ihva," came Cor's voice. "You have capable companions behind you, and you yourself are an able combatant. We will not fail."

How could he know that? Yet she wanted so much to believe him. Maybe she had to, too, if she wanted to succeed. She looked up at him.

"We won't. We can't," she said.

"I'm afraid the safest place is with us," the Prince said, looking at Cor. "If we hide her somewhere and someone finds out who she is, well, we can't protect her if we're not there." He turned his gaze to Ihva. "Will you accompany us, Ihva?"

"Of course," she replied without hesitation.

Of course she'd go with them. Even if she'd had another option, she'd accompany them. She realized she was looking the Prince in the eye, and she became nervous. He was giving her a careful look, and she wasn't sure what he wanted from her. His gaze sent a thrilling shiver up her spine, and she couldn't have spoken even if she'd wanted to. She wished he'd stop staring at her as she didn't seem to have the power to look away herself. The others were surely noticing at this point.

"That's good," Malach said, breaking the silence.

At that, the Prince turned to the dwarf, allowing Ihva to exhale the breath she'd been holding. She relaxed the muscles she hadn't been aware of tensing.

"But we have to get back first. Does anyone know how we're supposed to get there?" Malach asked.

It was the Prince who answered first. "Who has the compass? I think I understood his instructions."

Malach already had it out and was staring at it, but at the question, he handed it to the Prince.

"And we were supposed to be going south, right?" the Prince asked.

"South-ish. South by southeast. There's a small port town, Tamrath, in that direction according to Emett," Malach replied. "My question is how we're supposed to get there without a sail."

Yidda knelt down and reached under the bench, then produced a long wooden oar.

"Oh," Malach replied with lackluster enthusiasm.

"There are places here and here to place them for stability," Yidda said, pointing to four notches directly across from each other on the sides of the boat. "There are four oars so we must take shifts."

"We will need partners of comparable strength," Cor said. "Kronk and I can take two, then Jasper and Malach, then Yidda and Ihva, if that is agreeable to you all."

He looked at the others. They nodded their approval of the plan with no further comment, and that was that.

Cor, Kronk, Jasper, and Malach took to rowing for the first four hours. Yidda suggested those who weren't rowing try to rest, and Ihva took the woman's advice. She curled up on the bench, and listening to the comforting tones of Cor, Malach, and the Prince discussing heading with brief interjections from Kronk, she fell asleep.

Chapter 17

ROWING WAS TEDIOUS WORK. MINUTES turned into hours, and hours turned into a few days. Ihva and the others had gone through more than half of the rations at this point, though they'd stretched the supplies from the beginning. However, with no land in sight, Ihva was nervous. Would the small bit of jerky and tack last? Did they have enough water for the rest of the trip? Already her throat felt parched. Where were they?

"Kronk want to know how far from home now?" Kronk had been asking the same question for the last few hours.

"Five minutes closer than the last time you asked," the Prince answered, his voice strained.

"Kronk, asking how far we are all the time won't get us any closer," Ihva tried to explain to the woman.

"But Kronk *bored!* Kronk *tired!* Sleep not good on floor of boat."

Ihva began to lose patience. "Well, just be quiet anyway," she burst out.

Kronk looked at Ihva with hurt at her sharp tone.

"Please," Ihva added.

"Now, children, quiet yourselves. Arguing will not help us reach our destination any more quickly, either," Yidda said.

Ihva focused her energy on rowing and stared off into the distance to try to let her frustration diffuse. If she was honest, she was as curious as Kronk about how much longer they would be at sea. She wanted to hit something. Traveling in a boat in such close quarters with the knowledge she couldn't swim ever in the back of her mind, she'd grown anxious and upset.

Her eyes still on the southeastern horizon, she saw something in the distance. Could it be land? She almost leapt up with joy, but then she watched the horizon grow dark, then the black crept slowly toward them. She looked closer. That couldn't be land. Her heartbeat faltered.

"What is it?" the Prince asked from behind Ihva.

"I cannot be certain," Cor replied.

After some minutes, it filled an eighth of the sky, and their paddling became halting and jerky as they watched it.

Malach cursed. "It's a storm," he muttered, then Ihva saw it as well. Huge, dark clouds were the reason for the blackening horizon. "It's a storm, a blasted storm!" Malach cried out now, his voice trembling.

Ihva almost fell from her seat, and commotion overtook the tiny lifeboat. Kronk looked to where Malach was pointing and scrambled as far from it as possible. The Prince and Cor peered into the distance but said nothing. Ihva stood up as though that would give her a better vantage point. She couldn't swim. The thought repeated itself in her mind like a horrible chant. Meanwhile, Yidda told the others in a calm voice to look for anything else that could be used as paddles.

"What use will paddles be in a storm?" cried the Prince.

Despite his protest, he picked up packs and looked under the seats, searching for anything that might help. Cor and Malach nodded in agreement with Jasper, and Malach cursed again.

Yidda asked, "Does anyone know how to swim?"

Everyone shook their heads except Kronk, who gave a vigorous nod.

Yidda sighed and admitted, "Neither do I."

"We'll have to hold tight to the boat, then," Malach told them, his words whisked away by a sudden breeze.

The waves began to increase in size and tip the boat so much that Ihva had to grasp at the side to keep from falling out. At least she didn't have to worry about Kronk. Kronk would find her way to shore somehow. Ihva, on the other hand, was almost paralyzed with fear. Over the next hour, the wind howled across the water. Ihva braced herself as large drops of rain pelted her back. She huddled on the floor of the boat and grabbed the bench, trying to take cover under the seats. It was useless.

The waves became larger and tossed the tiny boat among them as though it weighed nothing. Ihva and the others clung to the small vessel with strength she hadn't known they possessed. Without the sun or compass for a guide, directions became muddy in Ihva's mind. She no longer knew which way the waves were pushing them, but then she didn't care as long as they were headed toward land.

For what seemed like hours, the lifeboat was lifted by the waves and hurled back into the water. Ihva stopped trying to anticipate the boat's movements and closed her eyes. She focused all her energy on maintaining her hold on the side. It felt like ages had passed since the sea had been calm. The rain and waves had soaked the side of the craft, making the wood slippery, and she fought to maintain her hold. Terror overtook her, and all semblance of thought vanished from her mind. All she was conscious of was the sickening tossing of the boat, the roar of the wind, and the rawness of her hands from losing her grip on the wood. She tried to pray but soon gave up and simply screamed, "Help! Please, *please*, help!" She couldn't hear her own voice.

She was growing tired and was sure the others were, too. She didn't know how much longer she could hold onto the boat. The last of her strength was fading, and despairing, she was about to loosen her hold and let the waves take her when the tiny vessel crashed into something. Ihva saw a large gray rock break through the wooden planks, splintering them to pieces. Somehow, she managed to grab hold of the rock and remained there, then looked down.

Kronk was swimming in the midst of the storm and waves or trying to. Ihva watched as the woman gave up and allowed the waves to carry her past the rock and out of sight. Cor and Malach took hold of some larger planks and were carried away in a different direction from Kronk. Yidda awkwardly grabbed hold of another piece of wood that was floating beneath Ihva. She knew Yidda didn't see her as the waves tossed her to and fro. Only the Prince noticed her on the rock.

"Come down, Ihva!" he shouted, his voice somehow carrying over the sound of the wind and the waves.

"I can't!" she screamed back, hoping he could hear her. She had no energy left to fight.

"You have to!" he called to her. "Please, Ihva!"

The water threatened to carry him off. He had to be fighting hard to wait for her.

"I'll die down there!" she screamed, clinging harder to the rock as a large wave swept over it.

As dangerous as the stormy waters were, though, she knew she couldn't cling to the rock much longer. She'd be torn off within minutes, and it would be better to at least find a plank or something to hold onto before that happened. She braced herself to jump into the sea.

At the same time, the Prince was struggling to keep his grasp on the section of wood he was using to float. A wave dragged him under, and his head disappeared beneath the water. Ihva screamed, calling for him to come back. A few seconds later, he still hadn't reappeared. Her shouts became sobs. She was alone. Her body wracked with terror, she failed to stabilize herself and was torn from the rock by another wave. She hit her head on the stone, and everything went black as she was washed into the sea.

Chapter 18

JASPER BURST FROM THE WATER in time to see Ihva dashed against the rock and plunged into the sea near him. He kicked hard against the current to reach the place where she'd fallen. She didn't resurface immediately. He focused all his energy on kicking to remain where he was, waiting, watching for her. He couldn't let go of the wood from the boat, part of a bench, but he wasn't going to leave without her. He couldn't.

After what seemed like minutes but couldn't have been more than a few seconds, she appeared next to him. She wasn't moving except where the waves took her. He paddled over to her and grabbed her around the waist, then hugged her to himself as though she were his very life. She was, she really was. Dear Oer, don't let her be dead.

The waves carried them away from the rock faster than they'd been rowing by far. Jasper held her to himself and propelled them with the waves toward wherever the ocean was taking them. He couldn't tell which direction they were heading anymore, but it didn't matter as long as they reached land.

He didn't have to wait long before he spotted a beach in the distance. He kicked even harder than he had been, and within a minute or so, the waves deposited them on the shore. The rain was letting up, and the dark sky was brightening. Dear Oer, don't let her be dead.

Without waiting to catch his breath, he dragged her up the sandy beach, out of the waves and water. Then he knelt beside her and held a finger to her neck. She had a pulse. He looked at her chest. She wasn't breathing. Blessed Light, what was he supposed to do now?

He brought her farther up the beach to where the sand was wet from the rain and not the waves, then knelt again and watched her chest. Still not breathing. He'd have to help her breathe. He'd seen it done to a servant who'd dropped unconscious when he was ten.

No more hesitating. Just do it. He leaned down. As he was about to open his mouth, though, she coughed. Water spewed onto his face, and he jerked back. She kept coughing, then sat up and looked around. He moved back to give her some space, wiping his cheek.

"Where are we?" she asked, sounding dazed.

Where were they, indeed. How was he supposed to know?

"Good question," was all he replied.

She looked at him and her eyes seemed to come into focus. She wasn't fazed by him, just regarded him with an innocent look. Oer, he hoped she didn't realize what had been going on when she'd regained consciousness. He'd been trying to save her, but now, looking at her, all he could think of was how he wanted to hold her. She was alive.

"Where are the others?" she asked, interrupting his guilty reverie.

"I don't know," he replied quickly, too quickly.

He glanced around. There was no one in sight, though the clouds were dispersing and letting sunlight through in bright beams.

"We should find them," she said.

Find them and interrupt the small bit of time he'd have with her alone, he thought to himself, begrudging, but she was right. They needed to find the others.

"We need to pick a direction," he told her.

She looked up and down the beach. "I say that way," she said, pointing left as he'd been about to suggest going right.

"Alright, then. That way it is," he replied.

He stood and held out a hand to help her up. She took it, and a moment later, they were making their way up the beach. He realized he wasn't sure how close to her to walk. Too far and she'd think him distant, that he wanted to be left alone. Too close and she might start to understand the reality of his feelings. If she found him out, if she knew he reciprocated, she'd be inclined to go after the Lady for him, and that was the last thing he wanted. Still, he didn't want to act too aloof or she'd think him "cool-natured," as she'd put it. Maybe he should just talk to her.

"So," he started. So what? "So, you're from Calilla?"

He realized he knew little about her background. Strange how traveling together, you could learn so much about a person—their likes, their dislikes, their idiosyncratic habits, their fears—but not much except mention of where they'd been.

"Yes," she replied in an instant, then seemed to think for a second. "Yeah, I lived there for more than half my life."

"I've never been."

"It's nice."

"Nicer than Agda?"

She glanced at him. "Well, I liked it a lot."

Jasper remembered her conversation with the young dwarf at the farmhouse. Maybe he'd picked a bad subject. Too late now. "What did you like about it?" he asked.

"Well, I had friends for one thing. That and it's beautiful, the ocean I mean. Looking at it, though, not being in it. I'd rather not be in it again."

Jasper laughed. She looked at him, and he wondered for a split second whether he'd made a mistake, then she laughed, too.

"I get that," he said.

They'd stopped, but he resumed walking. He felt uncomfortable with her staring at him.

"The friend part, I mean. The ocean part, too, though," he added.

She was looking at him again, but he decided to ignore it.

"You didn't have friends at the palace?" she asked.

123

"Um, not really." How to explain? "I guess anyone who thought themselves worthy of befriending me was rather pompous, and those who I would have rather been friends with were too deferential to assume that role."

"I'm sorry," she said with a tone of genuine regret.

It wasn't her fault. Why was she apologizing?

"It's just how it was. I suppose I had enough mentors to make up for it," he replied.

"Oh?"

"Yes, there was my weapons trainer, my tutor, our priest, Lydia, and Cor, of course."

"Has he always been around, then? Cor, I mean."

"Yes, he's been there my whole life."

"I like him."

"Cor? Yes, he's something else, but a good something else. You never have to doubt his loyalty, and he's never steered me wrong." Except perhaps about this Oer's Blessing stuff, but that wasn't important right now.

"You've never had a best friend, then?" she asked.

"No."

"Oh," she said sadly.

"Not that I haven't wanted one. Sure, I've wanted one, as dearly, I suppose, as I've wanted to fall in love, but it's never happened."

"Oh," was all she said.

There was silence for a moment.

"Did the other one happen, though? You falling in love, I mean?" she asked. She was definitely not looking at him now.

"Um," he stalled. Why had he brought up love? "Yes, once."

He'd had to tell the truth. She'd have known if he was lying. She was thinking it was with Jessica, though. She had to be thinking that. Her murmured response confirmed it.

"She was fortunate." The hurt in her voice was buried beneath her forlorn tone, but he knew it was there, and it pained him. He couldn't tell her, though. Maybe she'd fall out of love with him, and he'd never have to send her in the first place.

"I refuse to use another woman like I did Jessica, though." He stopped and turned to her. "I won't use you, Ihva. I won't do it. As it is, I wish you'd forget me, but I realize that's a bit difficult with me being all of a pace away." He realized it all too well. It was torment, having her within reach yet completely beyond him. "You're safe with me," he added softly.

She gave him a wounded look. What had he said wrong?

"I realize that now, that you won't use me. It's just I feel a little too exposed," she returned.

He knew what she meant. Had it been the other way around, had he confessed to her and had her neatly brush it off, he would have felt vulnerable, too.

"I won't hurt you, Ihva. I won't use you, and I won't use anything you've said against you," he impressed upon her.

"You don't have to." She turned and started walking again.

What was he supposed to do with that? His mere presence, his *existence*, was agony to her, and he knew it. At least, if she felt what he did, even half of what he did, that was what it would be. He jogged to catch up to her.

"It's fine," she said when he reached her. "Don't worry about it."

"But I *will* worry about it."

"Why do you insist on torturing me?" she burst out as she stopped and spun toward him.

How was he torturing her? He was trying to make things easier for her. Why wouldn't she want him to do that?

"Why *shouldn't* I worry, then?" he exclaimed. "You're hurt. You're distressed. You're upset with me. Why *shouldn't* I worry about that?"

"Because I shouldn't matter to you! I'm your subject, your charge for the time being, but when it's all done and over, you'll go your way and I'll go mine, and I won't matter anymore."

"That's not true, Ihva. That's simply not true."

"Then tell me, why should a prince, Oer's Chosen Son, find any interest in a common merchant's daughter who also just so happens to be fated to destroy half the world and leave the other half in shambles? I know you don't believe Cor. I have a hard time believing it myself that I'm going to somehow save Gant. I know you think I'm a danger to everyone. I know you think I'm a menace to Oerid, that I'm a menace to *you*. You can't but despise my presence, my existence, for the mere fact I'll obliterate all that matters to you. You probably wish they'd found me in Agda before Cor did so all this Oer's Blessing stuff could be done and over with. You—"

Jasper wanted it to stop, the torrent of hurt and bitterness, and besides that, the way she was standing—a pace away, looking up at him, her eyes alive with vehemence—set aflame the desire he'd had to kiss her. She was so near, within reach, close enough for him to put out his hand and touch her, but he couldn't. He shouldn't. But dear Oer, she was beautiful, and he wanted to return every bit of the anguished love she was expressing. He hardly knew what was happening as he closed the distance between them, tilted her head up, and kissed her.

Her lips were even softer than he'd imagined, and he kissed her gently. She froze for a moment, and he pulled back a little, his lips an inch from hers, her breath warm on his face, but then she moved toward him and was kissing him back. Time seemed to stop, and all he knew was her—her mouth on his, her cheek in his hand, her hair intertwined with his fingers. He shifted his other hand to the small of her back and pressed her closer. She moved willingly. Kissing her felt like coming home. It was a relief, like something that had been very wrong had suddenly righted itself. A vague question—why hadn't he done this sooner—flickered in his mind, but it didn't matter. They were here now. It seemed like an eternity and no time at all when she broke away.

He looked at her. There was something new in her eyes, some intensity, some fervor he hadn't seen there before. He couldn't stop himself.

"Because I love you, Ihva."

"I... I..." she stammered.

"I'm sorry. I didn't mean to. I didn't mean for any of it, but there it is. I love you, Ihva Marchand."

Light above, what was he doing? But this feeling was a tidal wave compared to his feeble intent to hide it.

"I didn't realize," she said and trailed off.

"I didn't intend for you to realize."

"I see that."

"I'm sorry. It makes everything a thousand times harder. I'd take it back, but I don't even want to."

"No, no! Don't take it back!" she exclaimed.

He was still holding her, he realized as she strained to move away.

"No, I can't. I couldn't," he said.

She slackened in his arms.

"Ihva, I'm sorry. I'm so sorry—for telling you, for not telling you, for all of it. I don't know what I've been doing. I thought I could keep you safe, but it seems I don't know how. I'm so sorry."

She stared at him but didn't speak. Guilt reared up inside him. He couldn't take it back. What had he done? Words came spilling out of his mouth.

"I don't know what this looks like, I don't know how it's supposed to play out, I don't know where we're supposed to go from here. I don't know anything except I don't think I can undo this," he said, keeping his eyes on her bravely.

Finally she said something, her voice quiet. "I don't know either."

He drew back and lowered his eyes. "I shouldn't have. I'm sorry. That was wrong of me."

He glanced up, but as soon as he met her gaze, she looked away. Her eyes were glossy.

"I don't know what about it was wrong," she replied, her voice unsteady and sounding like she might cry.

He faltered.

"I knew it would never work, but I never expected *this*." She looked back up at him. "I'm sorry to be your mistake."

"No!" he exclaimed, then went on in a calmer voice. "You're no mistake. Dear Oer, you're the furthest thing from a mistake. What I mean is I've dragged you into something I never wanted to drag you into."

There was a pause, then she asked, "What if I want to be in it?"

"No, Ihva, you don't understand. You don't know who or what you'd be dealing with."

"I'm not stupid. I know who the Lady of Shadows is, and according to Cor, I'm going to battle her one way or another."

Jasper stopped for a second. Did she have a point? Hope he hadn't been aware he possessed mounted up within him. Maybe things *could* work out. Maybe if he just made her pledge not to do anything risky, not to try anything stupid...

"You have to promise me you won't do anything dangerous because you know I care for you," he replied slowly. "No sacrificial acts of bravery, no running after what the Lady of Shadows holds over me. I won't have you risking your life for my sake. I can't do that to you. It's the last thing I want. I fear if you do, neither of us will survive the outcome."

She nodded but didn't say anything.

"Do you promise?" he asked.

"Yes, Highness," she replied dutifully.

"And call me Jasper, for goodness' sake."

"Yes, Jasper," she said softly.

A thrill ran through him again as she used his name. At a loss for words, he watched her. So this was going somewhere. The decision hadn't been conscious, but it had been conclusive, nonetheless. This was going somewhere. He relished the notion and didn't even care about the small part of him holding out resistance to it. No, that was easy enough to push aside as he stared into the depths of her shimmering green eyes.

"You meant it, then?" she asked in a quiet voice.

"Meant what?"

"What you said. That you, well, what you feel about... You know," she said, trailing off as she looked away.

"That I love you?" He wasn't certain what she was asking about. She glanced back at him and swallowed, then nodded.

He stared at her for a moment before he could answer, trying to tone down his intensity. "Yes, I meant it."

There was a pause during which he wondered if he should have added something else. Finally, she turned her face in the direction they'd been walking.

"We should get going," she said but then turned back to him and didn't move. What was she waiting for?

"What is it?" he asked finally.

"Nothing. I don't know. I'm confused."

Afraid he'd made another mistake and hoping to console her, he took her hand in his own and intertwined his fingers with hers. He made a small turn as though to leave, then thought better of it.

"Is that okay?" he asked.

"I mean, they'll find out eventually, I suppose," she said.

That was a good point.

"Besides, I wouldn't put it past Malach to already suspect," she added. "He's been looking at us kind of funny since Eshad."

"Since Eshad?" Jasper exclaimed.

"Yeah. Maybe he knew what would happen."

Jasper felt himself gaping.

"I mean, he was right, wasn't he?" she said.

"Well, yes," was Jasper's reluctant reply. "But since Eshad?"

"Yeah. I don't know."

"Right, well, they'll find out eventually."

Hesitating for a second, he clasped her hand and started walking. He had no idea where they were going, but instead of panic, a sense of expectancy guided his steps. Of course there was fear, and it threatened to cloud his vision, but as the skies above were clearing from the storm, his mind was breaking free from its anxieties. Feeling Ihva's hand in his helped. She was warm whereas the temperature around was dropping. Most of all though, holding her hand reminded him that this was going somewhere, and the delight of that thought carried him as though on wings.

Chapter 19

HE'D KISSED HER. IHVA WAS still reeling from it. He loved her; he'd said. She couldn't understand. How had he gone from barely regarding her to loving her?

Her hand in his felt right. It just felt right, but something strange was going on. It made no sense, but like he'd said, there it was—he loved her. She didn't doubt it. His kiss had made it rather clear, and if she'd wondered about her feelings for him at all, she now had an acute awareness she cared for him, too. All of a sudden, everything in her wanted to withdraw. She'd thought she loved him back on the boat, and maybe she did. At the very least, she now knew she cared for him deeply, in *that* way, not just as friends.

She glanced at him. He wore a small smile, the same smile he'd had a few times in practice, the same rare smile from those nights around the fire, the same smile he'd worn when they'd danced. The same but different. It was less distracted now—he had no faraway look at the moment. He was present.

He turned his head to look at her. "Are you alright?" he asked, a frown overtaking his expression.

"Yeah. Yeah, I'm fine. It's just odd, you know?"

"I guess so."

He didn't get it. He couldn't get it. Here she was, walking hand in hand with the Prince of Oerid on some unknown beach, strolling along like he somehow belonged to her.

"Where are we, you think?" she asked to get her mind off it.

"I can't tell. I thought Eshad was all cliffs."

"Me, too."

"And it looks like everything's to the north of us. I mean, it's possible we were carried far enough to be—"

"The Lost Isle?" Her voice was hushed as though whispering would somehow make it better. If they were on the Lost Isle, they'd never make it home.

"I mean, it's possible," he said.

She slowed at his words. "But how are we going to get back?" she asked him.

"We'll just have to figure something out."

She wasn't sure what was going on. He was usually the disconcerted one, but here he was telling her it'd be fine.

"Highness, Prince, Jasper, we need a little more of a plan than that."

He stopped and turned to face her. "I don't know, Ihva. I don't know what we'll do. But something has to work out."

"Okay," was all she replied.

"Look, I don't know what's going on anymore. I never planned for this. I never planned for Jessica to be kidnapped. I never planned for her to be killed or that I'd fall in love with you much less that I'd tell you I'd fallen in love with you, but it's all just happening, so let's just let it be what it will be. I can't believe this is all for nothing."

A far cry from what he'd said in the Jinadian prison, but Ihva didn't point that out. Instead, she replied, "Okay, I trust you. It's not going to be for nothing, I agree." Her voice was unsteady.

"I'm sorry," he said a moment later.

"For what?"

"It's a lot, I know. I didn't mean to overwhelm you."

"You didn't overwhelm me."

He arched an eyebrow.

"Okay, maybe a little," she said. "But I'd rather this than, well, anything else."

"I can give you some space if that's what you need."

He stepped away as though to demonstrate, but she tightened her grip on his hand before he could get too far.

"No, not that!" she exclaimed.

He took a tentative step back toward her.

"I just need time," she said. "Just some time, that's all."

He let go of her hand and nodded then watched her a moment longer. After that, he turned to start walking again but paused as he looked back at her. She was confused. He'd wait for her then, until she was ready. Of course, she'd admitted to liking him, to possibly loving him, but this was different. He wanted her commitment it seemed, to what she wasn't sure, but she did know she wasn't in a place where she could offer that—not with the world turning itself upside down and them stranded on an island cut off from it all.

"You ready?" he asked.

"Yeah," she replied.

She caught up with him and they continued up the beach.

"Jasper? Ihva? Is that you?"

It was twilight, and Ihva heard a male voice calling from the north. A second later, she saw Cor walking out of the flowered grasses beyond the beach fifty paces away.

"Yes, it's us," Jasper called.

Cor jogged over to meet them. He stopped at Jasper and eyed him for a moment. Jasper did the same to Cor, then smiles broke out on both their faces and the dwarf caught Jasper in a manly hug.

"I was not sure that anyone else had survived. Thank Oer you are alive," Cor said.

Jasper looked at the dwarf and smiled. "You think a little water would kill me after all we've been through?"

Cor chuckled and turned to Ihva. "And you, Ihva? Are you well?"

Ihva looked at Cor and smiled, too. "I made it. I hate the ocean, but I made it."

Cor chuckled and gave her a gentle pat on the back. "I found a small spring up there," he said, pointing inland. "No food, but fresh water will tide us over for a little while."

"Tomorrow, I'll hunt," Jasper said.

"I saw a few rabbits around," said Cor. "You should be able to gather a few in a morning's work."

"We'll rest here tonight, then," Jasper said.

The three walked inland beside a small tributary that Cor pointed out. He guided them to where the freshwater emerged from the ground. Ihva drank plenty, and Jasper did as well. Cor had gathered wood, which had dried enough in the hours since the rainfall, and soon they had a fire. Ihva spent the rest of the evening listening to Cor and Jasper reminisce and interjected a few times with laughter and questions. She avoided Jasper's eyes for the most part but caught him considering her a couple times during lulls in the conversation. Both times, she quickly asked something to get the other two talking again.

As darkness fell, they each found a space and laid down to sleep. The fire was dying by this point, but despite the cold of her drying clothing, Ihva fell asleep in an instant.

The next morning, Ihva woke while it was still dark. She looked around and saw Jasper sitting near her.

"Good morning," he said in a hushed tone.

"Morning," she replied simply.

She didn't want to talk. Her dreams had been off-putting, and she was worried about the others. Jasper must have understood her wishes and respected them, remaining silent. They stared off in different directions and listened to the breeze in the grasses. After a few minutes, Ihva heard Cor waking beside her.

"You two are awake as well?" Cor said.

Jasper replied, "It's a strange place. I think we're all uneasy."

Cor nodded, then asked Jasper, "Are you planning to hunt? I do not have anything to use for such endeavors. Otherwise, I would help."

Jasper glanced at Cor and smiled. "Not that a hammer would be much use anyway—unless, of course, we were looking for rabbit flatcakes."

Cor chuckled. "What weapons do we have left, in any case? I lost mine at sea."

"I have my daggers," Jasper replied. "I lost the rapier and crossbow at sea, too."

"I have Darkslayer," Ihva said, touching the blade at her side.

She was surprised the sword had stayed belted to her despite the tumult of the storm, but she didn't question it. She was grateful she had anything.

"So we're not weaponless except you, Cor," Jasper said. He handed the dwarf a dagger. "Take one. I have two."

"I do not know how to use it," Cor replied.

"It's easy enough. Just stab whoever's coming at you."

"Yes, but they will have greater reach with a sword or ax than I will have with this."

"Then throw it at them."

Cor looked at Jasper and raised an eyebrow, but Jasper had turned his attention to Ihva.

"Would you like to come with me? I can try to teach you to use a dagger for hunting," he said.

She looked at him. She wanted to refuse but felt force behind his request. She nodded but didn't look at Cor. Jasper stood without another word, and Ihva rose to follow him northward.

Cor called out after them. "I will wait here, then. And watch for the others."

Her cheeks grew warm, but she continued forward. As she and Jasper walked through the field, the sky was starting to brighten. For a few minutes, they explored their surroundings. Ihva saw a mountain range to the north. The ground to the west and the east varied in height, rising into cliffs in some regions, but for the most part, grasses and short trees covered the terrain. Wildflowers scattered about as well. It occurred to her that it was the wrong time of year for flowers. She stopped for a closer inspection of the plants and found the small white blossoms looked compact and hardy. Maybe they grew year-round. She straightened and saw Jasper standing a few paces away, looking back at her, so she jogged to catch up.

They continued wandering through the inland region when Ihva spotted something rising out of the ground in the east. She peered toward it and pointed it out to Jasper. He squinted his eyes too, looking into the distance.

"I can't be certain, but I don't think that's a natural feature of the landscape," he said finally.

She agreed with a nod. "Could it be a village?" she asked.

"It's too far away for a small gathering like that to appear."

"A city, then?"

"That sounds more like it." He squinted again. "We should visit it once we find the others. The people there should be able to tell us where we are and maybe how to get back."

The conversation tapered off into silence again.

As the sun peeked over the horizon, Jasper said, "Now we'll hunt. You need to stay close to the ground and step softly." He handed her the dagger. "If you see a rabbit or anything else, throw this at it. Try to spare the meat as much as possible."

She took the dagger from his hand and held it with an awkward grasp. He looked at her and chuckled, and she defended her lack of skill.

"No one ever taught me to use one before," she told him.

He nodded and maintained a grin, his eye teasing. Was he trying to flirt? "Like this," he said as he cupped her hand in his own and repositioned her fingers. She grew uncomfortable as his warmth seeped into her. When he withdrew his hand, though, the dagger felt more natural in her grip. She couldn't help smiling.

"Alright, but I think I'll watch you a few times first." She handed the dagger back to him, and he took it, a playful smile still on his lips. Smiles really did suit him.

She crept along behind him for the next three quarters of an hour. He managed to down three rabbits in that time. There weren't as many to be found as Cor had suggested, but part of Ihva found she didn't mind the slow going. Jasper made hunting look so easy.

After his third kill, he made Ihva take the lead. A few minutes passed before he pointed out a rabbit about thirty paces away. It was standing still, nibbling the grass around it. Ihva stalked around the creature until she thought she was close enough to hit it, then stopped and held her breath. The rabbit's ear twitched. It was now or never. In an instant, Ihva drew the dagger back, drove her arm forward, and released the blade. It sped through the air and landed harmlessly in the dirt in front of the rabbit, which took the opportunity to flee. Ihva cringed and looked at Jasper. Amusement marked his face, and wrinkles formed at the corners of his dark eyes, and she couldn't help giggling. His smile was infectious. After grinning at him for a second, she remembered herself, blushed, and looked away.

"Maybe I need some more practice," she said.

Jasper nodded, chuckling. He made her try a few more times, which didn't go any better than the first. A rabbit was a small target. She handed the dagger back to Jasper, and he took down another of the small animals within five minutes. Ihva shook her head. She'd never be as good as him with weaponry. At one point, she remembered they'd need fuel for a fire. She spotted a group of short, gnarled trees in the distance.

"I'll grab some wood," she said. She handed the now four dead rabbits to Jasper.

"I suppose four will be enough," he said, looking at the creatures' scrawny bodies. "It will hardly be a feast, but we hardly have time for a feast anyway."

As he mentioned the time, Ihva remembered that the others were still out there somewhere. She hurried to the trees ahead of her, broke off thicker branches, and gathered sticks from the ground for tinder. The wood was dry. Perfect. She carried the bundle in her arms while Jasper took the rabbit carcasses back to camp.

They walked for about half an hour before nearing their campsite again. Two figures appeared there. One was short and wide and had to be Cor. The other figure was tall and bulky. Ihva squinted and wondered if it could be Kronk. She quickened her pace. As she and Jasper drew closer, she confirmed indeed the larger figure had to be the orc-blood woman. At least, whoever it might have been was wearing a purple gown. About thirty paces away, Ihva broke into a run, hugging the wood to her chest.

It looked like Kronk and Cor were facing the beach as Ihva neared them, so Ihva called out, "Kronk!"

The orc-blood woman turned around and bounced in place. Ihva felt relief course through her as she reached the campsite, dropped the wood, and ran up to the woman.

"I was afraid you were dead!" Ihva said as Kronk drew her into a close hug.

"Why Kronk die?" The orc-blood woman sounded upset.

"The ocean, silly!" Ihva replied.

"Oh. But Kronk swim!"

Ihva shook her head and squeezed Kronk again. Her embrace brought comfort like a blanket, and Ihva realized just how anxious she'd been as her nervousness faded. Kronk was here, and with her she carried some semblance of normalcy, the feeling of home. After a moment, she let go of the orc-blood woman and turned her attention to Cor.

"Where did you find her?" she asked.

"She was wandering up the beach from the same direction as you two, talking to herself." Cor gave a lighthearted chuckle.

Jasper caught up to the group. He looked at Kronk. "Welcome."

The orc-blood woman looked back at him with her brow furrowed. "Welcome where?"

"To being stranded, I suppose," Jasper said.

Kronk tilted her head at Jasper, and Ihva interrupted.

"Don't worry about it, Kronk. Are you thirsty? There's some water up here, and we are about to cook breakfast." She patted Kronk on the shoulder and spoke in a soothing tone.

"Kronk *very* hungry." Kronk eyed the rabbits. "Rabbits for Kronk?" Her voice trembled.

"We have to split them, Kronk, but there'll be one just for you."

Ihva was grateful that they had an extra rabbit. She was even more grateful that Kronk had made it alive through the storm. Today might turn out to be a very good day.

Chapter 20

JASPER SAT WITH THE OTHERS by the fire while the rabbits cooked. He was markedly aware of Ihva as she knelt between him and Kronk—she was smiling but clearly reserved. What was she thinking?

He'd tried to teach her to hunt. It seemed her skill with the dagger didn't equal her skill with the sword, but it had been enjoyable to spend time with her. He was surprised at how easy it had been. He'd been resisting his feelings for so long that he hadn't realized how effortless it felt to move with them. He wasn't second-guessing or second thinking anything, just acting. It was living unforced and uncomplicated by extenuating circumstances. He could just be, and he didn't know how long it had been since that was the case. Possibly it had never been. In any case, it was marvelous.

Still, he didn't know what Ihva was feeling. She seemed to have pulled back. Not that she'd ever extended herself entirely, but she'd at least let him know she cared for him, and now she was withdrawing. She needed time; she'd said. He could give her time, time and space, but he wasn't going to let her retreat all the way. She needed some coaxing, and he was more than willing to do that coaxing, not to force her into anything but to allow her the freedom and safety to return his sentiments.

"Son?" Cor said. He sounded as though he'd asked Jasper a question.

"Yes, sorry. I was thinking about something else. What is it?" Jasper replied.

"We will need to work our way farther up the beach instead of just remaining here today."

"Oh. Yes, we should probably move on if we want to find anyone else."

"East, still?" Ihva asked.

"Sure," Jasper replied. East was as good a direction as any. Besides, that was the direction they'd seen the city.

"Well, we ought to be on our way. Perhaps we can leave the fire as a sign of our presence, should any come behind us," Cor said.

That was a good idea. Malach or Yidda would know someone at least had survived then.

"Sure, sounds good," Jasper said.

"Let us go, then," Cor replied and rose to leave.

Jasper got up, drew an arrow to the east in the dirt in the ashes from the fire, and followed. If Malach or Yidda was coming after them, at least one or the other might discover what he'd drawn and realize where they were heading.

The four trekked through the mid-morning sun. The temperature was cool, cold even, and even if it hadn't been, the ocean breeze would have had Jasper shivering. Still, this weather was preferable to M'rawa's and Jinad's heat. Kronk decided to walk in the shallows of the sea, and every now and then, a bigger wave would wash over her. She always emerged laughing to continue in the same manner. Jasper hadn't known Kronk was so fond of water, though he should have since she'd done the same thing in Jinad.

After a while of walking in the sand, the sun was high in the sky, so Cor suggested a short break. Jasper agreed, and Ihva called Kronk in from the water. The orc-blood woman returned to where the others were sitting and complained of hunger. Cor took it upon himself to explain to her they didn't have food with them anymore.

Kronk challenged him, and he grew exasperated. Kronk also believed that Malach and Yidda were hiding like Ihva had been and would come out eventually. Cor rested his forehead in his hand. Even the dwarf had only so much patience. Jasper chuckled to himself, though he was tiring of Kronk's arguing as well. At the same time, he gave Ihva a knowing look. She appeared startled at first, then returned a self-conscious smile.

Cor and Kronk's conversation continued onto other themes, mostly tales from Kronk's days on the road after leaving her father's tribe, as the dwarf tried to steer her away from the controversial topic of food. They all knew that Kronk would make her discomfort known every five minutes if given the chance, so Jasper mentally applauded Cor's decision to change the subject.

After half an hour, they got up to walk again. They searched inland and ahead as they went. Soon, it was mid-afternoon. Cor and Kronk eventually fell silent, and Jasper and Ihva continued, unspeaking as well. Concern furrowed Cor's brow, and Jasper felt worry creeping over him, too. Where were Yidda and Malach? Jasper spotted the cliffs ahead. His hope of finding the other two still alive was fading.

Minutes after Jasper saw the cliffs, though, they found Malach. He was lying in the sand, the water rushing in and out over his feet. Cor was the first to spot him and cried out, then rushed over to him.

"Malach!" he called.

Jasper jogged over as well with Ihva right in front of him. He watched her kneel by Malach's side. The dwarf was unconscious, but it wasn't clear why. He was lying on his back with his arms and legs splayed out, and there was no blood around or on him. Sand had gathered around his feet where the high tide reached.

"He needs Healing," Cor said, his voice strained. He looked up at Ihva. "He has been unconscious for a while. I do not have the power to restore him. You should, though, Ihva."

Ihva looked Cor in the eye, and her expression hardened. Kronk stood behind her, swaying anxiously. Jasper hoped Ihva could in fact Heal the dwarf, as he wasn't sure that she could handle losing Malach.

He didn't know how he'd take it either. He watched nervously as she laid her hand on the dwarf's chest and closed her eyes. White light spread from her, and soon Malach's entire body had a slight glow.

"It's his legs. They're broken," she said after a moment. She opened her eyes.

"You must Heal him, Ihva," Cor said.

She looked at Cor, nodded, and closed her eyes again. She murmured something under her breath that Jasper couldn't make out, and light shone from her hands again and spread more brightly over Malach's body, focusing itself on his legs. The light grew in intensity, and Jasper watched Ihva grimace. He nearly reached out a hand to her shoulder but stopped himself, not wanting to interrupt her. The light pulsed, then faded. Ihva opened her eyes and looked at Malach's face.

"It's done, I think," she said.

The dwarf stirred, and she drew her hands back. She looked concerned. Cor was watching as well, and Kronk nudged Ihva aside to make space to see Malach herself. Malach's eyes fluttered open. They looked out of focus at first, and he rubbed them, peering at the others.

"Cor? Is that you? Jasper, lad? Ihva? And Kronk?" His eyes moved from one to the other. His voice was groggy and weak. Ihva touched his arm.

"He needs water," she told the others. She looked at Cor.

"We must find a spring," said Cor. He turned back to Malach. "Do you think you can walk?"

Malach hesitated and tested his strength, trying to lift himself from the ground. He fell back. "Muscles aren't working like they're supposed to."

Jasper held out his hand to Malach, and Malach grasped it. Jasper had to strain to raise Malach from the ground, but soon, Malach was standing, leaning his weight between Cor and Jasper.

"I'm not sure this walking thing is a good idea," Malach said, unsteady on his feet.

"We have to," Jasper said. "I'll help." It'd be a struggle and their going would be slow, but Jasper could manage. He wrapped Malach's arm around him, and the dwarf eased his weight onto him.

"We must be watchful," Cor said as he shaded his eyes against the glaring reflection of the sun with his hand and looked into the distance. "Without water, no amount of Healing will keep him."

Malach wasn't out of danger yet. Jasper glanced at Ihva. She was frowning, and there was worry in her eyes. He tried to catch her gaze, but she didn't look at him. They all started east again toward the cliffs. Jasper and Cor agreed they needed to climb the sandy incline to reach the grassy inland region. Cor reasoned that he could walk on the edge of the hill and watch for both Yidda and water at the same time. Jasper agreed.

Trekking up the hill, practically dragging Malach along, took a good five minutes. As they reached the top, Jasper looked into the distance and saw the structure Ihva had spotted that morning, albeit much closer. It looked like a wide cone with the largest part at its base. He couldn't make out the details, but he pointed it out to Cor.

"We saw that earlier. Looks like a city," he told the dwarf.

"We must be wary of the inhabitants. We do not know if they are friendly," Cor replied.

True, but they didn't have any other leads on how to get back to the mainland. Then again, the inhabitants could be the reason no one had returned from the Lost Isle. Jasper nodded at Cor and continued walking. After about half an hour, Kronk, who was running ahead, stooped down. Jasper and the others drew closer, and the sound of trickling water met Jasper's ears.

"Thanks be to Oer!" Cor said in a loud voice.

Ihva let out an audible sigh of relief, and Jasper heaved Malach into a more comfortable position. Malach groaned, and Jasper increased his pace toward where Kronk stood. They arrived at a small spring flowing out of the ground much like the stream Cor had discovered previously. Jasper lowered Malach to the ground, and the dwarf crawled as best he could toward the stream. He was gulping the water when Cor cautioned him against it.

143

"Easy, son," Cor said. "You will sicken if you drink too much at once."

Malach pulled back and crawled out of the others' way. Jasper, Ihva, Kronk, and Cor took turns sipping from the spring. After they finished, Cor instructed Malach to get some more.

"We need to rest here for a while until he restores himself." Cor indicated Malach. "The water will help. Maybe you can go hunting again?" He was looking at Jasper. "He will need food to regain his strength as will the rest of us."

Jasper nodded and glanced at Ihva with a question in his eyes. She must have known what he was asking, but she shook her head.

"I'll work on getting firewood with Kronk," she said.

Unfortunate, but she probably didn't want Malach asking questions. Time. She needed time, and Jasper would give her some. He shrugged at her and nodded again, then made off through the grass.

Three rabbits in an hour's work. It wasn't much, but at least they were bigger rabbits than before. Perhaps the animals could feed the five of them. Jasper didn't mind hunting more, but the others would wonder where he'd gone, and he didn't want to worry them.

He walked back toward camp at a quick pace, not at a stroll though not so quickly that he couldn't think. He had a lot to contemplate. Of course, his first thoughts were of Ihva, but he couldn't start there. He had to think about getting back. To what? To Oerid, to his father, to Agda. He *had* to make it back, but how? They didn't have a ship or any means of traversing the ocean that most certainly separated them from the mainland. Where else could they be but the Lost Isle? The Lost Isle, of all places to be stranded!

But they'd found the others, all except Yidda. They had to find her, too. Jasper felt a strange connection to the woman. She understood his secrets, perhaps his most closely held secret. He couldn't be certain if she knew, but even if she didn't, she'd had the same problem, and something had freed her. He needed to know what it was before something like what had befallen her happened to him. Besides her knowledge, though, she'd gotten them out of the Jinadian palace and out of Alm'adinat. She was with them, and he wouldn't leave her behind.

Which brought him back to how they were getting back. He'd told Ihva they'd have to figure it out, and he'd been right, but now it came to the figuring it out part, and he was stumped. He remembered her face when he'd told her to just let it be what it would be—frightened wasn't quite it, more overwhelmed. He knew it was a lot to handle at once, but he'd told her he loved her, and he had to stick to the course. Not that he minded. He'd told her, she knew, and she cared for him, too. He'd kissed her! He hadn't known himself to be especially audacious, but there it was. He couldn't take it back, and he wouldn't take it back. He hated how messy it made things, though. The Prince of Oerid tagging along and in love with Oer's Blessing. The one chosen to maintain peace and stability in Oerid to make romance with the one fated to bring ruin and disaster on the very nation. Never had Jasper hoped Cor was right more than now.

It was just that Ihva didn't seem the kind to bring disaster. Jasper had recognized once she was no havoc-wreaker, and now he was even more convinced of it. She could hardly stand watching a Shadow Bandit die. There was no way she could rain destruction on a village, much less on an entire nation or the world. She wouldn't be the cause of Oerid's fall, Jasper knew. If anyone would be, it would be him. He had to protect Ihva from the Lady—for his sake, her sake, and Oerid's sake.

He saw the others a ways away. They'd started a fire already. Remembering the city in the distance, he realized the inhabitants would certainly know he and the others were out here now. It couldn't be helped, though. They needed to eat. He hurried off to join them.

Chapter 21

IHVA AND KRONK RETURNED WITH arms full of wood to the stream where Cor and Malach were sitting. Malach had managed to steady himself enough to sit up. As the four waited for Jasper, Cor took some sturdier twigs and rubbed them together for a minute or so until he created a flame. Soon a fire was burning, and Ihva and her companions arranged themselves around it.

Jasper returned about forty-five minutes later with three rabbits, enough to give sustenance but not enough for a real meal. Ihva knew they'd remain hungry until they could find proper provisions. Soon they were enjoying cooked rabbit around the fire, though. They traded details of their experiences at sea and their time since they arrived on land. It turned out a wave had thrown Malach into a large rock, which was how his legs had been broken. He'd been unable to stand or walk, so he'd remained on the beach without food or water until they'd come along, thus his half-dead state when they'd found him. He thanked Ihva a few times for Healing him and expressed gratitude to them all for waiting with him as he recovered.

Soon, evening came, and the five decided to stay put for the night around the fire. They agreed that their first priority the next day would be to find Yidda. After Yidda joined them, they'd approach the city they could see in the distance. They spent the darkening hours talking around the fire. At first, the tone was grim, but soon Ihva and the others resumed their normal banter. Jasper told them about the time a rather rotund, middle-aged woman with a face like a mule had communicated her interest in Cor. Apparently, Cor had not realized her interest was romantic and ended up on a house call to "pray over her new home" despite his objection that he was not a priest. Cor's face turned red as he protested.

"She did not make her intentions clear until we reached the kitchen!"

Jasper looked at Cor, amusement playing at the corners of his mouth. "You said she couldn't keep her hands off you and kept calling you 'darling,' Cor."

Cor shot Jasper a look but laughed along with the others. The night proceeded with storytelling and teasing, and Ihva almost forgot her worries for a couple hours. Finally, the moon rose in the sky, and the fire had burned down to coals. Cor added wood to the flames, and they all set watches, leaving Malach and Ihva to sleep the night through. Exhausted once again, Ihva fell into a deep sleep minutes after putting her head to a pillow of grasses and flowers.

Ihva woke to sunlight. She blinked and looked around, stretching. Jasper was up adding the last of the wood to the fire. Cor and Kronk were gone, hopefully gathering some more.

"Good morning," Jasper said in a cheery voice, smiling at Ihva.

Was that affection she detected in his voice? Every moment, his manner grew more casual and unreserved. She wasn't sure how to handle it.

"Good morning, lass." Malach's greeting interrupted her thoughts.

She turned her eyes to see Malach sitting a few feet away. He seemed to have more strength than the day before.

"Good morning, Malach," she replied. "How are you feeling?" Her voice took on a motherly tone despite being younger than him. She walked over and knelt down to look at his legs.

"They're fine, lass. You did a mighty fine job," he assured her. "Now all I've got is a famished stomach, but the good fellow, Jasper, should be taking care of that this very minute."

Malach looked over at Jasper and winked. Ihva turned and saw Jasper skinning three more rabbits for breakfast. Her stomach rumbled, and she was grateful for the meal to come, but still, she was tiring of rabbit meat.

Meanwhile, Cor appeared by the fire with Kronk. Cor held a few dry branches, and Kronk carried what looked like half a tree trunk. Ihva saw Jasper's eyes widen.

"We're not staying here that long, Kronk," he told the woman.

Kronk's face fell.

"But a log like that will make for great fuel for the rest of the morning," he added before she could reply.

When had he become so amiable? Ihva stared at him for a long moment as he and Cor moved away to continue preparing the meat. Kronk went with them to try to help.

"He likes you; you know?" Malach's whisper broke her concentration.

She jumped, startled, and looked at the dwarf.

"You don't see the way he looks at you, do you?"

She remained silent, staring at Malach. He looked back at her and said nothing for a second. He must have taken her expression for interest, though, as he continued.

"I knew for sure back with them elfy folk. You know, when you were off dancing. Your Prince fancies himself a secretive man, and maybe he can fool the womenfolk, but I know the look of a man besotted."

Ihva looked down, fiddling with the hem of her blouse. Malach fell silent, and she knew he was waiting for her to respond. As she'd thought, the dwarf had known, which was fine, but talking about it with him was a different matter. Anyway, Jasper couldn't have felt

148

this way for that long, she was sure. It was no use arguing with Malach, though.

She drew in a tentative breath and said, "I know." She glanced up at Malach.

"You know, do you?" the dwarf said slowly. "Has he told you, then? Or you figured it out, intuitive lass that you are?"

"He told me." He'd showed her was more like it. With passion, too. She blushed thinking about it.

Malach chuckled. "He told you, did he? Good for him, good for him. It's been eating him up for a while now, lass. You might find him a different man than you've known thus far."

"What do you mean?"

"I suspect he wasn't always quite so tortured and brooding until you came around, and I also suspect he might drop the guise now that you're, you know, together."

"We're not together!" she said in an emphatic whisper.

"Oh, playing coy? I didn't peg you as quite that type."

"No, we're just not together. That's all."

"I know the look of a woman in love, too, lass, and you're the portrait of it."

"I'm not in love."

Malach looked at her with a raised eyebrow.

"I'm not. I just, I care about him. That's all," she said, sounding her best to make her voice confident.

Malach's expression didn't change.

"I can't be in love, Malach. There's too much going on. Besides, he's my *Prince*. He'll be my *King* one day. How can I presume to love him? It's completely insensible."

"Love is insensible, lass."

"But—"

"Think about it. Just think about it." He winked at her.

"Malach, will you help us with these spits?" Cor called.

Malach pushed himself to his feet and grimaced as he stumbled forward and fell to his knees.

"The Healing did a lot for me, but it seems there remains some recovery." He looked at Jasper.

"I don't know that I can carry you resting on my shoulder the whole day," Jasper replied, then looked at Cor and asked, "Maybe we should rest here for a while longer?"

Cor frowned. Ihva knew he was worried about Yidda. She was worried, too. If they didn't continue on their journey today, they might not find Yidda in time. Anything could have happened to the Jini woman, and she might need their help. On the other hand, if they stayed put, maybe Yidda was searching for them and would find them at their campsite. Cor finally spoke.

"I suppose we must. If we try to continue today, we will wear ourselves out and have to rest twice as long to recover. We will stay one more day."

Malach sighed. "I hate to burden you. I feel a lot better than yesterday. Maybe another day of rest will get me up to standards."

Cor, Jasper, and Ihva nodded. Kronk saw them and gave a delayed nod of her own.

"It is decided then," said Cor.

They all relaxed for the rest of the day. Jasper returned to the grassland to hunt, and they had roasted rabbit again for dinner. Ihva and Kronk walked to the beach and waded in the ocean. Ihva stayed in the shallows despite Kronk trying to persuade her to come out among the waves. Cor sat with Malach at the campsite, and the two talked for hours.

That night, the campfire was roaring. With Malach's pipe lost at sea, he decided to sing for the others. His voice had a beautiful, low timbre, but he was still weak. Cor took over when Malach couldn't sing any longer. Malach sang ballads and dwarven folk songs, and Cor added a few religious songs. Laughter and storytelling filled the evening as well.

While Ihva sat with the others by the fire, she remembered Malach's words from earlier. What *did* she feel for Jasper? She realized she'd started calling him by his name, at least to herself. It felt right, somehow—it was thrilling. Her Prince, and he loved her.

Somehow, she, Ihva Marie Marchand, had captured his affections, and he wanted to be with her in some fashion or another. He wanted that "together" Malach had been talking about. If she was honest, she wanted it, too. What would "together" look like anyway, though? Whatever it was, Jasper would have to help define it. She hoped he would approach her again about it all. She didn't want to go begging him.

She grew tired more quickly than the others as thoughts of Jasper preoccupied her mind. While the moon was still low in the sky, she excused herself from the group, picked a spot some paces away from the fire, and laid down. She listened to the drone of voices and laughter near her and wished it would drown out her thoughts as the hope that Jasper might say something more made her anxious. Soon, though, she was asleep. Her slumber was fitful, and each time she woke, she knew she'd been dreaming about him.

Chapter 22

JASPER WOKE TO MALACH'S WHISPER. "Time for your watch, lad."

Jasper blinked his eye open to find it was still dark with the fire burning low. Malach was going to make him replenish the wood, wasn't he? Then he remembered Malach was still recovering. With a sigh, he got up to take third watch.

He ambled over to the pile of wood they'd gathered earlier. There wasn't much left. He took what was there and carried it back to place on the charred remains of previous logs. Then he turned to find a place to settle himself down for a few hours. To his surprise, he found Malach still awake. He opened his mouth to ask what was wrong, but Malach interrupted him.

"You look like you could use some company," the dwarf whispered.

Jasper blinked. He looked like he could use some company? He didn't think he appeared upset or anything. Staring at Malach, he wondered what the dwarf was after.

"Come on, over here. They're all trying to sleep, after all," Malach went on, waving Jasper after him as he made his way away from camp.

Jasper watched him for a second, curious, suspicious, but after a moment Malach stumbled and Jasper caught up to help him. The dwarf didn't let them stop until they were thirty paces or so from camp, out of earshot if they talked in low tones. What was the dwarf intending to discuss?

"Looks like as good a spot as any," Malach commented as he sat down. "Wouldn't you say?"

Jasper didn't reply, just gave a reluctant nod and sank down to the ground beside the dwarf. There was silence, and Jasper wasn't about to fill it. One's best chances with Malach lay in not engaging him. To Jasper's misfortune, the dwarf shattered the tranquility of the night's stillness.

"Brisk out here, huh?" he whispered.

Jasper glanced at him. "It wouldn't be if we were closer to the fire."

Malach chuckled. "You're pretty quick-witted. Clever."

Jasper didn't know what to say so he didn't respond.

"Been sleeping well?" Malach asked after a moment.

"Yes, for the most part." Indeed, he'd been sleeping well for the first time in months. He had a guess as to why, too—his anxieties were calming, and he was no longer battling the sentiments that had been bound to overwhelm him. He was unified within himself, at least more so than before, and there was now something in his life he was becoming sure of.

"That's good, that's good..." Malach said, trailing off.

There was another silence, but Jasper could sense the dwarf was about to say something, so he tried to head him off.

"Do you have any ideas how to get home?" he asked the dwarf.

Malach chuckled. "No clue, lad, no clue."

Something like disappointment dragged at Jasper's mood, but had he really thought Malach would come up with something better than the rest of them?

"You got anything?" the dwarf asked.

Jasper shook his head. "No. Just that we might find someone in that city who can help."

Malach shifted in his seat. "Yeah, that or they'll kill us and roast us for their dinner. One of the two."

Jasper looked at the dwarf in alarm. "They won't kill us. We wouldn't let them. We'd fight them and escape."

Malach turned to him. "There's got to be some reason no one ever returns from here, lad. There've been some pretty able combatants who've been lost on these shores."

Agitated by the dwarf's words, Jasper frowned.

"Come on, lad!" Malach prompted him, the volume of his voice rising slightly and putting Jasper on edge. "That's no reason to despair. Sure, we're up against unknown forces that have taken down entire fleets of ships. Sure, we've no way to avoid coming in contact with them. Sure, we know the world's going to pieces, ourselves probably to blame, while we sit hundreds of miles across the sea with no way back. It's not all bad, though! We've got each other."

Jasper found himself gaping by the end of Malach's speech. "Was that supposed to be encouraging?"

"What, you don't feel cheered?" the dwarf returned. "Well at least you have your dear lass by your side. That should be a comfort."

Jasper gave a start. "What do you mean?"

"I mean you have your darling, your sweetheart, your, um, I don't know, that lass over there," Malach said, waving a hand back toward the others.

Jasper froze. "I don't know what you mean."

"You're going to make this difficult, aren't you?" Malach said, then muttered to himself. "A man shows some interest in his fellow's love life, and the fellow pretends there's nothing to it. What kind of friendship is that?"

Jasper stared at the dwarf, realizing this was likely the reason Malach had stayed up with him in the first place. Why did Malach think he needed to know anything anyway? Who was he to barge in on Jasper and Ihva's business? Everything between them was too fresh, too new. They hadn't had a chance to determine what anything meant. What did Malach think he'd get out of Jasper?

The dwarf heaved a sigh. "Fine, let's start at the beginning. You've been making eyes at her the past three months. Your lady love, Jessica, is gone, Oer rest her soul. This damsel is clearly enamored with you. You're beholden to none and in love with a lass who'd as soon flee your advances as she'd wade out into the ocean depths again, and you're sitting here pretending all you care about is getting back to the mainland. What are you doing, lad?" He drew in a breath.

Jasper's thoughts raced, searching for a way out of the conversation. Malach was peering at him with a frown, and Jasper couldn't figure out what to say. He ended up blurting something out in his confusion.

"I don't know," he said. "I don't know. I don't know what's going on, and I don't know how to answer you. I don't know!" He squeezed his hands into fists in frustration.

"Esh above, no need to grow angry, lad! Calm down! Just trying to help you sort through things." Malach gave a small smile. "Sounds like you need it."

Jasper inhaled a slow breath, then set himself to figuring out how to answer Malach. It was the dwarf's turn to head him off, though.

"Now you know the first step is to kiss her, right? Or well, the first step is to get her to spend time with you—a nice dinner perhaps. But you've already got that under your belt with all those lessons you've been giving her. Excellent idea, that! Getting her to practice swordplay all the time, I mean. Did you come up with that yourself? Well you had to have as I doubt Cor would have promoted for something like that with you engaged to the Lady Jessica and all. Has to have been your idea—"

"That was *not* the intent!" Jasper was thoroughly flustered now.

Malach gave him a long, doubtful look, then went on in a conspiratorial whisper. "Right, well, since you've already got the spending time part down, it's time to kiss her. Doesn't have to be prolonged or anything like that, just a simple kiss. More than a peck, though, and on the lips. She has to know you think of her as more than a sister."

Jasper felt his face growing warm, though he was certain Malach wouldn't notice in the dim light.

"Now how to get close enough to kiss her is the tough part," the dwarf went on. "Some just walk their sweethearts home and give them a goodnight kiss, but obviously that won't quite work in this situation. You have to find a reason to draw close but be casual about it. Don't want to scare her."

Malach paused to draw in a breath, and Jasper found his muscles were tense. He tried to relax them and put on a patient, attentive look. Anything to get Malach to finish his speech.

"The other thing is you should probably be alone. Women like their privacy. You don't want to go kissing her in front of all of us, for example. Your lessons might be the only time, or maybe you can take her hunting, or I don't know, make up some excuse to go on a stroll down the beach, just the two of you, maybe at sunset—that'd be romantic—and do it then. Whatever the case, you've *got* to get her on her own. But don't be creepy about it, either. That's a major turn-off for women."

Now Jasper was growing aggravated. Was this really necessary? He was desperate for Malach to stop talking and tried tuning the dwarf out, but Malach's low voice was the one thing disturbing the night air.

"Now you're just going to figure out how to get near her on your own. I mean, I have some ideas, but you have to do what works for you. And her. What works for you and her. If you want some advice, though, I'd say—"

"Stop!" Jasper exclaimed, then continued on in lower tones. "Stop. It's fine. I appreciate your help, but it's fine. Everything's just fine."

"Oh," Malach replied, drawing back. "Sorry, not meaning to overwhelm you. The point I'm trying to make is this—kiss the blessed lass!"

Jasper kept his gaze on Malach, afraid to reveal something by looking away. Still, something must have shown on his face as the dwarf was peering at him.

"You've already kissed her, haven't you?" Malach asked in a hushed tone.

Jasper flushed but didn't respond.

"Ha!" the dwarf whispered with a grin. "Good for you, lad! And here I was thinking you're one of those poor souls who's afraid of women."

Jasper drew himself up. "I'm not *afraid* of her."

Malach had a wide grin on his face now. "Clearly!"

"Stop! There's nothing amusing about it. It was just a kiss."

"*Just* a kiss? Don't let her hear you say that!" The dwarf's voice had to be carrying back to camp at this point.

"Malach!" Jasper said using the most assertive tone he could while whispering. "For the love of Oer, be quiet!"

Malach frowned but looked behind him toward the others, then lowered his voice. "Sorry."

Then there was a charged silence as though Malach was waiting for Jasper to say something. Jasper watched him warily.

"Well, you going to tell me or not?" Malach asked after a long moment.

"Tell you what?" Jasper felt genuine confusion over the dwarf's request.

Malach raised an eyebrow, then replied as though his meaning was obvious. "About what happened."

Jasper stared at him in shock. The dwarf really thought Jasper was going to relate the tale?

Malach shook his head. "And this is why I avoid subtlety. Too many of those between-the-lines things never even come across," he muttered, then he turned his attention back to Jasper. "What I'm asking is what happened with you and her? Was it back on the boat? She ran pretty hard from you back there, and there wasn't even anywhere to run. Or was it before that even, or—"

"I was engaged then, Malach. Engaged," Jasper cut him off in a steely tone. "I was *not* about to go kissing her when I was involved with someone else. You really think me faithless?"

Malach blinked and grew quiet. His frown, rather than looking annoyed, appeared almost pained. It was like he was hurt. It struck Jasper that the dwarf was trying to help in his own bizarre fashion, and he wondered if he ought to feel bad for putting Malach off so harshly. The dwarf was one of his companions, one of the few who knew the truth about him, someone he could count as an equal and maybe even as a friend, yet here he was sidestepping an offer of camaraderie. Sobered, Jasper lowered his eyes.

"Sorry. I don't mean any disrespect. I'm not trying to be rude. It's just…" He trailed off, then glanced back up at Malach.

The dwarf was watching him with a guarded look. Jasper swallowed.

"It's just," he started again, then decided on a different approach. "There really wasn't much to it. We landed on the beach, and it was just us two. I knew her feelings for me, and I was aware of my feelings for her, and we kissed. That's all."

A small smile crept into Malach's expression, but he didn't say anything.

"You're right," Jasper went on. "I've felt this way for a while. I don't know about her. But now she knows about my regard for her—I told her, after all—and it seems too late to turn back now."

Malach gave a slow nod.

"So that's it," Jasper said. "I don't know what's going to happen going forward, but it all kind of depends on us getting back to the mainland. I know I love her. I love her more than I knew it was possible to love. There's just something about her—her innocence or her optimism maybe—it's beautiful. *She's* beautiful and inspiring and striking in her own unpresuming way. I want it to go somewhere, to turn into something. I've never considered a woman the way I consider her. Oer, I'd marry her if the opportunity presented itself, but this isn't quite the place for—"

"Whoa, whoa! I wasn't planning on covering any of that tonight. A proposal's down the line a ways, lad," Malach cut in.

Jasper stopped, realizing what he'd said. He'd marry her? He would, though. He'd been engaged to Jessica without any real attachment for a while, and he hadn't realized what it was like to *want* to marry someone. Indeed, he'd marry Ihva if it was possible. Was that premature? Was he getting ahead of himself? It wasn't like he was planning to propose tomorrow. It just seemed clear to him he'd never find a woman comparable to her.

"You're not one to jump into something lukewarm, are you?" Malach observed after a moment.

Jasper looked back at the dwarf. "I've never thought about it in those terms."

Malach grinned. "Well, try not to go asking her to marry you just yet. My guess is the lass needs a little time to sort through things."

Jasper swallowed and nodded. She'd said as much a couple days ago.

"Glad to know you're moving right along, though," Malach went on. He gave Jasper a hearty slap on the back, knocking the wind out of him. "Always a pity to see love neglected or worse, sworn off, when there's a perfectly good opportunity for it to flourish." There was a strange strain to Malach's tone that made Jasper wonder about the dwarf all of a sudden.

"What about you?" he asked Malach, surprising himself with his boldness.

The dwarf tilted his head. "What about me?"

"Do you have a girl back home you've been missing?"

Malach gave a start. "No, no I don't," he replied in a gruff voice. "I mean don't get me wrong, there are plenty of eligible young lasses. Plenty of them, I assure you. Just none of them has ever worked out. Not their fault, not mine, just not the right fit. It happens like that sometimes. But no reason to stop trying, that's what I say."

Jasper regarded Malach with a careful look, thinking to himself he'd rarely seen the dwarf flustered before. It was odd. Malach interjected before Jasper could think further on it.

"Well, good talk, lad, good talk. Appreciate your honesty, I really do," he said as he stood. "Time for me to get some sleep, though." He yawned and turned back toward camp. "You coming?" he asked.

Jasper blinked and frowned. This was a rather abrupt end to a conversation. Malach was looking at him, though, and he didn't want to make the situation any more uncomfortable by asking what was wrong. Instead, he got up as well and helped Malach back to the fireside.

"Good night, then," Malach whispered as he went to lay down, then he made a quick turn back to Jasper. "Remember what I said. Take it easy, but make sure she knows that, you know, that you like her and—"

"I know," Jasper interrupted him. "I'll do my best," he added in a softer voice while his eyes strayed to where Ihva lay sleeping. He turned them back to the dwarf as soon as he realized. "Thank you, Malach," he said quietly, then turned to face north at the edge of the circle they'd made around the fire.

He spent most of the rest of his watch formulating a plan of how to approach things with Ihva. By an hour before dawn, he'd resolved what to do. They were going to have sword practice this morning, and he was going to clear up any confusion then. He'd make sure they were in accordance with each other concerning what was going on between them, and he was going to set the course for the one thing he knew he wanted out of life. Not that he'd tell her, but he'd decided it this morning, and his talk with Malach had solidified it. He wasn't seeking some silly play at love. No, he wanted her hand. A swell of emotions overcame him at the thought—exhilaration at the possibility, anxiety about how she'd respond, visceral fear that she'd reject him, and a spark of desire that set aflame eager imaginings. He had to block them out for fear he'd set his hopes too high and they'd end up plummeting to destruction. Maybe she didn't even want that. Maybe she wanted something superficial. How could he know? He determined to find out this morning and spent the rest of the time until he woke her rehearsing lines in his head.

Chapter 23

IT WAS STILL DARK WHEN Ihva woke to a gentle touch on her shoulder. She opened her eyes and saw Jasper's face in the dying firelight. Startled, she decided at least he wasn't just standing over her this time.

"What's wrong?" she asked in an urgent whisper. She looked over and saw the others still asleep.

"Our lessons are still in order," Jasper said.

Ihva looked around, then back at him. "But we don't have the practice swords. And you don't have your rapier either."

"You still have some to improve with your progressions and footwork."

"Oh. Okay." The last word drew out as she wondered how they could work on those things without proper equipment. She stood up, picked up Darkslayer from beside her, and shivered. The night air was chilly. She followed Jasper to a clearer spot among the grasses where he stopped in the dirt and turned to face her.

"Take a ready stance," he instructed.

She felt awkward as she positioned her feet beside each other and held her sword out in front of her. They hadn't focused much on starting position. She figured she must look silly and was glad it was too dark for him to see her blushing.

"Mhm," was the only sound he made for a moment.

He closed with her, and she swung her sword in front of him, trying to fend him off without actually striking him.

"Stop, stop," he said, waving her blade aside.

He moved closer. If he didn't want her to swing at him, why had he entered her combat zone? She held Darkslayer still. He reached her side. She looked at him out of the corner of her eye, maintaining her position and posture. He reached his hand toward her arm.

"What are you doing?" she exclaimed softly.

"I'm showing you where your arm *should* go and where you ought to place your feet." He put his hand to her left arm and pushed it down a few inches. He bent her elbow more as well. "This will help maintain your balance." He bent and touched her left calf, pushing her left foot forward in front of the other. She wasn't sure whether her upper body should follow, and she ended up twisting at the waist to face more east than she had been.

He rose from the ground beside her, and she looked at him. He muttered something unintelligible under his breath and straightened.

"You'll need to face the same way as before," he said.

Ihva turned at her waist to face the direction she'd been staring a second ago. He stepped back and looked her over.

After a moment, he told her, "That's it. You need your foot there to give you a launching point." He pointed at her left foot. "With your arm there, you can move it wherever you need to keep your balance." He moved to point at her left arm. His dark hair rustled in the breeze and framed a smile. Her stomach fluttered.

"Thank you," she told him, looking away.

There was a pause as he stepped back in front of her. "Now parry as though I am coming at you from here."

He motioned a strike from her left. She swung Darkslayer, moving her feet and arm to stabilize herself. Her eyes caught his, and she gave him a tentative smile. He walked over to her again and shifted her feet slightly.

"Now try it again," he told her.

She returned to the starting stance he'd shown her, watched as he made a swinging motion, and shifted her weight to meet the imaginary blow.

"Good, very good," he said.

For the first time, she heard respect in his tone, though she realized there had been hints of it all along. He'd never used quite so many words, which was probably why she hadn't caught it.

"Now notice your stance with each form and how you move between them. Be aware of the transitions," he told her.

Then he led her through various swings and jabs and twists of her body. It was pleasant, delightful even, heeding his directions and receiving his approving smiles. He spoke more than he ever had, too. She experienced the new candor in him as a rain shower during a dry summer, a welcome easing of the tension she now realized had been oppressing her since their first exchange. He *was* changing, like Malach had said, and so was she.

As they practiced, she remembered his instruction to notice how she was moving from one form to another. She marveled at the fact that she'd never thought about the in-between moments, the transitions as he'd called them. She'd always focused on the end result, the objective, the intent of each motion, and in doing so she'd failed to understand her movements with any clarity. Now that she was paying attention, she discovered how things flowed into each other, how one move was the natural sequel to another, how fluid her motion could become when she understood its stages and sought perfection in each one. How was it she'd never known about this before?

"Perfect," Jasper said as she dodged an imaginary blow and came around with a stab.

She stopped and smiled at him. The in-between moments, the moments of transformation, had a strange magic to them, or maybe it was his soft tone that had her heart aflutter. Whatever it was, all of a sudden, it felt like the world had been opened to her. She realized that transitions, far from being a waste of time, were the means by which anything was accomplished. They could be as beautiful as the final realization of one's purpose if one stopped to think about them.

"You've always been a quick learner," he said after another one of her swings. The serious look on his face broke into a smile again.

Ihva surprised herself with her own daring as a coy grin came over her. "Have I been? You could've told me earlier. All this time I've felt I was barely keeping up."

He gave a small chuckle. "You're an excellent student and have become a capable swordsman. Consider that making up for lost time." His face was bright and playful, his eyes shining.

A few seconds passed as he continued to look at her. She shifted in place, suddenly unsure what to say. The transition. Something was happening even at this moment. His eyes grew somehow deeper, and she felt a sudden tug, a magnetic pull, toward him. She resisted, not because she didn't want to go to him but because she wasn't sure what she'd do when she got there. In the end, it didn't matter that she hadn't moved, as he stepped closer.

He stood above her; his face turned down to look at her. She stopped breathing, and her body tingled. His look was intent, and her heartbeat quickened. She became torn. She wanted him, she knew, but something in the back of her mind whispered to her telling her it wasn't right. He was her prince. She couldn't beguile him like this. His fingers brushed her sword hand, which still held Darkslayer, and moved it aside. He took her other hand in his and stepped even closer until she could feel the heat radiating from his body.

"I'm sorry, Ihva," he said, his voice low.

"Why?" she asked, confused by her inner turmoil as much as by his apology.

"I kept you at arm's length, Oer, at greater length than that, for so long."

"It's okay," she replied, everything inside still muddled.

"I care for you, Ihva."

She broke his gaze and looked toward the distant sound of the waves. His words were welcome, but she couldn't shake the fear that the foundation of this interaction was unstable, that it would all come crumbling apart. She looked back up at him. His eyes were full and pleading.

"I believe you," she managed to whisper.

She was telling the truth. He'd changed so much from the taciturn prince she'd met in the palace. Even now, tenderness showed in his gentle gaze.

"It's just," she started to say. She couldn't find the words, though.

He picked up as she left off. "I love you, Ihva. I'm sorry. It's complicated, I know. It's more complicated than anything I could have imagined, but that's just how it is. I promised I won't use you, and I won't. That's the last thing I want to do. I love you, and I know you feel something of the sort, too, but I pressed that confession from you, and it's not the same to hear it that way. I regret forcing it from you, Ihva. I'm sorry."

Her breath caught. It wasn't the same speaking her confession that way either, she knew. Did she love him after all? Standing here, with him so near, she couldn't think straight. Whatever she felt was powerful, and it drew her to him. He loved her. Since when?

"How long have you felt this way?" she asked.

She tried to look past the intense look on his face but couldn't shift her eyes from him. At her words, though, his expression turned sheepish even as he smiled to himself.

"I don't know that I noticed at first," he replied. "I was in no position to think further on anything I might have felt, in any case. Besides being betrothed, I was determined I wouldn't involve one person more than necessary in my tangles with the Lady. It must have found a way to break through, though. I know I was jealous over you after we left Irgdol."

With Aaron. That had to be what he was talking about. All the way back since Eshad?

"But I realized in M'rawa. The second or third day, I don't remember which," he went on.

"Since M'rawa?" she asked, incredulous.

"I mean, yes."

"But—"

165

"I know. I was engaged to Jessica, but I didn't mean to. It just happened. It didn't help that you were around every second of every day."

"But you barely considered me back then. All you did was glower up to that point, and after that, you didn't look at me more than to instruct me how to hold my sword."

"And why do you think that was, Ihva?"

"You wanted nothing to do with me. That's what I thought."

"I suppose I feigned my disinterest well, then." He moved his hand to the small of her back and pulled her closer. "I'm sorry, I know it must be bewildering. It didn't make sense to me, anyway, until just two days ago. I didn't want to involve you. I wanted you to forget me, but I suppose I wanted to tell you more. Now you know, and there's really only one path from here, if indeed you feel similarly."

"I do."

She surprised herself with her answer. What had she spoken? She fell silent, though, as she watched his expression. He remained quiet, just looking at her. What could she even say? She wanted to tell him that she loved him too, but caution held her fast. What if she was deluding herself? At the same time, she saw his manner become more intense. He pulled her gently to himself, and she allowed him to press her body to his. He was trembling. His warmth invaded her soul, and she felt like she was floating. He used a hand to tilt her face up toward his. She looked into his eyes, his beautiful, dark eyes, and her heart leapt.

Just then, she heard a rustling behind her, and he glanced up toward the fire. She turned her head and spotted Cor stretching, and beside him, Malach was stirring too. She turned back to Jasper. He frowned and let go of her, then pulled away. She felt a sort of pain as he withdrew. He walked back toward the campsite and motioned for her to follow.

As she walked, she turned her face to look at the sky. It was still mostly dark, but somehow the stars appeared brighter than when she'd awoken. It was then that she recognized it—the transition.

Something was changing between her and Jasper, indeed something already had. They were in a moment of passage, and he was letting her determine whether the transformation would complete itself. She realized she'd never made a choice like this before as her parents had sheltered her from real decision-making, but her next move held significance. The weight of the moment held her in place. Jasper was her prince, her sovereign, but might he be meant to be even more to her than that? Light in Heaven, what was going on? Her heart pounded within her as she came to herself, and she jogged to catch up to him.

Chapter 24

"YOU TWO ARE UP MIGHTY early," Malach said, looking at Jasper.

The dwarf stretched and sat up as Jasper lowered himself to the ground on the opposite side of the fire. Ihva was standing as though deciding where to sit. Jasper knew the last thing she wanted was to discuss what they'd talked about with Malach, and she was probably trying to allay suspicions as best she could, but Malach glanced at her with a sparkle of mischief in his eye. She looked away and knelt on Jasper's side of the fire close to the sleeping Kronk.

"The same could be said of you," Jasper replied. His voice was not exactly sharp but firm.

"Getting some sword practice in, huh?" Malach asked, his tone knowing enough that Jasper could tell he understood what he and Ihva had been up to.

He looked Malach in the eye. "She still needs some help with her blade and footwork. We're Oer knows where. She needs to be as prepared as she can be."

Malach nodded slowly, and silence settled over the group for a moment. Then Cor broke in.

"How are you, Malach? Do you feel you can walk today?"

Cor's distraction worked as Malach turned his attention to the other dwarf.

"I feel much stronger, to be sure." He lifted himself to his knees and then to his feet. He stood for a moment, then turned from the fire to step forward. He wobbled but maintained his balance for about ten steps before stopping. Cor let out a slow breath.

"We will set out with the sunlight, then. We can stop for a late lunch if we haven't had any luck finding Yidda by then," he told the rest of the group.

"Lunch?" Kronk said in a muffled voice.

Jasper looked and saw her yawning. Her voice sounded sleepy.

"Not now, Kronk. It's not even morning yet, really," Ihva said.

"Breakfast?" Kronk suggested instead.

"No, Kronk," said Cor across the firepit. "We need to find Yidda. We are already a day and a half behind."

A frown overtook Kronk's face. Jasper knew she was hungry. *He* was hungry. They all had to be, eating a small bit of rabbit meat each day after almost a week on limited rations at sea. Nonetheless, Jasper agreed with Cor. They had to find Yidda. Besides that, he was eager to see about the city on the cliff.

Without packs, they had little to gather from camp. As the sun peeked over the horizon and brightened the sky, they set out east, again walking on the divide between the sandy beach and the grasslands. The going was slower than normal as they cut their pace in half to help Malach keep up. Besides that, their path was ascending to reach the level of the cliffs ahead. They hadn't walked for more than half an hour when Jasper stopped and peered into the distance. Two figures appeared on the cliff. He held out a hand for the others to stop as well. They obeyed.

"There," he said, pointing. Two figures? That couldn't be Yidda. It had to be city dwellers.

"What do we do?" Ihva asked.

"They've likely seen us. We can't run," Malach said. He had a sheepish look. "I, at least, can't run."

Cor and Jasper looked at each other, then Jasper spoke.

169

"It seems we're going to meet them, one way or another. We don't know if they're hostile, and only Ihva, Cor, and I have weapons. We must do our best to be diplomatic," he said.

"I have my dagger," Malach replied.

"Right, then four of us have weapons, three of them daggers," Jasper said. "Still not enough to defend ourselves if it comes down to it."

Cor nodded. "I suppose we must continue, then. We ought to minimize the time we spend worrying," he said.

Malach started forward with Jasper beside him. Cor, Ihva, and Kronk followed. Jasper watched the figures draw closer. Soon, he could make out general shapes. The figure on the left looked roughly human, and the other seemed to hover off the ground. What could these creatures be?

A few minutes passed. Jasper and his companions were about an hour out from the city and a hundred paces from the creatures approaching. Jasper could see the figures more clearly now. The figure on the left picked up its pace and appeared to be wearing something brown and unshapely—Yidda. Who could the other one be? Jasper didn't rush forward, skeptical of Yidda's companion. The others seemed similarly hesitant.

Kronk looked at Ihva and asked, "That secret talky lady?"

Jasper had forgotten Kronk's name for Yidda and nearly laughed despite his nervousness or maybe because of his nervousness.

"Yes, it is," Ihva said. "But don't go running to meet her. We don't know who the other one is."

A faint cry reached Jasper's ears. It was Yidda's voice. "Hail, friends!"

Jasper and the others continued forward at a slow pace, and Yidda met them a minute later. Yidda rushed up to Ihva first and wrapped her pale arms around her, squeezing tight.

"I was afraid you'd all been lost!" the Jini woman exclaimed.

"We're not, Yidda. We're not," Ihva said.

"We're all alive and well," Malach added. "I mean, we could use a little rest and some food, of course."

Jasper looked behind Yidda toward her companion.

"Who is with you, Yidda?" Cor stole the question out of Jasper's mouth.

"Oh, of course! His name is Grax," Yidda replied.

"Oh. What, um—" Malach began.

Jasper could tell what Malach was trying to ask and that he was trying not to be rude. "Who is he?" he finished Malach's question.

"He's, well, I'll let him explain that," Yidda said. "He found me wandering here on the cliff a couple days ago. A wave threw me onto the beach, and I made my way up here to look for you all. I hoped the height would help me see farther."

Cor nodded and said, "Indeed." The word lengthened as he continued to watch the distant figure.

"Perhaps you ought to bring him over here," Jasper said.

Yidda nodded and looked back, then hurried to the creature. After reaching it, Jasper heard some words exchanged in low tones while Yidda led it back. As it approached, what Jasper saw was a bizarre, orange-yellow creature. He tried not to gape as it reached him and his companions.

The creature stopped five paces in front of them. It was the size of an older human child, hovered above the ground, and had a tail that it swished back and forth every so often. Its orange-ish scales glimmered like sunlight off of a piece of glass, and its wings fluttered like a hummingbird, keeping the creature about a third of Jasper's height off the ground so it was eye level with him. Its body wasn't bulky but had some mass to it. Last of all, Jasper noticed its head. Its face was long and scaled and had heavy features. Two short, straight horns emerged from the back of its skull. Its eyes were slitted like a cat's eyes and shone a light golden-brown. Jasper could hardly believe what he was seeing. Before he could think further on the matter, though, the creature spoke, its voice masculine, deep and gravelly while still youthful.

"Greetings to you on this fine day, you travelers. What do you fine young men and women seek in these secluded parts?" it said.

Jasper was surprised in a few respects—that the being spoke at all, that it spoke Common (though a more archaic form), and most of all, by what he thought the creature must be. Were the Thousand Long Years over? Ihva must have thought the same thing.

"Are you a, um, dragon?" she stammered.

"Oh, no! Dear Gulur, no! I am a drake," the creature answered, sounding upset.

"Oh," Ihva replied simply, then introduced herself. "I'm Ihva Marchand."

"My name is Grax, young lady, and it is my pleasure thee to meet," the creature responded.

Jasper had been contemplating whether to give their real names, but Ihva just had. Then Cor chimed in.

"I am Cor Gidfolk, advisor to His Highness." He motioned to Jasper and proceeded. "And this is Kronk, companion to Ihva, and finally we have Malach of Irgdol."

"Again, a pleasure to make your acquaintance!" said Grax politely. "A pleasure to make your acquaintance," he repeated and trailed off.

If the drake had possessed anything to fiddle with, Jasper was sure he would have done so. They all stood, awkward, looking at each other and back at Grax, waiting for someone to take the conversation in some direction. It was Yidda who broke the silence.

"Like I was saying, we met two days ago, and dear Grax has been helping search for you ever since," she said. "He said you were likely to see the city from a distance and head toward it. It seems he was right."

Jasper and the rest of his companions were still eyeing Grax with varying degrees of suspicion and curiosity. Silence fell over them again for a moment.

"Kronk hungry!" Kronk exclaimed. "Sunny lizard man have food?"

Grax looked at Kronk, seeming unperturbed by what she'd called him. He smiled, baring two rows of pointed teeth—a disconcerting sight.

"I have none with me," Grax replied. "I fear Yidda and I ate the last of my provisions this morning. I have returned from Skatteby, after all, delivering Lord Gulur's share of treasure. The journey took a few days less than usual, what with the winds in a favorable direction, but a few days' sustenance can stretch only so far…"

Jasper stopped listening as the drake rambled on. There was edible food in the city ahead, then, if Grax had shared his with Yidda. Jasper's stomach felt hollow, and he knew if they didn't find something more to eat soon, the effects of malnourishment would set in. He already felt weaker and lightheaded. Besides that, they had no other leads on how to get home. He turned his attention back to Grax.

"…so you see, the journey to Skatteby is long, and it is a wonder I arrived back so quickly."

Jasper waited until the drake had finished his sentence to speak. "Master Grax, if I might interject? We're stranded here without provisions and without a way home and are in desperate need of assistance."

The drake nodded along.

"If you would please show us into your city and guide us to someone who might help us back to the mainland, we would be appreciative," Jasper went on.

At that, Grax gave a start and drew back. "Dear Gulur, no, I cannot do that!" he exclaimed, then began muttering to himself. "They desire to see the Onyx Voice. He will not like that. No, he will not like that at all."

Jasper interrupted again. "Who is the Onyx Voice, may I ask? Can he help us?"

Grax turned his attention back to Jasper and his companions, his eyes flitting between them. "I suppose he hath the means and authority to help, but I very much doubt he would do so."

"Why wouldn't he?" Jasper asked.

Grax gave a furtive glance around, then answered in a hushed voice. "He does not take kindly to foreigners." He glanced back at the city. "He has probably already noticed you. It might be that there remaineth no hope of escaping him."

"Escaping? What will they do to us?" Jasper replied, his words hurried.

Grax didn't respond, just kept his gaze on Jasper, who stiffened. It sounded as though walking into the city was a trap, as though being on the island had already sprung it. They were caught, and Jasper figured the best way to extricate themselves was to be upfront and forthright. There was nowhere to run, nowhere nearby at least. They weren't going to escape this Onyx Voice. The best thing to do might be to walk straight up to him and try to negotiate. Surely with two princes in their midst, they could convince this Onyx Voice to keep them alive and send them on their way. Surely this authority, whoever he might be, would see the danger of not doing so. Jasper gathered himself.

"Will you take us to him?" he asked, his eyes on Grax.

Grax jerked back. "Thou knowest not what thou askest."

Jasper couldn't make out the drake's expression, as the reptilian features were new to him, but he caught the warning tone in Grax's voice.

"You said we can't escape him," Jasper replied.

Grax peered at him, then said, "Indeed, you cannot escape."

"Then we march forward," was all Jasper responded.

Then he glanced around at the others. They were giving him careful looks, and he knew he should ask their opinions, but there seemed to be only one option. It was just a matter of time before they'd meet the Onyx Voice, and it might as well be on their terms. It occurred to Jasper the Onyx Voice might be a dragon. He tossed the notion aside. It didn't matter.

"If thou art certain," Grax replied, letting the words draw out.

Jasper turned back to the drake and nodded. "If you would, please take us to the Onyx Voice."

Grax peered at him again for a second, then turned and fluttered up the incline toward the cone-like city. Jasper looked at his companions and found them waiting for him. He turned his gaze to

Cor, who wore a grim frown. Then Jasper turned to Ihva. When he met her eyes, she gave him a small, faltering smile and nodded. Turning back up the incline, he told himself it didn't seem like they had a choice. He'd been all for entering the city a couple of days ago, but now he felt fearful. What had kept all those expeditions from returning? Whatever it had been, he and the others had to press forward. He nodded and started after Grax.

Chapter 25

THE SOUND OF MANY FLUTTERING met Jasper's ears as he stepped through the tall, plain, stone city gates. He peered around inside the city and saw drakes of all colors flitting about. As he and the others stepped into the city, though, the motion around them stopped and silence overwhelmed Jasper's senses. It thickened the air, almost as if he could reach out and touch it. It was at this moment it dawned on him they were trapped now, completely and utterly trapped.

Grax's voice called out, "Be at ease. These are friends."

"Friends? What makest thou so sure, young Grax?" a maroon-scaled drake called out from a stall to the right. "What purpose have they in entering the Sheltered City?"

"Why, Master Brognev, they seek—" Grax faltered.

"If I may, Master Grax," Malach interrupted, then bowed and turned to address the drake who'd spoken. "Master Brognev, my companions and I have been stranded on your shores and simply seek a way back home."

Whispers filled the square as the drakes spoke to one another with a fearful timbre. Jasper looked around. As he caught their gazes, they drew back behind doorways and windows to escape his vision.

The tension heightened as Brognev's voice rang out in anger. He spat, "How darest thou bring these *foreigners* here? Yet ought I expect any more from a follower of the amber Gulur?"

Grax's wings sputtered to a stop and he landed on the ground, cowering.

Malach's polite, lilting voice chimed in. "We will be on our way as soon as possible, if you will provide us a way back to our homelands."

"You shall never again see your homelands or did foolish Grax forget to inform you—strangers who find themselves inside the gates of Wymon never pass out the same gates, save in death," Brognev explained. "Grax, thou art to lead the prisoners to the Onyx Voice, and he will inform you as to their specific sentencing."

"Master Brognev, surely an exception can be made," Grax argued. "I believe these are remarkable individuals in their respective kingdoms."

"Young Grax!" Brognev's exclamation thundered through the square, and the other drakes withdrew into their hiding places. "The Onyx Voice will see to their fates. There are no *exceptions* in Wymon."

Jasper stood for a second in shock. So this was what Grax had been talking about—they were going to be made captives, exiles from their homelands for the rest of their lives. The prospect of such a thing gave rise to a defiant resistance in Jasper. They weren't going to lie down and allow this Onyx Voice to do with them whatever he wanted. Jasper would attempt diplomacy first of course, but he decided now that if it reached the point when force became necessary, he wasn't afraid to use it.

"We'll find a way home," he muttered under his breath.

Grax moved on up the street before them, his head bowed. Yidda went after him, as did Cor and Malach. Kronk looked at Ihva, but Ihva was watching Jasper.

"We have to," she told him, and he realized she'd heard him.

Before he could think to be embarrassed, though, she took him by the hand and started forward. He fell in stride beside her. As they walked, she intertwined her fingers with his. If he hadn't been so distracted, it would have been pleasant. As it was, he firmed his jaw and squeezed her hand. He had to be strong. He couldn't lose hope.

Grax led them along the winding streets of the city (Brognev had called it Wymon?) for what seemed like hours, though it could not have been more than thirty minutes.

Along the way, Jasper noted stone buildings made of what looked like granite with small flecks of color on a background of gray. They were mostly one-story buildings with an occasional two-story structure. Each had a simple rectangular opening in the front for a door and a square window beside it. The buildings were rarely decorated, though Jasper could see the flooring inside was often colored. There were patterns in the coloring, too. For a while he would only see blue floors, then just green floors, then some red floors, and then yellow, all occurring in groups on their way up the city.

By the time Jasper and the others reached their destination, they were breathing hard from the ascent. What met their eyes when they reached the top of the city was astounding—an extraordinary, tall building. It differed significantly from the rest of the city's structures and was magnificent in dimension. It towered, protective, over everything else, standing four or five stories tall. Instead of the white stone of the city walls or the flecked granite inside the city, an obsidian-looking stone, deep black and reflective, composed the building's walls and roof. Grax stopped and looked up with hesitation in his stance. Jasper wasn't sure what was stopping the drake but knew it wasn't good.

Grax stepped through the open doorway with a jerking, cautious sputtering of his wings. Malach and Cor entered together, and Yidda pulled at Kronk's sleeve to keep her from following. The Jini woman bowed her head to Jasper and allowed him to proceed before her, so he started forward, his face smoothed with feigned calm. They couldn't let the Onyx Voice know how desperate they were for permission to leave the city. If politics had taught Jasper nothing else, they'd shown him that letting someone know you needed them gave them the upper hand. He strode through the doorway with Ihva at his side.

The sheer size of the room overwhelmed him. Large, high windows let in sunlight, which was the only thing illuminating the room. He looked up at the ceiling. The same black stone from the walls created a seamless, narrow dome high above his head. There was nothing between them and the roof, and the stark contrast between the earthy stone abodes throughout the city and the grandiosity of the building he'd stepped into left him speechless. He was careful not to let it show, though.

His eyes wandered down to what lay before them as he sensed another presence in the room. In front of him stood a large stone desk and looking over the desk at him was a drake with deep gray scales sitting high above Jasper and his companions, foreboding. So this was the Onyx Voice. At least he wasn't a dragon. Jasper stepped forward to the desk and opened his mouth to speak, but the drake interrupted.

"Unwelcome you are here, as you might have gathered." He had a deep, grating voice.

"Well we know, Your Majesty," Jasper replied, employing a most respectful title.

"'Your Honor' is sufficient to address me. I am merely an elected official, after all, the Onyx Voice. We drakes do not live in such an unsophisticated political regime as others, bowing to a figure whose sole qualification for office is his pedigree." If this drake was as unforgiving as his tone made him sound, Jasper and the others were doomed. Jasper shifted, uncomfortable, as the gray drake went on. "The question remains—what are we to do with you? We have not had intruders enter our land for many years and certainly none come through our gates, and we cannot allow you to bring more to us. Indeed, we must imprison you here within our walls."

The Onyx Voice did intend to keep them in Wymon, then. At least he wasn't planning to kill them. Certainly the drake could be reasoned with.

"With all due respect, Your Honor, I believe it might be in your best interest to have us return to our homelands." Jasper had been about to mention that he and Malach were princes but thought better of it at the drake's diatribe against monarchies.

"Thou art saying we would do better to let you go?" The Onyx Voice laughed. "Let me hear thy pitiable argument."

Jasper bristled inside at the drake's condescension but remained outwardly calm. "There is a certain peace about Gant that cannot be maintained without us. Already it is unraveling, and I doubt the calamity will exclude you when it comes into its own. The longer you detain us, the more irreversible the situation becomes."

It was true. If Jasper didn't return, Oerid would fall. If Malach didn't return, Arusha would rule and bring chaos to Eshad and eventually to all of Gant. If Ihva didn't return, who knew what would happen?

"Thou soundest so certain of thy import," the Onyx Voice observed. "What dost thou intend to tell me? That thou servest a leading role of one of these wretched kingdoms? Are you generals, perhaps? You do not appear military."

Great. It would be unwise to lie at this point, but to tell the truth didn't seem the most hopeful option either. It was Malach who spoke next, though. He sounded like he was choosing his words carefully.

"In truth, there are two royals among us, if you are interested to know, and we have reason to believe upheaval is at hand in both of our nations. Our common foe seems to have arisen from her slumber to make war with us and between us."

Well put. Jasper wasn't sure he could have done a much better job of explaining the situation himself. Certainly the mention of their common foe would not go over the Onyx Voice's head—the Lady of Shadows wasn't one to be underestimated. Surely the drake would understand the threat to his own city.

"Thou believest in a common foe?" The Onyx Voice let out a humorless laugh, then gathered himself. "There is no 'common foe,' as thou namest it. The problem lieth in the hearts of mortals. Men and dwarves and elves have long attributed their faults and disasters to this 'enemy' when it is the evil within them that produceth their calamities. Sending you back would not alleviate the tragedies but exacerbate them. No. You shall not return. Perhaps we do your peoples a favor by impeding your homecoming. In any case, keeping you will spare you at least. You ought to thank me."

He didn't believe in a common enemy? The drake was insane. He didn't believe in the Lady of Shadows? Jasper had never heard of anyone not believing in her. Not respecting her or fearing her, certainly, but not disbelieving her. Had isolation driven the drakes mad?

More importantly, though, the Onyx Voice wouldn't allow their departure from Wymon. Not only would he not provide them a way back to the mainland, but he would confine them within the city walls. Jasper grasped for words. They could never hope to fight their way out the city gates, and even if they did, where would they go from there?

"And what when Eshad and Oerid fall to armies of Raised?" Malach asked, sounding as panicked as Jasper felt.

"It is not our issue. We knew you to be volatile races when we decided to disengage, and it is in the spirit of this disengagement we forbid you to leave the island of Hildur and city of Wymon. We grant you the mercy of your lives but no more. You will establish trades to earn your food and lodging. Your lives are yours, but your freedom is not. This is the final word!"

The Onyx Voice slammed a gavel down onto the desk in front of him, then turned and exited the room out a back door, leaving Jasper and the others gaping after him.

Chapter 26

IHVA HAD TO LET GO OF Jasper's hand when they'd entered the room and was now hugging herself around the stomach with her arms as they exited through the yawning doorway behind them. They were exiled. They were confined to the city and wouldn't leave its gates "except in death," as the drake, Master Brognev, had said earlier.

No one said anything as they made their way out of the building, and it took Ihva a moment to notice that Grax was missing.

"Where'd he go?" she asked aloud, piercing the oppressive silence.

Everyone looked at her, then glanced around. He was nowhere to be found.

"Well, now what are we supposed to do?" Malach asked. "Stuck on this blasted island with these Esh-forsaken fools under the threat of death," he muttered loud enough for Ihva and the others to hear. Ihva noticed Cor didn't bother to rebuke him for his language.

They continued to stand around for a minute or so, and Ihva avoided meeting anyone else's gaze. Instead, she observed them out of the corner of her eye. Cor had an impassive expression and was standing with a firm stance while Malach was busy wringing his hands and muttering to himself, this time too low for Ihva to hear. Yidda's mouth has twisted in such a way Ihva wondered if the woman was about to cry, and Kronk stood looking around at the others as well, wise enough to keep silent with the questions Ihva knew she had. Then there was Jasper. He was looking out over the city, his eyes scanning the southern horizon where the sea met the sky, and he had his lips pressed together in a frown. His posture, though, was what caught Ihva's eye—he had that small look about him again. He was afraid, and she wished there was some way she could allay his fears. Not all hope was lost, she knew. There had to be some way to get out of the city and back across the sea. One step at a time, though, she told herself.

At that moment, Ihva caught sight of movement out of the corner of her eye. She turned and found Grax fluttering there lower to the ground, below eye level for her. She was about to say something when a flash of an image caught her attention. Her eyes jerked toward it.

It was a picture of the tall obsidian building they'd exited floating an inch or two above Grax's head. It loomed over the city, which looked miniscule by comparison in the image. As Ihva watched, something blinding struck the building from above, and it shattered, then crumbled to the ground, not one piece of it left standing. At the same time, she noticed the rest of the city lay in shambles, and a horrified sense of foreboding crept over her. She was about to cry out but caught herself in time. This was another "viewing," she knew, and she realized now it wasn't only necessary but vital that they find their way out of the city or they'd be destroyed along with it. Whatever force had leveled all the buildings and struck the Onyx Voice's palace, for she didn't know what else to call it, would have no trouble taking them along with it. She shivered, then the image faded. She tried to bring her eyes back into focus as it felt like they'd been peering far off into the distance. What she noticed once her vision cleared was that Grax was staring at her. She couldn't make out his expression, as his face wasn't something she was used to interpreting. His posture was drooping, though.

"It's okay, Grax," she said in a quiet voice. It wasn't his fault. It had been their decision to enter the city despite his warning.

"I do not know what I can do to rectify this," Grax replied.

She didn't say anything. She didn't know either.

"We ought to be on our way," Cor broke in. His voice was heavy, something Ihva wasn't used to hearing from him. The dwarf wouldn't give up hope until the last shred of it had vanished, though, and she wasn't sure that it had. She caught Cor's eye. The spark of resolve to fight hadn't disappeared, at least. They'd find a way. They had to.

Ihva and her companions made their way down the city street in a tight group. Ihva became aware of the walls that held them captive, as she had clear sight of them from this height. This wasn't the first time she'd been confined to a city before, she realized, and a wave of nostalgia passed over her. Did her parents miss her? Had her father even noticed her absence in the midst of his busy schedule, or had it been the prohibiting of his meeting with Lord Rinaldo that reminded him of her? What had happened with the trial anyway? Had Mother cried when Ihva hadn't come home that night months ago? Did she still cry? Ihva's heart ached. As much as she'd resented their overprotective thinking, she realized her parents had been right. Look where adventure had gotten her—jailed in a city far from home by strange creatures with only a few companions to count on. Had she listened to them; she'd still be safe in Agda. Well, she would have been until someone discovered she was Oer's Blessing.

Anyway, Mother was right about Ihva and her romantic life as well, all too right. Sure, Jasper loved her, but he'd never marry her. Either they were stuck here on the Lost Isle and there'd be no point, or they'd find their way back to the mainland and he'd find someone more suitable to his station. Guilt weedled its way into her again, telling her she should never have entertained his advances in the first place. She was making things harder for both of them. The phrase "common blood" ran in repetition in her mind, so she tried to think of something else.

Her mind's gaze shifted to Linara and the elves. A sudden weight took hold of her, dragging her down. If they couldn't make it off the island, they couldn't return to fight the Shades. What if the elves couldn't defeat the Shades without her? She had a sinking feeling they indeed needed her, and she gripped Darkslayer at her side. The elves were doomed without her, and not only would Linara not see her parents again but the Shades might take the girl as well. Ihva had failed Linara and Laithor and all the citizens of Rinhaven. Now dejection overwhelmed her like it seemed to have done to the others.

They walked back down the streets of Wymon at a slow pace. Their speed was dragging as they were in no hurry. There was nothing to hurry to. Before Ihva knew it, though, they were entering a house. The floors were yellow, tiled and swept clean. As she stepped through the doorway, she noticed the home was larger on the inside than she'd suspected from the outside. It felt comfortable and spacious in a bare, stony way. Neat and tidy, the entry room opened up into a living room and kitchen and led into a bedroom separated by a wall. The doorways lacked doors. Ihva didn't understand why, but the place started to calm her. Perhaps it was the plainness and simplicity of the space. It reminded her of home in Calilla. Interrupting her thoughts came Grax's voice, and she realized he'd already been speaking for a while.

"...my home, humble as it mighteth be, should be spacious enough for us all for the time being. We ought to take lunch now, then venture out to buy your supplies. You will not endure long without proper provisions." He went to his cupboards and pulled out some food.

The rest of the group was silent. They all seemed to be in shock, and she wasn't in the mood for small talk either. Grax provided a hearty meal of dried fish in seaweed. Of course, Ihva hated dried fish, but her stomach demanded that she devour every bite given to her. As she chewed, she remembered the savory, salty taste of seaweed-wrapped rice and bits of cooked fish she used to eat as she sat on her father's lap. If only she could return to that time, that younger time when life was simple and adventure had been playing hide-and-seek behind tree trunks or spying on farmers from behind corn stalks, not watching a gruesome assassination, fighting incorporeal creatures who were after her soul, fleeing Jini attackers in the night, and struggling against waves larger than her house to not fall out of a boat and drown. All that was behind her now, and even her monotonous life in Agda was out of reach. Father was an ocean away, head of a booming merchants' guild, and Mother was likely passing the time designing the latest decor change in the Marchand home while Ihva was condemned to live forever on the Lost Isle, never to return. Ihva chewed her fish slowly as she ruminated on these things. Finally, Grax spoke.

"Well, are you prepared to go purchase some supplies? I have a stipend," he said.

"That'd be helpful," Malach replied, his voice flat.

"Indeed, we will be needing things to eat and drink." Cor's tone was strained.

"Let us depart, then," said Grax.

He spun around and exited the dwelling. Ihva and the others filed out after him. They made their way through the streets, once again receiving suspicious looks from the other drakes. After fifteen minutes, they arrived in a market district, one of the multiple sections of the city containing shops that Ihva had noticed on the way up. She noted that all the flooring on the inside of the shops yellow. She wondered what the color signified when Grax answered her unspoken question.

"We are in the amber market district, my preferred marketplace and the only place we can be sure no one will cheat us," he informed the others.

"Why is that?" asked Cor.

Grax replied, "Why, the Lord Gulur frowns upon cheating and general misconduct."

Ihva and the others looked at each other. Who was Gulur? Ihva had heard Grax mention this person a couple times. She tucked the question in the back of her mind for later and joined the others as they followed as Grax stepped up into a small shop on the right.

"What might I do for you strangers?" asked a plump-looking, violet-colored drake with a womanly voice.

She fluttered barely above the ground with small, sharp wings that contrasted with her mass of a body. Her voice was low-pitched but feminine and her words melodious. If she hadn't been glaring, one might even have mistaken the tone of her voice as friendly.

Grax looked at her. "Mother, these are my new friends. They require food to last a few weeks until they can start their own shop to sustain themselves."

"Well, I *sell* food, so unless they have coin, I can be of no help," the other drake replied.

Jasper pulled out a rather full money sack, but Grax put a hand out and indicated for him to put the pouch away.

Even as he did, the female drake spoke in a disparaging tone. "The Lord Gulur doth not accept the gold of foreigners, and neither shall I!"

"*I* have coin, Mother, and I will purchase their provisions until they can manage for themselves," Grax replied.

Surprised at Grax's words, Ihva asked, "I thought you said you received a stipend for us?"

Grax sounded sheepish. "I have received wages, and no one said they must be used for me, so I am using them for you."

Ihva looked at Jasper. He had an eyebrow raised, and she wondered if they should accept Grax's aid. How much of a sacrifice was the drake making for them? They'd lost almost everything at sea, though, and she knew they needed his help.

Yidda spoke first. "We appreciate your assistance, Grax, as we are in a rather humble situation."

Grax didn't respond. It seemed he and his mother had entered a staring match.

His mother spoke first. "This is unwise of thee."

"But Mother—" Grax started to say.

"But nothing. I should not have expected anything more from thee. Thou refusest to build up Gulur's hoard and instead givest precious gems and coins to children in the streets. For *food*, of all things."

She spat her words at Grax. Ihva felt sympathy for him.

"Thou hast always been a selfish one, Grax, and I should have expected nothing more honorable now. Give away thy money, fine. At least when it is mine, I will take it to Gulur's temple where it belongs."

Grax's desire for her approval was clear. Ihva felt tempted to touch his shoulder to comfort him but didn't want to make things worse. He and his mother started bartering, and his mother piled fish jerky, rabbit meat, a bag of grain, and dried seaweed on the ground in front of Ihva and the others. Ihva shuddered. More dried fish. She tried to think of ways to make the upcoming meals more palatable while she and the others continued onto other shops to buy water skins and other necessities.

Chapter 27

BY THE TIME THEY ALL arrived back at Grax's house, Ihva was exhausted. Deep blues were overtaking the eastern sky, and it had been a long day. It had been a long couple of months. Everything was catching up with Ihva, and all she wanted to do was to lie down and sleep.

Instead, she sat with her companions on the tile floor since Grax had no chairs. They watched Grax tend to a small fire in a brick oven where he was cooking some rabbit meat. At least it wasn't dried fish again. Like the rabbit meat they'd eaten in the wilderness, this rabbit had no spices and no salt. Ihva sighed. She wanted to think of ways they might sneak out of the city and find a way home, but she was too tired for such creativity. Instead, she sat, staring at nothing in particular, waiting for dinner. The others sat in silence as well. Soon enough, they were passing around a plate of food, picking up pieces for themselves and eating with their hands. The mood in the circle was somber.

Grax broke the silence after a few minutes. "I pray the meat is to your liking." He looked around at each of their faces.

"Yummy!" Kronk exclaimed.

She seemed relieved that conversation had resumed. Licking her lips, she leaned over Ihva and grabbed another piece of rabbit from the plate. There was plenty more to go around, so no one begrudged Kronk her large portion. Looking at the feast before them, Ihva noted Grax withheld nothing from his guests. He was a generous soul, she realized. A sudden appreciation for him welled inside her, and she decided that whatever happened, she'd try to find a way to repay him. Someone needed to value him, and if his own mother wouldn't, then perhaps Ihva could. If she and the others had to stay, if she could do nothing more for Gant, maybe she could at least do something for Grax.

As they finished their meal, the drake fluttered his wings and returned to hovering a few feet off the ground. "Perhaps after this tiring day you might like to retire?" he asked Ihva and the others.

"Excellent idea," Malach replied with lackluster enthusiasm.

"Well then, let us retire. I will take watch outside," Grax told them.

His offer surprised Ihva. Were they in need of protection? Jasper had the same question, it seemed.

"I was not aware that we needed guarding. Are we in danger, Grax? Will your brothers harm us in the night?" he said slowly.

"Not as such," Grax replied, trailing off. After a pause, he added, "Only inasmuch as some think you might steal our secrets and find a way to return to your homes with them. Few believe you are capable of doing so, and even fewer are willing to take action against you. It is a crime to harm a guest in Wymon, after all. You are safe. In the event that I am wrong, however, I will stand guard."

Grax avoided Jasper's gaze, but for his part, Jasper eyed the drake. Ihva could tell Jasper suspected something was amiss, and a moment later she learned his reasoning.

"You're here to keep us from leaving, aren't you?" he said in a stony voice.

There was a short silence, then Grax spoke. "Yes." He hid his eyes. "But I pledge my life to care for you in your stay here as well."

"Our *stay* here?" Jasper returned; his tone heated. "You say that as though we choose it, as though we can leave at any time."

Grax was silent, bowing his head. Jasper's voice was hard as he spoke again.

"You cannot be on both sides, Grax. Either you are for us, or you are against us. You are either bent on obeying the Onyx Voice or you are willing to help us. As things stand, you're as much an enemy to us as any other drake."

Grax's posture wilted, and Ihva's heart went out to him, though she understood Jasper's point. If Grax knew of any way for them to escape, he ought to tell them, not guard them against leaving. It was a miserable situation. Why should they expect the drake to betray his people for a group of adventurers he'd just met, though? Caught between the two sides, Ihva sensed tension filling the room and felt light-headed.

A few moments passed without anyone speaking. It felt like an eternity. Grax was the first to say something, his head hanging. His voice was quiet.

"I had hoped they had changed or that they could change, perhaps. There have been decades since any have arrived on our shores. I have tried explaining we cannot subvert the inevitable, but they do not listen. They refuse to heed wisdom, and now the judgment has been set against you. I beg your pardon for my brothers' ways for they are also my ways."

"It doesn't matter now, dear," Yidda said in a soothing tone. She shot Jasper a frown that demanded he stay silent. "Even the most profound change of heart or conversion to wisdom cannot undo what has been done. The future can't *erase* the past, but sometimes it can overcome it."

Grax looked up at Yidda. Ihva turned to her as well, wondering where she was going with her argument.

Faltering, Grax said, "What sayest thou I ought to do?"

"Grax, dear, what I mean is you can't do anything to undo the Onyx Voice's sentencing, but you can help us overturn his judgment." Yidda paused for a moment to let her words sink in. "You can help us escape."

Grax's eyes widened. "I have never disobeyed a judgment by the Onyx Voice," he said and paused. "I have never questioned the laws of the city, but I begin to see. We fear the prophecies, but that which resulteth is cruelty and barbarity. One ought not find himself an exile for the mere fact that he has stumbled into a strange land. And if you speak truly about the state of affairs abroad and your roles therein, I cannot but aid you. It is what is right." He paused and seemed to be thinking.

At the same time, Ihva wondered what prophecies Grax was talking about. He resumed speaking before she could ask, though.

"There is only one way I can imagine, but no, *that* is too dangerous," he said as though to himself. He gave a vigorous shake of his head, then looked at Jasper. "There is no way I can imagine that you might find your way back to the mainland, I am afraid. There is nothing I can do to help."

There was another short silence, then Jasper spoke. "Grax." The anger had left his voice. "I cannot say for sure whether the dangers present on the mainland will reach your shores, but I believe this island to be in as much danger as any other land. Even if you don't believe me on that, though, please hear me."

Ihva found something in Jasper's tone and expression that she'd never encountered in him before, and it puzzled her.

"I know you seek our lives to be preserved, but what are our lives worth if our countrymen, our own fathers and mothers and sisters and brothers, are manipulated or massacred by the Shadow? We seek to save our people. Living out our days here while the rest of the world is destroyed is no life at all. You sentence us to such a fate if you don't help us. Let us try, Grax. The cruelty of forcing us to succumb to this existence, the torment of having deserted our loved ones cannot escape you, can it? Surely you understand."

No, it wasn't that she'd never encountered this in Jasper, as she saw now it had been evident in every nervous glance around, in every time he'd looked helpless and afraid. She'd never seen through to what was behind all the desperation, though. It was something kinder than she'd imagined. Something strange came over her, listening to him. There was a zeal, a deep yearning, a passion in his words. His small looks over the past few months started to make sense. He cared for Oerid in a deeper way than she'd understood, and he was afraid for his people. She recognized the care in his tone now because she'd heard it before—it was similar to the tone he'd been taking with her lately. Listening to his voice, she started to fathom the depth of his affection for *her*, and it scared her, yet with a fear that drew her along instead of frightening her off. She felt driven toward the object of her fear, as though only the experience of it could cure it.

Grax was talking now. "I cannot imagine I would have much for which to live should I know my fellow drakes were suffering and dying at the hands of evil while I did nothing."

He thought for a long moment, and no one dared to speak. Finally, the drake opened his mouth and spoke woeful caution.

"I must warn you that you shall face the wrath of the Onyx Voice and of all my countrymen if you fail. They cannot imagine any good coming from your release, only evil and destruction. The wisdom of old bodeth not well for us concerning strangers." He looked around at the others. "One way back to the mainland from here existeth, and you must escape the city to find the ones who can help you."

"Who must we find?" Jasper asked.

"The gem dragons." Heavy force behind Grax's words drove his warning into Ihva's heart. There would be no turning back once they started on the journey to find these creatures, whoever they were.

"The gem dragons? Where are they?" Malach asked. "Better yet, who are they?"

"No one is aware of where they reside. They are lost to time, and mere legend of their existence remains. We know only their names and colors. They are Raidurr the Ruby, Blarr the Sapphire, Graiyent the Emerald, and Gulur the Amber. We have impressions of their personalities, but that is all. We drakes worship the gem dragons, each choosing one to hold his devotion. Each dragon lord's temple containeth a hoard of sacrifices offered throughout the years.

"I have read many scrolls and books concerning our dragon lords. I have learned much. There existeth a tale we tell that they all

193

hatched from the same egg. According to my research, once the pieces of the shell come together once more in unity, they will reveal the secret to the gem lords' location."

"Intriguing." The word Cor spoke lengthened to fill the silence as the others absorbed Grax's words, then Cor continued. "Where might the pieces of the egg be located, if you do not mind?"

"There are four pieces. I believe they are the holy relics on display in the temples, but that is just my guess. I have never seen the other pieces, so I cannot say whether they fit together," Grax said.

Ihva wondered aloud, "Why don't you all just gather the fragments and put them together to find out?"

Grax looked down. "If it were my prerogative, I would. Unfortunately, in Wymon, the majority ruleth, and the majority is so occupied building each gem dragon's hoard and authority within the Council that it hath little time for tales like this or actual pursuit of the beloved lords. We drakes prefer to argue with each other about the superiority of each one's liege. To do so, we compete to develop the greatest loyalty to our lords and perform the greatest generosity to our temples. It seemeth we care little for knowing the truth. In many cases, I feel a good number even fear discovering it. We would rather keep the gem dragons a mystery than a reality to which we are accountable."

The room went silent. Even in her tiredness, Ihva recognized how sad and tragic it was for an entire race to be alienated from their gods not by the nature of things but by their inability to move beyond themselves. The drakes were letting politics and competitive spirit keep them from reaching their lords. If human means could reach Oer, mankind would have reached him long ago. Or would they have?

A new wave of exhaustion overcame Ihva. Her eyelids felt like lead, and her consciousness was fading. She knew the others were still talking, but she couldn't pay attention. At one point, she lifted her eyes and found the others looking at her expectantly.

"Um, sorry. I think I missed the question," she said. Her words slurred into each other.

"Thou lookest weary, and I asked whether thou wouldst like to sleep in the bed," Grax said.

"Oh, sure," Ihva replied, taking note of the darkness outside and stars peeking through the doorway.

"Then, thou mayest enter that room to sleep and leave thy belongings on the floor within," Grax said, motioning to the bedroom on the left.

Ihva looked down at Darkslayer. That was really all she had with her besides her clothes. She nodded to Grax and thanked him, then bid the others good night.

As she walked into the room, her eyes went straight to the bed. It was simply a slab of unpolished granite, flat on the top and about six feet long. There were no blankets or pillows. It would do, though. Kronk appeared next to her. Apparently, the orc-blood woman was tired as well, or she might have been bored and hoping to escape the conversation in the other room. Ihva didn't mind, but she wasn't going to talk much. Kronk plopped herself down on the slab before Ihva had a chance to reach it in her stupor, so Ihva shrugged to herself and curled up on the tile floor instead.

"Good night, sleep tight," came Kronk's loud whisper from above her.

She looked up and found the orc-blood woman peering down at her.

"Good night, Kronk," Ihva replied, her words sluggish.

"Ihva okay?" Kronk asked just as Ihva was about to turn over.

Ihva stared at her for a moment, trying to comprehend her words. Finally, she understood and nodded.

"Yeah, I'm fine. Just tired," she said. She *was* tired, and nothing else seemed to matter at the moment—their predicament, their plan to escape, the plight of the world. Ihva told herself her despondency concerning those things was a result of exhaustion and that things would look better in the morning. A good night's rest could cure just about anything, she reasoned. She realized her eyes had closed and she'd drifted off for a second.

"I'm fine," she repeated, mumbling such that Kronk might not even be able to understand her. "We'll talk in the morning. It'll all look better in the..."

She didn't finish her sentence before she fell asleep.

Chapter 28

JASPER, COR, YIDDA, AND MALACH stayed up discussing their strategy for escape. Ihva and Kronk were long asleep, and Grax was out front.

"I am still not convinced Oer would permit this. There must be something else we can do. We cannot go through with it," Cor said.

Cor was trying to convince them to think of another way to flee the city and escape the island. Jasper sighed inwardly. Cor always made things more complicated than they needed to be.

"We have to. It's the only way!" said Malach, his voice low and tone urgent.

"But it is theft of their most prized artifacts. Are we capable of such a crime?" Cor asked.

Jasper retorted, "We have to be! Not all of us see in black and white, holding tight to so-called righteousness, Cor. This time, there is no *right* answer. Our choices are between one evil and another, worse one."

Yidda interjected in a gentle voice. "He's right, Cor. Either we're responsible for theft from the drakes, or we are responsible for the collapse of two kingdoms and the loss of many lives by the theft of two nations' leaders. I believe we must choose the less impactful of the two options. No one here will die for the fact that the eggshell pieces are missing as it sounds like they pay them no attention anyway."

Cor gave a slow nod, and his voice grew reverent. "Oer, forgive us."

"Are we agreed, then?" said Malach.

Silence followed, though everyone nodded.

"Anyway, we're just looking around tomorrow," Malach said.

Cor was still frowning.

"We'll tell Ihva and Kronk in the morning," Jasper added.

No one said anything. Jasper wasn't sure why the others were looking at him, but he conceded. "*I'll* tell them in the morning."

Cor and Malach nodded again, and Yidda put a hand on Jasper's arm.

"We will find a way home," she said.

Uncertainty gripped him despite the woman's reassurance. The others broke from the conversation and looked around for somewhere to sleep. Ihva and Kronk had the bedroom, so the rest of them had to find a place in the living room or kitchen. The residual heat from the cooking fire earlier left the kitchen warmer than the rest of the house, so Jasper left it to Malach or Yidda. He and Cor took opposite corners of the living room and laid down, but he didn't fall asleep right away. His thoughts kept him awake, as usual.

He wondered how they would manage to steal or even get close to the eggshell fragments. He had no idea how the drakes guarded their artifacts. Grax had told them about a pedestal in Gulur's temple amidst what sounded like a large library. The shelves should hide any activity at the pedestal from prying eyes. They had no idea about any of the other temples, though.

It made Jasper anxious, thinking about the unknowns, so he turned his mind to other things. He thought of Grax. The drake seemed trustworthy enough. Jasper knew he wouldn't like Grax's mother, though, if given more time to get to know her. Oer, he already despised her. Her reproach of Grax's compassion and generosity was reprehensible. Jasper wondered about the other drakes. Did they have more in common with Grax or his mother? They sounded foolish at best from Grax's description.

They were an alien race, to be sure, but Jasper couldn't help but note some similarities between them and the Oeridians he was to rule. The political system for example—the Onyx Voice was elected, he'd claimed, but he seemed to rule with absolute authority like Oer's Chosen Son. From what Jasper had observed, the ruling drake had decided Jasper and his companions' fate without any outside input. At least Father had advisors. Besides that, the drakes were too busy vying for power to notice what was right in front of them, the chance to find their beloved gem dragon lords. Jasper wondered whether Oer's Blessing might be something of a similar situation. Perhaps Oer's Blessing was meant to bless, to bring Oer's presence back to Oerid and to Gant, but Oerid was so distracted by the Shadow and in-fighting that she missed the favor meant for her. Maybe Ihva could bring peace after all. Maybe she *was* a blessing.

Ihva. Jasper still hadn't gotten used to the wave of emotion that washed over him when he thought of her. They were different emotions than before. In Rinhaven, he'd felt an ache, a joyous ache to tell her, knowing he never could. Traveling to Jinad, it had been a sharper pain as he tried hard to bury his feelings beneath necessity. Now he felt no pain at all but instead an overwhelming sense of affection and desire. She was beautiful and fascinating, and he adored her. She seemed to be responding better as well. She hadn't said anything concerning her affections since the time he'd forced the confession from her on the Wandering Whale, but she was clearly attracted. She'd been trembling when he'd almost kissed her the second time. He cursed the fact that Malach and Cor had awoken in that moment. There would be more moments like it, though. He was determined of that. The problem right now was privacy. It was completely lacking, and there were certain things that could only be discussed in private, especially considering her tendency to confidentiality. One more reason they had to get out of here.

Jasper rolled toward the wall to hide his face. He was so frustrated, frustrated and frightened. It was the fear that was disturbing him the most, though. He hadn't expected to be able to fathom remaining in Wymon, but somehow he could almost see living out his days here. If he remained, then so would Ihva. He'd have *her*.

What troubled him was that he knew he wouldn't be happy that way. He wouldn't feel fulfilled or satisfied with himself as he would have abandoned Oerid. Father had raised him to care for his people as for his own life, and he took his role as their guardian seriously. In a strange way, he loved them. He'd never noticed before, but the thought of Oerid invoked a sense of care and attentiveness, something akin to what he felt for Ihva but with less specificity and therefore less intense and precise. The thought of his people sparked a certain vigor in him. Something must have veiled these feelings to him until now, but in this moment, it was as though a blindfold had lifted and he was seeing for the first time.

If only he'd recognized it all sooner. He was finally learning what it meant to rule, that was, to serve his people and offer his life for them. He was finally grasping what it meant to be king, but it didn't matter now. None of it mattered. If they didn't make it back, his care would be squandered. He cursed the day they'd entered the city. No, he cursed the storm that had brought them here, but again, that wasn't it either. None of this would have happened if it hadn't been for Jessica, and the Lady would never have taken Jessica if it hadn't been for him. He cursed the day of his birth, the day everything had gone wrong. He cursed the Lady, and he almost cursed the power by which his heart was sealed away, but that power was Oer, and he refused to allow such blasphemy to dwell in his mind. Even so, it dawned on him that he was resentful and that his bitterness had an object. It was a gross impiety to resent Oer, though, so he refused to discern the emotion any further.

Instead, he let out the breath he hadn't realized he'd been holding. He had to accept his lot. He was an exile, and whatever keenness he was feeling to defend Oerid was likely worthless now. He'd told the others it took courage to admit defeat. Now he needed to prepare that boldness in case it all went wrong. Unless they could

200

escape, it was all over. He didn't feel optimistic about their plan, and he knew there was little he could do if it didn't work, but he still felt responsible. If they failed, then he'd have failed, and he had to be ready to shoulder that guilt. Yet maybe he was getting ahead of himself. More than preparing for the worst, he had to throw himself wholeheartedly into the fight to escape. He couldn't let Oerid fall if it was within his power to return to her. They had to get back.

He shifted again and turned over. He couldn't let fear paralyze and defeat him. They'd go to the temples tomorrow and come up with a plan to take the fragments. Then they'd gather the shards, piece them together, find the gem dragons, and ask their aid to get back to the continent. It would work. It had to. It crossed his mind that they might have to take Grax with them. They couldn't leave him to his fate with the drakes when it was found that the prisoners were missing. Grax seemed young, but he seemed to know something of the adventuring life and could make it out with them. Jasper determined he wouldn't abandon the drake, whatever that meant.

Jasper sighed. He had to get some rest. He couldn't afford for weariness to overtake him tomorrow. He laid out flat on his back and tried to quiet his mind. It was still at least an hour before he fell asleep.

Chapter 29

JASPER WOKE BEFORE SUNRISE. HIS mind was clear, as it was most mornings before worry clouded it. He wanted to wake Ihva and talk to her but didn't want to disturb Kronk in the process. The mornings were his and Ihva's time, he'd decided. It was then when they'd practiced swordplay all these months, and it was then when they'd had most of their conversations. As it was, he slipped over to the room where she lay sleeping and looked at her. She was lying on the ground across from the doorway. She'd let Kronk take the bed. He smiled. He hadn't understood at first what Kronk was to her, but it had become clear the orc-blood woman was much more Ihva's friend than her servant. In fact, it seemed a lot like Ihva had been taking care of Kronk rather than the other way around—the irony. He shifted his attention back to Ihva. Her breathing was soft, but he could make out the sound of it in the early morning silence. His own breathing fell in sync.

Her loveliness struck him. It always had. He was sure it had been the reason for his discomfort at the beginning, back when he'd known her as "the girl" and "Miss Marchand." He laughed at himself inwardly. How could he have been so blind to it? He'd avoided speaking to her because it had made him uncomfortable. He'd avoided sitting near her because it had made him uncomfortable. He'd avoided interacting with her at all because it had made him uncomfortable. Of course, it had made him uncomfortable. He'd liked her—he'd been attracted to her. He thought of the moments in Eshad when he should have known. He'd been so upset about the dwarf boy, so delighted by their dance by the fireside, and so affected by her addressing him outside practice, even during practice.

It wasn't solely her beauty that held his attention, though. It was her being. She intrigued him with her optimism—her simple outlook and positivity. She didn't think as much as he did, it seemed, but she didn't think too little, either. She just evaluated situations and accepted them, something he'd never been able to do. He was always raging against something. She seemed so at peace, even with the burden of being Oer's Blessing set square on her shoulders. Watching her live her life enthralled him, and he was becoming increasingly desperate to be a part of it.

She stirred, and he withdrew behind the doorway. He didn't want her to know that he'd been watching her. He wasn't sure she understood all he felt for her, and he didn't want to scare her.

"Jasper," came her voice in a whisper.

She'd seen him. It was too late now to pretend otherwise.

"Ihva," he said quietly.

There was a rustle as she shifted and stood. He stepped out from behind the wall.

"Sorry," he said.

"No, it's fine," she said, stepping toward him. "I wasn't sleeping well anyway."

"Yeah, I just," he started. "Nevermind."

She neared him, and the next thing he knew, she was right in front of him, in his space. He stopped breathing. She was looking up at him.

"Um," he said, clearing his throat softly. "Maybe we should go outside."

It would be better there, in view of any passersby, true, but there would be none at this hour, and maybe Grax had fallen asleep or would at least let them be.

"Okay," was all she said.

He stepped back. Then, without thinking, he took her hand and led her out of the room and out of the house. She didn't protest.

Outside, they indeed found Grax asleep, but as soon as Ihva stepped out the front doorway, the drake's eyes shot open in the starlight.

"Hi, Grax," Jasper said. "We were wondering if we could get a moment, you know, to ourselves? We didn't want to wake anyone."

Grax's eyes widened. "Certainly," he said but didn't move.

"A moment alone, that is," Jasper clarified. "We promise we won't run."

"Oh," Grax said. "Oh, of course. You require a moment of privacy. Certainly. That can be arranged. Certainly."

Jasper got the idea that the drake was misinterpreting his request, but he didn't want to make things any more awkward, so he let it be. Grax nodded and sputtered into the house.

"Right," Jasper said after a moment, turning back to Ihva. He still had her hand in his, but he let it drop.

"Sorry," she said. "I didn't mean to make you have him leave."

"No, it's fine. I wanted to spend a moment alone with you anyway."

She looked at him, a question in her eyes.

"Just to spend a moment, that's all," he said.

She nodded, and he wondered if he detected disappointment in her face.

"We're going after the fragments," he said to cut the silence. "We'll visit each of the temples today and scout out the pieces, if indeed the temples house them. Then we can regroup and figure out how to go about it from there."

"Oh. What would we do then? Steal them?"

"Yes." He hoped she wasn't going to be like Cor. They *had* to do this. It was the only way. It meant saving Gant rather than leaving everything to destruction.

"It'll be dangerous," she said.

"Yes. That's why we're not trying it today. We'll have to come up with a plan, some way to do it more covertly."

"And when we've stolen them?"

"We'll have to find a way out of the city. Perhaps at night, something like that."

"And Grax? Does he know?"

"Yes. He needs to help us, and besides that, we need to take him with us. I won't leave him with them thinking he failed to guard us."

She smiled at him. "Thank you," she said, and Jasper grew embarrassed.

"Anyway, that's what will happen, if we can pull it all off," he said after a moment.

"We can do it."

It was his turn to peer at her. How could she be so sure?

"We can do it," she repeated with greater emphasis.

"How do you do that?"

"Do what?"

"Think like that? Hope like that?"

"I don't know. I've never questioned it. I've just always been this way," she replied, trailing off.

He gave her a searching look.

"Is there something wrong with me?" she asked, her voice strained all of a sudden.

"No," he said quickly. "No, not at all."

"You're not mad at me?"

"No. Why would I be mad at you?"

"I don't know."

"No, I'm not mad at you," he assured her.

He looked at her eyes, drank in their innocence. He *was* desperate to be part of her world, to be part of that optimistic expectation she had about life, about people, about everything. He'd told Yidda that the innocent could sometimes even redeem those touched by evil. How deep was his yearning all of sudden to find out if that was true, if Ihva's purity, her simple goodness, could cleanse him. For the first time, he considered what it would be if she did retrieve his heart, if he became whole.

"What are you thinking?" she asked in a low tone.

"Nothing. Nothing important," he replied quickly.

Something like surprise or maybe it was hurt flashed in her eyes, and it struck Jasper like a slap to the face that he'd lied to her. In the same instant, he decided that whatever he did from this point forward, he didn't want to lie to her again. Still, how to explain?

"I love you, Ihva, that's all." That *wasn't* all of it, though. "That and I'm wondering if loving you is in some way a good thing for me, a changing thing, something that transforms."

He looked down, uncertain how to proceed, but she said nothing. He looked back up and saw her eyes shining with moisture.

"Ihva, I don't know how to stop telling you. Forgive me for saying it again, but I care for you. I love you. I couldn't be mad at you, for your hoping least of all."

"It's okay," she said, her voice quivering.

"What's okay?"

He watched her swallow and gather herself.

"You can tell me again. I don't mind hearing it," she whispered.

He reached out to take her hands in his own, slow and hesitating.

"That you love me, I mean," she added.

He laughed softly. "Then I love you. Know it, Ihva. Believe it."

"I believe you."

"I cherish you; I treasure you; I prize you. I could say it a thousand times and never tire of telling you, Ihva. I love you."

"It's just surreal," she said, her voice wavering.

"It's more real than anything I've ever felt, Ihva."

"You can't, though. I'm nothing more than a commoner. You're my prince. I can't do this to you."

"You're nothing common to me. You've done nothing wrong, Ihva."

She gave him a skeptical look, but he could tell she wanted to believe him.

"Kiss me," she whispered. She turned her face up and looked at him, her eyes big, her hands trembling.

He quickly took his hands from hers, put one around her waist and one on her cheek. He pulled her closer, then hesitated.

"Please," she said.

So kiss her he did. He kissed her hard, and he kissed her thoroughly. He didn't want to stop. If he could tell her a thousand times he loved her, he could kiss her ten thousand times. She was supple, conforming herself to his body, and passionate, kissing him as hard as he was kissing her. He had to breathe, though, so he pulled back.

She withdrew slightly, and her eyes opened with a fire in them. He didn't want to break the moment, so he didn't say anything.

"I love you," she whispered.

He lost his breath once more.

"I love you," she said again, then laughed a quiet, joyful laugh. "I wasn't sure for a while. Maybe I was deluding myself, I thought. I've wanted to fall in love so badly, I thought surely this was a trick of my imagination, but it's not, Jasper. I'm calling you that, I am."

Jasper laughed with relief. She'd confessed it, and in her confession, he felt a shift. She agreed to belong to him, perhaps not fully, not yet, but it was enough. He leaned down and kissed her again. He kept kissing her and would have kept on endlessly, with abandon, even as she kissed him back, if the first rays of dawn hadn't been peeking over the horizon above the city walls. He pulled away.

"We should stop. They'll wake soon," he said.

"Okay," she said, her voice airy. She was looking at him as though she hadn't just agreed to stop.

"Really, Ihva. They'll find us."

"Let them."

Jasper felt a thrill of surprise. He smiled at her. "Malach won't let us be about it. He'll be asking all manner of uncomfortable questions."

She returned a mischievous grin. "I suppose you're right." She drew back a little, but only a little, then went on. "He's already thinking we're together. He told me you'd change, and maybe you have."

"What's that supposed to mean?"

"I don't know entirely."

"Yeah, he badgered *me* a couple nights ago," Jasper told her. He felt a slight flush come over himself thinking about it.

She laughed, then said, "I suppose we shouldn't give him more to ask about."

"Definitely not," he agreed.

She stepped back, gave him a sly grin, and walked back into the house.

Malach had said that Jasper would change, had he? He wondered what the dwarf had been referring to. Jasper had become bolder, truly, kissing Ihva in an open street. Kissing her at all, really. She'd said she loved him. She *loved* him. She'd meant it, too. The certainty of it grounded him. Maybe it wasn't just Jasper who was supposed to change. Maybe love was a mysterious force that emboldened and encouraged in a way nothing else could, and maybe it *would* change him. It just might be that he was meant to share in that hope Ihva carried, in that life she lived, in a deeper way than he'd imagined. He strolled into the common room, only half hiding his smile, ready to face the day and the challenge ahead.

Chapter 30

IHVA WALKED INTO THE ROOM, feeling the joy written on her face. Cor was waking as she entered and looked at her, though, and shyness overcame her, very unlike how she'd felt outside. She turned to avoid his gaze. She'd been so unrestrained out there, and she hoped Cor didn't realize what had happened. She heard Jasper's footsteps behind her and blushed, then glanced at Cor. He'd been looking at her and smiled but averted his gaze when she looked at him, graciously letting her slip by without addressing her. Malach was stretching and gave a loud yawn, and Yidda sat up.

"A fine morrow to you," Grax said loudly. Then, his voice grew softer. "We will proceed to the temple district when you are prepared to do so."

Cor turned to Ihva and spoke to her. "I assume Jasper has informed you as to the plan." She nodded, and he continued. "I have been reluctant to admit our only option right now, if indeed we intend to escape, is to take the fragments. I would like to think we can return the pieces to their proper places when we are finished, but I realize that might not be possible. This act of thievery is our one chance." Cor looked at Ihva with a remorseful expression.

"Art thou amenable to this proposition?" Grax asked Ihva once it was clear Cor had finished speaking.

Ihva paused. It wasn't that she hesitated to steal from the drakes. The fate of the world lay with her and the others. Surely Oer would forgive them. However, she wondered how well they could get away with their crime in a city where all eyes followed them with fear and contempt. Yet there was no other way, as Cor had said. The memory of Linara cowering before the Shades flashed in Ihva's mind, and she straightened. They'd have to try.

"I pledge any help I can offer," she told Grax.

"Excellent," Malach said. "Perhaps we can have a bite of breakfast and be on our way?"

"Certainly," Grax replied.

He scurried toward the pile of sacks in the corner of the kitchen and pulled out some dried fish. He opened a bigger bag and brought out some seaweed, then passed out some of each to the others. He got to Kronk, who was emerging from the bedroom, and held out the dried fish, but Kronk looked at what was in his hand and screwed up her face.

"Why flying lizards only eat fish?" asked Kronk.

Ihva giggled and heard the others snort and chuckle. She felt the same way, though, as she tore off a piece of the jerky and wrapped it in seaweed, trying to disguise its flavor.

Yidda responded, "It's really all that can sustain them here. There are no crops, and it would seem there are few sources of meat other than the fish in the sea and a few rabbits."

Grax looked about to interject when Kronk interrupted him.

"But Kronk need chicken!" she whined. "Kronk need yummy herb-roast chicken!"

Yidda soothed her, "Fish will do just fine, Kronk."

Kronk shook her head, but Ihva was still laughing inside. She hadn't realized how much anxiety had been present in the room until mirth over Kronk's exclamation had broken it.

Ihva looked around at the others while they continued breakfast and felt her fears melt within her.

Their plan might be outrageous and fraught with danger, but at least they were in it together.

***

Thirty minutes later, Ihva and the others were strolling behind Grax down the main street of Wymon back toward the front gates. Ihva noticed once again, all eyes turned toward them as they passed. This time, the drakes' faces contained as much curiosity as anger and fear. Word must have gone out about Wymon's "guests." Ihva and the others reached the bottom level of the city where buildings and streets spread out, and Grax motioned for the others to stop. He waved them closer so that they ended up squished together around him.

"I must warn you again should any of you be caught stealing *anything* from *any* temple, a mob would soon be upon you all, and the protection of the Onyx Voice would be forfeit." Grax looked around at the others, his eyes hard and his whisper stern. "We shall walk into each temple, locate the fragment, and exit—nothing more. Attempt to look reverent, I beg you."

"You drakes certainly take your gem lords seriously, don't you?" Malach said, amusement in his voice.

Grax looked at the dwarf with narrowed eyes and nodded. "Thou wouldst do well to refrain from making such comments as well."

The drake glanced at Ihva and her companions, then turned toward the archway that separated the temples from the rest of the city. He drew in a breath and sped forward through the air. Ihva followed him, as did the others. Grax set a rapid pace, but Ihva caught up with him as a husky, black drake stopped them with a claw extended. Grax halted immediately.

"*Young* Grax," the black drake began. Condescension exuded from his tone and stance. "*First,* thou showest these wretched castaways into our city, and *now* thou purposest to defile our most sacred spaces by leading them here?" The drake's eyes bored into

Grax, and Ihva was surprised Grax did not cower beneath their contempt.

"Master Gunleik, sir, I mentioned our beloved dragon lords, may their hoards grow immeasurably, to these who follow me. We have come that they might devote their lives to the lords, each one to the gem dragon lord of his choosing. I mean no disrespect, Master Gunleik."

Grax's voice wobbled, and he bowed his head. It would seem to Gunleik that Grax was acknowledging the elder's superiority, but Ihva suspected Grax was actually hiding his guilty expression. Grax was a terrible liar as far as she knew. Hearing voices drawing closer, she looked around and saw a small crowd was gathering. She raised a silent prayer to Oer, awaiting Gunleik's pronouncement.

"Very well," Gunleik said. His words drew out. "They may pass, as mayest thou, Young Grax. Be warned, however, that if the tiniest gem or copper is found missing, they will pay with their lives and thou as well."

Gunleik's warning echoed in the square under the arch. Ihva was close enough to Grax to hear him gulp.

"Very well, Master Gunleik," the young drake replied. "We live at the mercy of the Onyx Voice and obey the prerogative of the people. May their voice ever lead us." Grax kept his eyes down and waited for Gunleik to pass.

The crowd slowly dispersed as the black drake exited the district through the archway. Grax looked back at Ihva and her companions, and Ihva nodded that she was ready to move forward. Grax led them down the winding main road and stopped in front of a large doorway.

"This is the temple of Graiyent the Emerald," he said simply, his words strained.

In front of them loomed a huge building that filled Ihva's view. It cast a cold, ominous shadow in the warming morning sunlight. Ihva's eyes followed the rooftop of the towering expanse from the left to the right. Then her gaze moved down where the walls met in a corner on the right side. There was a fence, presumably extending around the temple. It had to be decorative since the drakes could easily fly over it. They must have intended the pointed spokes with barbed ends for their visual value, sharp and cruel. They also defined the edges of the landscape and architecture. The exterior of the temple was a deep gray, speckled like granite. It had sharp edges and swirling embellishments, and the roof above the doorway ended in stone dragons snarling their ferocity at anyone who approached.

Ihva made ginger steps through the yawning doorway behind the others, and Kronk followed Ihva. Inside, an overwhelming amount and variety of greens assaulted Ihva's eyes. The smell was of wet earth, though most of the building was stone. The floor was deep forest green and made of moss. The walls were a smooth, sea green limestone, and in the high, vaulted ceiling were glowing stones that looked to be uncut emeralds. It seemed Ihva and her companions stood in a gigantic entryway that led to a central room, which took up most of the temple's space. Ihva saw a few open doorways in the back, which presumably led to smaller rooms.

As Ihva scanned the central space, something drew her eyes to the center. There lay the hoard. It was piled high with reflective gold and silver pieces, and it gleamed with colors of various gems. There were a couple drake worshippers in the temple—a skinny, dark purple one flitting about the hoard, carefully placing his coins on the pile and another drake, this one gray, coming forward from the back of the temple. The latter had a similar build to Grax, muscular but not large. A few other drakes were entering the temple through the doorway as well.

Ihva looked back at the hoard. It contained more than half the King's treasury she guessed, and it was just one of four temples. She marveled over it, and her eyes followed along the base of the hoard to where there stood a pedestal. On it, an ivory fragment hovered, held up by glowing green tendrils of magic. It was smaller than she'd expected it to be. She looked around, and seeing everyone distracted and wandering in different directions, she walked closer to inspect the pedestal. She made sure to keep enough distance to avoid looking suspicious.

Ten paces away, she confirmed that indeed the fragment was about the size of her two hands cupped together. Strange. She stepped closer and became mesmerized by the green rays that bent and crackled every which way. It should be easy enough to take the fragment. Whoever did it would have to lift it from above. She breathed a small sigh of relief, though she still had no idea how they would manage to do so unseen. Looking down, she spotted an inscription beneath the eggshell on the front of the stone. She read it in a whisper.

The day she flees shall be the end,
For the secrets of the ages are hers to tell.
The final judgment shall she portend;
With the prideful it shall not go well.

From those whose sins are like the evening light,
Scarlet and spanning the sky's end to its other,
From them shall she make away and take flight,
Destruction in her wake, the evil to smother.

She shall find what they have sought.
She shall steal what they had bought.
She shall destroy what they have wrought.

She shall run, their pursuit impend.
He who is righteous shall receive her end
Such that she shall neither break nor bend,
And that shall be the cost.

Ihva stood perplexed for a moment when a voice interrupted her thoughts.

"I was not aware thou readest the Ancient Tongue," Grax whispered beside her.

She lowered her gaze. Not this again.

Chapter 31

IHVA FROZE FACING THE PEDESTAL, knowing Grax was to her right with his eyes on her. What would he think if he knew who she was? Could it be the drakes saw her as the elves did, placing their hope in her? According to what she'd read, it would seem the drakes had an understanding more similar to the Oeridians. The drakes' prophecy seemed to center on destruction and suffering. Certainly they wouldn't welcome someone with that reputation.

"I hadn't seen it myself, but I can't deny she possesses the gift of Tongues." Jasper stepped up beside Ihva.

"Is that, how do you Oeridians call it, her Power?" Grax asked.

Ihva swallowed. It was her turn to speak up—the story was hers to tell. She needed to take responsibility.

"No, it's not. I haven't made the Exchange yet. I was preparing to make it in a couple months but then we left, and something else happened instead."

She paused to look at Grax. He had his eyes fixed on her, listening. She continued.

"It started with the prophecies back in our own temple to Oer. They're written in the Old Tongue runes, but I could read them. Cor found me and discovered what I was doing."

Grax looked at Ihva with sudden fascination. "Hast thou other powers?"

Ihva nodded. "Little things, sometimes. When the need is dire, things seem to just happen the right way. In Irgdol, I could open locks."

Jasper interrupted, saying, "She has learned to use a blade far more quickly than any other student I've encountered."

Ihva glanced at him and gave him a shy smile. He didn't drop his serious expression, though, so she continued to explain. "I can see things before they happen sometimes, I think. And, well, I can Heal. Cor told me that my Healing is strong."

"She has brought two of our number back from near death, one of them being myself," Jasper agreed.

Grax was silent a moment, thinking, and neither Ihva nor Jasper interrupted. Finally, the drake spoke, his tone low. "I have read many prophecies and commentaries. I cannot be certain for prophecies are complex and can refer to any number of things. Sometimes they appear to speak of one thing but pertain to something else entirely. It is not that I believe I understand it all, but there are specific foretellings concerning this day, though of course, I cannot tell you that I know that it is this day of which they speak." Grax was rambling and his voice wavering. He drew himself up and continued, saying, "I do not know this for a fact but, Lady Ihva..."

Grax laid his scaly hand on Ihva's shoulder. It was cool to the touch.

"Dear Lady Ihva, I do believe thy appearance signifieth the end for us. A new beginning, but the end." Sorrow filled the drake's voice.

"I was afraid of that," she said quietly.

The end for Wymon. Her appearance meant their end. She blinked back the moisture gathering in her eyes and went on.

"The prophecy there doesn't seem very hopeful," she said, pointing to the words on the pedestal.

Grax's eyes met hers. "The prophecies also speak of new beginnings. Many will perish. Indeed, we might all, but thou bringest a new start with thee as well. Thou mightest usher in despair, but thou art Hope herself as well. Do not fear, Lady Ihva."

She looked at him, torn. She realized she should tell him about the viewing. Maybe they could get the drakes out of the city before disaster hit if she did. Something kept her from speaking to Grax, though, and instead she turned to Jasper.

"There's something else," she said in a quiet voice.

Jasper nodded and watched her, waiting.

She swallowed again. "I saw something yesterday." How could she explain it? "Back in Eshad, Cor mentioned the Beholder's Sight or something like that." She paused, waiting to see if Jasper would show any recognition, but he didn't. "I don't know what to call them but viewings. They're like prophecies, I think. I saw something with Arusha, a dagger with blood on it. That was the first time, and I didn't know what it meant, except that something was going to go wrong. Then there was the one about Malach. He had a crown in my viewing, and I didn't know what that meant either—he hadn't told us who he was yet—but that was when Cor mentioned this Power I have, or at least I think this is a Power…"

Jasper was giving her a careful look, appearing both interested and heedful. As she trailed off, he replied softly, "What did you see yesterday?"

She looked down. "It was the city. It's going to be destroyed. Completely destroyed." She left it at that, not sure what she could add to make it better.

Jasper's eyes on her didn't waver, and after a moment, he took her hand. "I'm sorry," he murmured.

She nodded and gathered her courage, then turned to Grax. "We have to get everyone out of here. There was no sense of time to what I saw, but I can't imagine it's too far off if what you're saying about this is true." She made a small gesture with her hand to the writing on the pedestal.

The drake's posture had slumped, and he was hovering just a foot off the ground. "No measure we might take could accomplish such a thing."

"But we have to," she insisted. "Everyone will *die* if we don't." She stiffened her jaw to try to look brave, but really her knees felt like buckling and she was having a hard time breathing deeply. Her appearance signified an end for the drakes, Grax had said. Surely she could intervene, though. If she warned them…

"No one shall heed you," Grax said as though in answer to her thoughts. "Thou shalt endanger thine own passage from the city shouldst thou give evidence of thy function and of thy fulfillment of the prophecies. They shall kill thee."

Ihva froze her expression, not wanting to give away her distress. Was there truly nothing she could do about it? Everything was piecing together, the beliefs of men and of elves and of drakes, and the final product contained more suffering and devastation than she believed she could handle. She felt volatile, as though she might lose everything at any moment with herself to blame.

She remembered Jasper and looked at him. He met her gaze, his dark eyes sympathetic. She couldn't help letting a few tears slide down her cheeks. What was she supposed to do? Jasper still had her hand in his, and she realized she could lose him as well. More tears escaped her eyes until she could hardly see past them.

"It's okay, Ihva. You're strong, stronger than I've understood," Jasper said, his voice soft but sure.

He squeezed her hand lightly, but she continued to cry. Sure, she looked strong on the outside, but what about inside? How was she supposed to be encouraged with the world in pieces and her existence to blame? How was she supposed to believe it would all be okay when her very identity could destroy all she loved?

"Prophecies might indicate your path, but they do not dictate your actions. You have a choice," Jasper said.

She watched him, uncertain what he meant. What choices did she have then? Could she change anything in the end? She'd been trying so hard to be a blessing, to be the one to give hope when all looked dark, but now it seemed she *was* the darkness foretold. Jasper pulled her closer and took her in his arms. She leaned her head against his chest and let her tears fall, soaking into his shirt. She didn't care if the others saw her.

"You might be destined to watch the world fall around you, but I know you, Ihva. You will hope until the end, and that's what the world needs," he said.

"Why me?" she asked, her voice unsteady.

He withdrew a few inches and she turned her face to look him in the eye. Her vision was still blurry.

"I don't know anyone else whose love could endure the knowledge you have, who might save the world even as it breaks into pieces. You are brave, Ihva, braver than you know." He let a moment pass before he spoke again, his voice quieter now. "Your hope is infectious. We'll do this together."

Together. The word struck Ihva. She wasn't alone, she had to remind herself. As many as desired to strike her down, there were still five, at least, who were on her side. Five who supported her and more than that, who knew her—five who believed in her. Then she remembered Grax. There were six, then, but the elves trusted her as well. There *was* hope. There were many who believed in her. A few more tears fell, but she wiped them from her face and looked back at Jasper.

"I can't face it without you. You know that, don't you?" she told him.

He nodded, and she glanced at the others. They'd gathered about fifteen paces away in conversation and at intervals were looking over Ihva and Jasper, their glances brief.

"I need them, too." Ihva stopped, trying not to choke on her next words. "We're all in it together now. There's no turning back. There must be some we can save."

Jasper nodded again, and a moment passed. Finally, Grax interrupted, speaking just loud enough for her and Jasper to hear.

"Lady Ihva, Master Jasper, we must head onward. I understand now that it is vital that Lady Ihva returneth to Oerid. We must make our way to the next temple."

Jasper took his hands from around Ihva, and she gave him a needful glance before turning to face the open doorway to the street. The drakes she had seen entering the temple earlier skirted around her with annoyed looks, but she didn't care.

Without a word about what happened at the pedestal, Grax, Jasper, and Ihva rejoined the others.

"Now onto the temple of Raidurr the Ruby!" Grax announced as though he were leading a casual tour.

Ihva followed behind the drake, and Jasper fell in stride with her as they exited the Temple of Graiyent the Emerald.

Chapter 32

JASPER WALKED IN STRIDE WITH Ihva as they proceeded to the next temple. He was worried about her. She'd appeared so miserable. He'd tried to console her, and it seemed to have worked, but it had been strange to him being the one holding out hope while she despaired. What he'd told her was true—watching her graceful responses to what they'd been through threatened to turn him sanguine, something he'd never imagined he could be.

He looked over at the others. Grax's attempt to look calm didn't cover his anxieties well. He hurried along with not so much as a glance around. The rest of Jasper and Ihva's companions wore frowns and furrowed brows, and Malach and Kronk in particular kept looking in Jasper and Ihva's direction. After seeing the hushed conversation a few minutes ago and the way Ihva had cried, the rest of their companions must have been wondering what had happened. Jasper didn't care to explain right now.

Grax led them a short distance along the outside wall of Graiyent's temple toward the back of the building. They arrived at a massive fountain. In the center of the fountain was a statue of a dragon with its head tilted up toward the sun. Water spewed from its mouth and fell back down on the platform, flowing down into the pool below.

Grax led them past the fountain to another temple. It was made of the same stone as Graiyent's temple, a flecked-gray granite. Grax set a quick but comfortable pace toward the entrance. When he arrived some paces away from it, he put out a hand to signal the others to stop.

"This temple will be warmer than the Temple of Lord Graiyent. Take care to stick close to the path. I believe that is needless to say," Grax told them.

Jasper nodded his consent, though he wasn't certain what the drake was referring to. As they neared the entrance, Jasper noted a warm glow coming from within. Fire, it had to be fire. Grax stepped inside first, and Jasper and the others followed.

Within the Temple of Raidurr, Jasper found a path indeed marked by fire. It was about ten paces wide. Flames abutted it and surrounded a hoard of precious metals and gems. The room looked similar to the Emerald Temple's hoard room—a vast, open space with a pile of treasure centrally located. The path sloped downward, winding down to the hoard that sunk into the ground in the center. The temple was not busy with only a few acolytes flitting here and there. There were no visitors but Jasper and his companions. Jasper relaxed and searched for the eggshell fragment. He couldn't find it. Heat radiated from the flames as he followed Grax down the path.

"Where can it be?" Malach whispered loudly in Grax's ear ahead of him.

"Lower thy voice," Grax replied, his words sharp. "I am not aware of its location. I have only ever been in the Temple of Gulur."

Jasper and the others continued down the pathway. Finally, they reached the end where the flames opened to the hoard. In the middle of the entryway to the pile of gold, silver, and gems, there stood a pedestal, and on the pedestal lay another eggshell fragment. Grax stopped, and the others halted behind him. He pointed out the eggshell piece with a subtle wave of his claw. Jasper nodded his head slightly, and Grax turned around to head back up the path. Jasper and the others waited for the drake to pass to take the lead, then they followed.

Ihva, however, waited a moment. When Jasper realized she wasn't following, he turned back for her. She was peering at the pedestal, which Jasper glanced at as well. It had words in the Old Tongue carved into its face like the other had.

"It's the same passage," she told him, her voice somber.

He nodded. "It's okay, Ihva."

"It says the day I leave will be the end. The day I leave, Jasper. I doom Oerid if I don't go back but Wymon if I do."

"You doom more than Oerid if you don't return," he replied. She would, wouldn't she? If Cor was right, that was. Jasper hadn't realized how hard he was clinging to Cor being right.

"I can't do this. I can't be the death of anyone," she whispered.

"Doing nothing is doing something, though, Ihva. I hate it, I really do, but you're going to have to give up some to save the rest."

"I'm not a god, Jasper. I don't have the right to decide who's given up."

"Maybe you don't have the right, but you have the responsibility."

She looked at him and didn't say anything for a moment. She wasn't on the verge of tears this time. In fact, her tone sounded more embittered than upset. He knew it was a heavy choice to make. He'd had to make it with Jessica—he'd had to reconcile himself to the fact that she could be lost in the course of saving Oerid, and she *had* been lost. It didn't feel right at all, and maybe it had been a mistake, but he couldn't change it now. Ihva was on the other side of such a choice, but either way, she would face the same outcome, the loss of those she meant to protect.

"I'm sorry, Ihva. I didn't mean to sound harsh," he said after a moment.

"You didn't."

"It's not easy. I know it."

"How do you bear it?" she asked.

223

He peered at her. He didn't know how he bore it. He just did and always had, ever since he'd become aware of who he was.

"I just do, Ihva," he replied finally. "I have to, like you do. I didn't choose it. The choice was made for me, but I can't negate that choice and remain a good man. Maybe I'll do things as king that will compromise my character anyway, but I have to at least try."

She nodded but said nothing.

"We should get going," he said softly.

He looked and found the others had disappeared up the path. Hopefully they were waiting at the front of the temple.

"Okay," Ihva said.

He let her go ahead of him, glanced back at the eggshell fragment, then followed her up the path.

Jasper and the others reached the entrance to a third temple.

"The Temple of Blarr the Sapphire," Grax said as they approached.

Jasper was wary as he glanced around. The temple looked the same as Graiyent's and Raidurr's on the outside. A decorative fence of warning set it apart from the space around it, and rageful dragons made of speckled granite and dark metal sat at the corners of the roof.

Cool air wafted out the building, and the sound of falling water and gushing liquid grew louder as they neared the entrance. Inside, the sight was startling and breathtaking. Water fell from the towering ceiling to the floor through a series of intricately linked waterfalls. Indeed, to walk into the room at all, one had to descend some stairs and ended up ankle-deep in water. Walkways spread out before them from where they had entered, each one submerged to some depth in the pool. In the center of the pool rested Blarr's hoard. The mound extended down to the bottom of the pool for about one hundred feet and rose above the water a good forty more feet. Jasper had already witnessed the wealth of two temples, but the third pile still left him in awe. Malach waved his hand toward something in the far corner of the temple. Jasper followed the dwarf's eyes to another pedestal with another white eggshell fragment. Beside Jasper, Ihva started toward it, wading through the water.

"Don't," Jasper said.

Grax flew up next to her nodded. "They must all have the same inscription. I have found it in Lord Gulur's temple as well. We know where the fragment lies. That is all we need for now."

Ihva looked at both Jasper and Grax and turned back toward the entrance to the temple. Jasper couldn't tell by her face what she was thinking, but he suspected she was reviewing their conversation from Raidurr's temple. He hoped she was, at least.

Grax led them through the square once again. He stopped a few paces from the entrance to the fourth temple, then straightened.

"This is the Temple of Gulur the Amber." His voice was louder and more confident this time.

Jasper walked up to the entrance and peered inside. He found himself above the main floor and would have to go down some stairs to get to it. It was indeed a library, like Grax had described. The walls were full of books, and all up and down the center stood aisles filled with more books and scrolls. Some were newer and less tattered while others were worn with age, especially the scrolls.

"This is our temple," Grax said.

"Where is the hoard?" asked Yidda.

"Why, it is above us!" Grax looked up, and Jasper followed his gaze.

A huge, round pile of gold, silver, and gems was suspended in a tightly woven net above their heads. Beneath it, in the center of the aisleways between the shelving units, a pedestal stood with the eggshell fragment. Making sure the others had seen the pedestal, Grax turned to them and spoke loud enough for drakes nearby to hear.

"This should conclude our tour." He looked at the others closely and continued in a softer voice, "It is time we return to my home."

Everyone nodded. Grax spun around and led them out of the temple. He looked back briefly as they exited, sorrow in his face. Jasper caught the drake's eye and gave him what he hoped was a comforting look. They proceeded out of the doorway and back to Grax's dwelling.

Jasper and the others made the trek back through the city to Grax's home. Jasper tried not to act suspicious but was afraid Grax would give them away anyway. The drake was averting his gaze from the passersby and skirting out of everyone's way with obsequious jerking motions. Fortunately, they made it back without confrontation.

They filed into the small entry space and circled around in the living room. Jasper leaned back against a wall. Their purpose was far from fulfilled, and he still had no idea how they could accomplish the theft of the eggshell fragments. Maybe the others had thought of something. He looked around at their faces and found them similarly exhausted and defeated. Grax came back from peeking out the doorway. He gave one more furtive glance outside, then spoke in a quiet voice.

"Now you are aware of the fragments' locations. I have considered various means of retrieving them, but none has struck me as particularly feasible." He averted his eyes as he mentioned the word "retrieve," then scanned the group as he asked, "Hast any of you a suggestion?"

The others eyed each other with puzzled looks.

"There are so many of your kin present, it would be almost impossible to sneak in and steal away with so central an object, at least during the day," Cor said.

"Is night an option?" Malach asked, then glanced at Grax. "But if any of us are caught outside at night heading toward the temple district, I suppose that wouldn't look too good, would it?"

226

Grax shook his head.

"If any go, it must be one rather than all of us," Yidda said, looking around. "Whoever it is must be swift and stealthy, able to keep to the shadows and remain unnoticed. Grax, are there priests or caretakers in the temples at night?"

The drake thought for a moment. "I have never visited Gulur's temple by night, but I believe a few of the more devoted disciples of each lord sleep in the back rooms of the temples. They might also patrol the temples and their grounds."

"Whoever goes, then, must be able to hide in plain sight, else be fast enough the acolytes never see him," Yidda went on. She turned to look at Jasper.

"I'll go," he said. He might not be able to hide in plain sight, but his elvish cloak would do well enough if he could stick to the shadows.

All heads turned to him as soon as he spoke. It was Cor who answered.

"As unfortunate as it is that we must ask you to do this, you are the most suited to this task. Your cloak will aid greatly," the dwarf said.

Jasper nodded and glanced at Ihva. She was looking at him with worry in her eyes but covered it when he met her gaze. She set her mouth in a determined expression, and he suppressed a sigh. It couldn't be helped. He had to do it.

"Very well," Grax replied after a moment. "Thou shalt delay thy trek until midnight. Then go thou swiftly, stealthily, and silently. We will await thee here, and when thou hast returned, you will make to flee before any of my brethren can alert the rest about the missing relics. There are guards at the gates, but perhaps you can disable them? Then you shall away, you shall flee."

"*We* will flee, Grax," Jasper said.

"What dost thou mean?" the drake replied.

"I mean you're coming with us."

"But I belong here," Grax said, lowering closer to the ground.

It looked like Jasper was going to have to persuade the drake to come with them. "You're not going to survive long if you stay here," he told Grax.

The drake peered at Jasper, saying nothing, so Jasper went on.

"You said we'd forfeit the protection of the Onyx Voice should they find us making away with these fragments. I doubt your brothers will take kindly to the discovery that we are gone, and you remain."

Grax continued to look at Jasper. He opened his mouth to say something but hesitated, and nothing came out.

"Jasper is right, Grax. They will not take lightly your failure to keep us," Cor said.

The drake turned to Cor, then bowed his head. "I suppose thou speakest truly."

Jasper nodded and Cor spoke again.

"Jasper will go at midnight and retrieve the pieces, then we will make our way out of the city. It is best now we get some rest. We have a long night ahead."

The rest of the group looked at him, then at Grax. They all gave their consent, then rose and dispersed to separate corners of the house. Jasper considered following Ihva but decided against it. He needed time to think and prepare.

Chapter 33

ABOUT TWO HOURS INTO SECOND watch, Ihva lay on the floor still wide awake. The rest of the house was quiet, too quiet for her comfort. The silence allowed her thoughts to run amok, and she imagined a great number of catastrophes while Jasper made his way down the streets of Wymon to the dragon lords' temples. She shifted onto her side. There was no getting comfortable.

An hour or so ago, Jasper had slipped out of the house into the darkness outside. The shadows of the buildings had quickly hidden him from view. As he'd disappeared, Ihva and the others had made to await his return. Ihva must have looked distraught for Cor had placed a hand on her shoulder and assured her they would all soon be safely outside the city. Then he'd suggested trying to get some rest.

She couldn't rest, though. It was different when she threw herself into danger. At least then she had the illusion of control. With Jasper out there committing what she was sure the drakes would consider a capital offense, she felt at a complete loss for reassurance. She had no power over his fate while he was gone. She shivered, then turned her attention outward, listening for any sign of his return. For a few minutes, she listened in vain. The night was noiseless except for the whistle of a slight breeze past the front window. She was exhausted, and the frenzied energy from sending Jasper out began to wear off. She was drifting off when the sound of rapid footsteps came through the doorway.

Her eyes shot open, and she stood, then rushed out of the bedroom to Grax's front door and arrived alongside the others. Jasper was inside beside the doorway. He was trying to catch his breath as he leaned against the wall, and his eyes were darting back and forth from the entryway to the group.

"What's wrong?" Malach asked hurriedly.

Jasper's eyes shifted back to the others. "One of them saw me. In Raidurr's temple. Fire left no shadows. He's coming I think." He was still breathing heavily and paused to inhale.

"Dost thou have the fragments?" Grax asked, his tone low and words rushed.

Jasper pointed to the bag at his side.

"All of them?" Cor sounded somewhat incredulous.

Jasper nodded and looked back to the doorway. Ihva didn't hear any pursuers yet, but she knew that was no indication they weren't coming.

"We must flee the city," Grax said in a grave and urgent whisper.

He looked at Jasper and made for the doorway. The others grabbed the packs they'd prepared earlier and followed Grax as he propelled himself down the winding path toward the city gates.

Ihva tried to run on tiptoe down the incline. The situation would become more complicated and dangerous if other drakes woke up and joined the pursuit. She was grateful not to hear anyone behind them. They were running for about five minutes when angry shouts sounded from ahead, though. Grax slowed his pace, and the others followed in kind. The voices grew closer, and Ihva could distinguish three or four of them. Grax moved to the more shadowed side of the road, putting distance between himself and the group. He crept slowly around the bend.

Fire illuminated the pathway as it poured around the turn. Grax jumped back as flames came within inches of him. The shouting intensified.

"It is him!" cried a drake whose voice sounded young and feminine.

"They must be nearby! Search them out!" It was the harsh, cracking voice of what must have been an older drake.

Ihva and the others quickly hid themselves in the shadows, but she knew it would be useless. She turned to see Cor beside her. He reached for a weapon but grasped at air, and his eyes grew wide. She drew her sword and hoped Jasper had brought his daggers. They two and Malach were the only ones armed.

A dark-colored drake came into view. Ihva rushed toward it with her blade brandished as it saw her and the others. She was about fifteen paces away when Grax threw himself between her and it. A split second later, it opened its mouth and spewed forth some sort of liquid. The substance struck Grax and forced him back toward Ihva. The places it hit him began to hiss. He cried out but remained between the other drake and the group. Meanwhile, a lighter drake came around the bend.

"Traitor of traitors art thou!"

It was the older drake with the cracking voice. He stared directly at Grax and breathed fire.

"No!" Ihva screamed.

Even as she called out, a globe of white light appeared around Grax. The flames reflected off of it and curled around behind him. Ihva was glad to see the others had moved away as she felt heat against her eyes. What had just happened? She blinked, trying to readjust her vision. Her eyes felt like sandpaper.

A third drake came into her line of sight. It was large and burly. It took one look at Ihva and the others and opened its mouth wide. What would it be this time? Steam erupted out toward them. Ihva held out her hand and turned her face away, desperate to not be hit. The steam dispersed around another shield, this one around all of them. As Ihva was turned back toward the others, Malach caught her eye. His eyes were big and his mouth agape. She had no time to think, though, as she saw three more drakes coming down the path toward her and the others.

"Quickly! We must reach the gates!" Grax cried out. Then he gave a shout of pain.

Ihva turned to see him beset by two of the three original drakes. They were tearing at him with their claws, and he already had a few wounds with dark liquid oozing out. He reached out, and crackling rays of energy leapt from him to the two assailants. They were forced back.

Ihva turned. The three drakes coming down the path were twenty paces away when they stopped and opened their mouths. She put out her hand and this time was conscious of willing another wall of light to appear between the drakes and her companions. Flames diverted around the shield.

Behind Ihva, Grax cried out again. Three drakes were now attacking him. Ihva held out her hand to maintain the light shield around her companions and tried to come up with a way to help Grax. A wall of light would do nothing with his attackers in such close range. One of the drakes swiped his claws across Grax's chest, and Grax fell to the ground. A split second later, the three assailants were on him like vultures.

"No!" Ihva screamed again.

This time, she was as enraged as she was afraid. A pillar of light came streaming down from the sky. It struck the three drakes on Grax, and they flew backward and landed on the ground. Ihva readied herself for them to rise, but they remained motionless. She looked back at Grax. He was on the ground in the middle of a crater, but he lifted his head and waved her toward the others. He was safe for the time being.

She turned to look back up the path. A small mob had formed. At least ten drakes were making their way forward. Malach and Kronk stood in front of Jasper, Cor, and Yidda, and Malach swiped at drakes with his elvish knife, but Ihva knew the two in front couldn't withstand the claws of so many drakes. She hesitated a moment. She feared that the three drakes behind her were dead. If she tried what happened with Grax again, she might kill even more of them.

Kronk threw her fist at the closest creature, a heavy-looking drake. She connected with its side, and it flew to the left, crashing into the one next to it. This incited the group of drakes further. A new one dragged its claws across Kronk's chest, and the orc-blood woman screeched. Ihva's fury came boiling back over. She dropped the shield of light and called down beams of radiance with both hands. Two pillars came rushing down and four drakes flew backward and lay still on the ground. The other drakes seemed to panic, and their attacks became frenzied. They shouted for help, and as though on cue, five or six more rushed to join them. Seeing the walls of light were gone, a few of the drakes made to breathe destruction from their mouths. Ihva threw up a shield just in time.

The drakes began to push forward again, swinging their claws at her companions. She kept the shield up with one hand pressed out in front of her and drew her other hand down to call down another pillar. The pillar struck three more drakes and threw them back. As powerful as she felt, she didn't know if she'd be able to withstand the entire city's population. It would certainly come to that though with the drakes' roaring voices and explosions from the light pillars. She kept up the shield and tried to get her companions' attention.

Jasper was looking at her, and she motioned for him to follow her toward the gates. He said something to the others, and carefully walking backward, with Ihva maintaining the shield between them and the drakes, they made their way toward the city entrance.

Ihva managed to turn around as she looked for Grax. He was still lying on the ground, his breathing heavy. Four or five drakes were closing in on him, and hysterics nearly overtook her. She couldn't hold the shield, protect Grax, and get everyone to the front gates all at the same time, but she needed to if they were going to escape with their lives.

One of the drakes reached Grax and breathed fire from feet away. Grax was shuddering as the flames dispersed. Panicked, Ihva let go of the shield and began to call down light again. The drakes still heading for Grax were blown ten paces back, and another explosion sounded behind her. More drakes appeared, taking the place of the ones that fell. Ihva spun around, hardly seeing the scene before her. She called down bright beams in every direction. Radiance fell from the sky, and the ground erupted. Drakes flew in every direction. The pillars of light blasted buildings to pieces, and soon destruction was raining down on the whole city. Ihva saw as she started to demolish everything, but she couldn't stop herself. Something inside her compelled her to sustain the offensive. Flashes of light and booming blasts filled her consciousness for what seemed like hours.

Then, she felt the zeal within her fade. The sound around her diminished as she drew one more pillar down and hit the pinnacle of the city, the building where they'd met the Onyx Voice. Fragments of the walls flew apart as the final blast reverberated, then there was silence. Exhaustion overwhelmed Ihva. She sank to the ground as the dust began to settle.

Chapter 34

DESTRUCTION IN HER WAKE.

The words from the drake prophecy ran through Ihva's mind in ceaseless torment. What had she done?

The city before her lay in ruins. Not one wall stood intact, and bodies of drakes littered the ground, all motionless. She heard the scraping of boots on the ground behind her. The others! She turned around to see how they'd fared.

Kronk was standing and looking down at her chest, which was bleeding. Her dress was ruined with claw marks running across it. Ihva wasn't sure she had the energy to Heal Kronk at that moment. Beside Kronk, Cor was getting to his feet, as was Malach. It seemed the blasts had knocked the others to the ground, but Ihva saw no injuries on them, only Kronk's wound from the drake's claws. Yidda was checking on the others.

Jasper sat on the ground, staring at Ihva. She met his gaze. His eyes were wide, and she looked down. He was afraid of her now. Why shouldn't he be? She'd razed an entire city while standing in place. Who knew what else she was capable of? She couldn't bring herself to look at him again.

A groan came from her left. Grax! She turned and rushed to his side. He lay on the ground, and she could hear his labored breaths from paces away. She knelt beside him.

"Grax," she said.

He turned his head to look at her. "Lady Ihva," he murmured, his voice feeble.

His scales were scorched, and he was bleeding. Ihva put her hands to the wounds on his chest. Acid from the drake's attack earlier burned her skin, but she didn't withdraw. Instead, she closed her eyes and prayed. No energy went out from her. She pleaded with Oer, but nothing happened.

"I suppose this is farewell," Grax murmured.

"No, Grax!" she said forcefully. "You have to live. You have to!"

She willed her Healing to reach him to no avail. He gave a weak cough, and tears welled in her eyes. Her vision blurred, and she hardly noticed as Cor came to stand beside her.

"Even if you could, Ihva, the poison has already seeped into his veins," Cor said softly. "It is too late."

The last sentence pounded her to the ground.

"No," she said faintly.

"I am well, Lady Ihva." Grax's voice was soft. "I hope thou shalt remember me as one who fought valiantly by thy side. If thou mightest do that, it will be enough. I shall not have lived in vain."

Ihva could hardly see Grax's face through her tears. She reached out to grasp his hand and remembered more of the words she had found on the temple pedestals. She repeated them under her breath:

She shall flee, their pursuit impend.
He who is righteous shall receive her end
Such that she shall neither break nor bend,
And that shall be the cost.

As she spoke the words, it dawned on her—Grax died for *her.* She should have been the one the drakes killed, but instead, he lay there on the ground, life seeping out of him.

"It shouldn't have been you. It's not fair." Sobs threatened to choke her words, but she went on. "You saved us, Grax. I owe you my life. We all do."

She wiped the tears from her eyes, and her view cleared for a moment, long enough for her to see Grax smiling up at her.

"Thou art the most noble woman I know, Lady Ihva."

His face tightened, then he squeezed her hand and shuddered. Her tears multiplied. His eyes glazed, and he was still. She couldn't hold back her weeping any longer and staggered to her feet while her body shook with sobs. She'd slaughtered an entire city, and she couldn't even save its most worthy member. Cor was about to place his hand on her shoulder, but she drew back. She didn't deserve his comfort. She didn't deserve anyone's comfort.

She turned east to face the horizon where the sun would rise. Stars still filled the sky, but darkness seemed to overwhelm their light. It was the middle of the night, and morning seemed impossibly far away. She turned and stumbled down the pathway toward where the gates had stood.

"Ihva." Yidda's sympathetic voice came from behind.

Ihva didn't even turn her head to look back. She couldn't face the others, not after they'd seen what had happened. She fled down the city lane.

She didn't see anything on her way through the city. Even as her sobs became tearless, accusing thoughts assaulted her mind such that she wasn't paying attention to anything but surviving their battering. She didn't deserve to survive, though. A whole city, dead.

After ten minutes of making her way through the rubble, her crying had subsided, and she reached the city gates. She moved around to the front of what still stood of the wall and leaned back against it, out of view of the others. She slid her back down the wall until she was seated, knees bent in front of her, arms grasping them to her chest. Although her eyes looked out into the distance, she saw nothing.

She lost track of time as she sat. Thoughts so overwhelmed her that she couldn't distinguish between them, and she descended into a state of pure emotion. Grief, anger, fear, and disgrace flowed over each other like unceasing waves inside her. When one subsided, another would rush in to take its place, leaving her no room to understand, no room to breathe anything more than short, shallow breaths. She couldn't tell if minutes or hours had passed when she was finally interrupted.

"Ihva. Ihva!"

A male voice broke into her consciousness. She turned to look to her left and slowly distinguished Jasper's angular features. Startled and afraid, she jumped to her feet. What could he possibly want from her?

"What?" she replied curtly.

As quickly as she'd thrown up shields earlier, she erected walls inside. He looked at her. His fearful expression had gone, and he stood with his eyes transfixed on her. Nothing about his stance suggested he was there to reprimand her, but she felt sudden remorse threaten to crush her, nonetheless. She couldn't breathe.

"I'm sorry," she whispered. Tears began to blur her vision again. She didn't dare look back at the city as she was certain it would break her.

Jasper continued to look at her. "No," was all he said at first.

"No, I'm sorry!" she insisted. Wymon and its citizens were gone, and she was to blame. They were dead, all dead, and she was their murderer.

Jasper's voice was subdued as he replied. "You couldn't have stopped it."

His words startled her. What did he mean? She let him go on.

"You know as well as I do that this was foretold," he said. "They were fated to die the day we set foot in this city, on this island even."

"But—"

"You saved us, Ihva."

His words perplexed her, even angered her. Saved them at what cost? An entire city's citizens massacred in the night to save six individuals. Was it worth it? Besides, Jasper had told her she had some power over her destiny. He was contradicting himself, and it confused and upset her. She replied with bitterness in her voice that she didn't intend to come out, even if she felt it.

"Didn't you say I have a choice? That I could decide?" she asserted.

"You can't overturn Foretellings, Ihva. No one can do that, perhaps not even the gods." He spoke the last words with resentment in his tone.

"What choice do I have then? If I cannot save a city or even a single drake, what will come of the rest of the world?"

His next words were forceful. "You can't save any more than are meant to survive, but you can bear up under your fate with nobility like you have all this time. You can choose dignity even when the world tries to blame you. That is the choice you have."

"You said I could change it, though! I could choose whether to heal or kill. You said that!"

"I didn't say that. And even if I did, maybe I was wrong. Maybe I'm learning even as you are."

Ihva hated that her face twisted into a scowl. It wasn't fair. It wasn't his fault that he hadn't understood. She hadn't either. Besides, maybe he was right. She couldn't reverse what the prophecies foretold, but she could live her dreaded role with noble faith. She could bear up under it with grace and carry her head high. She could always determine where she'd set her own heart, if she had no other choice, and she could place her belief firmly in the camp of Truth and Light and Good, even if she ended up destroying everything. She was called Oer's Blessing, after all, not the Lady's. Her gaze on Jasper softened. She worried people would misunderstand. She worried people might resent her, no, she *knew* they would.

"People aren't going to believe me, you know. They'll think I'm here for the sake of Chaos and Darkness on behalf of the Shadow. How can I convince them I'm pursuing the Light when all they can see is destruction?"

"You don't need to. You're not here to convince people you're doing the work of the Light. At least, from what Cor says, you have some other job, a different role, than that of a leader. Yes, it'd be nice to have people love and trust you, but maybe that's not for you, Ihva." He paused, then taking her hand, he added, "I'm sorry."

"When did you start believing Cor?" she asked quietly.

Jasper paused before answering her, and she refused to fill the silence.

"I don't know," he replied finally.

His answer was much too ambiguous for her. All of a sudden, she *needed* to know what had persuaded him there was truth to Cor's words.

"No. Tell me what convinced you," she insisted. She needed to know so she could believe it, too. As it was, her hope was wavering. She knew she hadn't intended to slaughter anyone, but intentions didn't seem to matter. She'd done it all the same.

"It wasn't just one thing, Ihva," he began. His gaze on her was intent, his eyes unwavering. "Maybe it was when you Healed, or maybe it was when I fell in love with you, or maybe it was you Reading the prophecy in the temple yesterday. I don't know. You have no Power yet you have magic more varied and powerful than anyone I know. You're Oer's Blessing, Ihva, but you're no havoc-wreaker. You're the farthest thing from purposing pain and destruction. You're hardly ever even disobliging unless there's good reason to be. Gant might not believe you desire good. Oerid might interpret in you purposes to traumatize and cause anguish, but I don't. You're Oer's Blessing, but you intend no harm, and only Cor's interpretation of things even allows for that. You're no power-hungry, bitter, hateful force of destruction. You love and hope and care. If you want someone to believe you, I do. I really, really do."

She stared at him in surprise.

"If that counts for anything," he said, then looked away.

"That counts for a lot," she replied.

He looked back at her, and they gazed at each other for a while in silence. Something settled on his face, in his eyes, that Ihva didn't understand. It was a mixture of intensity and tenderness, and it both frightened and thrilled her.

"I told you we're in this together. I'm here, Ihva," he said.

He raised his hand to brush aside a lock of hair that had fallen in her face. He was standing rather close. He reached out his other hand and settled in the small of her back, and she stepped closer as he drew her near. He believed her. He didn't think her a blind terror bent on destroying the world. He didn't believe that at all. She was looking up at him in wonder when he leaned down to kiss her.

She hadn't realized that was exactly what she'd needed from him until suddenly his lips were gently caressing hers. Some tension or perhaps uncertainty fled in that moment as she closed her eyes. Her heart calmed from its anxious state, and she kissed him back. He wasn't afraid, then. Not of her, at least. She relished the thought.

He drew back after a moment and whispered, "You are nothing short of a miracle, Ihva. I couldn't have dreamed of anything as marvelous as you happening to me."

Ihva blinked her eyes open, feeling his breath against her lips. He was still there, inches from her.

"Me neither," she replied breathily.

All the troubles that had been burdening her seemed to grow wings. He kissed her again, sweetly, innocently. His tender movements—the way his hand moved around to cup the back of her head, the way he pressed her gently nearer—she felt as though she could stay in this moment forever, but finally he broke away. She opened her eyes. He was looking at her, his own eyes earnest.

"We should get back, or they'll start to wonder."

She nodded. He let go of her and gave her space to walk beside him back into the city. As they made their way back toward the others, she couldn't suppress the hope bubbling up inside her even through the pain. Jasper believed her. He'd stand by her even as the world was crumbling around them.

Chapter 35

JASPER ARRIVED BACK WITH IHVA where the others were sitting among the debris. The others were talking in lowered voices. Yidda looked over at and indicated Jasper and Ihva to the others. Cor, Malach, and Kronk turned. They were about twenty paces away from the others when Kronk yelled to them.

"Ihva okay?"

The others hushed Kronk.

"Ihva okay?" she asked again in a whisper that still carried through the otherwise silent night air.

Ihva nodded. Jasper knew the redness of her eyes and the tear stains down her cheeks would imply otherwise, but she seemed in better spirits now. The worst of the storm was over.

Yidda came to meet them. She reached Ihva and stopped, taking Ihva's hand in her own. "Are you sure, dear?" she asked.

Ihva nodded again. Yidda gave her an intent look.

"I'm alright. Really. I mean, as alright as I can be," Ihva said finally.

Yidda's expression was kind. "You are god-touched. You saved our lives."

Ihva looked down. "But at what cost?"

"The world is a dark place, Ihva," Yidda said, sounding pained.

"Perhaps there are some who cannot be saved," Cor said. He was walking toward them. "Oer himself will not bend the wills of his creatures. He honors each one's decisions, be them for good or for evil, and there comes a time of judgment."

Ihva looked up at Cor, and he continued.

"Since shortly after I met you, Ihva, I have wondered whether your hope and purity of heart might be an indictment against Creation. So many have chosen bitterness. So many have fallen to the Shadow. Yet they all have had a choice, and each one might have chosen the Light instead. There are some who have made their choice for evil, and Oer's mercy reveals itself in their eradication."

Jasper turned Cor's words over in his mind. Ihva as a judgment in her innocence. He could believe it. He himself felt a conviction around her, a conviction to be better, to think more hopeful thoughts and act with greater courage. If Oer were to judge the world by one person, Ihva would be an excellent standard.

There was silence for a few moments, then Malach came over with Kronk and said, "I'm not sure what the plan is, but I know we'll need a fire if we plan to sleep anymore tonight. I, for one, am rather cold." He looked around. "If we dig enough, we should find food too. Maybe we can even find some packs."

"Indeed, we should start looking," Cor said with sudden pragmatism, and his eyes turned to search the area as well.

"Look for food, wood, bags, water. Anything that could be useful," Yidda called.

She'd already broken from the group and was making her way toward a larger pile of rubble. The others spread out as well. Jasper wanted to follow Ihva as the group dispersed, but he'd seen Cor looking at him and knew he needed to talk to the dwarf. Cor probably already had some idea what was going on between him and Ihva. Besides, if Jasper didn't talk about it, he wondered whether the intensity of his feelings would not overpower his ability to conceal them.

If he was honest, he had no problem with letting everyone know. He loved her, and he'd tell anyone who'd listen if it were up to him. He wasn't sure how long he could contain it, anyway. She was more reserved, though, at least when it came to disclosing what was going on between them. He'd sensed that in her ever since their conversation on the ship, and he was determined not to upset her, even if it meant keeping everything secret. He could trust Cor, though.

He jogged to catch up to the dwarf. At the same time, as he turned his head to gaze after Ihva, he caught Malach's eye, and Malach gave him a knowing grin. Jasper shook his head, remembering their conversation a few nights ago. After a few seconds, he made it to Cor and fell in stride with the dwarf. All of a sudden, he wasn't sure what to say. He hadn't thought that far. The two walked in silence for a moment.

"You have something to tell me, son? It will remain between us." Cor's tone was reassuring.

"Um, yes. I do," Jasper started.

Where should he start? What would Cor think if he knew how it had all come about and how long Jasper had been carrying this? Jasper hesitated. Maybe he shouldn't tell Cor anything. Ihva might prefer it that way. Yet the thought of her brought it all surging up within him again. She loved him! The layers of impossibility had fallen away, one by one, and now she loved him. When he started speaking again, it was like a dam had broken open. His words poured out with force.

"Cor, I love her. I really love her. I never knew what that's like. It's different than anything I'd imagined. It's, it's, I don't know… Glorious?" As he stopped, awkwardness immediately overcame him. What was he talking about? He felt his face flush and peeked at Cor out of the corner of his eye. The dwarf was looking straight ahead and had a small smile. Jasper appreciated the privacy Cor afforded him by not glancing in his direction and wondered if he should say something else. Cor remained silent, waiting and looking pleased.

Quietly, Jasper asked, "You knew?"

"Yes, I knew." At this point Cor turned, and his eyes met Jasper's. In a serious tone, the dwarf continued. "Love *is* a beautiful and glorious thing. Do not be ashamed."

"Did you know she feels the same?"

"I suspected. I could not determine the strength of her feelings, but I knew their direction."

Jasper felt a grin on his face but tried to hide it. He hadn't realized how *happy* he was until this moment. He was acting like a fool, a lovestruck fool. He tried to tone it down and sober himself.

"I know it's complicated, Cor. After that display and all, especially." He waved a hand at the rubble all around them. "I should be afraid, I know. I just can't be, Cor. She doesn't intend harm at all. In fact, I'm not sure that she's capable of intending it, and if she does end up destroying the world, well, I guess I'm just committed to watching it alongside her. I can't leave her to face something like that alone."

Cor stopped and turned to Jasper. "I hope you fear, son. These are dark times, and dark things are to come. Yet I believe Ihva is not the one to fear."

Cor always had been wise.

"What ought I fear, then?" Jasper asked.

"The Shadow and its persuasive power. Evil and its conniving ways. The Lady and your attachment to her."

The last sentence struck Jasper silent. He'd nearly forgotten his own predicament in the midst of it all. The Lady of Shadows still possessed his heart, and he needed to get it back. Ihva was the one who could do that, but he'd promised not to use her. He wouldn't. Yet he realized he could never offer himself to her unless he retrieved that piece of himself. Maybe she'd *have* to go after his heart. How could he send her, though, knowing the danger the journey posed?

"Cor, what if I can't protect her?" His voice was hardly even a whisper. At first, he thought Cor might not have heard him, but then the dwarf answered him.

"Only Oer can truly protect any of us. We have illusions of control, but true power belongs to him." Cor paused. "You cannot protect her, Jasper. She knows what burden you carry. She is a wise young woman. She knows choosing you subjects her to the same burden. Do not make the choice for her. If she decides to have you, do not spurn her for the sake of what you think is nobility."

Jasper stopped in his tracks. Indeed, Cor was wise. Jasper was afraid, but he understood the dwarf's words, and he played with the idea of permitting himself to love Ihva, to have her, to be loved by her. Perhaps she *could* return his heart to him. Maybe they'd find a way to do it all. The idea overwhelmed him. He wasn't accustomed to such grand hope.

He was relieved when Cor changed the subject, pointing at something in the rubble. Jasper quickly walked to the place the dwarf had indicated and pulled out a basket of dried fish. The two continued to converse, but Cor didn't speak of Ihva again, so neither did Jasper. Instead, the conversation turned to the situation at home, and the two discussed everything from the king's health to the rising price of cloth before they'd left to the potential for civil war in the kingdom. The subject matter left Jasper discouraged, but beneath his dejection, he felt intoxicated by hope.

Jasper and Cor arrived back at the place where the others had gathered. They were the last ones to return. They'd found a few baskets of dried fish, some wood, and three bags woven of seaweed. Jasper dropped his findings on a pile that had already formed. It was still a few hours until sunrise.

Then he looked around. The others looked exhausted. Malach had collapsed on the ground, and Kronk sat on a piece of stone nearby. Yidda looked out into the distance. Jasper sensed that everyone was too tired for conversation, so he gathered some wood, knelt, and started building a fire. The night air was colder on the top of the bluff where cool breeze rushed past, and he was grateful for the coming warmth.

"Do you still have the fragments, Jasper?" Yidda asked, breaking the silence.

Jasper looked up at her. "Yes. They're right here," he replied.

He set the piece of wood in his hand in the pile for the fire and pulled the pieces of eggshell out of the pack at his side. The exterior of the fragments was a pearly white, and it shone even in the moonlight.

"You have all of them." Cor spoke his words as an affirmation.

"What are we supposed to do with them, again?" Malach asked.

It was Ihva who answered. "He told us if we put them back together to form the whole egg, the dragon lords' location would be revealed."

She was referring to Grax. Jasper pushed away the thought of the drake. He couldn't let Grax's death distract him right now.

Yidda nodded. "It can wait, though. We'll need rest if we are to pursue the gem dragons."

"Can we bury him?" Ihva asked in a small voice. Jasper noticed she still wouldn't say Grax's name.

"Perhaps it would be better to use a pyre," Malach replied in a subdued tone unusual for him. "Since we don't have shovels," he added.

Jasper looked at Cor. They did need to do *something*. Jasper had been resolved the drake would accompany them in their flight, and he was no less resolved that they respect Grax in his death. Without waiting for Cor's approval, Jasper spoke.

"In the morning. We'll build a pyre in the morning." He glanced at Ihva. Her eyes were filled with moisture, but she wasn't letting her tears fall.

"We need rest before we can do anything," Cor said.

The others nodded, and Jasper went back to building the fire. He'd found some flint lying on top of the pile of wood, so he used it. The wood ignited, and flames soon warmed the surrounding area.

They each laid down on the cold ground near the fire. Jasper chose a spot between Cor and Malach, facing Cor of course, and pulled his blanket around him. He fell asleep quickly with hardly a thought crossing his mind before he faded from consciousness.

A few hours after falling asleep, with the sun still low on the horizon, Jasper awoke. The flames beside him were burning low, so he quietly added some wood to the fire. He looked around to see if any of the others were awake.

Malach was still fast asleep, as was Kronk. They were snoring in unison. Yidda shifted her body with her eyes shut tight. Cor didn't seem about to be close to waking, nor did Ihva, so Jasper slipped away from their makeshift camp to about fifteen paces away to watch the sun rise. He found a large chunk of what must have been a wall and sat down on it, then watched the horizon and mused about last night's events.

It was hard to believe that a handful of hours previous, the city had been standing intact and he'd been moving furtively among the temples. He'd been doing fine until the fire temple. That Lord Raidurr had such an affinity for fire had been the problem. Flames on their own didn't cast shadows, so there was little Jasper could have done but what he did—slip quickly down the path to the relic, take it, and flee back up the path hoping the drakes on watch did not see him. They hadn't until the last second, and it wasn't even him they'd seen but the missing fragment. Jasper had heard one of them cry out about it and then an argument, but he'd fled before he could hear the conclusion. He'd heard another shout as he slipped around the corner of the temple, but he hadn't stopped to find out what it was about.

Maybe it was his fault Wymon had fallen. If he'd gone unseen, he and the others might have made it out of the city unnoticed, too, then they wouldn't have had a standoff with the drakes in the streets. Had Jasper had something to do with the fulfillment of the drake prophecy? He scoffed at the thought. He had nothing to do with prophecies save the one concerning himself and then as one being acted upon. He had no power to determine anything about such things. Like he'd told Ihva about her own role, the choice he had now was how he would bear up with dignity under his place in Gant's history and current situation. While he could fight for Oerid with everything he was, he couldn't change his predicament except by one path. He'd have to send Ihva, but he decided he wouldn't leave her to fend for herself. He would accompany her. Besides that, she might be able to protect herself anyway. If she could destroy a whole city, certainly she stood at least a chance against the Goddess of Hell. Maybe.

He looked around at the ruins of the city. It was complete devastation, yet the sun rose as if nothing had happened. If you could depend on nothing else, you could depend on the sun to rise—callous, unfeeling, disinterested in the events of Gant beneath. Jasper grimaced at the thought but smoothed his expression when he heard someone moving behind him. He turned to look who it was.

Chapter 36

IHVA WOKE AND FOUND THE flames burning with new wood. Someone must have added to the fire. She looked around to see who was awake and found Jasper missing. As she glanced out among the rubble, though, she found him. He was sitting on a large piece of stone and looking out toward the horizon. He appeared relaxed. She walked toward him, and he must have noticed she was awake, as he turned to look at her. She grew shy as her eyes caught his, but then he motioned her over and she went. She sat down beside him with about a couple handspans between them as they faced the eastern horizon.

"Nothing more dependable than the rising of the sun, you know?" he said, wearing a wry half-smile.

Ihva looked toward the bright orb in the distance. What was he getting at?

"I suppose so," was all she replied.

"A city leveled in the night, and the sun still rises in the morning. Makes you wonder what would happen if the whole world were destroyed. Would the sun even notice?"

He was talking about Oer. The god of Light and all that was good, Oer was said to raise the sun every morning and receive it to rest every night. Jasper was resentful. That much was clear.

"You don't care much for religion, do you?" she asked.

Jasper's mouth twisted slightly, though with pain or scorn, she couldn't tell.

"You see how well it's served me. They loathe me," he said.

"Who does?"

"Oer. The gods. Hell's Mistress. They all do. They're fighting to control me, and I'm the one who loses. I do, and Oerid will, too."

Ihva sensed his bitterness. She couldn't blame him. Sadness came over her, and her voice was quiet as she replied.

"I understand what it is to feel cursed." She paused. She *did* know. She'd leveled a city last night. She had to shield her mind from the memory of it as she went on. "Yet I know somewhere inside Oer has not designed all this for our affliction. I know that."

Jasper frowned.

"Or at least I hope so," she added, trying to bolster her faith within herself. There *was* hope. There had to be. Silence reigned for a few long seconds before Jasper replied.

"You have more confidence in him than I do."

Ihva peered at him. To be threatened by the Lady of Shadows his entire life, he must have felt like giving up many times. Somehow he was still fighting, though.

"Why do you persist? Wouldn't it be easier to abdicate and appoint someone else as heir? No one could really blame you," she asked.

Jasper turned his face to her. "What else can I do? I was born Oerid's prince. To give in and give up the responsibility I've received, what kind of coward would that make me?"

His answer struck her silent.

"Being at the mercy of the Lady consigns me to a life of fear, but I don't have to let that fear rule me," he explained.

"I guess that makes sense." Her words trailed off.

"How else would you propose I handle it all? How do you do it?"

"I don't know, really."

She stopped to think. His words reminded her of Linara, unaccompanied in facing an impossible task, only Linara had trusted Rawa for help. Jasper was trying to face it all with himself alone to count on. Ihva took his hand in her own.

"It seems so lonely to bear the burden by yourself," she said. "Surely Oer wouldn't place duty on his children without also giving the means to accomplish it. He intends to help us. If he doesn't, what hope do we have? We're up against the goddess of Darkness and Hell."

Jasper looked into her eyes for a moment, his face pensive. Then he squeezed her hand and withdrew from her grasp. She watched as he turned back to face the sun and could tell he wanted to be alone, so she got up and went back to tend the fire.

By that time, Cor had arisen and was sitting. He looked up at Ihva as she walked over. His gaze bore a look of comprehension. He didn't say anything, but it was clear he'd seen what had passed between her and Jasper. Ihva finished adding some more wood to the flames, though they didn't need it, and sat down next to the dwarf. She hesitated a moment before deciding to confide in him.

"I understand a little more about him now," she began.

Cor didn't turn his head as he spoke. "He is a tragic figure in many ways. None of it was his fault, but he bears the repercussions of the sin that saved him."

"He despises Oer. You know that, right?"

"I do, Ihva. He has stretched my patience and my faith. I see that Oer's purposes are larger than a single life and a single moment, but he cannot see beyond what is right now."

"I'm not sure I can either," she said quietly. Compassion for Jasper threatened to overcome her convictions. "It's not fair," she added.

Cor's tone became grave. "The opposite of faith is not doubt. It is capitulation. It is surrendering to that doubt."

Ihva looked at the dwarf with resolve. "I won't give up, if that's what you mean."

"Neither will he." Cor paused. "He is not as far from hope as you think. He is wrestling right now, but he is stronger than he knows. Not fearless, but strong. He will find his way."

Ihva didn't say anything as she pondered Cor's words. She wished she could say or do something to make it easier for Jasper, but she realized she couldn't. As she lifted a silent prayer for his relief, for his pain to subside and hope to find him, she knew that was the only help she could offer.

"He is not the only one struggling, though," Cor said.

She looked over at the dwarf and found his eyes on her. "What do you mean?" she asked, though she realized he was referring to her.

"You contend with your function in this world and grapple with the mantle placed upon you," he replied. "Such guilt is a heavy burden to bear, Ihva. You must find a way to lay it down if you are to continue."

She stared at Cor even as tears began to blur her vision. The guilt was hers, though. How was she supposed to surrender it when she was the only one who could carry it?

"I saw it before it happened," she said in a quiet voice. "I knew it was coming, and I wanted to warn them. It was the only way to keep them safe, getting them to flee the city. I didn't warn them, though, and it happened."

Cor was watching her but let her go on speaking.

"And I'm the one who did it," she managed, her words choked at the end. She tried to blink away the moisture in her eyes, but it just collected there until she could no longer see Cor's face.

"I do not understand it all either, Ihva," he replied in a soothing voice. "I only know there will come a time of reckoning for us all. This was one such time, the judgment of the city of Wymon. That you were the instrument of that judgment, I do not envy, but neither do I or any of your companions hold this against you. Rather, we are grateful. You saved us, and you saved yourself. Gant is in your debt for that."

She stared at him, tears escaping down her cheeks. She wanted to believe him. She wanted him to be right.

"But what if this is a judgment for all of Gant, Cor?" she asked through halting breaths. She wasn't going to let herself break down. She wasn't going to weep, she promised herself. She gathered herself and forced her words to come out steady. "What if this happens to the whole world because of me?"

"I wish I could assure you it will not. Alas, I cannot be certain," the dwarf replied, and she stiffened. So this *was* going to happen to the whole world? Was that what Cor was saying?

"I can't do it!" she burst out. Tightening her fists, she declared, "I won't do it."

Cor placed a hand on her knee but said nothing. His calmness irked her, and angry words came spilling out of her mouth.

"I never asked for this! I never wanted it. Why does it fall to me to destroy the world? What did I do to deserve this? It's not fair. I never wanted to murder them, to wipe out an entire city. I never wanted to annihilate them, but I did. I don't even know why I did it! I just couldn't stop. They were all coming at us so fast, and everything was confusing, and I was terrified they would kill one of you. I couldn't stand if they had! Jasper said I'm strong, but I'm not. I'm so weak. I couldn't stand if one of you died. I don't know what I'd do. But that made me kill *them*. If I'd stopped to think for even a moment, if I'd tried to be brave and thought about what was going on, maybe I could have saved them, too. Maybe they would have survived, but now every last one is dead. They're all dead..."

She trailed off as sobs choked her words. She didn't know what she wanted Cor to say to make it better, if there was even anything he could say. She felt him withdraw his hand from her knee, and a sense of panic subdued her. He was going to leave her to this. He stood and was murmuring something to someone who'd come over. Ihva didn't look up to see who it was, rather just kept weeping. She'd massacred an entire city.

"Ihva," came Jasper's soft voice from beside her.

"Leave me alone," she spat.

He sat down next to her. She could tell by the way the piece of debris they were sitting on shifted. Everything was in ruins.

"Ihva, it's okay," he said softly.

She looked over at him, her eyes burning with resentment, but when she saw his face, the rage within her faltered. He was watching her, his body turned toward her and his gaze gentle. Part of her wanted to lash out, to make him feel what she was feeling, to make him take it away. It was fortunate he didn't try to take her hand or touch her as she was sure she would have turned on him. Part of her was ready to set itself on him or on anyone who tried to convince her that what she'd done was okay, that she wasn't guilty. She'd done wrong, and she knew it. She'd done something horribly, horribly wrong.

"Ihva," Jasper began again.

"Don't!" she exclaimed. "Please don't. Don't say it's alright, that everything's fine, that it was all justified. Cor's trying to convince me what I did was right and that there's nothing to feel guilty for, but he's wrong. He's wrong, Jasper! I killed them, every last one of them, and there's nothing I can do to take it back. There's nothing…" She was about to cry again, so she stopped.

He waited until she was finished to speak and then in a quiet voice she almost couldn't discern, he said. "I know how it feels, Ihva."

She stopped and stared at him.

"I know what it's like to have blood on your hands," he went on. "So I didn't destroy a city. It doesn't matter. I killed Jessica as surely as if I'd driven the sword through her myself, and what difference does it make how many died, only that they did. Bloodshed is bloodshed." He paused, and Ihva remained silent, transfixed by the pained look in his eyes. "I'm sorry you have to bear it, too," he concluded.

Ihva opened her mouth to speak but realized she didn't know what to say. What she'd done was wrong—it was a crime, a misdeed, an irreverent sin against living creatures—but she wasn't alone in carrying such guilt it seemed. She didn't blame Jasper for Jessica's death. Could it be he didn't blame her for the massacre of the drakes of Wymon? He hadn't intended evil, and neither had she. Could it be their intentions absolved them?

"They're still dead, though," she replied, her words feeble.

"I know," he said in a sad voice. "I know."

"There has to be a way to make it right. There has to," she asserted.

He looked at her for a moment before responding. "I don't know that there is. Nothing can bring them back, and short of that, would anything count as redemption?" She made to speak, but he went on. "We can't do anything about it, Ihva. We just have to accept that." He paused. "And try harder going forward, I guess."

She knew her face looked skeptical, but she didn't know how else to feel. Tentatively she replied, "Maybe you're right."

He watched her for a while, then looked away, saying, "We should get some food. There's a journey ahead of us today, more than likely."

She swallowed and nodded. "Okay," she told him.

He glanced back at her and said in a low tone, "We're in this together. Remember that." Then he got up and went to join the others.

Ihva stared after him. Her heart felt like it had been wrung of emotion and all that was left was emptiness. She rose and followed Jasper the short distance back toward the rest of the group.

Chapter 37

HALF AN HOUR LATER, EVERYONE had eaten their shares of fish jerky and was sitting around the fire waiting for someone to speak. It was a somber feeling they shared in the quiet, and Jasper worried about Ihva. Silence meant time to think, and that was the last thing Ihva needed right now. Jasper decided to get the day started, though he had little idea what that meant and worried things might get worse before they got better. He drew in a breath and addressed the others.

"We must be on our way soon. It is time we honor Grax," he said.

Cor and Yidda nodded, but no one said anything. Malach glanced at Ihva, then nodded as well and strode over to the pile of wood that remained from last night. Jasper watched Ihva, but she didn't move even as the others rose to help Malach. A second later, Kronk was at her side and sat down next to her. Ihva looked up and gave the orc-blood woman a forced smile. Jasper decided to let them be for a minute. Instead he joined the others. He walked to the center of what used to be the city street. There he set the wood down and returned to the pile to grab some more.

Jasper's gaze strayed to the surrounding area as he helped build the pyre. Drake bodies littered the scene. It crossed his mind that they might include the other drakes in the pyre. It seemed disrespectful, irreverent even, to leave them strewn about as they were, but he realized they had barely enough wood left to burn Grax's remains. He searched for the young drake's body. A second later, he found him. Grax's body was lying across the street, propped against the remainder of a stone wall. Jasper glanced over at Ihva. She was still sitting with Kronk's arm around her, her eyes shut tight. She felt guilty, he knew, and there was nothing he could do to assuage that. Last night had been horrific.

At that thought, images from the battle flashed before his mind's eye. The ground erupting, light flashing in all directions, drakes being hurled like rag dolls every which way. It had been all confusion and mayhem, and in the end, all the drakes had perished, even Grax. It wasn't Ihva's fault about Grax. If guilt belonged to anyone, it belonged to Jasper. He was the one who'd gotten caught stealing from the temples. If he'd been more careful, they might have made it out of the city unnoticed or at least with less destruction, certainly without Grax being killed. Jasper shook his head to rid himself of these thoughts. It wouldn't do any good to dwell on them. Grax was gone, and that was that. He turned his eyes back to the pyre.

It was almost finished. A hollow had formed in the center for Grax's body, and Jasper was about to turn to where the body lay when Cor and Malach came into view carrying Grax between them. The sight of their living arms holding his dead ones created an eerie feeling in Jasper, and he turned his eyes from the gruesome look of the burnt scales and blood and gashes. Instead, he made his way over to Ihva and Kronk.

The two women were speaking in low tones when he arrived. Kronk was the first to notice him and pointed him out to Ihva, who gave a start as she turned to him.

"It's time," he said in a quiet voice.

She swallowed and gave a slow nod, then Kronk got up and helped her to her feet. The three wandered over to the pyre where the others were now covering Grax's body with the remaining wood.

Jasper wanted to take Ihva's hand to console her, but he decided against it. It would just as likely startle her and cause her distress. Instead, he stood next to her, near enough to feel the warmth radiating from her but not touching her. There, he watched.

Cor struck a spark into the kindling at the base of the pyre and moved back. The wood caught fire. After a couple minutes, flames began to spring from the larger pieces of wood as well. A strange smell began to emanate from the pyre, something akin to burning flesh, and Jasper realized Grax's body had caught as well. He kept himself from wrinkling his nose, but the stench was nauseating. He tried to focus his attention on Ihva instead.

When he looked over at her, he found tears rolling down her face. She glanced at him, and something about seeing him seemed to break her. She fell to her knees and cried out.

"No!" she cried. "No, no, no! It's my fault!"

"It's okay, Ihva," Jasper said, kneeling next to her.

"No!" she exclaimed. "It's wrong! He shouldn't be gone!"

"Ihva," Jasper said in what should have been a soothing voice, but it seemed to make her angrier.

"How dare you?" she exclaimed. "How dare you try to justify it? He should never have died. It should have been me!"

"Ihva!" Jasper's tone was sharp now.

"It's true!" she shouted, then collapsed to the ground.

The crackling of flames had intensified, and the reek of burning flesh made Jasper almost wretch. That didn't matter, though. It was the fact that Ihva was sobbing harder than this morning that had Jasper disquieted. He reached out to put a hand on her shoulder, but as soon as he touched her, she jerked away. What was he supposed to do? He looked across at Kronk, but the orc-blood woman was watching Ihva. He ended up just kneeling next to Ihva as she wept for a few long minutes, then finally, something interrupted them.

"Are you okay, Ihva?" Cor asked, his words gentle.

Jasper looked up and saw everyone was gathered around them, watching Ihva with hesitant stances. She'd stopped crying, Jasper realized. No one spoke for a moment, but Yidda walked over and held out a hand to help Ihva up. Ihva faltered but accepted it and got to her feet. She must have been dizzy as she wobbled in place, but Malach was beside her and caught her before she fell.

"Careful there, lass," he told her, holding her up.

Jasper stood as well, still watching her. There was a poignant silence, then Ihva spoke.

"I'm sorry," she said, barely audible.

She drew back from Malach and glanced over the others, her eyes landing on Cor.

"I'm sorry," she repeated, louder this time, her voice shaking. "I'm so, so sorry! I didn't mean to; I really didn't mean to. I'm sorry I scared you, I'm sorry I freaked out, I'm sorry I destroyed everything! I'm sorry they're dead, all dead. I'm so, so sorry!" The tears in her eyes overflowed again at this point, and it seemed distress choked her words.

"Ihva, dear, no one is angry with you," came Yidda's voice.

"She speaks the truth, Ihva," Cor added. "We cannot pretend to understand what happened here, but it is clear that you intended no malevolence or evil. This was not the Shadow. This was Oer, and it was through you he accomplished his purposes. Do not apologize for enacting his will, however little we understand it."

Jasper grimaced at the mention of Oer but managed to quickly smooth his face.

Ihva looked at the ground. "But…" she started to say.

"I told you already, you saved us, and with us, many more. If we hadn't survived, if *you* hadn't survived, where would Gant be, Ihva?" Yidda said.

Ihva looked up at the Jini woman and whispered, "I don't know."

"Lost, lass," Malach told her. "Gant'd be lost."

Ihva swallowed as she looked Malach in the eye and nodded. The dwarf was still frowning, and his eyes shone mistily. She watched him, her eyes wide and tearful as well, then turned and hugged him.

"Thank you," she said simply.

Malach stood stiff and coughed as though she'd knocked the wind out of him. A moment later, he gave her a slow pat on the back.

"Uh, yeah, no problem, lass," he said. "It's no problem at all…" He trailed off as she withdrew. "I'm just not the best at this affection thing. Blame it on me not having a mother or whatever, but I don't do hugging very well. It's kind of awkward, to be honest, I'm not sure why, but don't worry, doesn't mean I don't care, just, well…" He trailed off again, his face red.

Ihva let out a small laugh, and Jasper couldn't help smiling as well. For all Malach's forwardness about romance, he was rather uncomfortable in friendship. Jasper couldn't blame him, though.

"Thank you," Ihva said, looking around.

"Of course, Ihva," Yidda replied as she returned a kind smile.

Cor nodded, and Kronk caught Ihva in a hug, this one not nearly as stiff as the one with Malach. After a moment, Kronk let go.

"You mean a lot to me," Ihva said. "A lot," she repeated, though the words teetered on the edge of tearful.

Jasper regarded her carefully as a wave of affection washed over him, which quickly turned to adoration. She was bearing up under this burden with grace. She was innately beautiful and his in some small way. It was delightful.

"And you to us," he replied, trying to subdue the intensity in his tone.

Ihva turned to him as though startled, then blushed and turned her eyes down again. "Thank you," she murmured.

No one said anything for a minute, and the sound of the pyre's flames reminded Jasper why they were there. He was just wondering what they should do to honor Grax when Cor spoke.

"Let us perform the rites, then," he said. "I do not know the ceremonies of the drakes, but I believe Oer's ritual will do well enough. I trust Oer, sovereign overall, will receive Grax to rest wherever he might arrive."

Jasper looked at Cor and nodded. A couple minutes later, they'd all gathered around Grax's pyre and were listening to Cor's steady voice pronouncing blessing and farewell. Jasper stood near Ihva and watched, his thoughts wavering between mournful and pleased as his attention cycled between Grax and her.

Chapter 38

IHVA AND HER COMPANIONS WATCHED as the flames continued to consume the pyre. Cor had finished the rites, and no one had spoken for some time. Ihva's thoughts had drifted from Grax some minutes before, and now she wasn't thinking about anything in particular, more just resting in the cathartic quiet. Then Cor broke the silence.

"We are confined to this island until we find transportation back to the continent," he said. "Grax told us the gem dragons might be the only hope we have. I pray the fragments work as he presumed they might." He looked at Jasper.

"We can certainly try," Jasper replied.

Ihva reacted against his words. "We have to try," she told him.

He raised an eyebrow at her but went over to his pack and reached inside. The others turned their attention to him as he set the fragments on the ground. He pulled out the fourth and final piece and looked up.

"That's all of them," he said.

Ihva glanced around the group and stood, starting toward the eggshell shards. The others watched her with uncertain looks but didn't stop her. She arrived where the pieces lay on the ground and picked one up. The fragment was heavier than she expected and shone a milky, reflective white as she turned it over in her hands. After a moment of inspection, she looked back at the other pieces and picked up another one. Positioning the two fragments together, she found they fit perfectly beside each other. Holding the pieces together with both hands, she realized she couldn't pick up a third piece. She looked up at Jasper.

"Can you get another one?" she asked.

He hesitated but then picked up a piece, stood, and moved it to fit on top of the two in her hands. The third fragment settled in place. Then he balanced the third piece with one hand and bent to take the final fragment in his other hand. Her pulse quickened when she saw that the fragment's shape would fit into the remaining space. She held her breath as he situated its edges to match the rest of the pieces—a flawless fit.

The moment the last fragment fell into place, the egg began to glow and the cracks where the pieces fit together mended and disappeared. Wonder filled Ihva as the complete egg ascended into the air. She caught astonishment in Jasper's face as well.

The egg stopped level with her eyes and started to spin, whirling about until it became a blur of white. It made a soft whirring noise as it spun, and a surge of awe left Ihva trembling. She blinked, and when her eyes reopened, the spinning had stopped. The egg was perfectly still. Ihva sensed great tension, though, like something inside the egg was struggling to burst through. The next thing she knew, a crack appeared on the perfectly smooth surface. It became a longer fracture and branched off. Soon, fissures covered the shell. Suspense thickened the air.

The eggshell splintered apart with a small shattering, and a creature appeared. It crawled out of the shell and remained in the air as the egg dropped to the ground and splintered into hundreds of tiny pieces. A burst of anxiety filled Ihva as she realized they'd never get the eggshell back together again, but for now that didn't matter. She turned her attention to the creature in the air.

She'd never seen anything like it before. It was about two hand-lengths tall and had a drake-like face—a long snout with wide nostrils, slitted dark eyes, and two horns protruding from the back of its head. It had wings as well, which were beating slowly to keep it suspended in the air. Its body was horizontal instead of upright, though, and its scales were the same pearly white as the eggshell. Its tail flitted back and forth, reminding Ihva of when they'd first met Grax. A pang of nostalgia hit her, but she kept watching the creature before her. She couldn't be certain what it was. It seemed too small to be a dragon, but it certainly wasn't a drake.

Then the creature spoke. "Who is it who summons me?" it asked.

Ihva glanced around at the others. Everyone's eyes were wide, but no one spoke.

"There are a few of us," Ihva replied, wondering why everyone else was silent. There were two princes among them. Shouldn't they be taking point? Then again, the creature had its eyes on her. "There's Jasper Aurdor, Prince of Oerid, and Malach Shemayim, Prince of Eshad, and—"

"I did not ask about your companions. Who is it who summons me?" the creature interrupted her.

Ihva stopped. The others were still watching her, but she got the sense they weren't following the conversation. She swallowed and replied, "It is I, Ihva Marie Marchand. Who are you?

"I am Durnena, dragonling servant of the Blessed Dragon Mother, Ashildur," the creature said.

Ihva wondered who Ashildur was but chose to save that question for later. "We seek a way back to the mainland. Can you help us?" she asked instead.

"You have need of much more than conveyance to the continent, my child," Durnena answered. It was hard to discern what emotion accompanied her words with her face as unreadable as the drakes' faces had been and her voice light and otherworldly.

Ihva wasn't sure what the dragonling was referring to exactly. She and the others *did* need more than a way back. They needed direction and guidance, and an army behind them wouldn't hurt.

"You know little of Truth and Eternity," Durnena went on. "You will fail your assignment without a greater understanding of the matters in which you are involved."

Ihva balked a little at the dragonling's suggestion. She wasn't *that* ignorant about Reality. Of course, things were muddled and mysterious in her mind concerning her own role in it, but she'd been a devoted student in her religious studies, in all her studies really, and anything she didn't know, Cor was teaching her. Still, Durnena was probably right. There was much more to learn, and Ihva wouldn't turn down an explanation of what was going on.

"Please, what is it we need to know?" she asked the dragonling.

"I cannot tell you, my child. My function is simply to guide you to one who can," Durnena replied.

"The gem dragon lords, you mean?" Ihva responded, her awe returning.

"No. The gem dragons are merely guardians of secrets long forgotten. Rather, you will seek the Dragon Mother herself. She will enlighten you as she can reveal Reality as it is."

Ihva stared at the dragonling floating before her in bewilderment. Reality belonged to Oer. What could the Dragon Mother know and need to tell her that Oer could not communicate to her directly? Was it above Oer to descend to the level of his creatures, even the one he'd chosen himself to be his Blessing?

"Where can we find this Dragon Mother?" Ihva inquired, trying to keep her skepticism from filtering into her words.

"You will find her beneath you," Durnena replied. "The base of this bluff houses a cave where she has hidden herself. The Father opens the eyes of the worthy to the entrance to this cave. Inside the cave are four caverns. In them, you will find four tests. Passing these tests will gain you access to the Dragon Mother."

Ihva quickly recorded Durnena's words in her mind. A cave with four chambers and four tests to get to the Dragon Mother. Were the tests dangerous? But almost half of her companions were unarmed. Ihva was about to voice a question when the dragonling began to fade.

"The Father has placed His mantle upon you, child. Wear it well, knowing you have already been deemed worthy."

As soon as Durnena had finished speaking, she vanished in a wisp of smoke. Ihva was left staring apprehensively through the air at Jasper. He had an eyebrow arched, and his eyes were fixed on her. She took a moment to gather herself, knowing the others were watching her, waiting.

Chapter 39

JASPER STARED AT IHVA, TAKEN aback. She'd been watching the small dragon that had appeared between them with rapt attention, speaking a strange language he'd never encountered, then the dragon had disappeared. Now Ihva was looking at him like he should be saying something when all he felt was confused.

It was Kronk who spoke first. "Where little dragon go?" Kronk was staring at the space where the creature had been, appearing wary.

"What did it say?" Jasper asked.

"You didn't understand her?" Ihva asked.

Jasper shook his head.

"It seems the Power to Read is also the Power to Speak," Cor explained. "You were speaking the language of dragons."

Ihva swallowed and looked back at Jasper. "Her name is Durnena," she said after a moment. "She said we need to find the Dragon Mother. I think Durnena called her 'Ashildur?'"

She looked around at the others as though they might elucidate, but of course no one did. Jasper had never heard of an Ashildur.

"Did Durnena explain where we could find the Dragon Mother?" Cor asked gently.

"She told me about a cave system somewhere beneath us. I guess the entrance is hidden except to those he deems 'worthy,' which I don't know what that means. Hopefully we are worthy." She took an uneven breath. "She said the Dragon Mother can inform and guide me, or us. Ashildur knows something we must know, too."

Ihva's words were faltering, and her attention drifted as she was considering something. There was an unfocused look in her eyes. Jasper cleared his throat softly, drawing her attention back to those before her. Her gaze re-centered itself on him.

"This Dragon Mother will provide us a way back to the continent?" Malach asked.

"I think so," was all she replied.

Malach shared a look of uncertainty with Jasper while Cor said, "The drakes themselves seem to have lost knowledge of her." He trailed off.

"Do you think she's safe, then? Can we approach her?" Malach asked.

"Would it matter if she isn't? All the counsel we've received has led to her. What other choice do we have?" Yidda replied.

Ihva turned to Jasper. He wasn't sure what she wanted him to say.

"I agree," was all he ended up answering.

"Finding the Dragon Mother seems indeed to be our only option," Cor said.

"We look for dragon?" Kronk's voice faltered, and Jasper could tell the woman was frightened—as she should be. Legend had it the dragons had fled in anger and spite and that they resented the other races. At least, every Oeridian depiction of dragons centered on their ferocity.

"I wonder whether finding the Dragon Mother might be the purpose of our ending up here," Ihva said.

The others turned back to her, and she drew back. Jasper wasn't sure she was right. It seemed too contrived for the gods to have intervened in that way. They'd arrived on the island by chance. If this Ashildur had useful information for them, it would have been a fortunate accident that they'd ended up here, but an accident, nonetheless.

"Very well, Ihva. We must heed Durnena's instructions then," Cor said.

"We should probably carry what provisions we can with us," Ihva replied.

Jasper nodded. Who knew how long it would take them to reach the cave, much less how much time it would take to get through it? He stood, as did the others, then they quietly gathered the food they had found into seaweed-woven bags and shouldered them as they readied themselves to follow Ihva.

Jasper and the others walked an hour along the descending cliffside to reach the shoreline, then turned to walk back along the bottom of the bluff. Tidepools and rocks dotted the beach, and it took some creativity to navigate the way at times. From the dampness of the sand, Jasper guessed the high tide left about fifteen paces between the edge of the water and the base of the cliff. He hoped they made it to the cave before then. He wasn't interested in getting wet.

He, Yidda and Ihva had taken up the front with Ihva in the middle. Everyone was quiet for a while until Yidda spoke.

"You're doing well, Ihva," she said.

Ihva turned her head to the Jini woman, and Jasper could no longer see her expression.

"Maybe I am," she replied in a small voice. "I'm trying, at least."

"There exists much confusion concerning you, Ihva. The world doesn't know how to receive you," the Jini woman went on.

That was true enough. Jasper had felt the confusion himself, though it was love that had won out.

"I know," was all Ihva replied. Her tone was subdued. Jasper felt an urge to take her hand but resisted.

"It's not easy, bearing the burden placed on you." Yidda spoke quietly, too, but Jasper could still hear her.

"I didn't ask for this." Ihva had a touch of bitterness in her voice. It weighed on her, this role she had to play, he knew. Maybe her sentiments mirrored his own more than he'd understood. She'd leveled a city—he wasn't sure how he'd take that either. He'd drawn the parallel between their situations to her earlier, but he was starting to understand how deeply what had happened was affecting her.

"You didn't need to," Yidda replied. "It's not by your request or by your merit but by divine will and Heaven's devotion to the world of Gant that you've been chosen, in this place, at this time, perfectly ordained."

Yidda's sanguine interpretation of events struck Jasper wrong, and it must have done the same to Ihva, as her words were pointed when she replied.

"You're a Jin. What do you know of the gods?"

Yidda didn't react with the defensiveness that Jasper expected.

"It's true, I'm cut off from certain celestial knowledge by my heritage as a Jin." She paused. "Yet, I sense something deeper than my own limited experience of the world."

Though Jasper didn't like to admit it, "limited" didn't seem quite the right word to describe anything about Yidda. Apparently the Jini woman had traveled through Gant and collected its knowledge for many years previous to this. At least, that was what Jasper had gathered from conversations over the past month. If Yidda's knowledge was limited, Jasper's knowledge was infinitesimal. Could Yidda have a point? Yidda's voice interrupted his thoughts.

"I've seen something more purposeful in the events of history and in the lives of those I've watched, something more profound going on than a cycle of life and death. Everything is headed in a direction, and though I don't know how it all ends up, I've witnessed enough to know these things can turn out for the best. So I will hope, Ihva, and I urge you to do the same."

Jasper recoiled from the notion Yidda was proposing, but he allowed himself to rethink and consider it a moment. Things could turn out for the best? They certainly could—Jasper wasn't going to deny that—but that they would was a whole different matter. Hoping in something so uncertain and tenuous seemed a recipe for discouragement and disappointment, at best. Yet he recognized some form of hope was necessary to maintain the will to fight. The knowledge that things could turn out right must have fueled his struggle against the Shadow in some small way. Yet the desire to do what was right, no matter the cost and chances of success, drove his efforts, too. He wasn't sure which force was stronger in him. In any case, they were working together. At the end of the day, he couldn't understand Yidda's anticipation of victory, only her desire for it. Ihva was speaking now, though.

"I try, Yidda. I don't know that I can withstand it all," she said, then straightened her posture. "I will keep fighting, though. I have to."

Yidda's tone was sympathetic. "That is all you are called to do, dear. You are no deity. You cannot control anything but your own actions. You can, however, serve the one who has power over it all. You can serve and trust him."

Trust was another one of those tenuous things, one of those shaky foundations, especially trust in Oer, especially for Jasper.

"Yidda, what are you going to do?" Ihva asked suddenly. "I mean, will Oer even receive you, you know, once you, um, die?" She was looking straight ahead as she spoke.

"I don't know," the Jini woman replied in a quiet voice.

"Why do you even involve yourself in all this? You might never see reward for any of it," Ihva pointed out.

"The most righteous deeds are not done with reward in mind but with a devotion to see good effected no matter what the personal outcome," Yidda said. "I expect I will find my eternity in the Prison of Souls. Whatever good I now accomplish; I cannot change the fact many Jini perished by my sins. No, I don't seek eternal reward except for the knowledge the world will find at least a slightly better ending than it would have without me."

Respect for Yidda grew in Jasper as he listened to her. He resonated with her words and wished he could say the same, but he was seeking his own reward alongside that of Oerid. He was seeking his own freedom even as he sought the freedom of his kingdom. He felt guilt creep over him, a familiar guilt that he'd somehow forgotten in the midst of everything with Ihva. He cringed as Ihva spoke.

"I guess I want that, too," she said softly.

Then, she and Yidda fell silent as they continued along beside each other. Jasper tried to escape his thoughts, but he couldn't with everyone being so silent. Even Malach was quiet, surprisingly.

After another hour of searching for an opening in the bottom of the cliff, Kronk told the others she spotted something in the distance. As they moved forward, it became clear—a small cave entrance in the side of the cliff. The sand had eroded a path such that water from the ocean flowed onto the floor of the cave. It looked like they were going to get wet after all.

Soon they were fifteen or so paces from the hollowed space. They gathered in close, anxiety drawing them together. Jasper had positioned himself beside Ihva and intertwined his fingers with hers. She didn't withdraw her hand but held his tight. She must have been as nervous as he was. They were headed to find a dragon, and not just any dragon but the Dragon Mother. If she was friendly, it might be an awe-inspiring experience, but if she was hostile, there was little chance of it being anything other than terrifying and disastrous. Jasper remembered only he, Malach, and Ihva had weapons, as Cor had given Jasper back the dagger he'd lent him. There was little chance they could fight their way out of this. Jasper was considering giving his second blade to Yidda when Cor interrupted.

"There is one path forward," the dwarf said, breaking the tense silence that had settled over them all.

They all took some last glances at each other, then Ihva let go of Jasper's hand and stepped out to lead them through the opening.

Chapter 40

JASPER TOOK HALTING STEPS FORWARD. Ahead of them was a passageway wide enough to fit four men side-by-side, albeit rather tightly. The others' footsteps sounded behind him, but despite their presence and Ihva by his side, he felt alone. He inhaled a sharp, nervous breath.

The passage curved to the right about twenty paces past the entrance and wound back to the left shortly after that. Water was dripping from the ceiling and down the walls, making the smell damp but not unpleasant. As the brightness from the sun outside grew distant, Cor whispered, and a ball of light appeared. It radiated to fill the space around them and followed as they continued walking. There was nothing but rock and dripping water, and Jasper began to wonder if they'd come into the wrong cavern. Then they rounded a corner, and he came to a sudden stop.

He found himself facing a mass of scales. He froze. Whatever it was appeared massive, much larger than any creature he'd encountered before. It was lying on the ground maybe twenty paces from him inside a cavern that seemed to billow out from where the tunnel ended. As Cor's light drifted into the room, Jasper could make out the crimson shimmer of the scales, and he knew—this had to be

Raidurr the Ruby. His breaths became shallow.

The rest of his companions weren't moving either. In fact, almost everything had an eerie stillness to it such that Jasper finally noticed the steady rise and fall of the mass before him. It was breathing. He was just wondering how they should approach the creature when it shifted, and its neck swung around. The creature's head, when it appeared, evoked fear in Jasper. It was the same deep red as the rest of its body and had a long snout with flared nostrils. Rows of scales led up to reflective yellow eyes with black slits that expanded and contracted as the creature's gaze fell on Jasper and his companions. Straight, ivory horns extended from the back of its head, and huge fangs in the shape and size of daggers protruded from its closed mouth. It was indeed a dragon.

The creature's head moved, and Jasper was tempted to back away. Instead, he stood his ground. The dragon turned to face him, and Cor's light danced in its eyes like fire for a long moment before it spoke. Jasper swallowed in apprehension.

"Salutations, Seekers of Truth, saints of the Father," the dragon began.

It was speaking in Common, and not in the archaic Common of the drakes but the everyday Common Jasper was accustomed to hearing at home. He watched the creature warily.

"My name is Raidurr. I am the Ruby Lordess, and I greet you with the blessing of my Mother."

Now that he thought about it, the dragon's voice had something feminine about it, a melody and wistfulness, despite its low pitch. The dragon scanned the group silently for a moment.

"Greetings," Jasper said, feigning calm in hopes he might start to feel it.

"You arrive seeking answers to questions you were not aware you ought to be asking," Raidurr replied. "I am prepared to respond, but I must warn you that the answers you seek, rather than satisfying your desire for wisdom, will rather induce further inquiry. I will supply you with as much counsel as I am permitted. You must proceed farther in to know the Truth as it is. First, I require you to solve a puzzle.

The correct answer is a key to what I must tell you. Are you prepared to answer?"

Raidurr had been looking at Ihva for most of her speech, but as she spoke her final question, she looked over the group.

"We are prepared," Ihva said, her quiet words piercing the hush around them.

Raidurr's eyes shone brighter as she began speaking her riddle, and Jasper listened carefully.

Holding up for estimation,
Dross to burn and veil withdraw,
Flames revealing the formation,
These make clear both strength and flaw.

At a loss to mask each fault,
The circumstances dire,
One is bared by their assault,
Passing through them as through fire.

"What are they?" Raidurr concluded.

Jasper set to puzzling over the dragon's words. Dross to burn and veil withdraw, they made clear both strength and flaw? Whatever "they" were, they revealed the truth about things or maybe about people. One was bared by their assault and passed through them as through fire? They were harrowing, it sounded like. Jasper tried to remember the rest of the riddle, but the words kept slipping from his mind as he watched Raidurr's face. Nothing about it changed, and that frightened him. What else had she said? Something about being dire? Holding something up? He couldn't recall the rest and began to panic when Cor spoke.

"They are trials," was all the dwarf said, though it was enough to trigger Jasper's mind to start fitting the pieces of the riddle together. He didn't get much time to think, though, before Raidurr turned her gaze to the dwarf and replied to him.

"You answer correctly, Cor Leviel Gidfolk," she said, her songful voice approving. Cor bowed his head, and Raidurr continued. "You have endured various trials to arrive at this point, and you shall undergo further trials as you move forward. I cannot rescue you from them, only warn you of them and exhort you to prepare yourselves for what lies ahead.

"You might ask how I know. Long ago, I was named the Afflictor by those who did not understand my role. I do not myself afflict, only the Father reveals to me the woes which might come to pass should his creatures continue on their paths. There are times this adversity might be avoided should such individuals rectify their ways, for their own evil invokes their misery. This is not such a time. It is by your righteous acts and courageous deeds that you shall come into hardship. Indeed, devastation shall fall upon you for your valor and resolve. Do not let this frighten you. Rather, when distress comes upon you, take heart that your way is straight, and you are following it. Without swerving, you might make your way through Hell itself, but on the other side is Heaven. Only by moving through Shadow shall you find the Light, and it is your dauntless love that shall carry you."

The dragon lordess drew in a long breath while Jasper found himself speechless, brought low by her words. He understood enough of their gravity and truthfulness to stand in silence soaking them in.

"Our love will carry us?" Malach asked slowly.

"Indeed, love has been the theme of the universe from before time," the dragon lordess replied. "My mother was born of love, but the affections that drew her mother and father together grew sour. Jealousy turned them against each other. The Heart of the Universe was broken, and where once Light and Shadow beautifully mirrored one another, tenderly gazing into their reflections, they began to war against each other. No longer can a child of the Light find solace in her shadow. Darkness and Night are no longer a place of rest for the righteous but rather are an enemy to flee. Love has broken. The world has broken, well each of you know. Yet Love will restore what has been lost, for it is Love that can heal those who have been wounded."

It seemed as though Raidurr were looking directly at Ihva for a second, and Jasper fought a shudder. The dragon lordess was talking about something deeper than he understood. Surely he'd experienced moments that touched on love, but under Raidurr's gaze, he felt childish, like he was gazing into the depths of love's true power, like it might drown him.

"It is time for you to move forward," Raidurr said. "My brothers anticipate your arrival, and I do not intend to keep them waiting."

The dragon lordess turned her head and opened her mouth. Out poured a sea of fire so intense Jasper thought the mere sight of it would incinerate him. However, as the flames dispersed, he found they left a comforting warmth. They lit a path to a dark opening he hadn't noticed before in the opposite wall. He glanced at Ihva; whose eyes met his but quickly darted away. Maybe she was experiencing the same shame or smallness he was. It didn't matter, though. They had to continue on. He started forward on the path between the flames. Too late, he realized he'd made no parting salutation to Raidurr.

Chapter 41

IHVA WAS SHIVERING A LITTLE as the temperature continued to drop. The farther from the outside world they went, the farther from the sun and its warmth and comfort, the more she longed for daylight. Cor's light had an eerie glow to it in these caves. Without the sun, she couldn't gauge how long they'd been walking either. Cor's voice interrupted her thoughts.

"Are you well, child?" he asked quietly.

She'd known Jasper was walking next to her but hadn't realized Cor had made his way to the front of the group as well. She considered his question. Just hours ago she'd destroyed Wymon, Grax was dead, they had an ocean between them and home, they were in a freezing, damp cave system, and Raidurr had just informed them that only with Love could they overcome the great trials that awaited them, yet Ihva was suddenly unsure she had any idea what Love meant. Would it do any good to not be okay, though? It seemed the path forward required her to be strong.

"Do I have a choice not to be?" she replied, trying to sound detached.

"You always have a choice," Cor said, peering at her intently, then spoke in low tones she alone could hear. "You must learn to share

278

your burden. To regard those fated to destruction as you do, to save those whom you can save and grieve those you cannot, you must apportion your sorrows and allow others to carry you in them."

Ihva glanced at Cor out of the corner of her eye, chastened. She'd been lamenting the way Jasper suffered on his own, and here she was trying to hide her struggle just like he was. She was about to answer Cor when Yidda interrupted.

"Careful, dear. We near the edge of something," the Jini woman warned.

Ihva looked and saw a dark space ahead. It seemed the path ended about five paces in front of her and dropped off into nothingness. There was black beneath, though as she looked up, she found a large ledge far above her head. They'd hit a dead end and the only way to go was up. But how? Then, she spotted movement and a flash of green out of the corner of her eye. She whipped her gaze toward it and saw a tail disappear behind the outcropping.

"Greetings to you, the Elected," a deep voice said.

Ihva suspected from the tone and pitch this was a male dragon and guessed from the green tail they'd found Graiyent the Emerald. As if to answer, a dragon's shimmering head appeared over the edge of the overhanging rock, its coloring like a dark orchard or forest. Ihva met its eyes, and their eternity mesmerized her such that she didn't reply to him. He spoke again.

"Welcome, Chosen Vessel of Destiny."

Ihva still didn't speak. The silence of reverence bound her, and she felt herself transfixed.

"You have come far, weary travelers," the dragon went on.

Malach surprised Ihva as he replied, "Indeed, our journey has been long."

"You have a long way yet, but our strength will be yours if you will have it," Graiyent said.

"You are Graiyent the Emerald, are you not?" Ihva asked. She'd found her voice again.

"You speak correctly. For your wisdom, I offer you an opportunity to further distinguish yourself from the foolish. Respond to my question without error, and you shall add Truth to what I proffer."

"We are ready." Somehow, Ihva's words came out steady.

"Very well," Graiyent said. When he spoke again, he did so lyrically.

This want of happy bond
Craves a comrade, kind and near.
This need for darling fond,
It is sorrow vast, severe.

This doleful, friendless ache,
It laments and does beseech
Its forlorn jail to break,
Its seclusion now to breach.

"What is it?" Graiyent concluded.

Ihva grew nervous as soon as he finished speaking. She felt like she'd missed a lot of what he'd said. Something about a "happy bond" and a comrade. It was sorrowful, doleful, friendless, whatever it was. She sifted through her memory for more clues. This thing, it sounded like a feeling or emotion of some sort, being a want and need according to Graiyent. It was an "ache" or something of the sort. Ihva's thoughts swirled, and she became lost in a sea of words and ideas. It was Malach's voice that called her consciousness back to the room where they stood.

"Loneliness," he said in a small voice, then glanced at the others. "The answer is loneliness," he said, a bit stronger this time.

Graiyent gave a looming nod and replied, "Child of Light, this world is dark, overtaken by Shadow, and it has stolen from you those you have held most dear. Friendless you have been but not forsaken, solitary but not alone."

There the dragon paused, and Ihva glanced at Malach. The dwarf's eyes were wide, and he stood as though he wanted to shrink back but couldn't, or maybe it was he wouldn't. Lonely was never a word she would have used to describe Malach, not with his outgoing friendliness and incessant attempts to make conversation. Yet here he stood, looking fearful and small, exposed. Something about the situation, the revelation, unsettled Ihva. Had she been that blind? But Graiyent was speaking again.

"There have been those who have named me the Sunderer for I foretell the heartache of forlorn solitude. Indeed, you shall find it breaks you as well before the end. It must be so. One cannot know himself by mirrors alone. There comes a time when he must lance his pride and sever his dependence on his companions to discover who he truly is within himself. Assuredly, you will shed many tears as struggle and unprecedented suffering lie in your path. My sister has informed you of this. I myself exhort you to pursue growth in your desolation."

Ihva's heart felt dull and heavy, and it sank like lead in water at Graiyent's speech. What did the dragon mean, saying desolation and sorrow lay in their path? What was she supposed to do with that? She couldn't go back—there was no way to return to the simple life of a merchant's daughter—but she wasn't sure she knew how to go forward either. Graiyent interrupted her thoughts again.

"The Father has empowered each of you to fulfill a distinct role," he said. "Each one will find himself as significant as the next. Indeed, the Father foresaw this story in the aftermath of the Breaking. You appeared in his mind's eye as he arranged for the redemption of Gant, and we have all awaited your arrival with sorrow and yearning. None of you has the strength or wisdom in himself to accomplish your task. However, in your journeys, each of you will grow in the knowledge he needs such that you all will grow in fellowship and amity to pursue the Father's purposes."

Graiyent's eyes swept over Ihva and her companions, and when his light blue eyes landed on her, she shivered.

"My brother awaits your arrival," he said.

Then Graiyent's enormous wings extended and beat the air to lift him. He maneuvered through the cavern, which seemed smaller as he extended to his full length, though it had to be one hundred feet wide at least. Ihva and the others stepped back as Graiyent descended. He landed in front of them, balanced on the edge of the stone platform. Angling one wing down to the ground, he motioned with his front claws for Ihva and the others to step up onto his back.

As nervous as Ihva was around water, she was rather daring when it came to heights. Soon she'd climbed atop Graiyent's back. His wings beat again, creating cool currents around him, and exhilaration tingled in her extremities. They rose through the chamber slowly, and Ihva relished the journey. Too soon, they'd reached the upper platform and she was sliding off Graiyent's back. She awaited the others. When Malach, who'd come last, had gotten back on his feet, the dragon addressed them all again.

"For many years, I have prayed for this moment. I shall continue to intercede on your behalf. Much depends on you—all of you."

Then Graiyent nodded to her and the others and turned to look down at the doorway beneath him.

A type of heartache came over Ihva, but she knew they had to continue. She turned toward the back wall of the cave to find a passageway extending farther in. Cor motioned his hand forward, and his ball of light moved toward the opening. With a sigh, Ihva walked forward into the darkness once again.

Chapter 42

AFTER FIVE OR TEN MINUTES, the next tunnel opened up into an extensive space with a large pool blocking the path forward. Jasper peered down into the water and realized it was many feet deep. Remembering his time in the ocean, he realized there was no way they would all make it across the pool. Had they reached the end?

He looked back up. The water spanned twenty paces across the cavern, and in the middle of a shelf protruding from the opposite wall lay another dragon. Curled up, it looked like it was sleeping. Its scales were a deep turquoise-blue and shimmered even in the dim illumination of Cor's light. Blarr the Sapphire.

As Cor came out of the passage into the room, his sphere of light brightened the cavern. Jasper quickly motioned to Cor to stop. The dragon's left eye, the one facing them, fluttered open. Dark blue or black, it had a slit of white down the center. The dragon lifted its head and turned to look at Jasper and the others.

"I have been waiting for you, Beloved of the Father," the dragon said in a booming, masculine voice.

"Are you Lord Blarr?" Ihva replied

The dragon's eyes shifted from Ihva to Jasper and the others. His gaze was piercing, and Jasper got the impression that the dragon could see many things, like nothing any of them was thinking or feeling was hidden from this creature. It was a vulnerable sensation but not exactly fearful. The dragon certainly understood Jasper, but Lord Blarr's knowledge of him didn't feel invasive or condemning. Rather, Jasper found a surprising sense of relief as he looked into the dragon's eyes as though his unspoken fears and desires had found a place to rest. He didn't have time to wonder about it as Lord Blarr answered Ihva.

"You speak correctly. Many have sought me, but not one has found me until today. Those who pursued the furtherance of their own wills proved themselves unsuited to know the Truth." The look in Blarr's eyes intensified like dry tinder catching fire. "You, however, have been deemed worthy, Ihva of Oerid, you and your companions."

Ihva didn't say anything for a moment, and in those few seconds, Jasper marveled over Lord Blarr's words—worthy. They'd been deemed worthy. The pronouncement came as a solace to Jasper, but he shook it off. Worthy was never a word that described him. He was a captive struggling against his bonds, persistent perhaps but not worthy.

Ihva shook her head. "I've done nothing very different than my fellow Oeridians," she said.

"Perhaps not. Yet the Father's power has descended upon you all the same." The gem dragon broke off, letting his audience ponder his words.

Jasper suspected Blarr was speaking of Oer when he named "the Father," but things had become so perplexing he couldn't be sure. Three months ago, he'd been convinced dragons no longer existed, yet here he was listening to one converse with them. Who knew what other beings existed outside Jasper's experience? The Father could be anyone, another dragon even. Jasper puzzled over this while Ihva remained silent, and finally, Lord Blarr spoke again.

"With the power you possess you have received a task none but you can accomplish. The Father has provided you each much already in the way of companions." His eyes swept across the group. "It remains now that he enlighten you as to your undertaking."

"We would like that," Ihva replied meekly.

Blarr nodded and explained, "Our knowledge remains hidden, as we ourselves have been for many years. Mysteries and puzzles conceal what we know, as you have seen. You and your comrades must unravel these mysteries yourselves if you are to truly understand."

"We will answer your riddle," she said. Her voice had a tremor to it, and Jasper let out a slow breath.

"Very well," Lord Blarr said. "You must decipher the meaning of my words. The answer will fill your coming days, but you must not yield an inch to them."

Ihva nodded. Then the dragon closed his eyes and started speaking, his intonation musical.

They move like the rain,
Twinkle like a star,
Are love's refrain
And bitterness's bar,
Leave trails one can trace,
Though not very far,
Wound not the face
But pain's etching are.

The dragon opened his eyes, his gaze was on Ihva once again. "What are they?" he asked.

Jasper quickly sorted through the dragon's words. Love's refrain, bitterness' bar, were an etching? They moved like rain? The words jumbled together. Trails one can trace, though not very far. What left a short but traceable trail? A shooting star, maybe? Yet stars weren't painful. Far from it. And besides, Blarr had compared whatever the answer was to a star. What could it be? Jasper turned the clues over in his mind, but as soon as he came up with an answer that satisfied one part of the riddle, he remembered another part his answer did not fit with. He was still deliberating when Yidda's voice resounded in the cavern.

"Tears," she said.

Jasper turned to look at the Jini woman. Tears. Was that the answer? Tears moved like the rain, falling to the ground, and twinkled like stars in the light. Tears could express both joy and sadness, love and bitterness. Tears left a noticeable trail down one's face, a short distance, before they fell. Yidda was right, then.

"You answer correctly, Yidda of Alm'adinat," Blarr's voice reverberated. His eyes were gentle as he looked at the Jini woman. "Well you know tears, Yidda. Yours have not been wasted, and neither have those of your companions. Some have called me the Mourner and not without reason. Shed tears are of deepest gravity to me, and I have collected those of the righteous since my birth. Not one tear has gone unnoticed, and for every teardrop I have account. They have all flowed together into the rivers and oceans around us, but I have recorded each one."

As Blarr spoke, he immersed his audience in another compassionate gaze, the look in his dark eyes soft but strong. The sense of being known returned with power, and Jasper squirmed uncomfortably. It wasn't so much that Lord Blarr understood him that fazed him but the empathy in the dragon's eyes. Jasper always felt uneasy when someone expressed that type of kindness toward him. Such a sentiment felt unseemly to Jasper. Fulfilling one's duty deserved no accolades and struggling to satisfy his responsibilities was no reason for someone to pity him. It was what it was.

"The Father instructed me in this task. As the first elves and dwarves made their homes in the world, before they felt the effects of the Breaking, the Heart of the Universe shattered, and the Father bade me gather his tears for all the years to come. He told me the upright would shed saintly tears as he had and that he must have an account. He would repay their sorrows with joy. He told me the wicked whose actions precipitated the noble souls' sighing would drown in these waters I have gathered."

A solemn silence followed. Jasper wasn't sure what to make of Blarr's words. The Father, Oer? He'd wept? And continued to, it would seem. And he appointed Blarr as an instrument to bring redemption, somehow. What did this have to do with them? It occurred to Jasper that he hadn't shed tears in many years, not since his childhood over a scraped knee and things of the sort, never in self-pity. He'd never wept over his plight. Was there no record, then, of his sorrows? It was well there shouldn't be, though. Jasper just hoped he wouldn't be among those drowned in the tears of the righteous.

"You shall find yourselves in an ocean of tears in the days to come. While you must suffer grief, do not surrender to it. Do not let it overcome you for hope still lives and one day shall reign supreme." He paused. "You have much left to learn, and my brother is waiting for you. I regret our time together is at its conclusion."

With that, Blarr extended his tail across the cavern to the shelf where the group was standing. As the dragon shifted his body, an opening in the wall behind him became visible.

Jasper averted his eyes from the dragon's gaze as an unpleasant feeling seeped into him. It was a heavy feeling, the burden of Reality. If tears were the price paid for righteousness, Jasper had accomplished nothing good in his life. He didn't plan on lamenting any of his experience, either. He'd rage against this Father, but he'd never accept the Father's pity. Jasper tried to smooth his frown as he watched Ihva in front of him. She made a ginger step onto Blarr's tail and walked along the dragon's back and neck to reach the doorway on the other side of the cavern. Jasper didn't wait for the others but followed immediately after her. He didn't want anyone to see his discomfort.

Chapter 43

IHVA AND THE REST OF the group entered the passageway extending back from Blarr's cavern. Ihva was in sort of daze. As they left the dragon lord's presence, some of his words, his warning, replayed in her mind. *The answer will fill your coming days, but you must not yield an inch to them.* Tears. Tears would fill her future. How could Blarr know? Yet he seemed to know many secret things.

Besides informing Ihva that sorrow would greet her soon, Lord Blarr had exhorted her not to give herself up to grief. While she'd always been determined not to surrender when things became perplexing and painful, she knew she needed Blarr's reminder. The distress and suffering of the last couple months oppressed her, though she was doing her best to push them back. She focused her efforts on bending under the weight of it all, trying so hard not to break beneath it instead. She squeezed her eyes shut for a second. How was she supposed to endure this?

Opening her eyes again, she led her companions through the tunnel, still guided by Cor's light. As she rounded a corner, she found herself facing a brighter room with a huge space and high ceiling. It was roughly hewn with irregular jutting and curves. Cor's bright orb disappeared in the light of the cavern, and in the illumination, Ihva saw words upon words carved on the walls. She tried to read them but found her eyes overwhelmed by their sheer number.

She realized she'd stopped when someone bumped into her. She looked back and found Jasper stepping back, his eyes on the walls as well. Before Ihva could turn her attention to searching for the final dragon lord, Lord Gulur, a deep, male voice echoed in the cavern.

"Welcome, Children of Anticipation."

Ihva looked around, and her eyes landed on something on the far side of the room about fifty feet away. There rested another large dragon, this one with reflective, amber scales. Above it hovered a bright sphere of light, the source of illumination in the large space.

"Lord Gulur," Ihva said, yet again breathless in the face of such magnificence.

"Yes, daughter," Gulur replied. "You have arrived at the final phase of your journey before you may present yourselves to the Dragon Mother. You have also reached your final test. Are you prepared to answer me?"

Ihva swallowed and nodded. "We are ready, Lord Gulur," she said.

Gulur's tail, which was curled around in front of him, shifted out of the way as he made his way over to Ihva and her companions. He gave them an intent look as he approached. When he reached a space about fifteen paces in front of them, he came to a halt and spoke his riddle rhythmically.

Concealed, veiled, in the dark,
As though they can evade
Vision, notice, and the mark
Of being seen and weighed.

Indeed and yet, some can elude
The shame of plain display.
One might think this makes him shrewd,
But their sly schemes can slay.

The last word rang out, then in more normal tones, Gulur asked, "What are they?"

Ihva lowered her eyes and sorted through the clues in her mind. Whatever these were, they were hidden. Who hid them? Did they hide themselves? Someone who thought himself "shrewd" concealed these, but their slyness could kill. What else had Gulur said? Ihva puzzled over the riddle for a minute or two before she heard Jasper beside her shift. Glancing over, she found he was standing with his hands clasped together in front of him. He'd inclined his head slightly, but his eyes flickered toward Lord Gulur.

"The answer is secrets," he said in a quiet voice.

A spark flashed in Gulur's eyes, and he nodded his enormous head. "You are correct, Jasper Thesson Aurdor," the dragon said. "Well you are acquainted with secrets, young Prince, for they have driven you to the loneliness of which my brother spoke. They will only continue to do so. Known as the Whisperer, I am aware of that which each of you withholds from your companions." His gaze passed over Ihva and the others, and Ihva shivered. "Your secrets press you into hidden corners and dark places, and yet it will not always be so. It shall come to pass that you find yourselves exposed, vulnerable, and defenseless against your companions' scrutiny. You shall find yourselves revealed and known, and it shall be your candor that saves you."

Gulur paused, and Ihva wondered at his pronouncement. Secrets? She didn't have secrets, really. There were things the others didn't know about her, but it wasn't because she was withholding information, only that such things hadn't come up.

"Saves us from what?" Jasper asked, interrupting Ihva's thoughts.

Gulur turned his eyes to Jasper and replied, "You have heard now of the Breaking when the Heart of the Universe split. Never can it be restored to its unbroken state. However, our hope lies in the expectation that it can be healed. Darkness fell, and with it, the Wholeness. It shall be Light alone that must triumph now. The Father enjoined all who remained loyal to the Truth to help guide you in your journey. In this way, he has shepherded you to this place.

Here shall his daughter bestow on each of you the required knowledge.

"You will not survive the Truth, however, unless you yourselves speak it. If you neglect to be open with yourselves and each other, the Truth will consume you like a fire, leaving nothing but ashes of what once was. Ashes scatter in the wind, and you will find your fellowship dissolved and yourselves divided if not for faith in each other. Encourage each other, day by day, moment by moment. The world may be rescued yet, but it will not be without sacrifice. With honesty and love, you shall find the necessary oblation worth its cost."

As Gulur finished speaking, the final word rang heavy through the cavern. Despite the dragon lord's talk of truth, gloom and fear colored Ihva's thoughts. What sacrifice would be required of them to rescue the world? It was up to them, then? Doubt crept in about whether she would be able to give what was necessary when the moment came to offer it. She became queasy.

Gulur's voice boomed in the cavern once again. "It is time. She will receive you now."

"Are we to see the Dragon Mother, then?" Cor asked.

"Indeed, you are to see her, and she will reveal the Light as it is, just as she has revealed in pieces through her offspring. She shall honor you, the pure, with the Truth," Gulur replied.

Ihva trembled and had a sudden inclination to flee. Who was she anyway? Over the past couple of months, she had grown to think more highly of herself. More highly and less, really. Oer's Blessing, the Dread Prophet, Doomspeaker—these titles were hers. But really she was Ihva—Ihva Marie Marchand, wealthy merchant's daughter, naive, ignorant, seeking love and adventure without the awareness that such things were fraught with deadly danger. How could she come before this Dragon Mother, pretending to be pure and honorable? She might have experienced a few victories in her journey, but she'd made just as many mistakes, one costing the lives of an entire city. What would the Dragon Mother think when she learned Ihva had destroyed the drakes? Ihva squeezed her eyes shut.

She had to move forward. They were going to see the Dragon Mother, and she was just going to have to apologize and hope for the best. She gathered her wits, opened her eyes, and looked up at Gulur. He was looking back at her. She inhaled a breath of resolve.

"We are ready," she told him.

The dragon lord moved to the left side of the cave, and at the same time, the globe of light illuminating the room moved to the right and intensified. Soon, it was blinding, and Ihva had to cover her eyes. Heat radiated out from the orb as well, a comforting heat, not searing. It wrapped itself around Ihva, enclosing her in reassurance. The light became so bright she felt her eyes would burst even through her closed eyelids. Then, abruptly, the brightness and heat calmed. Slowly, Ihva lowered her hand from before her eyes and lifted her eyelids. The sight before her overwhelmed her more than anything she'd observed that day. She stood in stunned silence as awe overtook her.

Chapter 44

THE BRIGHT ORB ABOVE WHERE Gulur had been lying earlier was brilliant and blinding. It had also grown to many times its original size. Jasper shut his eyes against it but reopened them as the light softened. He looked toward the orb and saw a figure take shape. It was a gleaming, white dragon, this one twice the size of the previous ones. Jasper's eyes adjusted as he continued to gaze at the figure. With a softer sound than he would have expected, the creature took flight and drew near the group. Once it reached the center of the cavern, it landed with a mighty thud. The ground quaked, then the dragon spoke in a rich, songful voice.

"Salutations, Ihva Marchand, Oer's Blessing. Greetings to you, Jasper Aurdor, Bearer of the Light. Welcome, Cor Gidfolk, Beloved of Oer, and welcome, Kronk, Oer's Innocent. Salutations, Malach Shemayim, Holder of the Flame, and to you, Yidda, the Redeemed."

Jasper couldn't yet make out the face of the dragon for the brilliance of light, but he could tell it was looking at each individual as it spoke. Bearer of the Light? What was that supposed to mean? He had no magic associated with the Light. What was this dragon talking about?

"My name is Ashildur," the dragon continued in her canorous

tone. "You come seeking something meager, but I offer you something much greater. You come seeking passage to the mainland, but I offer you passage to the Courts of Oer. Truth itself shall transport you, though physically you shall remain where you stand. Come, now, what answers may I offer you? My children have afforded you their hints of my Father's mysteries. I have much to tell you, but first I must know what you understand already."

When no one answered at first, Cor stepped forward. His voice shook slightly, though Jasper could tell it wasn't with fear. Rather, it seemed a type of exultation caused the dwarf to tremble.

"Indeed, the dragon lords' and lordess's puzzles seemed a tight knot of intertwining secrets, part of some greater enigma of the one called 'the Father.' I would like to believe that this Father is the great Father of all, the Blessed Oer?"

Ashildur nodded in response to the question in Cor's voice and let him continue.

"What I have gathered is this. In the beginning, Oer, the Lord of Light and Life, was involved with Darkness in a favorable capacity. However, at a point early in history, the Blessed Lord divided from the Shadow. Somehow, this split, the 'Breaking' as your children called it, delineated good and evil by the severing of Light from Darkness. From that day forward, Oer has meant to vanquish evil and overcome the Shadow. He has chosen us as vessels through which he might accomplish this task. Your children hinted at hope. I pray you might grace us with a foundation for that hope. Of course, the Father himself must be central, but what further assurance might he provide to strengthen us?"

Jasper looked over at Cor in surprise. While he'd gathered some of what the dwarf had said, he hadn't deciphered the gem dragons' cryptic clues and speeches to mean all of that. Of course, what Cor had said made sense of the information the dragons had provided. Jasper had little time to awe over Cor's discerning ways, however, as Ashildur answered the dwarf.

"You have always proven yourself clear-sighted and perceptive, Cor Leviel Gidfolk." There was an approving smile in Ashildur's voice that Jasper still couldn't see through the haze of bright light. "I will tell you my Father's story from the beginning."

The white dragon shifted her wings and settled them beside her, then began.

"My Father, Oer, has always been. He always is, and he always shall be. He is the essence of Being, and as such, cannot cease existing. My Mother is the same way. They enjoyed their companionship immensely in the timelessness of Nothing, but one day, they imagined a world together, a world full of life and good. Together, they formed the Universe. My Father placed the sun and its many brothers, the stars, in their places. My Mother created the night as a time of peace and rest, a perfect complement to my Father's day. Together, they imagined and fashioned Gant. They created the lands and the oceans, using raising mountains from the earth and pressing into the land to create valleys. It was pure joy for them to create together.

"They decided the first inhabitant of the new world would be an offspring rather than a creation. Thus was I born. They gave me the whole of Gant to roam, and so I did, though I always returned to this island. It became my home. They created for me an egg that I myself might mother its hatchlings, and out of it were born the gem dragons. They also allowed me to create. So were formed the drakes.

"One fateful day, in the middle of Spring, my Father and Mother made a portentous decision. It would cost each of them what they most prized—each other. They chose that day to make their own creations, apart from each other, to populate Gant with creatures of their own individual imagining. Oer created the elves and gave them their own mother, Rawa. He placed them in the lush forests they now inhabit. Next, he created the dwarves and gave them a father and king, Esh. My Father felt a great joy in creating, and he took pleasure in establishing order among his creatures.

"My Mother, however, grew jealous when she saw the elves and their matriarch, Rawa. The elves were winsome and Rawa beautiful. Perhaps my Mother feared that Oer would create for himself a creature more beautiful than herself to replace her. Perhaps she simply had her own creative ambitions and feared that my Father would outdo her. Whatever the reason, she schemed her treachery and carried it through.

"First, my Mother created the Shades and the Black Monocero. The Monocero herded the elves like so many cattle to the Shades, whom she used to sever their souls from their bodies. To keep the souls and bodies from reuniting, she transported the immaterial essence of her victims away to the desert lands, where they now live as Jini. Their bodies she ferried away to the Land of Shadows where you know them as orcs."

Ashildur stopped, perhaps to catch her breath or perhaps to allow her audience a moment to process her words. Jasper stood, bewildered, as he turned the dragon's words over in his mind. He worked backward. Kronk, being the daughter of an orc, was somehow related to the elves? And Yidda was an elvish soul? That was one of the last things Jasper had expected as an explanation for the orcs' and Jini's existences. He'd certainly never imagined the two were in any way connected. Yidda had never spoken of a previous life, and Jasper suspected that she was as surprised as he was. He decided against glancing over at her. Besides the news about Yidda, though, there was the rest of what Ashildur had told them. The story was unlike any he'd ever heard. As far as he knew, Oer created Gant for Light and Life, and Darkness had always been opposed to what was Good and True. Who was this mysterious Mother figure in Ashildur's life? Jasper had a guess, but it was too preposterous to truly consider. Besides, to speak it, to even think it, would be blasphemy, and as much as Jasper disliked Oer, he wouldn't entertain such a thing. In the end, though, Ashildur's tale was so complex and had so many subtleties, unlike any other supposed explanation of the creation of Gant, that Jasper found himself believing it.

The Dragon Mother resumed her tale, saying, "When my Father discovered my Mother's deeds, he grew furious. He sought her out and found her atop the Mount of Beginnings in the land of Eshad. He discovered her about to rain down her terror upon his dwarves. He opposed her. My Mother and Father fought on the summit of the

Mount of Beginnings. Neither could gain the advantage, however. In the end, my Mother fled to the southern lands, leaving my Father's heart in pieces. That is what we call the Breaking—the Heart of the Universe, the union of my Father's and Mother's hearts, rent itself in two.

"Today, a piece of the Heart of the Universe remains atop the Mount of Beginnings. It is there my Father sends you, Ihva Marie Marchand, and your company to retrieve his half. With it, you might approach my Mother. We seek to banish her back to the Nothing from before the Universe existed to continue her eternal existence there. Without my Father, she cannot create Time, and she will be unable to reenter the Universe. Her influence will pass away with the years, and Life and Good will rule Gant once again."

Ashildur's words slowly faded into silence, and their echoes in the cavern grew quieter until they were nothing. At the same time, Jasper saw Cor's head shift from a respectful bow to look up at the dragon before them. Into the silence, he addressed the dragon.

"We thank you for relating this painful tale, Great Dragon Mother. It is tragic indeed, and I pray we might play our roles well in redeeming the Universe from the effects of the Breaking. I offer two questions. Where might we find this Mount of Beginnings, and where then might we find your Mother?"

Ashildur's voice was quieter when she answered. "You know the Mount of Beginnings by another name—the Shrieking Summit. As for my Mother, you will find her to the south of Oerid in a mountain range in the center of the Realm of Shadows. Her lair lies in the depths beneath the highest peak. You will recognize her when you find her, for you know of her already. Her name is K'shia, but you know her as Hell's Mistress."

Even as Ashildur confirmed Jasper's suspicions, the dragon's revelation sent his mind reeling. The Lady of Shadows. It always came back to her, and now Jasper couldn't deny the fact the god of the Universe was sending them on a mission not just to outsmart but also to defeat the immeasurably powerful Mistress of Hell. Indeed, Oer was sending them on a mission to save the world and all Reality.

Jasper couldn't understand how it was all coming together, but he recognized Cor had been more right than any of them had suspected. Ihva was Oer's Blessing, and now Jasper was starting to understand what Oer meant by that. His thoughts faltered, and he stood, staring at Ashildur, his eyes searching her as though her next words might make the truth easier to bear.

He had to wait a while as no one was speaking. The room was clearing of its misty brightness, and Jasper saw Ashildur more clearly. The Dragon Mother's scales shone a brilliant, translucent white, and her blue eyes gleamed something quiet but fierce. Her tail was as long as her children's entire bodies and wrapped around in front of her. Jasper's eyes traveled up the dragon's neck to her head. It contained many sharp angles and would have seemed menacing if it hadn't been for the gentleness and pain he'd just heard in her voice. The set of long, curved horns extending back from the top of her head accompanied by a set of shorter, smaller horns outside the first ones. Each horn came to a sharp point and would have added to any foe's terror. It occurred to Jasper how fortunate it was that the Dragon Mother had aligned herself with her Father rather than with her Mother.

Even as Jasper took in the majesty of the creature before him, he felt a prick of disbelief inside. Something strange was going on. If he thought about it, Oer's plan was quite perilous. He'd included Jasper and Ihva together, he'd allowed them to fall in love, and he'd thereby allowed the great danger of the Lady of Shadows—K'shia, as Ashildur had called her—overtaking the two of them and turning Jasper against the others. For years, Jasper had held his peace with Oer. For years, he'd kept himself from decrying his plight, but this was too much, and for once, he had someone to answer his criticism. He made a conscious choice not to stop himself from speaking.

"Perhaps Oer has the good of his creation in mind," he said. "Perhaps that is true, though I cannot know. Perhaps he intends us to defeat this K'shia, yet I cannot but question how he intends to carry out this plan with his Chosen Son in such a perilous position. We of Oerid like to think of our royalty as descended from the great

Lord himself. I cannot attest to this notion's validity, but I do know this—that if this Lady obtains the heart of the Crown Prince of Oerid, she will not be easily defeated, and she will have gained a great advantage over Oer and his champions. Even without that influence, she is surely more than a match for six finite beings such as ourselves."

Indeed, it was perplexing at best that Oer would choose Jasper as one to hunt down and banish the Lady of Shadows. The Lady as near as possessed Jasper's heart already and bringing Ihva against Hell's Mistress increased the chances Jasper would find himself at the Lady's command. As soon as she could access his heart, she would have complete control of his actions, whether his intentions aligned with hers or not. He would be her puppet. Why would Oer place the group in such a hazardous position, adding Jasper to their number? Why not lock Jasper away somewhere where he could do no harm while the rest fought K'shia to cast her out? Jasper began to think Ashildur didn't intend to answer him when he heard the Dragon Mother breathe a sigh.

"When my Mother fled, my Father hid his piece of the Heart away on the summit of the Mount of Beginnings," she replied. "Then he made his way to the large, uninhabited land to the east. Mankind was his final creation, the crowning glory of all he had fashioned. He named their nation Oerid and breathed his spirit into the first men and women he placed there. He appointed their first king and established him in Agda, and upon each king thereafter he bestowed his blessing. So indeed, Jasper Thesson Aurdor, the Father established you. The Aurdor dynasty was named for his love for the creatures he created."

"Yet he allowed it to end that night twenty years ago," Jasper interjected. He kept himself from glaring, but his voice was stern and accusing.

"He did not allow it to end, young Prince, as surely as you stand here before me," Ashildur returned in a patient voice.

"Without the aid of his treacherous Wife, I would not be standing here," Jasper came back. This was no way to speak to the daughter of the god and goddess of Creation, Jasper knew, but the force of years of confusion, frustration, and anger drove the words out of him.

"Oer has foreseen the potential of his creatures and their choices since he created them. He knew your father might accept K'shia's aid. He knew Theophilus's sin before Theophilus had the choice presented to him." Ashildur peered at Jasper as he grappled with her words. "Your situation is no accident, Jasper Thesson Aurdor, and neither is your place in this fellowship. You are every bit as essential as your companions to my Father's plans.

"My Mother stole your heart for reasons more complex than you could guess. For one, she knew that owning one of Oer's kings would be effective in breaking her Husband's heart further. As though her initial betrayal were not enough, she knew turning one of my Father's own against him would deepen the wound she had dealt him and that it would weaken him. She seeks to take the Universe for herself. You cannot allow her to do so."

"I cannot engage a Being who holds my very life over me," Jasper replied, now as perplexed and frustrated as he was upset.

"You must not allow your understanding of what constitutes feasibility to guide you." Ashildur looked hard at Jasper. "Do you find the peace of Gant worth your trouble? Do you know the value of a soul, even one soul, saved from the Shadow?"

Jasper looked back at Ashildur, not saying anything, and the dragon turned her eyes to Ihva.

"Do you, Jasper Thesson Aurdor, believe her courage and her peace worth the difficulty you might have in defending them? For she requires your hope as you require air to breathe. Without your support and that of your companions, she will fail. It is not up to her alone as Oer's Blessing to summon back the good of Gant. It is upon all of you and each of you to uphold her."

Jasper was quiet, feeling chastened. At the same time, he was trying to understand all Ashildur had said. His inclusion was no accident. His *existence* was no accident, and Ihva needed him to stand by her if she was to succeed, if they were to succeed. Jasper felt conflicted, torn between believing Ashildur, holding onto the hope she offered, and rejecting her words as preposterous jabberings of a strange creature from a strange land. He would have liked to choose the latter, but the former drew him, attracted him like a moth to the firelight. He yielded and hoped he wouldn't, like a moth, find himself incinerated by the outcome.

"Prince of Oerid," Ashildur went on. "Oer's Chosen Son, your love for this young woman will be your saving grace on the day of peril. You cannot break what secures you to her, and neither can she break her need for you. Do right, young Prince. Pursue justice and do good."

Ashildur seemed to be peering into Jasper's soul as she spoke, and indeed, he felt suddenly exposed. He realized at that moment the Dragon Mother knew his secrets, his most private sentiments. He couldn't hide. A sense of vulnerability overcame him, but he refused to look away. Ashildur's gaze bore into him, and he became intensely aware of his own frailty. Struggling hard against self-doubt, he grasped to maintain his hold on what little courage he had. Eventually, Ashildur broke his gaze and spoke to them all.

"I fear there is little time to waste, now," she said. "I know questions will plague you from this time until all becomes right again, but to explain it all would rob us of precious time we must use to oppose the Shadow. We must bring you to the mainland."

As Ashildur spoke, a trickle of light streamed down from above. The rays brightened, and Jasper looked up to see the ceiling of the cave parting and sunlight breaking in. He covered his eyes once again to keep from being blinded.

Chapter 45

THE GROUND ABOVE THE CAVERN split open, and sunlight poured in. The platform where Ihva and her companions stood shot upward. Balancing herself against the shaking, she watched the sides of the cavern rush past. There was a sudden jolt when the cave's floor settled level with the ground above them, knocking her to the ground. She made sure they were no longer moving, then stood, dusted herself off, and looked around.

They'd entered the caves when the sun had been a little past its zenith, but it now hung low on the western horizon. It was perhaps an hour before sunset. Ihva looked south and saw they were atop the cliff again, a half mile or so from the edge. She couldn't see the ocean from where they stood. As she turned to the west, the remains of Wymon came into view, about a mile away. She stopped breathing as visions of light pillars and explosions flashed in her mind. She hadn't apologized.

The sound of beating air interjected itself into her mind, though. She turned toward the noise and saw Ashildur descending from above her and the others and landing on the ground in front of them. The noise didn't stop, just changed as smaller wings sounded around them. Ihva spun to see all four of the gem dragons landing in a circle surrounding her and her companions.

"You sought transportation to the continent, and we will provide it. We will convey you to the mainland so that you might continue your journey," Ashildur said. Her voice didn't seem to surround Ihva in the same way as before without echoes reinforcing it.

The gem dragons took a moment to approach Ihva's companions, lowering their wings to the ground to make it easier to climb atop them. Blarr chose Yidda, Graiyent chose Malach, and Gulur chose Cor while Raidurr approached Kronk. The orc-blood woman looked back at Ihva with wide eyes, and Ihva started forward to join her when someone touched her shoulder. Looking back, she found it was Jasper. Beyond him, she saw the Dragon Mother motion her to her side with her tail. Ihva hesitated, then turned and tried to give Kronk an encouraging look. She was relieved to see the woman make her way onto Raidurr's back.

Once Ihva was certain Kronk looked comfortable on her own, she turned back to Jasper and Ashildur and gave herself no room for second thoughts as she strode ahead. The Dragon Mother had settled onto the ground and slanted her wing down. Ihva scaled her height first, and Jasper followed, then they settled in with Ihva behind him at the base of Ashildur's neck.

The dragons' wings began to move, creating currents of air around their riders. All five of the magnificent creatures ascended into the air. Ihva wasn't usually afraid of heights but looking down as the ground disappeared underneath them made her queasy. She turned her gaze back up. As they started forward, she squeezed her arms around Jasper and found him trembling. It surprised her, but then she felt her own heart fluttering as well. Something about soaring above the ocean's waters with him so near stirred a type of energy in her, and the moment became something timeless and eternal. It was a few minutes before either of them spoke.

"Are you alright?" he asked finally.

She rested her chin on his shoulder, unsure how to respond. Ashildur's flight was smooth, and everything around them was tranquil. The breeze rushing past was steady, the waves beneath them were even and small, and the clouds remained before them, high in the sky, unmoving. Everything was untroubled, and though Ashildur's tale had shaken Ihva, she realized that she was at peace.

"It's not every day you find out you're part of a story that started before Time itself," Jasper said after a moment.

He turned and gave her a small smile. It was reserved and distracted.

"I'm alright. Very much alright," she replied. "Are you?"

He didn't appear alright.

"Yes, I'm fine," he said unconvincingly. He glanced at her for a split second, then stared straight ahead.

"You don't seem alright," she replied, thinking she might as well take the direct route.

His mouth twitched, but he said nothing. He was going to make her pry. She hated prying. He hadn't taken it well back in M'rawa, but then again, he'd been trying to keep secrets from her back then. He wasn't doing that anymore, or at least she hoped he wasn't. She gave a small sigh. She knew what was bothering him, at least she had an idea.

"I don't think Oer hates you, Jasper," she said, then waited a second for her words to sink in. She didn't expect an answer, and she didn't get one. "It's a lot to take in, I know, but from everything she said, I can't believe he would include you if he hated you," Ihva went on.

"But if he knows so much about us, about our temperaments and views, why would he choose someone so skeptical?" Jasper returned. "If he knows I can't help but mistrust him and that I find myself infuriated whenever I think of him, why would he allow me anywhere near this company, much less be some kind of integral part of it? It makes no sense." He looked back at Ihva, then his tone became softer. "Sorry. It upsets you to hear this."

It did upset her, but she wasn't upset at him, rather she was upset for him.

"Sorry, Ihva. I don't mean to trouble you. I tell you about hope, I try saying it's worthwhile, but maybe I'm telling you as much to convince myself as to encourage you."

Sadly, that made sense, she realized.

"It's okay," she replied. She tried to sound soothing, but this was unsettling her. She wasn't sure how to convince him, how to supply him faith, when he was so obviously embittered against it all.

"It's all confused in my head, Ihva. I don't know how to untangle it. To be honest, I don't know if I care to untangle it anymore. Sometimes it's better to sever the knot than to try to unravel it."

She felt desperation surface, and she tried to calm herself before she spoke. "You don't have to untangle it alone," she said.

"No, I know I don't, but there comes a point when a person has to make a choice of what he's going to take as truth. There's a point he has to decide which reality is his reality."

"I can help you."

"You can't believe for me, Ihva." He turned and gave her a steady look. "No one can do that."

She looked back at him and tried not to let defeat show in her face. "Isn't there something I can do?"

Some emotion flashed across his face, but it was too fast for her to decipher what it was, then he looked sad. "I don't know," was all he replied.

He turned to face forward again, looking out over the ocean while she drew back. She was distraught. He *had* to get a grip. He *had* to figure it out. She wasn't sure what her role in that should be. As it was, his presence was leaving her more troubled than she would otherwise have been instead of lending her courage and faith. Was Ashildur wrong about the two of them? Ihva stared off into the distance, trying to understand.

"I'm sorry, Ihva."

Jasper's voice was so soft the wind almost tore his words away before Ihva could hear them. She guessed it had been half an hour since they'd last spoken. She didn't respond—she didn't know how to.

"I'm sorry," he repeated.

He shifted, then turned himself around to face backward on Ashildur, looking Ihva in the eye. He was frowning.

"Is it true what Ashildur said about me? You need my help?" he asked.

Ihva blinked as he took her hands in his.

"Yes. Yes, I told you that before, didn't I?" she replied.

"Yes, but I wasn't sure. You were distressed and I wasn't sure it wasn't just you feeling upset."

"No, I meant it."

"I'm sorry, then," he said. "I've been thinking of myself, my own predicament, my own troubles. I want to be here in what way you need—to support, to encourage, to inspire. I can't do that when I'm so focused on myself."

Ihva peered at him. How was he planning to do that instead?

"I love you, Ihva, and by that love, I pledge to do exactly those things," he went on.

She hesitated to respond.

"I'll stand by you. I promise you that," he finished.

She nodded slowly. He took one of his hands from hers and placed it against her cheek. Staring at him in uncertainty, she found her voice after a moment.

"I don't understand," she said quietly. "You mean you're going to believe for me? I thought you said that's impossible."

He blinked. "No. I mean, I know I can't, but I can point you in the right direction."

He wanted to bolster her hope, but how could he do that when he didn't believe it himself?

"But—" she began.

He interrupted, though, saying, "I'm sorry. I didn't mean all that earlier. I was confused. You've been chosen to save Gant, and we've been chosen to help you, and that's what we're going to do."

She stared at him for a moment in surprise, then in perplexity. She knew he was sincere—he had a genuine desire to help—but he lacked hope himself. He gave her another distracted smile, and her heart sank. She smiled back, though, and he watched her for another second before turning back around to face forward. Wrapping her arms around him again, she squeezed him tight with the strange feeling that she was losing him. To what, she didn't know, but he wasn't fully hers and she wondered if he'd ever be.

Chapter 46

IHVA WASN'T AWARE OF HOW much time had passed before she felt Ashildur descending. She removed her arms from around Jasper and looked down. She couldn't help but be discouraged. The world was in pieces, the Shadow threatened to overwhelm the Light, it was up to them to keep Gant from cataclysm, and the one she wanted to count on was struggling to hold even himself up.

Ashildur landed on the sand. Ihva's mind was still in the sky, but she forced herself to slide down the Dragon Mother's wing to the ground beneath. Jasper, who had gone before her, caught her arm at the bottom and kept her from falling. Finally, when everyone was standing together on the beach, Ashildur spoke her parting words. She described their location—the northwest corner of Oerid—and instructed them where to find the nearest port where they might purchase. Then Ashildur spoke of the Mount of Beginnings.

"On the Mountain dwell various hostile creatures, but none should prove too great a challenge for you, nothing more terrible than that which you have already faced. It shall be the temple that presents the greatest test, but do not be dismayed. The Father is with you. My Mother will not attempt to face you on the summit of the Mountain. She knows her greatest chance lies in luring you into her cavern, into her lair. You must obtain my Father's portion of the Heart in order to banish her back to Nothing. The Father will aid you when the time comes to expel her from this domain, but you are responsible to reunite the Heart of the Universe.

"Now, I must bid you farewell. I have fulfilled my duty, and though I yearn to do more, I am limited to supplying the information I have provided to you. I will remind you once more of these things—maintain hope, encourage each other in confident conviction, and remember your fellowship in love for one another. These things alone will sustain you to the end."

As Ashildur finished saying these words, she immediately turned north and beat her wings against the evening air to take flight. The gem dragons nodded their departing salutations and took to the air after the Mother. Ihva watched them disappear into the distance, where stars began to appear in the twilight.

An hour later, Ihva and the others gathered around a small fire. After the dragons had disappeared from view, they had split up to find firewood, mostly driftwood washed up on the beach. No one was particularly hungry, so they each ate a small portion of the dried fish left over from Wymon. No one spoke for a while either. Instead, everyone stared into the flames. The dancing light mesmerized Ihva, and she wasn't exactly thinking, rather she was feeling, filtering through the various emotions of the past twenty-four hours, sifting through them to experience each one individually.

"There is much to consider, tonight," Cor said finally. He looked around at the others.

"I'd say!" Malach replied, then began to mutter to himself. "A visit to blessed dragons, for Esh's sake. A dwarf's not cut out for these things."

Ihva turned her attention back to Cor.

309

"There's much we need to discuss," Yidda said. "Our course of action is set before us, but we must first decide the steps we plan to take to obtain our objective."

"It might be best that we first consider the revelations we have received," Cor replied gently, his gaze on Yidda, who in turn lowered her eyes.

"Yidda's right, Cor. We can discuss as much as we want, but it doesn't matter what we think of it all. It remains true no matter what we believe, and the only thing to do is obey the instructions given to us," came Jasper's sharp response.

Ihva looked over at him. He was watching Cor with a guarded look, his arms crossed in front of him.

"Yet each of us must grapple with his role, Jasper, and one cannot obey an instruction he has not accepted except with reluctance and resentment," Cor returned, an edge to his words as well.

He and Jasper stared at each other for a long moment, and the tension in the air became palpable. Ihva shifted, uncomfortable, and turned her eyes to the ground.

"And how do you propose we go about 'accepting' all these divine instructions and such?" Malach asked, breaking the silence.

Cor turned toward him and replied in a softer voice, "We have received information vital to our task, and it is incumbent upon us to try to understand it."

Malach nodded but didn't say anything, and Ihva's eyes flickered to Jasper, who was sitting with his arms still crossed.

"Where do you propose we start?" Yidda asked quietly.

"With what we know," Cor answered her.

She nodded and murmured her agreement, as did Ihva.

"Well, I don't know about you all, but I know blessed little except we're supposed to be finding some shard of a heart or something like that and taking it to the Shadowed Realm," Malach said with a shiver. "And that Ihva's going to lead the way," he added as an afterthought.

At the last statement, Ihva shivered as well. She was going to face the Lady of Shadows, just like Cor had predicted. At least she wouldn't be alone.

"Indeed, that is true," Cor replied. He opened his mouth to continue speaking, but Malach cut him off.

"My question is, how in the world are six humble souls such as ourselves going to go up against the Lady herself and even think we might defeat her? Makes no sense! Even if we have the Blessing on our side, there's no way!" He glanced at Ihva. "Not to dismiss you, lass. I mean, what you did back there was quite a feat to be sure, but this is the Mistress of Hell we're talking about."

Ihva shook her head. She knew exactly what Malach was talking about, and she agreed. She didn't know if she could repeat what happened at Wymon. She wasn't sure she wanted to. Malach started to go on, but it was Cor's turn to interrupt.

"Peace, Malach," he said, then scanned the group. "We are not to defeat her, merely to reunify the Heart of the Universe to allow the Father to banish her."

"Oh, right," Malach came back. "We've just got to steal her most precious artifact from under her nose—from her own realm, I might add—and get it reunited with its other half, which we also must steal, and wait around until Oer figures out how to get rid of her. No big deal. Should be home in time for dinner."

Cor watched Malach for a moment after he finished speaking, then responded, "I did not say it would be easy."

Malach grumbled something and crossed his arms as well.

"They didn't indicate it would be effortless, Malach. In fact, they spoke repeatedly of the difficulty of our task. They didn't say it was impossible either, though," Yidda said.

At this point, Ihva decided to speak up. "I don't know how we're supposed to do any of it, but they told us we have to so there must be some way to do it." She glanced around, afraid of the others' reactions. "Oer wouldn't tell us to do something if it was hopeless," she went on. She turned to Jasper and found his brow furrowed. "I mean, I don't think he would," she added.

"It doesn't matter either way," Jasper said. "We have a task, and we must do it—possible or impossible, favorable or hopeless. It sounds as though Gant will fall without us. We have no choice."

"I do not agree. Rather we must rely on hope or we will inevitably fail," Cor began. "Without confidence and reliance on the power that enables us to this task, we have nothing."

Jasper stared at Cor for a moment. "Rely on hope, then, Cor," he said finally. "Rely on belief and conviction and trust in your blessed Oer. It doesn't matter. It's all the same. When it comes down to it, it is our own choices that will determine the fate of the world, and we're going to have to live with that, one way or another. If I act rightly, it is for the sake of Oerid and for the sake of all of you, and whatever comes of that will come of it. That's just how it is." He paused and took a breath. "In any case, I'm going to bed. It's been a long day."

Cor watched Jasper with a frown but didn't say anything. Ihva and the others looked around at each other, then watched Jasper get up and rifle through the packs.

"No blankets," he said.

"We did not find any in Wymon," Cor said. "We must rely on the warmth of the fire tonight."

Jasper frowned at Cor but made to settle on the ground near the flames. He glanced at Ihva for a brief moment, a pained look in his eyes, then a mask of stoicism covered whatever emotion he might have had.

Then Ihva and the others laid themselves out around the fire, and Ihva heard snoring a few minutes later.

As tired as she was, she couldn't immediately fall asleep. She glimpsed Jasper looking at her from across the fire. As soon as he saw her notice him, though, he shut his eyes. She slowly shut her eyes as well. What in the world had Ashildur been talking about?

Chapter 47

IHVA MUST HAVE BEEN EXHAUSTED as she was still fast asleep when Jasper awoke at dawn. He was disappointed but used the time when no one else was awake to watch the sun rise and try to sort through all that had happened and all they'd learned.

What he had a hard time believing was that Oer had meant for everything to turn out like it was, that Oer had chosen him, of all people, for this task. Jasper was a grave danger to the rest. His presence with them generated a need to protect him from the Lady, from K'shia. Jasper's company created certain dilemmas they could otherwise avoid. It complicated their assignment and needlessly so. Still, Jasper remembered Ashildur's reprimanding words, her reproachful questions. Ihva needed him, and he couldn't focus on his skepticism if he was to help her. He needed to believe it all for her, or at least he had to act like he did. He wasn't sure if he could, but he had to try. At the very least, he'd make a valiant effort.

He turned to look at her. She was still sleeping and appeared at peace. There was the thrill of knowing she was his, somehow, and it competed with despondency for his attention. Ihva believed Ashildur, and she seemed so unconflicted as a result. She had focus and resolve and was bent on a single, noble purpose. Jasper wished he could say the same of himself, but he was desperately torn. He shook his head and turned his attention back to Ihva.

She was beautiful, but for the first time, her beauty felt completely out of his reach. Even in M'rawa, when he'd known she'd never be his, there had still been a sense of nearness to her. Now it was as though she existed in some other world, some other Reality, or perhaps he was the one who did, but either way, something intangible yet completely impassable separated them. He'd wanted to share in her hope, in her life, and maybe he'd walk with her through it all, but something fundamental divided them. He'd never take part with her in how she was living—her existence, her aspirations, their fulfillment—not as he so longed to do.

He was still looking at her when Cor awakened and caught his eye. Shame washed over Jasper. Cor had only been trying to encourage everyone last night, and Jasper had ruined it. All of a sudden, Jasper didn't know what to say, but Cor stood and walked over to where he was sitting. There the dwarf sat down. He was quiet, and Jasper sat in painful silence for a few minutes. Finally, Cor spoke, his voice soft and his tone solemn.

"I have not seen you so troubled in a long time."

Jasper didn't respond. What could he even say? Was Cor not going to reprimand him?

"Perhaps you intend to keep silent, but I cannot abide it." Cor paused again, and it dawned on Jasper that the dwarf was trying to encourage *him* now. Jasper stiffened as Cor went on. "I have seen you through many trials, Jasper, but none as grave as the one you face now. It is understandable that you are distraught, but you know as well as I that hiding from it and from us will do nothing to resolve the tensions you feel and cannot assuage your fears."

Jasper turned to look Cor in the eye. He wasn't hiding from it. He was considering the evidence and evaluating the options. Maybe he was delaying the inevitable choice between hope and despair, but it was because he wasn't sure how to make the decision he needed to make.

"I'm not hiding, Cor."

Cor raised an eyebrow.

"I'm not," Jasper said.

Cor was silent. The dwarf knew trying to convince Jasper was useless and that his silence held more sway than his words. Once again, it worked. Jasper gave in. He'd confide in Cor again, even if there was no wisdom in all of Gant the dwarf could offer that could resolve things.

"What have I done, Cor? I should never have told her. I should've let her be, let her feelings fade. There'd be no danger then." He slumped his shoulders and looked back at the ground, then continued. "It might have even worked. She didn't love me until I made it absolutely clear how I felt for her. If she'd had no idea, if I'd kept silent, she might have escaped this menace. She might have escaped me." His final words trailed off. He hadn't known he felt this way until the words escaped his lips. He was the danger posed to Ihva. He was the one she needed to fear.

"The greatest risks sometimes offer the most precious rewards, Jasper," Cor said.

Jasper looked at Cor, and the dwarf went on.

"Do you recall what your father told you about your grandmother, Lady Gianna?"

Jasper remembered. His mother, Theresa Richolle, was the daughter of Lord Daxton and Lady Gianna Richolle, who'd ruled Tarda, the southwestern province bordering the Cibelles' charge. Gianna had died in a battle with orcs, so Jasper had never known her. Like the Cibelles in Hestia, the Richolles and the Tardans faced the constant onslaught of orcs into their lands, and the men of Tarda pledged themselves to defend Tarda and Oerid. The Tardans also had ties to the elves, protecting them from the menace as well. Lady Gianna was a noble and courageous woman who'd sacrificed her life to save her children.

"Gianna, your grandmother, was besieged in the walls of the Richolle manor with your mother and her two younger brothers. Daxton, your grandfather, was away with his soldiers trying to drive another band of orcs back into the Shadowed Realm. Now, your

315

mother was already wed to young Theophilus at the time and was in Tarda for a visit. She'd always been homesick in the palace in Agda, after all. Gianna knew there was little chance of them all surviving with orcs at the walls of the manor and a small company of soldiers to defend them. The soldiers were of the royal guard, being your mother's escort, but there were many more orcs than soldiers."

Jasper nodded. He knew this story well. Gianna had let down the manor's defenses and sent Theresa and her brothers along with some guards through the underground passage that led out beyond the manor walls. Then, Gianna had lured the orcs into the manor, away from where the passageway opened on the other side. She'd fought valiantly but eventually surrendered her life to save her children. What did this have to do with Jasper?

"Your grandmother risked the last thing she had, her life, and she saved your mother and Oerid."

Indeed, she'd saved Oerid, too. If Jasper's mother had been slaughtered along with the rest, Oerid would have lost her Queen and the chance of an heir by her.

"Gianna knew her death was not merely a possibility but a probability. She risked everything to gain something even greater. Ultimately, she gave everything to gain an even more precious reward. It is Oer's way, Jasper. There is always an exchange."

An exchange. Jasper could see the logic of Cor's argument. Still, what did that have to do with Jasper?

"I get it, Cor, but I don't see how it relates. It's not just me I'm placing in danger but *them*." He swept his hand toward where the others lay sleeping. "I'm endangering *you*, Cor. If it was just me, fine. I'd understand. I don't mind sacrificing myself for Oerid or for Gant, as it may be, but I can't put all of you in danger for the sake of Oerid and Gant. Your lives are not mine to offer."

"As I told you concerning Ihva, we are making our own choices. Do not make them for us."

Jasper was about to respond but realized he didn't know what to say and closed his mouth. It was Cor who spoke next instead.

"Oer has pronounced you a part of this company, Jasper. You would do well to heed him. He will not be mocked."

"You might die because of me, Cor!" The words burst out of Jasper's mouth before he could contain them, and he spoke them with vehemence.

Cor gave him a hard look. "It is true. I might die, you might die, we all might die, but if that is the price to be paid for peace in Gant, I believe it is a small one compared to its outcome, and if it is the price we must pay trying to achieve peace in Gant, then it is what must be paid. An exchange must be made, our security and perhaps our lives for our brothers and sisters, for the world. We cannot dismiss our task so easily, though, simply because it might be costly. Surely you would say the same."

Jasper stared at Cor. He hated to admit that Cor's logic was valid. He found it interesting the dwarf had approached him with this tactic. Of course, Cor could have tried to convince him it would all turn out fine, that hope was what would carry them through, but the dwarf hadn't. He'd appealed to Jasper's sense of duty, and Jasper was becoming quickly convinced that Cor was right. Jasper couldn't spurn his responsibility, god-given or otherwise, especially not if he professed to care for the nation that held that deity as her god.

"You're right," Jasper admitted quietly, then fell silent.

He refused to sulk. If he was going to accept his task like Cor had told him to, he had to do it unswerving, not with half a mind to turn around and reject it again. He raised his shoulders and straightened his back, then turned his eyes up to the eastern horizon. The sky was becoming steadily brighter. He set his mouth firm with resolve.

"What do you plan to do about Ihva?"

Cor's question jolted Jasper. What did the dwarf mean, what would Jasper do about Ihva? He'd support her, encourage her, raise her up when she fell down. What was the dwarf asking?

"What do you mean?" Jasper turned to look at Cor and found the dwarf giving him a steady stare.

"You can continue your secret, circumspect cuddling, enjoyable but directionless, or you can make your intentions clear," Cor replied.

"What do you mean?" Jasper repeated, though he thought he knew what Cor was getting at.

"It will not be long before you are again in the public eye. It would not do to continue as you are. A prince cannot go around as you have with her in the view of his subjects. Oer's Chosen Son is not one who can let things remain undefined."

"What are you saying, Cor?" Jasper asked again, refusing to acknowledge what he realized the dwarf was saying. He felt suddenly uncomfortable where he was sitting. The rock beneath him was sharper than he'd thought, and the muscles in his back felt tight. He refused to shift though and kept looking the dwarf in the eye.

"I think you understand, son." Cor's voice was suddenly kinder, empathetic, and Jasper let himself relax. The dwarf wasn't trying to challenge or criticize him but to make him think. It was an important thing to think about, too. Of course, Jasper knew he'd ask her to marry him. He'd known that night talking to Malach, and he'd wanted it since long before that, if he was honest with himself. It occurred to him, though—what would Father think?

"I know what I want, Cor. I'm certain of it." Jasper paused and took a breath. Cor waited for him to go on, so he did. "I know it might sound ridiculous, but I want to marry her. I want to—I've never been so sure of anything before—only that I can't just do whatever I want. There's a lot more to it."

"With Lady Jessica's passing, you are free to do so."

"I know, Cor."

Jasper hesitated. Even with Jessica gone, dead, something Jasper still hated himself for, he couldn't imagine Father would take kindly to the news his son wanted to marry a common merchant's daughter who also happened to be Oer's Blessing. Jasper looked to Cor for an answer, and Cor gave it.

"Your father would not begrudge you such a union," the dwarf said. "You are already bound to her, Jasper. The honorable course of action is to marry her."

Jasper didn't respond, at least not with words. A slow smile of relief spread across his face, and he didn't mask it. If Cor had said it, it was likely true. Maybe Father wouldn't disapprove. Jasper felt suddenly grateful and immensely indebted to Cor. He wasn't sure what else to do but express his gratitude, and he was about to when he heard a shift of gravel behind him. He turned quickly to see who it was and felt himself flush when he saw it was Ihva. How much had she heard?

"Ihva." He spoke her name awkwardly and was searching for words when Cor interjected.

"Good morning, Ihva," the dwarf said.

"Good morning," she replied.

She looked at the ground and moved a pebble with the toe of her boot. What had she heard? Jasper cringed when he recalled Cor's last statement about "such a union" and marrying her. She knew what they'd been talking about. She had to.

"I didn't mean to sleep so late," she added after an awkward second.

"We all needed our rest," Cor replied. "Join us, Ihva. It is a beautiful morning."

She stepped forward and sat down in the space Cor made between himself and Jasper. She was looking at the horizon. Jasper couldn't tell if she was making a point not to glance at him, but he feared she was. Did she not want to marry him? It was all a little fast, he had to admit, but they'd traveled together for months, for Oer's sake. It wasn't like they were strangers.

"How are you, Ihva?" Cor asked.

Ihva didn't say anything, and Jasper wasn't about to stare at her, waiting for her response. He realized he was making a point to watch the horizon, too.

"It is a lot to take in, what the Dragon Mother told us," Cor continued.

"Yeah," she replied a second later. "There's a lot we didn't know."

"It is easy for her words to trouble us, Ihva, but we must not allow them to. She spoke as much hope as she did danger and

319

darkness. We are not as insufficient as you might believe. Take Wymon as proof."

Ihva flinched again at the mention of the drake city, and Jasper sensed the tensions in her rise. He wished he had something comforting to say. The sound of horses' hooves on the ground behind them interrupted his thoughts, however. The three turned toward the path at the edge of camp.

Two men on horseback approached at a canter. As they came closer, Jasper could see they were dressed in leather armor and carried longswords at their sides. He spotted bows and quivers on them as well. Then, something moved behind the horsemen and caught Jasper's eye as well. A coach was coming toward them along the path. Four more men on horses were with it.

Jasper rushed back to the others and shook Malach awake. At the same time, he called out to Kronk and Yidda.

"Wake up! We have visitors," he called out.

The three lying down began to stir, and at Jasper's warning tone, they shot up. Jasper saw Ihva rush over and pick up Darkslayer, and his eyes shot to Malach to check if he had his knife handy. A sword and three knives. Jasper slipped one of his daggers to Cor and turned to face the horsemen.

The horses stopped about ten paces from Jasper and the group, and the men dismounted. One was tall and dark-haired with piercing eyes and a trim, black beard, and the other was shorter and more wiry with red hair and a matching red beard. They both touched their swords as the dark-haired one stepped forward and spoke.

"Greetings," the man began in a cautious tone.

He glanced at Ihva and the others, and his eyes kept returning to Yidda. He seemed on edge.

"Good morrow," Jasper replied, stepping out in front of the others.

He had a hand on a knife at his side. This was his kingdom. He ought to take point.

"What business do you have along this stretch of road, may we inquire?" It was the dark-haired man who spoke again.

"We might ask the same of you," Jasper replied.

The coach approached along with the four other horsemen, as well-armed as the man before him, and a woman on horseback alongside. As Jasper got a better look at the coach, he realized it was fitted with armor, too. It made him anxious. The wealthiest of traders often sent armored carriages along land routes, but they boasted at least three or four coaches at a time with three times as many guards. Seeing just one, Jasper was wary.

"We are but simple travelers on our way to seek our fortune in the capital." The man's voice jarred Jasper's attention back to the present conversation.

Cor had made his way forward and was standing next to Jasper. "Well-armed for simple travelers," the dwarf said.

"Roth, they don't have anything. Let them be, and let's be on our way," came the voice of the woman riding up.

"Perhaps not. We shall see," the dark-haired man replied.

The other man on the ground slowly unsheathed his sword. Ihva had crept to stand beside Jasper, and Jasper saw her go to unsheath Darkslayer.

"I wouldn't do that if I were you, young lady," the red-haired man said. His eyes were on her blade.

Jasper narrowed his eyes at the horseman. What were these people hoping to get out of them?

"Check their purses," the man called Roth ordered.

"Seriously, Roth?" The woman sounded annoyed.

"Yes, Anna. They are well-dressed. That one wears royal garb, tattered as it may be. Who knows what they might have hidden in purses or pockets?" Roth replied, indicating Cor with a wave of his hand.

Ihva started at something Roth had said, but Jasper wasn't sure what. She might have been afraid of what Jasper now recognized as bandits. He drew his dagger, and at the same time, Roth unsheathed his sword and made ready to come toward the group. Jasper and the others didn't have much, and Jasper knew enough to suspect the bandits might turn to violence in their disappointment.

"Anna!" Ihva cried out. She spoke as though she knew the other woman.

"Yes, dear?" Anna said, sneering as she peered at Ihva, but then her tone changed. "Ihva, is that you?"

"Yes, it's me."

Jasper could tell the confidence in Ihva's voice was feigned. The men slowed their advance as Anna spoke again.

"What are you doing out here? Aren't you supposed to be in Agda?" Her tone had a touch of bitterness as she added, "What could possibly tear you away from your life of wealth and ease?"

Ihva recoiled, and Jasper remembered back in the first days of their journey together, Ihva had mentioned an Anna. Could this be the same one? The armed men had stopped, though they continued to brandish their swords. Before anyone else could speak, though, Malach's voice called out with authority, and he indicated Jasper with his hand.

"You dare advance in this manner on your Prince? Stand down!"

Jasper froze. That was probably the worst thing Malach could have done. Perhaps the dwarf thought the invocation of such authority would bow the bandits into submission, but Jasper knew otherwise. They'd ransom him before they stood down. The other men on horseback came closer and were about to dismount when they heard Malach's words. They looked at each other, ignoring Anna. Glances of understanding passed between them.

"The Prince, you say?" Roth looked to be scheming, then glanced at Cor. "And I take it you with the royal emblem are his guard?"

Jasper drew his dagger.

"Excellent," Roth mused. "Quite excellent."

At his sneer, Ihva raised her blade, and Jasper hoped Malach would do the same. It was up to them to save the group.

Chapter 48

IHVA HELD DARKSLAYER IN FRONT of her, ready to attack. She stood in front of the others, as did Jasper and Malach. The horsemen closed. She struck out at the one called Roth, slicing toward his side. She didn't want to kill him, just disable him. He dodged and swung his sword with both hands in her direction. She parried, and the clang of metal against metal split the air. He tried to push her blade out of the way. She struggled to force him back but found Darkslayer inching closer to her.

Then she found a sword point at her throat. Her eyes ran up the blade to the red-haired man's face. He looked at her, his mouth twisted in a sour expression. She stopped pushing against the other man's sword, but she didn't lower Darkslayer.

Out of the corner of her eye, she saw Jasper and Malach were similarly subdued. For a brief moment, she considered calling on Oer's power to disperse their attackers, but she wasn't sure whether she'd catch Anna in the explosion. What was Anna doing here anyway? Roth circled around as the other swordsman kept his blade against Ihva's neck. He was pressing it hard against her, and she was afraid he would pierce the skin. Roth wrenched Darkslayer out of her hand and tossed the blade on the ground out of everyone's reach.

"Release her," Jasper said, his voice cold as ice.

"Oh, does she mean something to you, *Prince?*" Roth pronounced Jasper's title mockingly.

Ihva turned her head slightly to see Jasper's face. His eyes were narrowed as he stared at Roth with contempt. He didn't say a word.

Roth chuckled. "You won't say, then? I guess you won't mind then if, let's say, something were to happen to her." He signaled the red-haired man. "Go ahead, Justin."

The sword's point at Ihva's throat dug in, and she felt a painful prick as it broke the skin. She tried not to wince, but she couldn't help jerking back. A small trail of blood must have begun to flow, as she felt a slow, thin stream down her neck.

"Stop!" Jasper shouted.

Suddenly, the sword that had pierced Ihva's throat freed itself from the man's hand and spun around in the air. Its tip flew to Justin's throat and remained there. She could see the pressure it had against his neck from the indent it made in his skin. She searched for the source of the movement. As she glanced at Jasper, she saw a look of intense concentration on his face and heard him muttering words under his breath. He'd dropped his dagger and held his sword-hand out in front of him toward the blade in the air. He was trembling.

"I wouldn't do that if I were you." Roth's voice shook, but he maintained an outward appearance of calm. At the same time, he grabbed Ihva's shoulder and roughly shoved the tip of his blade between her breasts toward her heart. She could tell from Roth's violent motions he wasn't afraid to kill her. She glanced at Anna pleadingly, but the girl didn't meet her gaze. Instead, she directed a look of vexation and disgust at Roth. Ihva looked back at Jasper. He looked pained, like he wanted to shut his eyes but couldn't.

"If you come quietly, we won't hurt your ladylove here," Roth said, his tone scornful.

Jasper looked about to try something, but he must have thought better of it. He glanced at Ihva with apology in his eyes and lowered his sword-hand. The sword he'd animated dropped to the ground with a clatter. Justin retrieved it and trained it on Ihva once again.

The man behind Jasper pulled the prince's hands behind his back, keeping them from making any further motions.

"Now come with us." Roth motioned for Jasper and Ihva to walk toward the carriage.

"What about the others, Roth?" Anna sounded irritated.

Ihva looked back and saw the other horsemen had created a wall between her and the rest of their party. Kronk was glaring and her mouth twisted with fury, but with a sword point trained on her throat, she must have known enough to remain compliant. Everyone else's expressions were a mixture of alarm and indignation, but they too stayed put.

"We won't be needing them. Just the Prince here and his little pretty to make sure he behaves. Lady Cibelle will certainly pay a high price to receive her prince back, not to mention the King himself."

Ihva's breath caught. Lady Cibelle? She was alive? Ihva turned her eyes to Jasper once again. His eyes were wide as well.

"Lady Cibelle has returned to the capital, then?" he asked.

Ihva picked up on the shock in his voice, though he masked it well.

"About three weeks ago. Why? What did you think, she was dead?" Roth laughed.

Jasper didn't answer but exchanged a look with Ihva. She couldn't tell if he was trying to communicate something or was simply sharing the bewilderment she felt.

"Oh," came Anna's voice behind Roth. The word drew out in recognition. "No, Roth. He's afraid we'll share our little discovery here with his betrothed, this dalliance with the precious commoner of his." Anna studied Jasper's face. "Don't worry, darling. We won't tell. Not unless you force us to."

With that, Anna spun her horse around and trotted back to the cart, which had stopped some paces behind her. The man behind Ihva shoved her forward, and she nearly fell. She turned her gaze to Jasper. He looked miserable but motioned for her to follow. They made their way toward the coach. Behind them, Ihva heard a tussle and looked back to see Kronk trying to wrestle a sword from one of the men's hands. Two other men were quickly upon her and slashed at her arms. She cried out as their swords connected.

"Wyatt, Mason. Stop." Anna had turned too and barked her command at the two men.

They kept their blades pointed toward Kronk but stopped slashing at her. Kronk whimpered as blood dripped slowly from her arms.

"Let them be," Jasper called back to the others. "We'll be okay."

Cor, Malach, and Yidda restrained themselves well, but Cor had to grab Kronk's arm before she could start after Ihva.

"It's okay, Kronk," Ihva said, trying not to sound frightened. What were Roth and Anna planning for her and Jasper? It sounded like they would ransom Jasper. What about her? And what of Lady Jessica? She was supposed to be dead. Had Sultan Sasar lied about killing her? Ihva's heart thudded in her chest as she wondered whether falling into Jessica's hands would be any better than her current situation.

Roth yanked on Ihva's arm, jerking her toward the carriage. Soon, she and Jasper were leaning with their faces shoved against the back of the cab, and Justin was tying their hands together behind them.

"Gag them," Anna commanded. "Else our mage prince here might find a way to escape." She spoke as though unconcerned about his abilities.

The same man who tied them wrapped cloth around Ihva's head and stuffed some of it into her mouth. She nearly choked. Jasper yelled something, but his words were muffled. As soon as the gags were in place and both Jasper and Ihva were restrained with rope, the men opened the door to the coach and heaved the two of them inside. Ihva felt the places on her body where bruises would form. The door slammed shut, and everything went pitch black.

Ihva desperately wished she could talk to Jasper. She had so many questions. Jessica was alive? How had she survived the Jini? Was it safe to be heading toward her? Ihva shivered. As she thought about Jessica, she suddenly remembered that Jasper was engaged to the woman. Her breaths quickened, and her thoughts whirled. She was terrified of losing Jasper. Yet, honorable man that he was, he'd likely be unwilling to break his pledge to Jessica. Jealousy speared Ihva through the chest. The pain was visceral.

For a few moments, Ihva only felt. Hurt and dismay drowned her thoughts. When she became aware again of her surroundings, the coach had begun moving. As it bounced, Ihva bumped up against a bench at the side of the cabin. The journey was going to be painful in more ways than one. The floor jounced more sharply and threw Ihva to her right. Falling onto her side, she shifted her weight, and her hands met Jasper's. His fingers felt along her palms, intertwined with her fingers, and closed around her hands in a comforting gesture. If only they could talk!

The memory of concentration on Jasper's face flashed in Ihva's mind. Alarm struck her. What had he done? She'd forgotten he possessed powers like the ones she'd seen. Come to think of it, there were only two times she'd seen him attempt anything magical—when they were fending off the Shades, though his magic then had failed, and in the Jini prison with the keys. Yet he was twenty. She should have known he had some kind of Power. The Prince of Oerid would certainly not have neglected to make the Exchange. Why had he kept his powers hidden until now? Incomprehension mingled with Ihva's distress. Frightened tremors took hold of her, and her hands shook in Jasper's grasp. He tightened his grip. In the darkness, it felt like the air thickened, and Ihva had a hard time breathing. The walls felt like they were closing in. So many unknowns. So much uncertainty, danger lurking in the answer to every question she had. Ihva squeezed Jasper's hands. He was the only one she could depend on now.

Chapter 49

IHVA JERKED AWAKE TO A violent lurch. She shook her head and tried to piece memories together as she took in her surroundings. It was pitch black. Disoriented, fear came over her as she remembered—they'd been kidnapped. The coach jostled, and she wondered how far they were from Agda. They'd been about a week from the city by horse where they'd been captured, but it was unclear how long they'd been traveling. Less than a day, probably, but she couldn't be sure. Her stomach ached with hunger, and her throat was parched. What would happen when they reached Agda? What would happen in the meantime?

Her thoughts turned to their captors. Who were they? Bandits, greedy brigands marauding the countryside, that much was clear. Roth seemed especially avaricious. Maybe he was their leader. But then, Anna had seemed nearly as authoritative when she'd questioned Roth's decisions. The other men were certainly subordinates, though. Ihva tried to remember their names. The one she knew for sure was that of the red-haired swordsman, Justin. As Ihva reviewed her memories, she concluded neither Anna nor any of the men seemed particular to the Lady's purposes. Everything they'd said indicated that they were serving their own interests, so they probably weren't

Shadow Bandits. Still, what was Anna doing keeping company with thieves and outlaws?

The woman's stinging words sounded again in Ihva's mind. She'd sounded so embittered, but Ihva couldn't think of anything she'd done to incur Anna's resentment. They'd cried together when Ihva had learned her parents were moving her to the capital. Ihva had been ten and Anna eleven at the time. Had Ihva done something wrong? Her parents had given her a large sum to buy Anna a present, and she'd chosen a beautifully embroidered red cloak since that was her friend's favorite color. Ihva's last memory with the girl was of her opening the gift. Anna had been uncharacteristically quiet during those final moments. She'd looked at the cloak with an expression Ihva had been unable to read. Ihva had always assumed Anna had been trying to cover up her sadness, but maybe her twisted mouth and glinting eyes had been something else entirely. In any case, Anna now seemed to care little for Ihva's welfare. Ihva wondered if the woman might even hate her. She shrank from the thought, the betrayal. What was Anna intending for her? Would she hand Ihva over to Jessica, and what story would Anna tell the noblewoman?

Anxiety began to overwhelm Ihva again. She rolled onto her right side and shifted toward Jasper, who had let go of her hands. Maybe he'd fallen asleep, too. She found him with his back toward her still. She struggled to position her hands against his and grasped them tight. A mere second later, he pulled his hands away. Surprised, Ihva tried to find them again. What was wrong? Maybe she'd startled him. Her fingers brushed against his again, but he'd folded his hands into fists. What was going on? He shifted his body away from her. He was acting so cold. She pushed desperately at her gag with her lips. It held fast, and she coughed as she tried to inhale through her mouth. Frantic, she kept trying to remove it. It took a few minutes of struggling, but she managed to push the cloth far enough out of her mouth to speak.

"What's wrong?" she whispered.

Silence met her words. Jasper gave no sign of struggling against his gag. Did he intend to not answer her? She tried to stave off the painful emotions building inside her. Finally, after a long moment passed, he spoke quietly.

"I'm sorry." He choked on the words, but Ihva could tell it was not from the cloth tied around his head. He must have freed himself earlier while she was asleep.

"What's wrong, Jasper?"

His apology made her nervous. What was there to be sorry for? There was another long pause.

"I'm so sorry." His voice trembled.

Her worry intensified as she braced for his explanation.

"It was never supposed to be this way," he said. He'd gathered himself, and his voice was steadier. "He said she was gone."

Understanding flooded Ihva's mind. It was about Jessica. It was what Ihva had been dreading, what she'd been expecting but raising desperate prayers against. Her heart sank, or rather, pain came rising to submerge it. She should have known. She couldn't speak.

"I can't break a pledge like that. Not when half of Oerid knows about it, probably all of Oerid now," Jasper said, his tone now resolute.

His words struck Ihva like a heavy blow to the stomach. She lost the ability to breathe for a moment. Painful tears flooded her eyes, but she wouldn't let them fall. Not now. It was clear the decision grieved him. She knew, or perhaps she hoped, that he couldn't hurt her like this without as deep a misery afflicting him. She tried to collect herself, but her voice still shook.

"I don't know that I could expect you to," she said truthfully, much to her anguish. She wouldn't want him to forgo his duties and promises. He'd have to desert his honor to have her, and she knew she couldn't ask that. Even if she could and he abandoned his commitments, he wouldn't be the same man she'd fallen in love with. Her thoughts tormented her.

"I can't lead you on anymore. As it is, I've been cruel," he told her.

"You couldn't have known." She was about to say his name, but the word stuck in her throat. For some reason she couldn't understand, she reached for his hand to comfort him. She found it, but he immediately jerked away.

"This is it, Ihva. I'm sorry." His voice had become hard.

The deluge in Ihva's eyes began to overflow. She understood what he meant. His cool manner was already returning. He would become callous or pretend to be, and his demeanor toward her would soon be as unwelcoming and frigid as before, maybe more so. She suppressed her sobs. It wouldn't be fair to express her pain. He was trying to sever things cleanly. He had obligations. It wasn't as simple as loving each other, not with him as Oerid's prince, and she didn't want to injure him further by letting him know what she felt.

She moved to the other side of the cab and prayed he couldn't feel her shuddering motions through the floorboards. She'd be strong. She'd be okay. She wasn't meant for royalty anyway. What did she think, that he'd marry her someday? She berated herself for letting her hopes overtake the consciousness of the limits that constrained her. Anyway, she had her own task and destiny. She couldn't count on Jasper's encouragement and comfort anymore. No matter. She was her own woman.

She tried to muster the faith to pray to Oer for his aid, but she felt pain smother the words within her. Anger filled her. No, she wouldn't be angry, not at Oer. Still, her grief was turning to outrage. Oer had assigned her to the torturous role of watching the world shatter, her presence the cause, and now he was stealing away the one remaining person she could count on.

She squeezed her eyes shut, willing her tears away. She was angry. She was truly angry, and it would have to be that anger that fueled her actions from now on. It would have to be her rage at the injustice dealt her and her resolve to live despite it. Gant would be saved if it was the last thing she did, and it would be with no thanks to Oer. It likely *would* be the last thing she did. With no one beside her, all she possessed was her rage, her fury, to drive her onward. The fury of a heart undone—it was all she had left, and she would have to depend on it if she wanted to save Gant. At that thought, her tears overflowed.

Chapter 50

JASPER COULD HARDLY BREATHE. HE felt Ihva shifting away from him, and he knew she was crying. He didn't have to hear her to know it. He couldn't expect anything else, though. He'd struck down, negated, everything from the past few months in one fell swoop, in a few cutting words. He'd wanted to tell her he loved her, that he'd never forget her, that he'd do anything he could for her, but the words had lodged in his throat. It was as well they had. They would have given her hope, and hope was the last thing she needed right now, hope concerning him, at least.

Hope was a horrid thing. He hadn't realized how heavily he'd been relying on it until it whipped itself out from underneath him. He was glad he wasn't standing, as he wasn't sure he was capable of it right now. His words had seemed to be coming from somewhere outside him when he'd spoken them, and he staggered under their weight. He'd been repelling Ihva as best he knew how, but he'd been tearing himself apart in the process. How was it that this morning he'd discussed marrying her with Cor? He was suddenly, painfully thankful the news of Jessica's return had reached him before he'd proposed to Ihva, "painfully" being the strongest part of the sentiment.

He cursed inside. He wasn't sure who he was cursing at first, only that everything in him seemed to writhe. It was all too much. So much had happened in the last thirty-six hours, and he wasn't sure it wouldn't implode him.

Then he realized—it was Oer. That was who he was cursing. Oer was at the root of it. It was his fault that Jasper had needed Jessica in the first place. It was Oer who'd allowed her to be kidnapped. Jasper had done everything in his power to protect her, and it wasn't his fault if it seemed even the Lord of the Universe couldn't guard his charges. It had been Oer's fault that Ihva had come with them. If it hadn't been for the prophecies about Oer's Blessing, Cor would never have "discovered" her, much less insisted on her accompanying them. It was Oer who hadn't taken Jasper's amorous sentiments when he'd offered them, morning after morning, to the only one he'd known to consult. It was Oer's fault that they were sent on this ridiculous quest for the Oer-forsaken "Heart of the Universe," and it was the blasted Lord of Gant who was tearing Ihva from Jasper now, Jasper was sure of it. It was Oer who'd raised Jasper's hopes so high, who'd "inspired" Ihva and Cor to their starry-eyed faith, both of whom had somehow convinced Jasper toward the same belief in Good and Truth and fairness, and it was Oer who'd dashed Jasper's hope to pieces on the rocks of Reality. Was there even going to be a Final Battle like Cor imagined, or would everything just crumble and choke like Jasper was at this moment?

Jasper was raging again, but this time he knew he was justified. This was the farthest thing from equitable. He'd been trying. He'd been trying so hard to make good on the duties Oer had placed on him, and this was what it had come to. He'd return to Agda, marry Jessica, abandon Ihva and the others, retrieve his heart apart from their help (apart from Ihva's help), and watch from the sidelines, by Jessica's side, as the world either stood or fell. He knew he'd remain faithful to his responsibilities. He'd fulfill his vow to make Jessica his wife, and he'd make a plan to recover his heart and execute that plan. Those were the only commitments he had. He'd never pledged anything more for Ihva than to support her—from his love, of course, and he doubted that would change. He'd have to support her from afar. He'd deliver on his commitments, but he wouldn't make any more. He was tired of being answerable for things outside of his control, and he was done trying to do the noble thing. He was done with Oer and all things divine. He was done, just done.

He shut his eyes against the blackness of the cab. At least when he closed his eyes, he was choosing darkness. At least he had that choice left.

GLOSSARY

Agda (AHG-dah) — capital of the human nation of Oerid located near the center of the country

Alm'adinat (ahlm-ah-DEEN-aht) — port city and capital of the Jini land of Jinad where the dwarves and Jini do trade

Arusha Molech (ah-RUUSH-ah MOH-lehk) — High Counselor to the late King Cherev-ad and head of the Council of Neved, murdered King Cherev-ad and shifted the blame to Jasper and his company

Charles Marchand (mahr-SHAHND) — Ihva Marchand's father and wealthy merchant

Cor Leviel Gidfolk (COHR LEHV-ee-ehl GEED-fohlk) — Oerid's dwarven ambassador to Eshad and mentor to Prince Jasper Aurdor

Council of Neved (NEHV-ehd) — the ruling body of Eshad that advises the dwarven king and enforces his decrees

Esh (EHSH) — the god of the dwarves said to have descended from Oer

Eshad (EHSH-ahd) — the dwarven nation of forests and mountains to the northwest of the continent

Exchange — a ceremony performed in the temple to Oer in Agda during which an individual offers an item of value to receive magical abilities from Oer

Gant (GAANT) — the name of the world in which everything takes place

Hestia (HEHS-chyah) — a province in the southwest of Oerid

Ihva Marie Marchand (EE-vah mah-REE mahr-SHAHND)— daughter of Charles and Isabella Marchand who discovers she might be Oer's Blessing while traveling with Prince Jasper

Isabella Marchand (mahr-SHAHND) — wife to Charles Marchand and mother to Ihva Marchand

Jasper Thesson Aurdor (JAAS-puur THEHS-sahn ahr-DOHR) — son of Theophilus and Theresa Aurdor and Prince of Oerid

Jessica Selene Cibelle (JEHS-sih-cah seh-LEEN SIY-behl) — daughter of William Cibelle, Lord of Hestia, and fiancee to Jasper Aurdor

Jin/Jini (JIHN/JEE-nee) — mysterious, hostile creatures from the land of Jinad who trade with the dwarves in Alm'adinat

Jinad (JEEN-ahd)— a dry, hot land to the west of the continent where the Jini reside, the capital of which is the port city of Alm'adinat

Kronk (KRAHNK) — orc-blood guard servant to Ihva Marchand who has an affinity for pretty things and a decided lack of courage in combat

Lady of Shadows — the nemesis of Oer and of all that is good, also known as Hell's Mistress

The Lost Isle — an island north of the continent where the dragons are said to have fled from which no one has returned

Malach Lam Shemayim (mah-LAHK LAHM sheh-MIY-yihm) — the jovial and straightforward only son secretly born to King Cherev-ad of Eshad, the Prince of Eshad

Marcia Polenya (MAHR-shah poh-LEHN-yah)— an adventurer from about 1000 years ago who traveled the world and kept journals of her activities, disappeared after she traveled to the Lost Isle and has not been heard from since

M'rawa (Mah-RAH-wah) — forested land of the elves in the southwest corner of the continent

Oer (OHR) — the creator deity of Light and Life, father to Rawa and Esh and worshipped primarily by human Oeridians but also by other races, such as the elves and the dwarves

Oerid (OHR-ihd) — a land of forests, hills, and fields in the northwest of the continent inhabited primarily by humans

Oer's Blessing — also known as Doomspeaker and the Dread Prophet, appears every 500 years, a young woman mysteriously chosen by Oer whose appearance brings doom to the land of Oerid and to all of Gant

Ohebed (oh-HEH-behd) — Yidda's Companion with whom she has fallen in love

Rawa (RAH-wah) — the elven deity said to have descended from Oer

Rinhaven (RIHN-hay-vehn) — the capital of the elven nation of M'rawa

Shadowed Realm — a land to the south of the continent where the orcs lives and where the Lady of Shadows is said to live and rule

Shrouded — dark beings of great power with unknown origins who serve the Lady of Shadows

Theophilus Aurdor (thee-AH-fih-luhs ahr-DOHR) — King of Oerid, husband to the late Theresa Aurdor and father to Jasper Aurdor

Theresa Aurdor (teh-REE-sah ahr-DOHR) — the late Queen of Oerid and wife to Theophilus, mother to Jasper Aurdor

Yidda (YIHD-dah) — a Jin who is leading Jasper and his company in their pursuit of Lady Jessica Cibelle, fled Jinad after a tragic encounter with the Sultan's guards

ACKNOWLEDGMENTS

To Nathan, my love, thank you for attending to my ceaseless requests to listen to and discuss the innumerable details of this work. Thank you for your gentle and apt suggestions and for dreaming with me about what this could be. I am so grateful for you and how you have helped foster this story within me. I would never have come this far without you.

To Kimberly, my dear friend, I dedicated this book to you because you have helped shape it. Your advice has opened new possibilities to me and helped me understand what I am writing. Thank you for your unfailing support and for joining me on this journey, sticking with me through easy times and difficult ones.

To Rebecca, I am so grateful for your time and enthusiasm as well as for your patience and gracious interest in my writing. Listening to one of the first drafts of this book, you inspired me to keep working on it, and your commitment to make space in your schedule for "story time" has been more encouraging than you might know. Kaitlin, I am thankful for your willingness to beta-read and your ability to offer practical and beneficial suggestions. Your feedback and advice have been key in helping me both revise and appreciate what I have written. Thank you to both of you who read or listened to this story in its unfinished form.

To my family, thank you. Mom, I cannot tell you how much your support has meant to me, from reading *Light of Distant Suns* to spreading the word about it. Dad, I appreciate how much you have believed in me through this process. Rachel and Nick, thank you for keeping up with the ins and outs of my writing and publishing process and being interested in my world and how I function inside it. Curtis and Debie, I am flattered and touched by how much interest you have shown in my writing and your astute observations about it.

Ryno and Megan, thank you for your sweet encouragement along the way.

Thank you also to my publication team. Jana, I would be nowhere without you believing in me and taking a chance on me. I am so grateful for this opportunity and look forward to seeing what the future brings us both. Kaylee, thank you for your help with marketing and encouragement, support, and motivation in the process. To the other INtense authors, thank you all for your kindness in promoting and strengthening each other.

Finally, thank you to all of you who have uplifted me, whether through a cheering word, a kind review, or even prodding questions about when the next book is coming out. I am honored by your support.

ABOUT THE AUTHOR

Lauren C. Sergeant, author of the *Children of the Glaring Dawn* series, adventures through life as a wife, mother, author, and assistant property manager. Having dabbled in over a dozen languages and taken more than a handful of international trips, she expresses her fascination with people in the novels she writes. The relationships of her characters with each other and with themselves draw readers into her keen attentiveness to what it means to be human. She spins epic tales of love, humor, and struggle, but in the end, she is just another individual on this quest called life.